Poms Down Under
Emigrating to Australia

J D Waterhouse

Copyright © J D Waterhouse 2014

The Author asserts his moral right under the Copyright, Designs and Patents Act, 1988, to be identified as the author of this work.

All rights reserved, including the right to reproduce this book, or portions thereof, in any form. No part of this text may be reproduced, transmitted, downloaded, decompiled, reverse engineered, or stored in or introduced into any information storage and retrieval system, in any form and by any means, whether electronic or mechanical without the express written permission of the publisher and author. The scanning, uploading, and distribution of this book via the Internet or via any other means without the permission of the publisher is illegal and punishable by law. Please purchase only authorised electronic/print editions, and do not participate in or encourage electronic/print piracy of copyrighted materials. This book is presented solely for entertainment purposes. No account of any persons living or dead that may be seen to be defamatory are intended as fact. The author and publisher make no representations or warranties of any kind and assume no liabilities of any kind with respect to the accuracy of the contents. Neither the author nor the publisher shall be held liable or responsible to any person or entity with respect to any loss of respect or incidental or consequential damages caused, or alleged to have been caused, directly or indirectly, by the text contained herein.

FOREWORD

Poms Down Under is set in the picturesque city of Perth, Western Australia, and follows the experiences of a group of British migrants in their quest to build new lives for themselves and their families in Australia. It explores how different people respond and adapt – or fail to adapt, as the case may be – to the challenges of their new country, what they think about Australia, and what the Australians think about the Pomes.

The characters all embark on their new lives in the sun with high hopes and expectations. For many, Australia proves to be the land of opportunity they had hoped for, and they readily embrace their new country and its culture. But as the story unfolds, others become disillusioned when they fail to secure the highly paid jobs and affluent lifestyles they had been led to expect.

Disagreements and discord amongst family members, whose views on the merits of their new country differ drastically, threaten to tear families apart, and send couples - who had previously enjoyed long and harmonious marriages - hurtling towards divorce.

The story travels inland with our migrants, through outback farming towns and eastward to the gold mining areas of Coolgardie and Kalgoorlie; from the massive and spectacular redwood forests in the south, and east again to Norseman - the last town along the Great Eastern Highway, nestling on the very edge of the Nullarbor Desert - and the continent's infamous Red Centre.

It is estimated that over the past sixty years, more than a million people have migrated from Britain to Australia, and though many have returned disillusioned, the vast majority have settled successfully. Thanks to this mass migration over the years, millions of people in Britain can now claim to have relatives or friends living in Australia. Conversely, a good percentage of Australians can trace their families back to Britain. There exists, therefore, between the British and Australians, an intense and reciprocal interest in each others' country and culture. Many might describe our close ties as being something of a love/hate relationship. Certainly, our relationship has always had a very 'competitive' edge, not only in the field of sport, but often in social activities, and in the workplace, too, where the British cautious, health-and-safety approach often clashes head-on with the Australians' notorious 'no worries' philosophy.

Work ethics are somewhat different, too. Early in the story, one migrant complains when discussing Perth's unemployment situation:

".... The truth of the matter is the Australians hate the British. Whinging Pomes, they call us. No way will they offer us decent jobs around the city. All the employment office want to do is issue you with a pick and shovel and pack you off into the never-never to dig their roads and railways for them. I'm a tradesman, I'm not about to be Shanghaied into the desert, onto some chain gang."

And later in the story, an Australian viewpoint is:

"The trouble with a lot of Pomes is they don't expect to have to graft when they come out here; they expect to walk straight into cushy, managerial jobs. Their attitude seems to be that of the old colonialists, coming to a backward country to modernise its antiquated industry with their technology and expertise, and expecting the whole of Australia to be eternally grateful. Then someone thumps a shovel in their hands and says, 'there you go, cobber, let's see how you handle a day's work', and suddenly it's shock-horror time, and let's all get the first boat home."

Given the enormous gulf in attitudes and opinions, the question posed by Poms Down Under is: how difficult is it for British migrants to be accepted and make new lives for themselves in Australia?

CHAPTER ONE

The ship was rolling gently and Geoff Patterson's mind lingered stubbornly in that surreal world mid-way between sleep and wakefulness. His eyes blinked open and tried to focus on the cabin walls, but they were not there. Familiar objects refused to reveal themselves. He saw hovering above him a strange, curved ceiling that swept down on both sides, as if to encircle him. It was as though he was looking up at the inside of a section of tunnel. Geoff blinked hard, hoping to disperse the illusion, but it became clearer and the gentle roll of the ship began to subside, the dream world faded away and reality came flooding in on him. He was no longer aboard ship. He had finally arrived. He was in Australia.

It was 1962, and Australia was thirsty for migrants to populate its vast and empty country, and expand its fledgling economy. Thousands of families, eager to escape a cold and austere post-war Britain, were responding to the Australian government's generous assisted passage scheme, hopping aboard a conveyor belt of ships and being ferried to the other side of the world to begin new and exciting lives in this land of promised prosperity, boundless opportunities and perpetual sunshine. Like so many other migrants, Geoff had been attracted by the huge advertising campaign and had decided to join the exodus. He had paid his ten-pound passage, enjoyed a relaxing month's voyage, and had now woken to find himself in Seaview Hostel, in Perth, Western Australia.

Elbowing himself upright, he cast a pair of bleary eyes around the arch-shaped, frugally-furnished room. Its appearance failed to impress; in fact, he found its most cheering feature to be the grinning portrait of Mickey Mouse that was crayoned on the back of the door. His bed, he discovered, was a short, iron-framed model that felt as though its mattress, too, had a large content of iron. It was paralleled along the opposite wall by a berth of similar discomfort. Between them stood two wooden chairs - buried beneath a tangle of discarded clothing - a dressing table and two small, bedside cabinets. At the foot of the beds, standing like sentry boxes, one each side of the door, were two tall, narrow wardrobes; their dark-brown finish contrasting sharply with the room's light-blue interior. The door stood ajar and Geoff could see through to a smaller, single room beyond. This he knew to be similarly furnished, and unoccupied.

Geoff's eyes crossed the room to where Craig Curran's six-foot-three frame was sprawled on the opposite bed; his bare feet protruding over its end rail. A muscular arm hung limply over the side, with the back of his hand draping on the floor beside a half-empty bottle of red wine. Even in sleep, Craig's casual, almost indifferent, outlook on life seemed to radiate.

They had met aboard the migrant ship four weeks earlier, and quickly become firm friends, even though, apart from a shared sense of humour, they had very little in common. At the moment, Geoff suspected they may well have one other thing in common: a mammoth hangover, this a relic from their previous night's "Hello Australia" drink.

Pushing back the sheet and single blanket that covered him, he stepped a little unsteadily out of bed and groped amongst the tangled clothing for his trousers. He grabbed them bottom first, and a shower of coins clattered to the floor.

Craig stirred and groaned, half into his pillow. "Oh, my head. What a night!"

"G'day, cobber," Geoff greeted him in an affected Australian accent, his breezy manner giving little indication of his hung-over condition. "I can see you are ready to sample the camp's healthy breakfast of eggs, bacon, sausages and black pudding, all swimming in frying oil?"

Craig turned a shade of green. "You've got to be joking." He rolled onto his side and reached down for the wine, took a swig and held the bottle out towards his friend. Geoff waved the offer aside.

"Unsociable slob. How come you're always so perky after a hard night's drinking?"

"Good clean living, that's the secret, my son." Geoff took a deep breath and slapped his chest. "I'll hop out and do a few laps of the hostel before breakfast, then I'll jog down to the beach and add to my golden suntan."

Craig chuckled smugly. "Pinky Patterson get a suntan? Now you really are joking. What you mean is you'll come back here looking like a flaming lobster, and spend all next week peeling chunks of skin from your back."

"Well, we can't all be blessed with that golden Latin complexion. Happily, neither are we all cursed with the horrendous Roman nose that goes with it."

"Jealousy will get you nowhere, Pinky," Craig said, with a rub of his ample nose.

Geoff sat on the edge of his bed and began pulling on his socks. "I wonder what the employment situation is really like?" he mused. "I doubt it's as bad as some people were saying, but there's bound to be a lot more work over in Sydney and Melbourne. They're much bigger cities, with more industry. That's why a lot of our shipmates chose to stay aboard and go there. Perhaps we would have been wise to do the same."

Craig laughed brashly. "I don't think so. The last thing I need just now is some well-meaning official offering me a job. Think on... we're in line for the holiday of a lifetime here. Glorious sunshine, miles of golden beaches, free meals and accommodation, and the government is even chipping in a few quid a week dole money to keep us in beer." He laughed again. "Work? Forget it."

"I didn't come out here for a holiday," Geoff said defensively. "We'll have to think about work sooner or later."

Craig took another swig of wine. "Later, my friend - much later."

To Craig, Geoff reflected, life was one long holiday. He seemed to regard life as something of a game, the object of which was to extract as much pleasure as possible while exerting the least amount of effort in return. Craig's ideal existence would be to laze on the beach all day, soaking up the sun, and then to party all night while soaking up free booze. The ten-pound migration scheme had provided him with a four-week cruise, halfway round the world to a land of perpetual sunshine and endless golden beaches; with free board thrown in. So, at present, life was getting pretty close to his ideal, and, to Craig, the present was all that mattered.

Geoff stood up, aware that Craig was still regarding him with amusement; his dark-brown eyes and heavy, studious brows conveying the impression of an attentive and sincere young man. Geoff gave a wry smile - just how wrong could impressions be. Certainly, in his relationships with women, Craig was anything but sincere. The quiet, attentive look was merely a mask behind which he disguised his predatory intent. His sincerity rarely extended beyond the carnal pleasures of a one-night stand.

Not surprisingly, it was sex that Craig was thinking of now. "Besides," he was saying, a twisted grin appearing on his wide, firm mouth, "I've been told these migrant hostels are hotbeds of lust. With so many of the men away working in the bush, the women become lonely, and with no cooking or housework to occupy them, they get bored and frustrated - and extremely randy."

"I'm sure their problems are solved now that you're here."

"Naturally, I will do my utmost to comfort them," Craig said, his grin widening with assumed modesty. "But I may need your valuable assistance from time to time. If you can tear yourself away from Susan's charms, that is."

"There's nothing going on between me and Susan, you know that."

"Sure, I know that. I also know that's not the way she sees it." He laughed teasingly. "Beware of that one, Pinky, my friend, she is dangerous, she has designs on trotting you down the aisle."

Geoff purposely let the subject drop. "I guess you're right - we can have ourselves a ball here. Why bother with work for a while? But right now, I have a bigger problem: will I go to breakfast, or won't I? My stomach says no, but if I don't feed my face before lunch, I'll starve. I guess I had better go and eat."

He gathered his cutlery and enamel mug from the top of the cabinet and moved to the door. "Carrying your cutlery around with you is like being back in the army," he observed.

"Well, be sure to remember the old soldiers' advice and don't drink the tea. They probably lace it with bromide to protect the women from us over-sexed new arrivals."

"I doubt that. With the government so desperate to get the country populated, they're more likely to feed us oysters three times a day. Totally unnecessary in your case, of course. But I'll be careful."

Outside, the sun blazed down from a cloudless blue sky. Geoff walked with his head bowed and his eyes screwed up against the light. His stride was laboured as he trudged through the fine sand of the walkways that ran between the chalets. Seaview Hostel was built on top of a hill, and had he raised his eyes from the sand and looked across the rooftops of the neighbouring suburbs, he would indeed have been able to see the blue of the Indian Ocean.

He was a tall, well-built young man with a fair complexion, reddened by the sun. His features were heavy, and while not handsome, they displayed an endearing good humour. His pale-blue eyes, set wide apart, held a steady gaze, and his thick-lipped mouth seemed always to be smiling.

"Welcome to Tin Town, young fellow."

The voice boomed in Geoff's ear like a clap of thunder. He lifted his head and saw a heavily-built man sitting on the wooden steps that led up to the door of his chalet. The man sat doubled over with his elbows resting on his knees, forcing rolls of fat to overlap the top of his khaki shorts.

"Good morning," said Geoff, and started to walk on. His head throbbed in the heat and he had no desire to stand talking.

"You've just arrived, haven't you? My name's Ryan... George Ryan." The big man waddled down the steps, extending a chunky hand. "You must have arrived yesterday on the Castel Felice. You have my full sympathy. It's nothing but a cattle-steamer, that one."

"It wasn't that bad. Quite an enjoyable voyage really."

"No need to tell me, son." George placed a consoling hand on Geoff's shoulder and shook him, almost affectionately. "I came out on it myself six months ago. There were thirteen hundred of us herded aboard that old tub, and she's only a twelve thousand tonner, you know. You'd think it were cattle they were shipping across."

"I guess it did get a little overcrowded at times," said Geoff, trying to edge away. The deep Brummie voice booming right into his ear wasn't doing his hangover any favours at all.

"A little overcrowded! That's an understatement if ever I heard one." George gave a false laugh, as if to cover his ridicule of Geoff's words. "And you could say the same for this dump, too," he added, indicating the hostel with a sweep of his hand. "Two families have to live in one of these overgrown tin cans, one on either side. Chalets, they like to call them. Makes them sound really grand, don't you think?"

Geoff's eyes followed the ark of the chunky hand to the rows of corrugated iron buildings. As George had said, they bore a close resemblance to overgrown tin cans lying on their sides. They stood two feet off the ground on wooden posts. The contour of iron sheeting that formed the roof and two sides was broken only by a door and two windows on each side.

"Come to Australia and enjoy a higher standard of living, they tell you. The only higher living you'll find out here is in these elevated tin cans. Look at them: perched up in the air like a monkey's tree house. I suppose you know why they have to keep them off the ground? To keep the snakes and spiders out, that's why. And the flies! You've never seen anything like it. I was in Africa after the war and I thought that was bad till I came here. Flies? Millions of the little blighters. You've never seen anything like it."

That, at least, Geoff was prepared believe. A swarm of them had been buzzing around his head since the moment he'd stepped from his chalet.

"You are not expecting to find work here, are you?" George ranted on, hardly pausing for breath.

"That was the general idea," admitted Geoff.

George gave a deep, rumbling laugh. "Forget it," he said. "There are three-hundred men in the hostel who came out with the same idea. I've chased jobs all over this city for six months now, and still I'm unemployed. The truth of the matter is the Australians hate the British. Whinging Pomes, they call us. No way will they offer us decent jobs around the city. All the employment office want to do is issue you with a pick and shovel and pack you off into the never-never to dig their roads and railways for them. I'm a tradesman. I've a right to be employed at my trade, that's what I keep telling them. I'm not about to be Shanghaied into the desert."

"Good for you," said Geoff. He was in no mood to stand listening to the fat man's laments. He wished only to bring their meeting to a speedy close, if possible, without having to resort to outright rudeness. He had heard there was much discontent at the hostel, but had hardly expected to be pounced on so soon, and have the country's shortcomings hammered home to him quite so rabidly.

It was Luigi, their Italian cabin steward, who had alerted them to the number of migrants who were returning to Britain unhappy and disillusioned with life in Australia. "The voyage from Britain to Australia is very happy; everyone is smiling." The comical little Italian had said, and with his two index fingers, pushed the corners of his mouth up to demonstrate. "The passengers, they all laugh. They look forward to their new lives in the sunshine. They are like adventurers; all full of hope and expectation. But the voyage from Australia back to Britain, that is so different." Luigi pushed the corners of his mouth back down and looked glum. "Everybody is miserable. No more hope and excitement, no more laughter - only grumbles and complaints. We call it the voyage of tears. And my Castel Felice, she becomes the heartbreak ship."

Eventually, Geoff made his excuses heard and continued to the dining room. It was late when he arrived there, and few of the modern, Formica-topped tables were still occupied. It was a large room, bright and freshly painted. Rows of fluorescent lights lined the low white ceiling, and the sun, streaming in through the large curtainless windows, reflected from the tables and blue and white tiled floor.

To his left, he could see a slender arm waving to him excitedly. The sun's reflection from the table behind her dazzled him, but he knew by the exuberant gestures that it could only be Susan. She was sitting with her parents, Ted and Joan Harvey. Geoff had shared a table with them in the ship's dining room.

He procured his breakfast from the cafeteria-type servery and made his way over to where they were sitting.

"Good morning, shipmates," he greeted them brightly.

"Good morning, Geoff, and how are you today?" Susan inquired with a big smile.

"Fit as a fiddle, as always."

"Oh yeah, and what happened to the appetite?" asked Joan, eying the boiled egg and dry toast he had selected for breakfast. She was a haughty-looking woman with piercing green eyes, a straight nose and a firm mouth. Her long, dark hair was brushed straight back and held by a comb-clip at the nap of her neck. For a woman of forty, she had a trim, youthful figure that she carried with poise. All her actions were graceful, almost regal. On first seeing her, Craig had dubbed her The Duchess, a title she had lost the moment he heard her cockney accent.

"My appetite?" said Geoff. "Yes, well... I must admit I'm not too hungry this morning – must be the weather or something." He gave a sheepish grin. There was no fooling Joan.

"Or something. You are certainly looking a bit under the weather," she said, regarding him sternly with those piercing green eyes. Geoff got the impression that he was being severely reprimanded.

"And how was your first night on the town?" asked Ted.

"Terrific! We must have made every bar in the city. Then, to top off a great evening, we caught the wrong bus back and ended up at the beach. Had to hire a cab from there and the crook tried to slug us three quid for the fare back. Needless to say, he wasn't successful. How do we get a cup of tea around here?"

"It's in that big urn by the kitchen door," said Susan. "Here, give me your mug, I'll get it for you."

"Tell me, is it my hangover giving me illusions or is the food really that bad?"

"It's not the best by a long way," said Ted. "If that's a sample of the food here, then the sooner we move into a place of our own, the better."

"Apparently you have to get in early while the food is still fresh," said Joan. "What did you think of the city, Geoff? I've heard Perth is very beautiful. We're all going in this morning for a bit of a mooch around, and compare prices."

"You mean you and Susan are going in," corrected Ted. "Leave me out of it. I can imagine the performance. They will be comparing everything from safety pins to washing machines. By the time they get back, we will know to the penny how much higher the Australian cost of living is."

Susan returned and placed Geoff's mug on the table in front of him. "Here you are," she said, "And I've brought you some bread and butter. You can't possibly eat that toast, it's much too hard."

"Susan, you're a real sweetheart. What would I do without you?"

She wrinkled her nose and sat down a little self-consciously. She had her mother's strong features, and her father's hazel eyes. Her smile was radiant, often mischievous, and always seemed to start in those clear honest eyes. She was very attractive, Geoff noticed, not for the first time. Craig was right, of course - he was very fond of her. Paradoxically, that was why he had no intention of dating her - well, not yet. A casual affair would not please or satisfy either of them, and Geoff was far from ready to commit himself to a steady relationship.

After serving two years in the army while doing his national service, he felt in need of a break from commitments and obligations. He needed a period of personal freedom, a time to please himself, without being obligated to anyone.

Joan got to her feet. "Come on then, Susan, we have a stack of unpacking to do before we go out."

"Okay, Mum. Aren't you coming with us, Dad?"

Ted shook his head.

"Old misery. See you later, Geoff. The luggage has all been dropped off in front of the reception hall... I saw your cases there." She turned and dashed off after Joan.

"They will be in their glory traipsing around all those shops," smiled Ted. "It will do them the world of good after being cooped up on the ship for so long. What are your plans, Geoff? I expect the labour exchange will be your first port of call, won't it?"

"I'll probably leave that for a day or two - there's no great hurry. In fact, while there's free board on offer, I'll probably take a couple of weeks' holiday, acclimatising and enjoying the beaches."

Ted leaned back in his chair. "No need to tell me whose idea that was," he said, knowingly. He was aware that Craig regarded himself as a well clued-up young man who had all the answers, and knew how to play the system. Ted, however, had him pegged rather more simply, and far less flatteringly as a freeloader. He failed to understand why a solid, dependable lad like Geoff had forged such a close friendship with him.

"You recognise our Craig's thinking when you see it," smiled Geoff. "He may have suggested the idea, but I was never in any great hurry to start work. After two years of having my life regimented by the army, this could be just the kind of break I was looking for."

"You weren't keen on army life, then?" Ted asked, steering the conversation away from Craig.

"It was okay, I guess. In a way, it was the best thing that could have happened to me. It got me away from home, and away from a job and a way of life that was fast becoming a rut. It gave me a sense of independence, so I'm grateful to it for that. But towards the end, the routine and regimentation was becoming unbearable. I was glad to get out. But army life changes you. I'd had a taste of travel and independence. I didn't want to leave the army and slip back into my old job and old way of life. I wanted to keep that independence and spirit of adventure alive. I still do. I guess that's why I emigrated."

"It's nice to be able to please yourself," mused Ted. "There are times when I wish I was still single. Oh, don't get me wrong," he added hurriedly. "I love them both dearly, but occasionally I think it would be nice to be foot loose and fancy free again. I envy you that."

The conversation lapsed while Geoff got on with his breakfast. Ted began drumming his fingers on the table absent-mindedly. Geoff had noticed he did that often, as though ill at ease and unsure of himself. Perhaps he was still agonising over whether or not he had made the right decision in emigrating.

Eventually, Ted leaned forward and said, "They say work is scarce around Perth at the moment. I don't suppose you'll have much trouble, though - mechanics are always in demand. I'm glad I have the driving job lined up with my brother. It will do nicely until I find my feet."

Having stopped drumming his fingers on the table, Ted now began fidgeting with the silver ashtray in front of him, turning it with his middle finger, and looking as though he had lost track of the conversation. He was a quiet-spoken man who seemed to weigh the value of his every word.

"If we like Perth and decide to stay, I'll buy my own lorry and start off the same as Harold did. He assures me it's a good line of business to be in... plenty of haulage contracts about."

Geoff found it hard to imagine Ted behind the wheel of a ten-ton truck. Not that he doubted his physical ability to do the job; he just didn't look the part. It was hard to see him mingling with a group of hard-drinking, hard-swearing truckers. Ted looked what he was - or rather, what he had been - a prosperous shopkeeper, even down to the ruddy complexion, slightly bloated features and soft friendly smile, moulded from years of sympathising with crotchety old women. He was not a young man, and it would not be easy for him to readjust to a new, very demanding, way of life.

"You'll find truck driving somewhat different to shop-keeping," Geoff ventured.

"I certainly hope so. After all, I emigrated to start a new life, not merely to continue the old one in a new place."

"All the same, I've done a spot of driving and, given the choice, I'd plumb for shop-keeping every time."

Ted rocked back in his chair and raised a monitoring finger. "Owning a shop isn't the idyllic existence most people seem to imagine. It's a full-time job, and hard work at that. Although, I'll admit it has its compensations. I was my own boss, nobody standing over me, and I was certainly earning more than I could by working for someone else." He paused, as though momentarily uncertain as to why he had thrown it all in.

"But a man can get into a rut, Geoff, even if he is onto a good thing. It got so I hated the sight of that shop. And the customers!" He rolled his eyes to the ceiling. "Every day, the same old biddies traipsing in one after the other, ramming all their troubles and woes down your throat until you almost forget there is any joy left in the world. Besides, I'm not an old man, and... well, I just didn't see myself stuck behind that counter for year after year till I eventually rotted into the floorboards. No, Geoff, I'm glad I made the break. I don't think I will ever regret it. The change is the big thing, the challenge of something new. Variety is the spice of life they say, and I reckon there is a lot of truth in that."

Geoff agreed, mainly because he sensed Ted's need for reassurance. It had doubtless been a huge decision for him to sell his home and business and migrate to the other side of the world. Perhaps it had been the courageous decision of a strong, independent man, determined to free himself from the rut life had been grinding him into - or perhaps it had been a foolhardy one made by a staid, middle-aged man, desperately trying to recapture the spirit and adventure of his lost youth. Time would tell.

"Good morning, Maureen," said Ted, as a willowy blonde-haired woman hurried passed their table. She gave them a faint smile and nod, and then hurried on to a table in the corner, occupied by her husband, two sons and four-year-old daughter.

Stan Taylor was a short, solidly-built Liverpudlian. An ex-army sergeant who ruled his family with military discipline. His two sons sat to attention opposite him, hardly daring to move. David was ten, a stocky lad; squat and broad-shouldered for his age, destined to grow up the image of his father. At seventeen, Peter already stood three inches taller than Stan. He had a slim, athletic build and his mother's blue eyes and fair complexion. His hair was combed into a low quiff at the front - the only wave salvageable from the regimental short-back-and-sides. He was a sullen, moody youth and the corners of his mouth dipped sulkily. His shoulders began to slump as he leaned on the table in weak defiance of his father's stringent discipline, then straightened sharply as Stan shot him a warning from beneath heavy brows.

"Horrible brat, that," said Ted, following Geoff's gaze. "It won't be long before Stan has a juvenile delinquent on his hands."

"Whose fault is that?" observed Geoff. "You can't suppress the spirit of a boy his age the way Stan does. He's bound to rebel sooner or later."

"True," Ted agreed half-heartedly. He gave a quick smile. "I had better go and see what those women of mine are up to. I'll need to watch how much they are taking out with them, too. They are liable to go on a wild spending spree when they see all those shops. I'll see you later, Geoff."

Geoff finished his breakfast and sat puffing at a cigarette. After a while, the Taylors got up to leave. He watched Stan stride to the door, noting again what a rugged-looking character he was. Apart from height, everything about the man was big: thick arms swung loosely from broad muscular shoulders, and an outsized head sat firmly on his short, thick neck. He turned, revealing a square jaw and broken nose. Not the sort of character you would want to meet down a dark alley, Geoff thought.

Geoff had met several like Stan during his stint in the army: tough, unyielding disciplinarians. As drill sergeants, they were priceless, but Geoff doubted whether those harsh, unyielding qualities were as appreciated by his children as they had been by the army. He felt especially sorry for young Peter.

"Pick those feet up, boy," Stan barked when Peter stumbled clumsily over the doormat.

Geoff smiled. Peter never seemed able to do right in Stan's eyes, but then the boy did appear somewhat guileless at times.

The dining room was almost empty now. A stout woman pushed a trolley between the tables, collecting dirty crockery and wiping the tables with a damp cloth. She sang merrily as she darted from table to table with the agility of a woman half her size. She, at least, seemed happy with life in Australia. How many migrants were, and how many became disillusioned like George Ryan?

Geoff began thinking of the people he had met aboard the ship: the families who had sold almost everything they owned, and said goodbye to all their friends and relations in order to start a new life for themselves on the other side of the world. What did they expect to find here to compensate for the things they had given up?

He recalled the huge advertising campaign being run in all the British papers and magazines. All those brightly coloured pamphlets with their beguiling pictures of sun-drenched beaches and smart new housing estates, all those promises of higher wages and a better standard of living. You could have it all for a mere ten pounds. But what if, like many advertising campaigns, it was all based on half-truths and deceptions? What if that better standard of living was a myth, and the high paid jobs were not there? What then awaited the families who had gambled all?

And what of George Ryan's claim that the Australians hated the British? Geoff found that hard to believe. While in the army, he had been stationed with a group of Australians. There had been a lot of rivalry and banter between them - as there tended to be between most regiments. But mostly it had been good humoured: the Australians would rib the British lads over their inability to win at cricket, and in response, the British would make fun of Australian Rules football; likening it to aerial ping-pong. But Geoff had never detected any malice in the exchanges. After all was said and done, the two countries had just been through a bitter war together - and in times of crisis and conflict, Australia had always been amongst Britain's staunchest allies. No, it was completely inconceivable that British migrants would encounter any hostility here.

Geoff himself was risking little. He was young and single and had no ties. If Australia was not to his liking, he would simply pack his cases and return home. But for the family man with a wife and children to provide for, returning home would not be such a simple or unemotional matter.

He began wondering about his fellow travellers - his newfound friends. For how many would the dream of a better life here in Australia be fulfilled? And, conversely, for how many would the dream be soured by disappointment? More poignantly, how many of them would soon be rushing to book their passages on Luigi's 'heartbreak ship' for that tearful voyage back to Britain?

CHAPTER TWO

It was hot, and the hostel drive was steep. Tom Henshaw found his breathing becoming heavier and beads of perspiration beginning to trickle down his forehead. He paused for breath and looked up the hill towards the rows of corrugated iron chalets, gleaming in the midday sun like rows of huge chromium-plated mushrooms. Not such a bad place after all, he allowed. He hadn't relished the idea of living in a migrants' hostel. His mind had conjured up distorted visions of dirty, dilapidated buildings where people of all nationalities were being herded together to live in semi-squalor - similar to the refugee camps he had seen in Europe after the war. He smiled faintly at his own pessimism. Whatever had given him such an idea? The hostel wasn't luxury, of course, but it was smartly laid out and the buildings all looked clean and well cared for - albeit somewhat utilitarian. In any case, they wouldn't be there long. They would soon have a home of their own.

"The heat getting too much for you, Tom?"

He turned to see Stan Taylor's squat form striding effortlessly up the steep drive, as though it were level ground. The man was like a miniature tank.

"Yes, I must confess it's a bit more than I'm used to. It must be near the hundred mark now." He took a large white handkerchief from his pocket and dabbed at his brow. A hint of newly-acquired colour tinged his sallow complexion, giving it the light, doughy appearance of half-baked bread. Tom looked much older than his forty-three years. His features were podgy, and lacking in any hard defining lines. Pouches of wrinkled skin hung beneath soft, watery-blue eyes, and his few remaining wisps of hair were spread across his scalp in an attempt to disguise its baldness.

"Ninety-six, according to the thermometer outside the shop," said Stan. "It will go higher yet, though. Mid-afternoon should see the peak."

"I've been admiring the gardens," said Tom. "It's amazing how they keep the plants looking so fresh in this heat. And the lawns are so thick. I've never seen grass like it before." He stepped cautiously onto the grass and felt the short, springy blades crinkling beneath his feet, like hundreds of tiny air bubbles.

"Buffalo grass, it's called, or so I'm told," Stan informed him. "Strange-looking stuff. Quite a few of the private lawns around here have it."

"I take it you've been out looking at the local neighbourhood then. The houses are beautiful, aren't they? Very American in style. I like the way they're all detached in their own plot of land, and the way the lawns come right down to the pavement, with no fences or privets. I would be in my glory with a garden like that to potter around in."

"A keen gardener are you, Tom?"

Tom chuckled. "I'd like to think so. But, to be honest, the only bit of green in our yard back in Sheffield was the weeds that forced their way up through the cracks in the concrete."

They laughed, and continued up the drive.

"But I had my allotment... my little oasis of peace and quiet. It was a sanctuary away from the hustle and grime of the foundry, and all the financial pressures at home. I had to cycle five miles to get there, but it was well worth it. I think I regret having to leave that little plot of dirt more than I regret leaving my job... or Sheffield."

Stan nodded knowingly. "To be honest, there isn't much I regret leaving behind. Cold, damp housing, overcrowded streets, everyone living on top of each other. That simply doesn't happen here." He filled his lungs. "The amount of open space out here in Australia is unbelievable. You won't have to cycle five miles to an allotment here, Tom. You'll have enough land to grow all the flowers and vegetables you want at home, in your own garden."

"That would be marvellous," Tom said wistfully. "My own garden." He was beginning to puff hard with the exertion of keeping pace with the striding Stan.

Stan slapped the rolled paper into his open palm. "Plenty of jobs going in the morning paper," he asserted positively.

"I did hear that there wasn't much work in Perth at the moment. They say some people were advised to stay on the ship, and carry on to Sydney or Melbourne. They are much bigger cities, bound to be more work over there," Tom offered hesitantly.

"Utter rubbish! That was just a stupid rumour," Stan said bombastically. "The whole country is growing so fast, every state is crying out for workers. If there was no work, the Australian government wouldn't be shelling out thousands of pounds to pay our passages out here. The very idea of there being no work is ludicrous."

Tom nodded in meek acceptance.

"It's a young country with a lot of growing to do," Stan continued. "The prospects and opportunities here are boundless, especially for the youngsters. There's bags of scope for them here in Australia." He gazed up at the cloudless blue sky and gave a deep sigh of satisfaction. "This is truly wonderful weather. I think we have made a wise move, Tom. There will be work, right enough. Of course, unlike you, I don't have the luxury of a trade to fall back on, or a job waiting for me. But if a man is prepared to get off his backside and do a day's work, he'll soon find himself a job. That's what I've always maintained."

"That's true," said Tom, not really knowing whether it was or not. He had never been unemployed and had to walk the streets looking for work, and the mere thought of having to do so terrified him. He was a cautious man, migrating to Australia had been a big worry to him. At first, he hadn't been at all in favour of the move. He'd had a steady job at the foundry, and would have been content to plod along there till his retirement.

The wage wasn't big, but they managed – the job was secure, that was the main thing.

But Edna had caught the emigration bug, and nothing he could say would change her mind. He shrugged despondently; nothing he said had much affect on Edna any more. She was a strong-minded woman; she invariably got her own way in the end. But he'd held out when it came to employment. He wasn't going to chase halfway round the world without having a job waiting for him – and he had told Edna so. For a while, he'd thought his stand had resolved the issue. Then Edna had spotted Drew's advertisement in the daily paper, and before he knew it, his application had been accepted and he had found himself left stranded, without a credible argument.

But there he was worrying again and, as usual, for no good reason. Hadn't he just been on the phone to his future employer? And hadn't he heard the gruff voice confirming his job at twenty-three pounds a week? Of course he had. Relief swept through his troubled mind like a cool, refreshing breeze.

They reached the top of the drive and made for the shade of the reception hall.

"Ninety-eight," said Stan, scrutinising the thermometer hanging on the wall. "It's shot up two degrees in the time it's taken us to walk up the drive." He turned, and with the proud air of a man surveying his own land, cast his eyes across the rooftops to the open country beyond. "I'm sure we have made the right move, Tom," he reaffirmed staunchly. "A man can really breathe out here."

Tom was looking in the opposite direction, at a compound where children were playing on a roundabout, pushing it round and jumping on, seemingly oblivious to the heat.

"It's a healthy climate for the kids to grow up in, too," he said. "Look at them. They're as brown as berries - like little Indians."

No sooner had the words past his lips than he regretted them. Politics in general and Britain's housing shortage and immigration policies in particular were touchy points with Stan. For a moment, Tom feared he was going to launch into one of his political tirades, but, to his relief, Stan merely grunted and rechecked the thermometer.

"It certainly is a beautiful day, Tom," he said, and walked on.

Tom watched him go with a sigh of relief. He liked Stan, but at times he could be somewhat overbearing with his opinions. He recalled the time on the ship when a group of them had been discussing England and their reasons for leaving. Stan had been voicing rather forceful views and someone had called him a communist.

"I fought for my country, and I'm as patriotic as the next man," he had bellowed, jabbing a thick, stubby finger in his accuser's direction. "Like others, I fought to secure a decent future for me and my family, for fair wages, and for good housing, available to all. I didn't go to war so that thousands of foreigners could be drafted into the country as cheap labour, lowering our standard of living, and taking up all our social housing. That is not what any of us went to war for. And I have a right to stand up and say so without some dozy twit calling me a communist."

Tom allowed himself a faint smile at the recollection. It didn't take a lot get Stan riled up politically. But he spoke his mind. And Tom respected him for it.

Tom turned and looked back down the drive. From this high vantage point, he could see how well spaced out the local houses were. Wide roads lined by trees and grass verges. All the properties appeared to have huge gardens. Soon, perhaps, he would be living in just such a property, and have his very own garden to tend. The possibility made him smile contentedly.

Tom had had a similar high vantage point from his allotment, overlooking the suburbs of Sheffield. That scene, however, was not such a pleasing one. Rows of small, two-up-two-down terraced houses, built back to back with only tiny yards and alleyways separating them. They were grimy, narrow streets, with barely a tree in sight, and overlooked by towering chimney stacks spewing out smoke and soot. The area had been built at the turn of the century to house the city's expanding number of steel workers. It was a cold, depressing scene - even when the sun shone. Tom gave an involuntary shudder at the thought. He felt the warm sun on his back. Surely Stan was right? Their move to Australia had been a wise one. They would all prosper here.

Tom's attention returned to the children's play area. A lonely little figure in a yellow shirt and big straw hat stood watching the other children at play on the roundabout. He edged towards them, as though wanting to be invited into their game, but he was shy and he didn't know any of them. He saw Tom, and came running up the steps to meet him.

"Can we go to the beach this afternoon, Dad?" His flushed face looked pleadingly at Tom.

"No, Kenny, there's too much unpacking to be done first."

Kenny's big brown eyes became hollows of disappointment, and a twinge of remorse stabbed at Tom's conscience. Kenny was such a frail, sickly child, always choked up with asthma or colds, or some other ailment. It seemed heartless to have to refuse him anything. True, the voyage to Australia had done him good; his cheeks now glowed with colour, and he was eating much better, but he was still weak and under weight for a ten-year-old. How different he was from his elder brother. John had always been a healthy boy, full of energy and a natural at most sports. Tom was duly proud of his eldest son, but little Kenny, he felt sure, would always be in need of a certain amount of parental support and protection.

"But it's only a mile away, Dad."

"No, Kenny." Tom was firmer this time. "And you had better keep out of the sun for a while, or you'll be getting burnt, then what will your mother have to say to you? Come on, we had best go and help her with the unpacking."

As they walked along, Kenny reached up and held onto his father's hand. Had his mother been there, he would not have done so. She would have scolded him and told him not to be such a sissy.

They found Edna outside their chalet, talking to a slim young woman with straggly, shoulder-length hair.

"And there's two Scots lads in that chalet over there," the woman's voice droned on disapprovingly. "Every other night, they're staggering back here as full as boots, singing and swearing, and throwing their empty beer cans onto the tin roofs. You wouldn't believe what a hell of a racket that makes."

"Why don't you complain to the management?" said Edna. "I shall if I have my sleep disrupted."

"The management? That's a good one, that is." The woman laughed thinly, and gave a rasping cough. "I went up and see Kertesz myself, I did. You know what he told me? 'Well, Mrs Bates, if you are not happy here you can always leave', he says, as though I was the one causing the ruckus. Didn't say boo to them, he never. The next night, it was twice as bad."

"This is my husband," Edna said, as Tom walked up to join them.

"Pleased to meet you, I'm Shirley." There was no intonation in her voice, just a flat monotonous whine that to Tom's ear seemed perfectly pitched for complaining. She had delicate, finely-chiselled features that should have made her attractive, but in common with her voice, her face was blank and almost devoid of expression.

There was an awkward silence. The two women stood looking at each other, as though awaiting a signal to resume their conversation.

"Well, how did it go?" Edna asked eventually.

"Everything is fine, love," said Tom. "I can start work whenever I like."

Edna gave a self-satisfied nod, indicating that some point of debate had been resolved in her favour.

"Maybe you'll be lucky," said Shirley, her voice holding out little hope. "But there's a lot in the hostel been brought out to jobs that don't exist. Trouble is the Western Australian government runs its own immigration scheme and gives tax breaks to firms that advertise for workers in Britain. As soon as they've had them here a few weeks, they find an excuse to lay them off. Then they bring out more migrants, and get even more tax breaks. I don't want to worry you, but that's the sort of thing that's happening out here."

What utter rot, thought Tom. The woman was obviously a born moaner, inventing faults that didn't exist. You were bound to meet them in a place like this. But his stomach gave a lurch. What if there was some truth in what she said, and in a few weeks he found himself out of work? How would he go about finding another job? Where would he start looking? He was in a strange country. He knew nobody - it would be impossible.

But surely no company would bring a man halfway round the world without having a job for him - the government wouldn't allow it. No, they couldn't get away with a thing like that. Deep in thought, he mounted the wooden steps and went into his chalet.

Shirley gave another rasping cough. "Never coughed in my life till I came out here," she said. "It's the dust that does it. Wait till the wind gets up, you'll see."

"It wouldn't be the cigarettes at all," suggested Edna.

"No, it's not the fags, love," she said, missing Edna's sarcastic intent. "It's the dust, it gets everywhere."

A toddler playing in the sand by the steps began to crawl under the chalet. "Tracey, you come out of there," Shirley called, her voice rising in volume, but barely altering in tone.

"There is God knows what living under these chalets," she said, turning back to Edna. "And all the nasty creepy crawlies out here either sting or bite. You have to keep an eye on the kids all the time."

A woman emerged from the chalet two doors along. She was tall and elegant with blonde hair swept high on her head, revealing a slender neck. As she descended the steps, she looked across, staring daggers at Shirley.

"Sandra Masters, the hostel madam," Shirley announced curtly. "Her husband is out in the bush, working on the construction of a water pipe. Went out there with my Terry only two months ago, and that hussy has had a different man in there almost every night since the day he left. Like most of us, she hates it here and wants to get back to England. She is trying to earn the fare - on her back, if you know what I mean."

"I'd say that is *her* business," Edna said brusquely. "She will not be interfering with me. Now, if you'll excuse me, I've a lot of work to do." She turned and strode purposefully into the chalet, leaving Shirley staring blankly after her.

Tom had seated himself beneath the window and was flicking through the pages of the morning paper. Edna stormed into the room, emitting a deep sigh of irritation.

"I can do without the likes of her coming neighbouring too often," she said." I hope she can take a hint."

"You're bound to hear a lot of complaints in a place like this," Tom said without looking up.

"All the same, this place leaves a lot to be desired. I must say I was expecting to be housed in something better than a tin shed. What do they think we are – gipsies?"

The accommodation buildings were uniform in their build and interior design, but the family units were a little less austerely furnished. The divan and matching armchairs had a look of newness about them, but the arms of Tom's chair were badly stained, and cigarette burns dotted the rug at his feet. The bedroom suite, too, was barely a few months old, yet scratches already scarred the top of the dressing table, and a certain J.B. had carved his initials deep into the wardrobe door. A writing table and two straight-backed chairs completed the furnishings of the main room. The small adjoining childrens' room contained either a single bed or two bunk beds, and a small bedside cabinet and wardrobe, similar to the ones in the single men's rooms.

Edna stood resolutely in the centre of the room, her hands planted firmly on her hips, a dour expression clouding her face. She was a big woman, full figured and round faced. Her large jowls and short, greying hair giving her a stern, formidable appearance, indicating that frivolity and fun did not rank highly on her list of priorities.

"Are you going to sit there all day?" she snapped at Tom, as she hoisted a case onto the bed and flipped it open. "There's a lot to be done yet, you know. And what are you reading the employment pages for? You don't need to take notice of anything that one says."

"I was just comparing some of the wages on offer," Tom said defensively. "The personnel manager said I can start as soon as I like, though he suggested I take a couple of weeks to acclimatise. Not a bad idea, this heat will take a bit of getting used to. But I think I will start as soon as I can, once we're settled, don't you think?"

"I don't know what we are going to do with the half of this stuff. There's no storage space in here at all," Edna complained, totally ignoring Tom's quandary.

"Why not leave most of it in the cases for now? We probably won't be at the hostel long. There appears to be no shortage of property for rent."

"I certainly hope not. It would drive me mad living in this rabbit hutch." She stood up and looked at her watch. "Anyhow, it's almost time we were over at the reception hall to hear what the manager has to say in his welcoming talk. Kenny, you are to stay in here out of the sun. And if John comes in, tell him to take the rest of his belongings over to his own chalet. And that's another thing I don't like," she said, swinging her attention back to Tom.

"The way they have split up the families. It's not right. Having the teenagers away from their parents, you never know what they are getting up to of a night. And I most certainly don't like the idea of our John having to share a room with that Taylor boy. He's no good, that one. He's sly and deceitful. I don't trust him."

CHAPTER THREE

The Taylors were already seated in the reception hall and were talking to Ted Harvey, and Tony and Janice Bradley when Tom and Edna arrived.

"My God! I never thought it could get this hot," said Edna. "That thermometer outside is up to a hundred and two!"

"It's truly grand," Stan said approvingly. "Think what the poor devils back home must be going through right now."

"I'm not so sure who the poor devils are – them or us. Right now, I would give a lot to see a nice crisp frost - even a refreshing drop of rain."

"Did you find out about your job, Tom?" asked Tony, his features contorted into their usual concerned, question mark expression.

He was a short, weedy-looking character. Craig had dubbed him "Mickey", as in Mickey Mouse, on account of his timid nature and protruding ears. Janice slumped in the chair next to him, a sulky, spoilt child expression on her face. She wore a white loose-fitting blouse and tight yellow shorts; an outfit that showed off her shapely and already well-tanned limbs.

"My job is fine, thank you, Tony. I can start whenever I like," Tom answered with a relieved smile.

"Good afternoon, Pomes," Geoff breezed from the doorway, his arms flung wide in a theatrical greeting. He wore a bright, multicoloured shirt and a white hat with a large, floppy brim. Craig had recovered from his hangover, and looked at ease in the hot weather.

Janice looked up at Craig and smiled sweetly. She had an angelic face, framed by loose curls. Craig ignored her. From this, Geoff surmised that Janice was already a notch on Craig's bedpost, and that having made his conquest, he had already moved on. Edna regarded both Craig and Janice with obvious disapproval, as though she, too, was aware of their indiscretion.

Joan and Susan came in, looking hot and weary after their trip into the city.

"Ah-ha, the hunters return," teased Geoff.

"My feet are killing me," complained Joan. "The pavements in town are red hot. You could fry eggs on them."

"Have you been into the city, Susan?" asked Maureen Taylor. She was a quiet woman, and rarely spoke unless spoken to.

"Yes, it's an absolutely fabulous place," Susan enthused. "Everywhere is so clean and fresh looking - tall white buildings and wide streets, and they have these lovely big shopping arcades that go right through from one street to the next. You'll simply love it, I know. One of the arcades is called London Court, and all the shops in it have those cute old-fashioned fronts with bay windows, and oil lanterns over the doors. It looks really great."

"Down along the Swan River is lovely, too," said Joan.

"Absolutely," Susan agreed. "Big colourful flowerbeds and palm trees all along the river bank. Perth is a really beautiful city."

"Can't say much for the buildings here, though," grumbled Edna.

"Don't you like the chalets, Edna? I think they're really sweet. I'm going to paint the ceiling in all different coloured stripes, then it will be like living under a rainbow," said Susan.

Craig rolled his eyes to the ceiling in exasperation and shook his head slowly. Susan smiled impishly at Geoff, indicating that this was just the reaction she had intended to provoke. Geoff smiled back. Susan, he had already realised, was nowhere near as naïve or dizzy as she sometimes made out.

"Good afternoon, ladies and gentlemen, and welcome to Australia. I am sorry to have kept you waiting. I am Mr Kertesz, your hostel manager." He turned to the two young men following him in. "This is Mr Preston of Amad Insurance, and this is Mr Smith of United Motors. They would both like a few important words with you while you are all together."

The salesmen smiled winningly, and then followed the manager to the low stage at the far end of the hall.

"If you wouldn't mind drawing your chairs round in front of me here," said Kertesz. He smiled, revealing gold fillings. "I am not going to make a speech, it's just that I have my desk up here, and I can spread all the necessary papers out in front of me."

He was a tall, thin man with sharp features and black hair brushed straight back. Edna was instantly doubtful of his sincerity. She could picture him dressed in a dark suit with a wide, colourful tie, looking every bit the wartime spiv. He had a clear, theatrical voice with a faint foreign accent. One got the impression that he thoroughly enjoyed delivering his little lectures.

He waved his arm in a sweeping gesture that encompassed the entire hall. "This is not the tidiest of reception halls, I'm afraid. As you can see from the toys and various pieces of equipment, it also acts as a nursery... and a youth club. Personally, I would rather see the hall being put to good use than being kept strictly for reception purposes. However." He dismissed the matter with a wave of his hand.

"I have some folders here that I would like you to have. I am sure their contents will answer most of your questions." He jumped lightly from the stage and began distributing the folders, like a schoolteacher giving homework to his pupils. "Not a very large party today," he observed. "I was expecting more."

"The others took the hint and carried on to Sydney," Edna commented dryly.

"So I believe. Well, that is our loss, and perhaps theirs, too.

Personally, I believe you lucky people have come to the best city in Australia. I say that quite impartially. I am not an Australian myself." He paused, as though expecting this revelation to be met by gasps of astonishment. "I am Hungarian by birth. I came to Australia twelve years ago, as a carpenter."

He continued to distribute the folders, and then began to stride up and down in front of them. Still the schoolmaster, he was now about to deliver a pre-term pep talk to his pupils.

"I believe this is a good country in which to live." He stopped to correct himself. "No, it is a *wonderful* country. The industry is expanding rapidly and there are many opportunities, especially for the youngsters. But it is not an easy country. If you wish to get on and earn high wages, you will have to work hard..." He paused again and looked self-consciously about the room, as though suddenly realising that his audience were not children, after all, and were, therefore, well aware of this simple fact.

"Nobody hands out wages for nothing anywhere in the world," said Stan.

"Quite so, Mr Taylor, quite so." Kertesz cleared his throat. "Before I explain the contents of the folders to you, I would like to say a few words about the hostel. Firstly, you must realise it is not a hotel." He smiled cleverly. "There is only one letter difference in the spelling, but like so many of your English words, that one letter makes a big difference in meaning."

"You can say that again," commented Edna.

He accepted the remark as a witticism. "I assure you, Madam, we do everything we can to make your stay here a happy one. But at the same time, the hostel is only intended as temporary accommodation. We have a continuous stream of migrants to cater for and we are constantly short of room; therefore, we do like to see you moving out into your own homes as soon as possible. I am sure this must be what you all want also. As regards tariff: you do not pay us anything at all until you start work. After that, you will find our rates to be reasonable, but not particularly cheap. As I have already explained, we are not competing for your lifetime patronage."

Craig gave Geoff a nudge and a wink at the mention of free board.

Kertesz climbed back onto the stage, where his two salesmen sat waiting patiently, one each side of the desk, like a pair of bookends. Their attire suggested they could be twins: both wore white shirts with their sleeves rolled up to one turn below the elbow, and light-blue ties. They sat in a uniform pose, almost to attention, their backs straight, their feet planted firmly on the floor and their arms extended over the briefcases resting on their laps.

To Craig's cynical eye, they resembled a pair of trained vultures, poised to swoop on an unsuspecting prey. Tell the new chumps anything, sign them up while they are still green, would be the salesmen's mantra. He wondered idly how much they had paid Kertesz for the privilege of those reception-committee seats.

Craig was bored, and the room's heavy atmosphere was making him drowsy. Vaguely, he could hear the manager's voice droning on, explaining various housing schemes, the education system, medical funds, transport systems and a multitude of other incidentals of not the least interest to Craig. He pictured himself relaxing face down on the soft golden sand, listening to the pounding surf while the sun's warm rays massaged deep into his back. Why had he allowed Geoff to drag him into this old woman's meeting?

Now the manager was introducing his salesmen, telling a corny story of some poor misguided fool who didn't buy from our trusted Mr Smith, and whose car, therefore, promptly began to disintegrate from the moment it was driven from the showroom.

How terribly sad, Craig thought sardonically. He noticed how well Kertesz told the story, and promptly doubled his previous estimate of the manager's perks.

Now Mr Preston was inculcating the dire necessity of investing in one of his medical funds and life-insurance policies. Craig was swimming leisurely through the rolling surf, turning and allowing the cool breakers to float him back to the beach.

Then Geoff was elbowing him in the ribs. "Are you going to join?" he was asking.

"Eh? Join what?"

"The hospital fund. Kertesz is filling out the forms now."

"Is it free?"

"Of course not."

"Then I don't want it."

"It's advisable, there's no national health service here."

"I'm in perfect health. I won't be needing a doctor for a few years yet. I'll wait for you outside."

The sun had moved across the sky, and the front of the reception hall was no longer in the shade. Craig leaned against the wall and let the hot afternoon sun beat down on him. Kertesz was right: the hostel was no luxury hotel. But it was free, and Craig had lived in much worse places. He lit a cigarette, drew on it deeply and gazed long and hard towards the horizon, trying to visualise the vastness of the Australian outback with its thousands of square miles of sun-drenched country. Craig was an impulsive traveller, always happiest when on the move; seeking out new places and new experiences. He yearned to be heading for the fascinating land beyond that horizon – and he would, he had promised himself that. But first there was Perth to see and savour - the beaches, the nightclubs, and, of course, the women. And when all of this became a bore, then would be the time to head for that horizon.

This was not the first time Craig had been to Australia. He had visited twice before, as a merchant seaman. On one occasion, he had jumped ship in Sydney, lived there for three months, and then signed on another ship for the return voyage to England.

"Aren't you joining the hospital fund, Craig?"

It was Tony Bradley. He stood looking up at Craig, his face its usual placard of perplexed anxiety. The expression never failed to amuse Craig. He smiled down rakishly.

"No, I'll gamble on my fitness, Tony."

Tony regarded him wide-eyed, as though he was about to stake his very life on a hundred-to-one chance. "You are taking a big risk – medical bills can cost you a fortune out here," he said worriedly.

Like all bills, that, of course, depended on whether or not one stuck around long enough to pay them. Craig didn't bother giving voice to his thoughts, aware that Mickey would grasp neither the logic nor the humorous intent.

The others were filing out now.

"You are a positive disgrace," said Susan, punching him on the arm. "Fancy going to sleep while the manager was talking."

"I wasn't asleep. I was merely resting my eyes," said Craig.

They all laughed, for the retort had become trite during the long days spent lazing on the deck while crossing the Indian Ocean.

"I was beginning to nod off a bit myself," confessed Ted. "I thought he was never going to dry up."

Janice came out and sauntered by without looking at them. "Tony!" she called back over her shoulder. Tony trotted obediently after her.

"Tony, Tony, Tony. Heel, boy," mimicked Craig.

"Don't be awful," giggled Susan. "Why does he put up with it?"

"She's bigger than he is," offered Geoff.

"Enough of this idle chatter. It's beach weather," declared Craig. "It's time I introduced you all to the thrills of bodysurfing."

"Bodysurfing! I can't even swim," said Joan.

"Are you coming, Mum?"

"You don't think I would let you go anywhere alone with this pair of rogues, do you?" She gave them one of her icy stares, as though wishing them into stone.

Craig laughed and put a long arm around her shoulders; aware that Joan's frostiness went no deeper than her expression.

Later, when they had changed and were walking down the drive carrying their towels, a Holden station wagon halted beside them.

"You are going to the beach?" the driver inquired. He was a young man and he had only a small boy in the car with him. "I will take you there if you can all get in. I, too, am going to the beach." He spoke slowly with a foreign accent.

They thanked him and climbed into the car.

"You have just arrived?" he asked when he had accelerated the car into top gear. "My name is Hugo. I am in Australia for three months only. I am come from Germany." He phrased each sentence as a question, as though wishing his English to be corrected. He liked to talk, and tried hard to express himself in neat sentences. He told them that he liked Australia, and the people... but he did not like the hostel.

"The people they are... different," he said hesitantly. "When they arrive, they are happy. Then, after a while, they become unhappy. They want to go home. They are... how you say?"

"Whinging Pomes," Craig offered dryly.

Susan nudged him. "Don't confuse him."

"Yes," Hugo said uncertainly. He had heard the Australians use that expression, yet he sensed it was more a term of abuse, and not quite appropriate in present company.

"They are homesick," suggested Susan.

"Yes, thank you, that is the word I look for. They are homesick. The happy ones they soon leave the hostel and find their own homes. But the homesick ones stay always at the hostel. And all the time they cry: 'Australia is no good, we want to go home'. The hostel is not a very nice place; there are not many happy people there."

"You see, I was right in the first place," said Craig.

Hugo was still looking confused. "This word... Pome?" he said hesitantly. He pointed to a dictionary nestling on the parcel shelf under the dashboard. "I don't find it here. It means, please?"

Ted turned inquiringly to Craig. "Yes, what does it mean?"

"That's a very good question," smiled Craig. "Unfortunately, there is no definitive answer. The true meaning or intent has been lost in time. There are several explanations kicking about. For me, the one that has most credence is that it's an anagram of Prisoners Of Motherland England, P.O.M.E. This raises an interesting point. Since the prisoners were the ones being shipped out here to become Australians, it must follow that it's the Aussies - not the British, who are the Pomes." He gave a defiant grin. "As you can imagine, the Aussies really appreciate having this simple fact explained to them."

"You're not getting me in there!" exclaimed Joan, as they pulled up at the beach and she saw the surf pounding in.

"That's only mild surf," Craig assured her dismissively. "The breakers are often three or four times that high in Sydney."

"It's still too rough for me. I'll settle for a paddle."

"You must swim always between the flags," Hugo informed them. "There it is safe. The lifeguards keep watch." He indicated the water's edge, where a line of young lifeguards were practising their rescue procedures. Their presence, however, served only to convince Joan of the perils.

Ted, too, looked somewhat apprehensive as they walked out into the surf. But once they had waded out beyond the breakers, the water was calmer and they could swim.

"This is absolutely glorious weather," said Ted. He stood with the water up to his chest, shading his eyes from the sun as he peered along the beach. "Miles and miles of golden sand. And so empty."

"Well over a thousand miles of it along this coast," confirmed Craig. "Farther than the whole length of Britain. Out here, you can have a whole beach all to yourself."

"It reminds me of the old music hall gag about our British seaside resorts," said Geoff. "If you happen to get a fine day there, the beaches are so crowded that only bald-headed men get a suntan. This is great. I think I'm going to like Australia."

While they swam, Joan confined herself to paddling along the shoreline with her sandals in one hand and her dress held high with the other.

The English abroad – how typical, thought Craig. To him, Joan's image seemed to crystallise the major differences in the beach-going attitudes of two nations – or perhaps it was more a case of how their different environments had moulded those attitudes. The beach and the surf were part of the Australian way of life, and Australian children would go to the beach for a swim as readily as their English counterparts would kick a ball on the street corner. But to the British, it wasn't the beach, it was the seaside - somewhere one went at holiday time, or on the firm's beano. And the water was approached with caution. Joan was at the seaside now, paddling along the water's edge fully dressed, with her sandals in her hand. Craig thought she could hardly have looked more English had she been parading up and down wearing a placard proclaiming: "I'm a Pome" written in big, bold letters.

The water was rushing by them, being sucked out to sea as a huge wave loomed in front of them.

"Dive! It's a dumper!" shouted Craig.

Then the solid wall of water came crashing down on them, bowling them over. Geoff felt himself being swirled over and over like the clothes in a washing machine, and then dragged along the sandy bottom on his back. The next thing he knew, he was sitting on the wet sand while the water rushed passed him on its way back out to sea.

Ted and Susan were sprawled nearby, Susan had lost her bathing hat, and her long hair hung in wet streaks about her shoulders and across her face. From out where they had been, Craig was standing laughing at them.

"You're supposed to dive under them," he called.

"Now he tells us," mumbled Geoff.

Craig pointed behind them to where Joan was running back up the beach, the bottom of her dress dripping wet.

"That's too rough for an old man like me," said Ted. "I'll leave my swimming for calmer days."

Craig swam farther out and waited. When another large wave started to build up, he began swimming towards the shore. The swell lifted him and he rode in the curl of the wave all the way back to the shallow water.

"That's what they call bodysurfing," he said.

"It looks great fun," said Susan. "Is it difficult?"

"Nothing to it. Picking the right wave is the hardest part. Come on, I'll show you."

They swam for a long while, diving under the breakers and trying to ride with the surf as it rolled in. Then, dripping wet, they ran up the beach to dry off and sunbathe.

"Mum, it's simply fabulous," panted Susan. "The English beaches were never like this."

"It looks dangerous to me," said Joan.

"No, it's not, it's great fun. I'm going to buy a surfboard with my first week's wages. Has your dress dried?"

"Almost. Nothing stays wet for long in this heat. I wish we had some deckchairs to sit on."

"Don't be such a Pome. The Australians don't use deckchairs. They all have big, colourful beach towels and spread them out on the sand."

She spread her own towel out and flopped down on it. "That's something else I must buy: one of those gorgeous beach towels. Why is it nobody seems to like the hostel? I think it's an exciting place to live. People arriving from all parts of the world, full of hope, and eager to make a new life for themselves. It must take an awful lot of courage for them to leave their homelands and migrate to an unknown country – especially when they have young children to provide for. And what about the foreigners who can't even speak the language? It must be an enormous decision for them to make. They must have the pioneering spirit, like the early settlers in America."

"I think someone has been watching too much *Wagon Train*," Geoff teased her.

Craig chuckled quietly to himself. "Can you honestly imagine the likes of Mickey or Tom Henshaw as hardy frontiersmen, pioneering the Wild West?"

"Must you always find something belittling to say about people?" she frowned.

"I'm sorry, little girl, have I trampled on your sandcastle? How remiss of me," he laughed. "But I'm afraid that today's migrants have no intention of pioneering anything. They want everything handed to them on a plate. Let's face it – most of them only left Britain because they found the going too tough there. And as soon as they realise that a quid is no easier to come by over here, they will sit down and bawl their eyes out, and start decrying Australia and everything in it."

"You only think it's great here because you see it as a scrounger's paradise," Susan said dismissively. "You've had a free cruise round the world, and now you'll be getting free board and lodgings, plus dole money. But once all the handouts stop and you have to start earning your keep, you'll soon change your tune. Then we'll see who bawls their eyes out."

"Absolutely," Craig agreed with a wide, annoying smile. He began slapping suntan lotion over his already well-tanned body before settling down to luxuriate in the sun. "The government promised to provide for me and keep me in the idle manner to which I hope to become accustomed. And I intend to make sure they do just that."

Craig raised himself back up onto one elbow and looked across at Susan with another taunting grin. "By the way, did I tell you the locals have a name for the hostel? They call it Septic Hill. They say it's like a boil on the landscape, oozing the puss and bile of discontentment out into their beautiful city."

"They do not. You're just saying that to try to wind me up. But you're wasting your time. On a perfect day like this, I refuse to bite. Anyway, I think it takes courage for young families to migrate out here. And I'm sure none of the people who came out with us are going to sit down and bawl their eyes out, as you put it. They are all made of much sterner stuff than that."

"We'll see," Craig assured her evenly, as he settled back down. "Give it a couple of months or so, and we will see."

CHAPTER FOUR

The night air was hot and clammy. Swarms of moths and mosquitoes buzzed angrily about the illuminated sign above the hostel entrance. Two drunks staggered in beneath the sign and made their way up the drive, chanting loudly and unmelodiously: "There's no a team like the Glasgow Rangers. No not one. No not one. Celtic knew all about their troubles..."

The taller of the two men stumbled and dropped the carton of canned beer he had been carrying.

"Don't drop those cans, Alex. Mind what happened last time you dropped them, we had beer sprayed all over the room."

"Aye, a hell of a night that was, Jimmy. We still have beer stains on the walls."

Alex groped about in the darkness, picking up the fallen cans and returning them to the carton. Then he swayed backwards and sat down heavily on the grass verge.

"What are you doing down there, Alex? Get up, man."

"This is a hell of a hill for a man to climb when he's had a few bevies," complained Alex.

"Get up, Alex. You're no drunk... not yet," Jimmy chided him. He pulled his friend to his feet, and they stood swaying unsteadily against each other.

They made a contrasting pair: Jimmy was slight and wiry, his features sharp and alert; while Alex was broad and burly. His dark hair hung untidily over his eyes and he looked slow and awkward. Both were in their early twenties.

"You cannae be drunk yet, Alex, we have all these cans to finish off ... and I still have half a bottle of Johnnie Walker in the chalet."

"Have you now? Oh, you little beauty. Come on then, we'll go and have a wee drop of Johnnie's."

As they neared the top of the drive, they could hear a group of teenagers laughing and joking on the reception hall steps. Most nights, the teenagers loitered outside the hall long after the youth club closed at ten o'clock. Predatory local youths, on the prowl for young girls, would often join them, adding to the general rowdiness by driving their cars around the hostel's narrow roadways.

An early model Holden stood at the curb. The front door was wide open and a long-haired youth in a white T-shirt and blue jeans sat revving the engine. A teenage girl sat curled up beside him, her arm draped loosely over his shoulder. In the back of the car, Peter Taylor puffed gingerly at a cigarette, trying to appear the seasoned smoker before his newfound friends. He sat low in the seat, ready to duck down should his father happen along.

"Got any grog for us?" he called to Jimmy and Alex as they staggered by.

"You'll be wetting your diapers if you drink this stuff, laddie."

The girls giggled.

"Get stuffed," sneered Peter.

Alex lurched over to the car. "You watch your mouth young'un," he slurred. "Or I'll bust your head."

"You and whose army?" Peter scoffed belligerently, making no attempt to step out of the car. Alex looked tough and formidable, even though he was drunk.

Jimmy took his friend by the arm and steered him away. "Come on, Alex, you're in no condition to fight. We have serious drinking to do."

"A fight, is it, you're worried about?" laughed Alex. "No worries there, pal. If there was ever any fight in that one, it ran down his father's leg."

"Watch the steps now, Alex."

"You watch them, I'm all right."

They staggered precariously down the steps, to be met by a sarcastic cheer from the teenagers on reaching the bottom without mishap.

"Cheeky young bastards," muttered Alex. They stumbled on towards their chalet.

"Can't hit a man when he's that drunk," said Peter. "Only have to push him and he'd fall flat on his face."

"Yeah," the long-haired youth in the driver's seat agreed without conviction. "Pile in, you guys, we're going for a burn along the beach." His call was met by excited shouts of approval, followed by the slamming of doors, then the Holden roared off down the drive.

"Here they come. As drunk as lords, by the sound of it," said Edna. She moved to the window, pulled the curtains aside and peered out. "Disgusting," she snorted. "Just look at the state they're in."

Jimmy was leaning against the door, trying to fit his key into the lock, while Alex, still clinging onto his carton of beer, leaned heavily against the handrail and guided his foot carefully onto the first step.

"Watch the step, Alex. It's the third one up that's broken, mind."

"Have they no fixed it yet? I'll be down to see Kertesz tomorrow."

"Don't do that, he'll be wanting you to pay for it."

Jimmy opened the door and they stumbled in.

"Disgusting," repeated Edna. She turned from the window. "If there's any trouble tonight, I'm going straight to Kertesz in the morning, and demand their eviction. Decent people can't get a night's rest. Those two are like animals."

Tom said nothing. They had been at the hostel for three weeks now, and he could see Edna becoming increasingly unhappy as the days went by.

"What with them, and that trollop Sandra Masters holding open house over there – and young Geoff and Craig are no better either, bringing their women back here overnight as though it's a... oh, I don't know what." She gave an exasperated sigh and sank back into her chair.

"Things will work out all right when we get settled into our own home," Tom consoled her. "It's just the hostel that's getting you down."

Her stare swung fiercely in his direction. "We are not moving from here until we're absolutely sure of ourselves," she decreed. "Where would we be if anything happened to your job? A fat chance you would have of finding another - half the hostel is unemployed as it is. None of those who arrived with us have found jobs yet. Look at Stan Taylor... he's out first thing every morning, walking the streets in all that heat, and he's not had a day's work to show for it. It's not right to bring people here when there's no work for them, and more pouring in all the time. The country is heading for mass unemployment, that's what."

Tom hung his head in resignation. He had long ago accepted the futility of vying with Edna's sharp tongue. He wasn't sure about Australia yet - in only three weeks, how could he be? - But he liked what little he had seen and wanted to at least give the place a fair try. The boys had certainly settled in well, loving the beach and the warm weather. But Edna was missing home, and he could see it was only a matter of time before she finally convinced herself that everything about Australia was intolerable, and stated outright that she wanted to go home. It really didn't matter what advantages the country might have, or what he and the boys thought of it. Edna's inability to settle seemed destined to drive them all back to England.

Tom wanted desperately to take the initiative and make her see things his way for a change; tell her straight that they were going to leave the hostel and its depressing atmosphere, find a place of their own and start living together as a family again. But caution restrained him. At the hostel, they had a certain amount of security, so if the unthinkable happened and he found himself out of work, then at least they would still have a roof over their heads. He was almost prepared to take the risk; after all, his job seemed secure enough - he had no reason to suspect it was not. But it wasn't a decision he felt empowered to make alone. He needed Edna's positivity and strength, needed her to lead the way, just as she always did, but Edna appeared to be locked into her own little spiral of ever-deepening depression, which was threatening to drag them all down with her. Tom was at a loss to know what to say or do to snap her out of it.

From outside, there came the clatter of an empty beer can bouncing along a tin roof. Edna moved instinctively back to the window and pulled the curtain aside.

"It's started," she said flatly.

A shirtless Alex stood swaying at the bottom of the steps, while Jimmy sat in the doorway holding a glass of beer in one hand and a can in the other.

"That were a good shot, Jimmy, did you see that?" Alex enthused, turning unsteadily to his friend.

"Aye, but you hit the wrong hut. He wasnae the one that complained about us. He's a Scotsman."

"Aye, but he's a Celtic supporter."

"Is he now? Well, have another go," Jimmy urged.

Alex was in the process of lining himself up when he overbalanced and fell onto the sand.

"What sort of a short was that?" scorned Jimmy. "You wouldnae even get a place in the Celtic team with a shot like that."

"Don't say that, Jimmy, you know I would never play for Celtic, even if they offered me a million pounds."

"Aye, that's right, Alex. Neither would I."

Jimmy came down the steps and they stood with their arms about each other's shoulders and began to sing.

"There's no a team like the Glasgow Rangers. No not one. No not one..."

"Hey, Jimmy, that's not the Scotsman's hut. That's where those two bludging Pomes live."

"Oh, aye, so it is. Lazy bastards they are, too. Lying on the beach all day, living off taxpayers' money. We have to work to feed yon' bastards – and it's a car they have the noo."

"A man is no a man if he cannae do a day's work, Jimmy."

"You're right there, Alex, a man must have his work. He's no good without his work. I'll stir them up." He hurled his empty beer can, and stood listening as it clattered along the roof.

"That's no use, Jimmy, they'll no be in. They'll be off out with their women."

"No wonder our tax is so high, it's women they have, the noo."

"I could just go a woman the right now, Jimmy."

"Well, go over and see Blondie. She's on the game, right enough."

"I've no money. I'm broke."

"You have ten shillings, have you, no? Sure that's all the cow is worth. Come on, we'll go over and give her a knock."

"Now there's going to be trouble," said Edna, turning to face back into the room. "They're going to Sandra Masters's chalet, and she has a man in there already."

Jimmy began thumping on the chalet door. It half opened. "What the hell do you want?" came a man's voice.

"Where's Blondie? My friend wants to see Blondie."

"There's no Blondie here. Clear off."

"Aye, there is. Your time's up, Mac. Come on, hurry up and get out."

"Get away from here, you pair of drunken louts," Sandra shouted, shouldering her way to the top of the steps.

"My friend wants to see you. He has money."

"What the hell do you think I am?" Sandra blazed indignantly. She raised the shoe she was holding, as if to throw it.

Jimmy backed apprehensively down the steps. "Well, what's *he* doing here? He's no your husband."

"That's none of your bloody business," said the man. "Now clear off, before I call the police."

"Wrap up, the bleedin' lot of you." A man raged from the chalet opposite. He stood at the top of the steps in his pyjama bottoms, and shook his fist threateningly. Nearby, a baby started bawling.

"You go boil your head," Alex slurred.

"You two are a bloody nuisance, raving and shouting like a pair of kids. Every weekend it's the same – nobody can get a night's sleep because of you. I'll have a word with Kertesz tomorrow and see about getting you thrown off the camp."

"It's you he'll be kicking out, no us," argued Jimmy. "You've no done a day's work since you got here. The tariff we pay is feeding you and your family."

The man went inside and slammed the door.

"That shut him up, Jimmy. He couldnae answer that. We're feeding them, right enough."

"I'm hell of a dry. I need another beer."

"Aye, he'll no be throwing us out; we're the only ones around here that pay our tariff."

They trudged through the sand, back to their chalet, mounted the steps and went inside.

"Disgusting," repeated Edna. "There are enough foreigners in the place to contend with, without having your own people behaving that way. I'll see Kertesz in the morning. If we all complain, he'll have to do something."

She remained at the window for a long time, her eyes glued to the scene as though hypnotised by its very drabness. The baby was still crying, and Jimmy and Alex began to sing drunkenly and stomp on the wooden floor of their chalet. It seemed the whole atmosphere of the place had been contrived specifically to depress her. Why, oh why, had she ever wanted to leave the comfort of her home and emigrate to this wretched place?

Edna's thoughts drifted naturally to home. But, in her reverie, she did not see the grimy suburbs the way Tom recalled seeing them from the vantage point of his allotment - the dowdy, terraced houses and huge chimney stacks that towered above them pouring smoke and soot over all below, the white-faced children wrapped in scarves and gloves to keep out the bitter cold, walking with heads bowed as they hurried against the driving rain or choking fog. All were mysteriously absent from her mind. Edna saw only the friendly, familiar neighbourhood where she had grown up. She was in her comfortable living room with its floral wallpaper and polished furniture, smelling faintly of lavender wax. She was reclining in her favourite armchair beside a bright, crackling fire while familiar faces smiled at her from the flickering television screen. What she wouldn't give to be back there now.

CHAPTER FIVE

Edna stepped from the manager's office and made her way between the chalets to the dining room. It was hot, as always, and the flies were out in force to annoy her, buzzing about her ears and crawling into her eyes. She was aware that other people were also making their way to the dining room, their cutlery and enamel mugs in their hands - like so many down-and-outs on their way to a soup kitchen, she always thought, and she hated being one of them - it was so degrading. Sand filled her shoes as she walked and a line of washing, strung from one chalet to the next, forced her to stoop almost to her knees to pass. A child sat dirty and semi-naked beneath a chalet, filling a dustbin lid with sand. Edna's face screwed up in distain. What a squalid place this was.

Inside the dining room door, she stopped to check the notice board.

"Have you seen these?" Shirley was asking over her shoulder, a light giggle in her voice. She was referring to some Andy Capp cartoons, pinned to the notice board. One pictured Andy running from the Labour Exchange. The original caption had been erased and beneath it someone had written: "No need to run, Andy, this is Australia, nobody wants you to work." Another pictured Andy's mate, Charlie, in a pair of overalls and carrying a toolbox. Andy was crying on his friend's shoulder, saying: "Tools! Overalls! Charlie, what have they done to you, lad?" And underneath was printed the explanation: "Charlie was a managing director in England, now he's a janitor."

"That will be old George Ryan up to his tricks again," laughed Shirley. "Not bad, are they? He's quite a wit, is our George."

Edna's expression remained rigid, refusing to show any trace of humour. "Too near the truth to be funny," she snorted. She turned from the notice board and went to join the queue at the servery. Against her will, she had found herself conversing more and more with Shirley lately. Only yesterday, Shirley had come knocking at the door, holding a letter from home that she insisted on reading out.

"It's from my mum," she sniffed. "I miss her so much. She's always been there for me. She says how much she misses little Tracey. She's her only grandchild, and she doted on her. Well, grandparents do, don't they? Look what she says here: 'Give her a big hug and a kiss from me'." Shirley began to cry openly. "It almost broke my heart when I read that. Mum loves her so much."

Edna had to steel herself from joining Shirley in her tears. She had received similar letters from her own mother. Of course, Edna's parents would be that much older than Shirley's, and it was highly probable that they would never see their grandchildren again. Why had this harsh but obvious truth not occurred to her before leaving for the

37

other side of the world? She had been so selfish and inconsiderate.

"Have you been to see Kertesz about the ruckus last night?" Shirley asked, joining the queue behind her.

"He's shifting them over the other side somewhere," Edna said with a vagueness that suggested she did not want to open a conversation on the subject.

"I didn't think he would throw them out. He doesn't like to see the place getting too peaceful, people stay too long. Still, I'll say one thing for them – at least they keep their drinking to the weekends. Not like the Australians, staggering around the city all hours of the day and night. I've never seen so many drunkards in all my life."

Edna glanced around the crowded room. She noticed with distain the number of Spanish and Italian migrants there were - dirty, smelly little people with dark skins and greasy black hair.

"What do you think of the place now?" asked Shirley.

Edna stiffened with indignation at the *I-told-you-so* tone of her voice. "Tom's getting a regular wage, that's the main thing," she said tersely.

"I suppose that's something to be grateful for. My Terry spent months trying to get a job in Perth. He's had to go right out into the bush to work - and he's had to lower himself to labouring. He's trying to scrape up enough money to get us home. We're not on our own, either," she added quickly. "Ninety per cent of this place would go home tomorrow if they had the money. It's the ten-pound scheme that's holding them here. If you return home within two years, you not only have to pay your own fare back, you also have to repay the government for your fare out here. By the time they pay off their debt to the government, it can cost a family over a thousand quid to get home. Poor devils ain't got an earthly. It's a trap to get people stranded here, that's all the ten-pound scheme is. It's a right con-trick.

"Take a look at her, will you, all dressed up to kill. I hear she's got her eye on the cook now, tired of the Italian already."

The woman joining the queue behind them was Mrs Hollins, whom Shirley often referred to simply as: 'that nosy old bag', She was a tall woman with hunched shoulders and short, frizzy hair. Her beady little eyes were constantly on the move, determined to miss nothing. A pair of large, round-framed spectacles sat squarely on her beak of a nose, making her look like an inquisitive owl.

Edna picked up her tray and turned to face the front of the queue. As far as she was concerned, Mrs Hollins was a malicious gossip and a liar, and she would have nothing to do with her.

Janice Bradley, preceding them in the queue, had been the object of Mrs Hollins's comments. She wore a skimpy pair of shorts and a bright yellow strapless top, which Edna thoroughly disapproved of as dining room wear.

"Hello, Rudy," Janice smiled sweetly at the man behind the servery. He was a short, swarthy-looking character with thinning fair hair and a neatly trimmed beard.

He winked at her. "And what can I do for you today, Mrs Bradley?" There was a humorous formality in his voice, as though they were sharing an in-joke.

Janice gave a girlish giggle. "I think I'll try the scrambled egg today, please."

"It is very good. I can thoroughly recommend it... with bacon?"

"Yes, please. And a slice of fried bread."

He smiled and handed her the plate. "Anything else I can do for you?"

She looked at him coyly and giggled again. "Not at the moment, thank you."

Brazen hussy, thought Edna. She moved through the servery and carried her tray over to where Tom and the boys were sitting. They appeared to be very pleased about something, though the sight of their elated spirits angered Edna, aggravating her own already thoroughly miserable mood.

John was a good-looking lad, in a clean-cut, college-boy sort of way. His appearance was always neat, and his hair well-groomed. He had his mother's strong jaw line, and his alert features had already become heavily bronzed from days spent at the beach, where he had become an enthusiastic new member of the local lifeguards club. Like his mother, he rarely showed any outward sign of emotion. But as Edna approached, his firm mouth widened into a broad smile as he flourished a sheet of paper excitedly in front of her.

"Guess what, Mum? Crowstone Engineering have accepted my application for an apprenticeship as a toolmaker. Isn't that great news? The college course won't start until March, but they say I can start in the workshop right away if I like, and get some experience on the practical side."

Edna stared at the letter for a long moment, hardly reading beyond the first line. "That's very good," she said unenthusiastically. "Though the education you've had merits something better than factory work."

She picked up her mug and walked over to the tea urn.

"Gee, Dad, Mum didn't seem very pleased about my job. Doesn't she want me to start work?" said John, his voice thick with disappointment at his mother's tepid response to his news.

"Your mother is missing home - and Granny. Of course she's pleased," Tom explained quietly. "She'll be all right in a day or two. Try not to bother her too much."

"She doesn't want to go home, does she? I hope not. I don't ever want to go back to England. I think Australia is terrific."

"Me, too," Kenny spoke up quickly, in support of his big brother. "I love the beach. I can swim two widths of the pool now. I'm going to do a full length before Christmas."

The furrows creasing Tom's brow deepened. All he wanted was a quiet, stress-free existence, be it here or back home in England, but he could foresee nothing but turbulent times and friction ahead, for himself and for his family.

"Flip, flop, flip, flop; everywhere the sound of big, flat, peasant feet," said Craig, as a plump Italian woman walked passed their table. "Have you ever noticed the way they pick their knees up and stamp their feet - as though they are on the parade ground? That action has evolved from centuries of stomping around the fields, breaking up clods of dirt with their bare feet."

"Just because they can't speak English, it doesn't mean they are ignorant peasants, or uneducated," reasoned Susan. She had been saying what friendly people the Spanish and Italian migrants were, and Craig had seized the opportunity to tease her about their living habits.

"Take a look at the way they eat and tell me they're not peasants; heads down in their plates like short-sighted punters studying form. And note the neat flick over the left shoulder with the scraps. That's to feed the chickens and pigs they are accustomed to having scratching about in the dirt behind them."

"They do not do that!" laughed Susan. She had ceased to take Craig at all seriously. "I think they're nice, anyway. At least the foreigners are honest, hard-working citizens, and that's more than can be said for you pair of layabouts."

"Listen to the hard-working girl," said Geoff. "And when exactly do you propose to start earning your keep, young lady?"

"I've been trying hard to get a job - you know I have. Trouble is, I'm not really experienced enough as a typist. I used to serve in the shop when I should have been studying. And I'm not experienced enough to do shop work, either. There's a big difference between serving in your *own* shop and being a sales assistant in a department store." She shrugged and gave a philosophical smile. "I'm not much good at anything, really. I can't see myself ever getting a job here."

"The kind of defeatist remark one might expect to hear from a three-week member, wouldn't you agree, Geoff?" asked Craig, after giving her his cool, professional scrutiny.

"Definitely," agreed Geoff. "I can see it won't be long now before our little sister becomes a fully-fledged member of Shilp."

"Shilp? Whatever is that?" she asked, suspiciously.

"It stands for Seaview Hostel's Institute for Lamenting Pomes," Craig was happy to inform her. "It's a club Geoff and I have founded for homesick migrants. Seniority of members is determined by their social status in England and their views on Australia. Both, we have noticed, undergo drastic changes as length of membership increases. For example: the social status of new arrivals is very low. The breadwinner's earnings were twelve pounds a week or less, they lived in a two-bedroom flat, with no bath, and naturally couldn't afford a car." Sensing that Susan was about to object, and interrupt his flow, he raised a monitoring finger.

"But then, after only one month's membership of Shilp, the same man will tell you he was earning fifteen pounds a week in England, and renting a three-bedroom house, with a bath - although, at this stage, he doesn't say 'bathroom', so we can assume it was probably a rusty tub that hung from a nail in the back yard. And now it appears he owned a car. True, it was only an old one, but good enough to get the family around in.

"On Australia, his criticisms are still rather mild. He might say: 'Jobs are hard to get, the money is a little better, but then the cost of living is twice as high – still, the weather is nice here'." He looked to Geoff, inviting him to continue. "And after two months' membership?"

"After two months," said Geoff, leaning back in his chair and taking up the story. "You will find that his English wage has risen to about twenty pounds a week, or at least equal to an Australian wage packet. He was buying his own house - 'A lovely home we had, too', he will say, 'I can't imagine why we ever left it to come out here'. And naturally he owned a car - for a two-month member, probably a late model Ford or Morris. By this time, he is finding all kinds of faults with Australia, and, unbelievably, even the weather is beginning to get him down."

"Hard to imagine, but so true," laughed Craig, as he continued. "Then, after three months spent amongst the optimistic, ever-cheerful inmates of Septic Hill, our new member is almost ready to graduate to our select group of diploma-holding members.

"To qualify for a Shilp diploma of whingemanship, a member must brag minimum earnings of thirty pounds a week in England, have owned his own house, in a very select area, and his car must have been nothing less prestigious than a Rover or a Jaguar. And to pass with full honours, he will also need to brag a second car for the wife. Naturally, the uncouth Australian way of life is in no way comparable to the cultured existence to which our diploma-holding members were accustomed. All of which begs the question: if life was so wonderful in England, why the hell did they emigrate in the first place?"

"And they wonder why the Aussies call us whinging Pomes," laughed Geoff.

Susan refused to join them in their mocking laughter. Craig could be very witty and amusing, even charming at times, but all too often, his humour was designed to ridicule and belittle.

"It's so easy to sit back and criticise people when you don't have their problems to face," she said cuttingly. "It's different for you – you're single and can leave here any time you like, but a man with a wife and family to consider can't. He has to stay and make the best of it. You don't seem to realise what a big step it is for a family to sell up everything they own and migrate to the other side of the world, then have to build a new life for themselves from scratch."

"Indeed, I do, my sweet," said Craig. He reached across and patted her on the head, as though consoling a temperamental child. "The whole crux of the situation is that our pioneer-spirited migrants don't realise it. They come out here with their heads crammed full of the rosy pictures painted for them by Australia House: jobs plentiful, average wage twenty-five pounds a week, new homes, theirs for the asking, and so forth. Probably they haven't had a decent holiday in years, and get wafted right into fantasyland by the prospect of a whole month spent cruising round the world on a luxury liner. Add the promise of free accommodation at Seaview Hostel - a name they immediately synonymise with Butlins - throw in a few coloured pictures of sun-drenched beaches and swimming pools, and the whole thing becomes a superb pleasure trip; all for a measly ten pounds. How can they possibly refuse?

"Once they get here, of course, reality hits them smack between the eyes. They soon discover that the holiday is over, and that twenty-five pounds a week average wage isn't an allowance doled out automatically by some benevolent uncle, it has to be earned by hard graft - the same as anywhere else in the world. That, my sweet, is when they wake up and appreciate what a big step they have made, and how hard it is to start from nothing in a strange country. Suddenly, they find themselves standing on the edge of a precipice, looking down and discovering they have vertigo. That is when the anal nerve goes and they start pining for the security of that dreary little rut they were so keen to get out of. And, before they have given themselves the chance to take an objective look at Australia and what it has to offer, they're feeling homesick... and Shilp has yet another dedicated member."

"You are such a cynic," said Susan, then admitted reluctantly. "But perhaps you are right, in a way. It's very easy to be taken in by all the advertising; it promises people too much, too soon. But I think most people really do try hard to get work and make a go of it. Look at Stan Taylor: you can't say he hasn't been trying."

"Ah, yes, our dear friend, Stanley. Certainly a very intense little man - and a born agitator. We are keeping him in mind for a position on the club's committee."

"Just because you don't like him, there's no need to insult him. He isn't an agitator at all."

"You obviously haven't heard him sounding off about dear old England. I'll let you into a secret: Stan didn't emigrate, he was deported, for fear he would start a communist revolution. If our Stan isn't successful in finding a job very shortly, I can see all that positive effort he's been putting in changing polarity - and when that happens, George Ryan may well have to relinquish the club presidency."

CHAPTER SIX

It was early morning, and the paper shop at the foot of the drive had yet to open. Stan Taylor sat on a bundle of papers that had been deposited in the doorway. He had slid a paper from the bundle and was running a pencil through the employment section. It was Monday, and the columns were scant, but he managed to circle a few possibilities.

The sun had barely risen and looked weak in the cloudless sky, but already its warm rays were beginning to penetrate the still morning air, stirring the flies back into life.

Stan had sat in the same spot at the same time for over a month now, and he knew the signs. Today, the heat would be intolerable, probably over the hundred. He would become sweaty and tired, and his feet would feel like red hot weights welded to the bottoms of his legs as he tramped around the factories and building sites in a futile search for work that wasn't there. He would return feeling thoroughly beaten and exhausted, as he had so many times before – and as likely as not, with the same negative result.

What was the point? Why didn't he stay home and sit and wait for someone else to find him a job, like so many other men at the hostel?

"Good morning, Stan." It was the shopkeeper, come to open up.

"Morning, Harry." Stan gathered the bundle of papers under his arm and followed the old man into the shop.

"Anything good in the paper today?" Harry asked with a hopeful smile.

"Not a lot, there never is on Monday," said Stan. He spread his paper out on the counter while Harry reached into a drawer for his street directory. Getting Stan headed in the right direction each morning had become the old man's first task of the day.

"Where are they today, Stan?" he asked.

"One in a timber yard in East Perth, and Subiaco Council are looking for a tractor driver. They look the most promising."

"Not much chance of you getting on the council, those jobs are always well spoken for. Still, it won't hurt to give it a try. It's on the way to East Perth, anyhow." He perched his spectacles on the end of his long nose and began flicking through the directory. He was a tall, straight-backed man with charcoal-grey hair and stern features. He could be a cantankerous old devil, and generally hadn't much time for the Pomes. But he had taken a liking to Stan; he was a grafter.

"Your wife was telling me that young Peter starts work next week."

"That's right," confirmed Stan. "He's got a job with the railways, in their maintenance sheds. It sounds a decent enough job. If he's got the gumption to knuckle down and pass a few exams, he could end up as a train driver in a few years."

"Make good money as an engine driver, right enough. It's a steady little number, too. He'll never be out of work. There seems to be more scope for the youngsters at the moment, quite a few of them have landed good jobs recently." He removed his spectacles and gazed wistfully through the open door.

"Ah, if only I was a young man again, with the prospects the way they are today," he sighed. "Why, in a few years this state of ours is really going to be booming. There will be big projects starting everywhere - steel works, power stations, irrigation schemes. They're all planned, Stan, no *perhaps* or *maybe* about it. Look at all the mineral resources we have here. There are whole mountains of iron ore up north, never been touched. They're searching for oil up there, too. When they find it - and they will - things will really start to take off. This country is going to be another America, Stan, you mark my words. And ninety per cent of the action is going to be right here in good old Western Australia."

Stan didn't argue. Harry had lived all his life in Western Australia and his opinions were biased accordingly. For him, it was "God's own country". Stan had noticed the same attitude amongst other Australians he had met; they were all fiercely patriotic and placed an enormous amount of faith in the future of their country, and their state. Perhaps they were right; perhaps it was the coming place, a budding America even. But Stan couldn't afford to hang around waiting for the development programme to get under way. He had a wife and family to support, he needed a job, and he needed it right now.

Finding the council chambers closed, he walked across the adjoining piece of ground to a row of sheds where men were taking out tools in preparation for their day's work. He was directed to the foreman, a stout man wearing a flannel shirt and a straw hat.

"Good morning," Stan greeted him. "I understand you're looking for a tractor driver."

The foreman straightened up from the mower he was tending. "Not me, mate," he said. "I'm only the foreman, I don't employ people. You'll have to wait and see Bob Crowley. You'll find his office over in the council chambers. But he won't be in till 8:30."

"The paper said to be here at 7:30."

The foreman shrugged, and returned his attention to the mower. "That's Crowley for you."

Stan checked his watch. It was quarter-past seven. He wandered back to the council chambers to wait. Soon other men began to arrive and by 7:30, there were eight of them outside the building. Yet another man strolled up to join the little group. He was tall and gaunt, and his clothes hung loosely about him, as though they were covering nothing but bones. Stan had seen him at other interviews.

"G'day, Stan. How are you going? Still having no luck, mate?" The man's breath reeked of cheap wine.

"Nothing yet, Dave."

"Keep trying, boy, you'll be right." He patted Stan on the shoulder, and gave a toothless smile. "Say, you wouldn't have the makings on you, would you, mate?"

Stan took a packet of cigarettes from his pocket and offered him one.

Dave's hands were shaking violently, and he had difficulty in lighting the cigarette.

"Put in a couple of days' with a builder over in Belmont last week," he slurred. "Been on a bit of a bender over the weekend." He looked despondently around the group of men. "Don't fancy the odds here much, though. Think I'll push off. Good luck, Stan. See you later."

Stan watched him totter away, his tall, bony frame jerking uncoordinatedly as he walked. Poor devil, he thought – who was going to employ him on a permanent basis?

By 8:15, the employees began filtering into the building, but it was almost nine o'clock before Bob Crowley came out to address the group of men. He was short and plump and had the drooping shoulders of a confirmed bureaucrat. He regarded them with a supercilious air.

"I take it you men are all here to lodge applications for the tractor driving position?"

They nodded as one.

"Actually, I need a man who has had some experience on graders, as well as on tractors. Have any of you driven a grader?"

Two of the men said they had.

"Then I'll concentrate on you two. I won't waste my time interviewing the rest of you." He turned to go back into the building.

"Never mind about wasting *our* time," called Stan. "If you wanted a grader driver, then why the blazes didn't you advertise for one? Keeping us hanging around here all morning for nothing."

Crowley ignored the remark and hurried on through the plate-glass doors.

"Ignorant little shit. Typical office worker," another man muttered after him.

Stan was seething. Jobs were hard enough to find without being messed around by some trumped up office boy. He was still cursing Crowley when he approached the foreman of the East Perth timber yard.

The foreman shook his head and pointed to a man stacking planks at the far side of the yard.

"Sorry... started a man at seven o'clock," he said. His manner was abrupt, and stated plainly enough: "It's no use you turning up at this time of day. You've got to be able to get your backside out of bed if you want to work here."

Stan's anger mounted steadily as the morning wore on, and everywhere he received the same negative response. How many miles had he walked and how many firms had he approached? He was at a loss to understand it. He was a fit man, willing to work, so why then, couldn't he get a job? Was Perth's unemployment problem really this bad? Or was it, as some at the hostel believed, the British were discriminated against, and it was his accent holding him back? If that was the answer, then there was nothing much he could do about it. He was sick of walking the streets hearing rejection after rejection, yet what alternative had he? He certainly couldn't afford to take the family home.

By midday, as he was almost ready to quit, he saw a corner hotel displaying a menu board for their counter lunches. He eyed the prices reproachfully - everything was twice as much as in England. But perhaps the prospects would look a little brighter on a full stomach.

He pushed his way through the heavy, wooden door. The pub's interior was dark and refreshingly cool, with large fans whirling overhead. A middle-aged woman stood behind the bar, polishing her fingernails. She had blonde hair with dark roots, and her face was heavily caked with make-up.

"What'll it be, mate?" she asked brusquely.

Stan ordered his lunch. Did he detect a sneer cross the woman's face on hearing his accent? It was impossible to be sure of any change of expression beneath that layer of make-up, it held her face rigid, like a mask.

"Be about ten minutes. Anything else?"

"I'll have a pint while I'm waiting."

"We don't serve pints here. You're not in England now," she said, jumping on his mistake. This time he was sure he saw her top lip curl.

"A beer," Stan corrected himself tersely.

As he waited for his beer, the door burst open behind him and a group of builders barged in. They wore tattered shirts and shorts, and heavy boots covered in brick-dust and cement. Stan found himself irritated by their rowdy intrusion, and resenting them their good fortune of having work while he had none.

"Come on then, Nelly, let's have some service around here," called one of them, swaggering up to the bar as though he owned it. He was a young man, and he towered a good head and shoulders above Stan. His shirtsleeves had been hacked away at the shoulders, and large biceps bulged at Stan's eye level.

"The usual five to lay the dust, sweetheart," he said, pushing his battered hat to the back of his head and smiling winningly at the barmaid, as though he was at a social event and she was a pretty young girl he was attempting to impress. "Then it's meat pie and chips for me." He turned to his mates. "What are you jokers having? Make it snappy, we haven't got all day."

"Suppose you try waiting your turn," Stan growled irritably.

"Hello, did someone speak?" The young builder glanced around the bar, purposely looking over the top of Stan's head. His mates roared with laughter.

The builder looked down. "Oh, here he is, I've found him. Hell, you don't want to sit down there, Pome, you'll get trodden on."

Stan bit hard on his bottom lip in an attempt to control his rising anger, but the ridiculing laughter proved too much. He grabbed the front of the builder's shirt and pulled his head down.

"Who the hell do you think you are laughing at?" he challenged between barred teeth.

"Let go o' me shirt, Pome, before I jump on you." The young man's expression was one of mild amusement, almost indifference. He was big, fit, and very sure of himself. He was, after all, Joe Lampton, captain of the Subiaco football team, a local hero with a reputation as a fighter. There were not many men around these parts who were foolish enough to pick a quarrel with Joe. He pushed Stan roughly away and turned to resume his place at the bar, still with that amused smile on his face.

Stan finally snapped. He lunged back ferociously, slamming a sledgehammer-like blow into the builder's ribs. As he staggered back against the bar, Stan moved in close and landed two more solid punches. Then Joe's muscular arms grabbed him and swung him round violently, and together they crashed over a table and onto the floor. They rose swinging wildly at each other while men bunched around shouting excited encouragement to Joe. Stan tasted blood as Joe's fist slammed into the side of his mouth, and then he heard Nelly's shrill voice screeching above the uproar:

"Break them up! Break them up, before they wreck the place!" she demanded.

Reluctantly, men stepped in to separate them. Stan was shoved roughly aside, feeling somewhat stupid and a little ashamed of himself for letting his frustrations get the better of him. He took a handkerchief from his pocket and dabbed at the trickle of blood at the corner of his mouth.

"You! Get the hell out of here. You're barred!" Nelly was screeching at him, and pointing to the door.

Joe was adjusting his hat with one hand and rubbing his ribs with the other. "No need for that, Nelly. There's no damage done." His broad, confident grin said he was not a man to hold a grudge, nor did he have to trounce every opponent in order to prove himself to his mates. Stan got the impression that he thoroughly enjoyed an occasional scrap. Perhaps he had himself at Joe's age, but he was older now and didn't consider it fitting behaviour for grown men to be rolling around barroom floors.

"I'm sorry. It was my fault. I've been having a bad day," he said awkwardly. "Let me get you a beer."

"Always ready for a beer." Joe extended his hand cordially. "No hard feelings. Joe Lampton is the name."

They moved back to the bar and Stan ordered fresh beers. The scuffle had served to release the tension and frustration that had been mounting within him all morning, and he soon found himself conversing freely with this tall, rather handsome young man. He perceived Joe Lampton to be the embodiment of the typical Australian male, as seen by the Australians: a tall, bronzed, hard-drinking, hard-swearing man. As rough as guts, yet a genuine bloke for all that.

"You don't want to take us Aussies too seriously, Stan – rubbishing people is a national pastime, nothing personal," said Joe. "The Pomes tend to get more stick than most because they rise to the bait more easily." He fingered his ribs gingerly. "By heck, you really pack a wallop, though. What do you do for a crust? I bet you're no office boy."

"Right now I'm not earning a crust at all, haven't been since I got here," Stan told him ruefully. "That's what I'm so uptight about. I've been chasing work all over Perth for weeks now, and I can't get a start anywhere."

"Yeah, there's not a lot doing around town at the moment. Always gets that way just before Christmas," confirmed Joe. He rubbed his stubbled jaw and studied Stan closely for a long moment.

"You look fit and active enough," he said eventually. "Done any hod carrying?"

"I've done most jobs on building sites, and more than a little hod carrying," Stan told him.

"One on each shoulder, I shouldn't wonder," smiled Joe, having already noted the width of Stan's shoulders. He straightened from the bar and once more nudged the battered hat to the back of his head. "To be honest, I could do with another hoddie," he began.

"Hold on there, Joe, it's always a joint decision who joins the team. It affects the bonus," said a thick-set man with a greying beard. Stan thought he detected a slight northern accent, but couldn't quite place it.

"But I'm the boss, Dave, and I say we could use another hoddie," Joe overrode the objection. "He has got a point though, Stan. We work as a team, and any new member has to fit in. Basically, that means you have to get on with the rest of lads. But most importantly you have to be prepared to work your arse off."

"You'll find no fault with my work," Stan assured him.

"Tell you what I'll do then, Stan. I'll give you a go for a week. If you're any good, you've got a job, if not, you're still looking. What do you say?"

Stan could hardly believe his luck; he was actually being offered a job. Yet, at the same time, he felt a vague unease at the offer. It had been made a little too casually, and there was something about Joe's effortless, self-assured style that reminded him of Craig Curran, a man he wouldn't have trusted any farther than he could throw him. But his suspicions were swamped by his elation at having at last been offered a job.

"Fair enough," he stammered. "When do I start?"

Joe looked at his watch. "In about twenty minutes, if Nelly gets her finger out. Come on, Nelly. Where are those pies?"

"They're coming," Nelly drawled from her makeshift kitchen.

"We'll need to find you some work clobber," said Joe. "There's an old pair of shorts in the tool shed, a shirt, too, I think. That's all you'll need for now. Don't get me wrong, Stan, you're on a week's trial, nothing more. We're on contract work and we don't carry any passengers, so if you don't shape up you'll be out. Come over and meet the team."

They went over to the corner table where the rest of the gang were now sitting huddled over their beers, and Joe introduced him around the table.

"Not another brickie, I hope," said Lee, a wiry young man with a dark complexion, and long, black hair, greyed by cement dust.

"He's a hoddie," Joe assured him.

"In that case, I'm pleased to meet you, Stan. I've been going like stink, trying to keep four brickies going on my own."

"Hark at this. You wouldn't work in an iron lung, you little rat-bag," said George, the oldest member of the gang. "We've been hodding our own bricks for a fortnight."

"You lying toad! It would kill you to hod bricks, you decrepit old git. I'll give you the drum, Stan. Don't take any crap from these brickies. If they get too lippy, stick their heads into the old cement mixer and give it a spin. That usually sorts them out."

Stan found them a loud and lively bunch. They laughed a lot, mostly at crude jokes aimed at each other. But once they started work, the clowning ceased, and Stan was kept on the run all afternoon, with barely a spare moment in which to take a breather. After almost three months of idleness, it was good to feel his muscles flexing back into action, and even the knowledge that they would be torturously stiff for the next few days failed to dull his elated spirits.

During the afternoon, it occurred to him that he hadn't discussed pay and conditions with Joe. He had been so eager to accept the job and start work that the thought had completely slipped his mind. Again, he sensed that vague uneasiness creeping over him. How simple it would be for Joe to put one over on him, and have him working all afternoon for nothing. Stan was already painfully aware of his hideous appearance, knew he looked a prize clown in the baggy shorts with their bottoms flapping about his knees, and the sleeveless shirt with the gaping rip up the back. How the gang had laughed when he had emerged from the tool shed. Stan hadn't minded their laughter then – it had had the effect of initiating him into the group.

But now he wasn't so sure. Had they been laughing with him or ar him? Was it a case of 'let's all take the rise out of the stupid Pome, so gullible and so desperate for a job, he could be duped into working for nothing? Well, it was too late to worry about it now. He would just have to see the day out, and if need be, endure being made the butt of the Australians' warped sense of humour.

When they knocked off at 4:30, and were washing under the water hydrant, Joe appeared satisfied with the afternoon's work.

"That's better, now we're getting somewhere," said George. "I told you last week we needed another hoddie."

"Good men are hard to find," said Joe. His manner was terse and noncommittal. Joe did not like being told anything, not even by George, the man who had taught him most of what he knew about the building trade.

"Put the job in at the employment office and they send you nothing but plonkies and no-hopers. It just means I lose a day's work, interviewing them and sending them back."

When Stan confronted him with the question of wages, Joe gave a slow grin. "Money? I don't remember saying I was going to pay you," he said. "I just thought you wanted to work." He finished drying his hands and threw the towel at Lee.

Stan felt his jaw tighten as he waited for Joe to deliver his punchline, followed by the inevitable eruption of mocking laughter.

"You know what, Stan?" Joe said in a measured tone. "You would be the first Pome I've ever met who didn't want to know the ins and outs of a pig's arse before he would roll his sleeves up and get stuck in. I like your attitude. I think you're going to fit in here just fine."

Stan breathed a sigh of relief as Lee threw him the towel.

"You'll be on nine-and-three an hour - that's the going rate, as laid down by the government. If the job is finished before time, you'll also get a share of the bonus. It breaks my bloody heart to have to pay it, but that's the only way I can get some of these old buggers to do any work at all." He looked around, expecting a response, but George had disappeared into the tool shed to change.

"Not a bad bloke to work for, ain't Joe," was Lee's appraisal of the boss, when they were in the pub washing down the afternoon's dust. "Him and his brother, Fred, got two gangs going at the moment. They subcontract the brickwork from larger builders, we get stuck into the job and finish it in half the time, and then they split up two-thirds of the profits between the team. I've averaged over thirty-five notes a week since I've been with him. You won't do much better than that in the building trade, not without going out bush."

Stan would have been happy with the basic wage, even without the bonus. But thirty-five pounds a week! It was more than he had ever dared to hope for. Wait until he told Maureen - she would be over the moon.

Maureen had been getting disheartened and homesick lately. She had tried to hide it from him, but Stan could tell. It was hard for the women to keep their spirits up while living in the depressing atmosphere of the hostel and having only other homesick women to converse with. But now that he had a job, everything was going to change. They could rent a house, and Maureen would have the running of a home to occupy her mind. She would soon forget her homesickness.

Now that he had a job, everything was going to work out fine.

CHAPTER SEVEN

Friday morning saw Craig and Geoff making their way to the employment office to lodge their sixth claim for unemployment benefits. At the door, Craig stopped, put a hand to his forehead, and then slid it slowly down across his face, as though pulling a mood of depression over himself. He considered the atmosphere inside to be such that it seemed almost sacrilegious to enter looking at all pleased life. He invariably found employment offices to be that way - quiet and overbearing, rather like the reading-rooms of public libraries.

A dozen or so men sat around the room. Some looked up as Craig and Geoff entered, others continued reading the racing guide in their morning papers.

Craig strode to the end of the long, partitioned counter and placed their forms in the metal tray provided. He casually lifted the contents of the tray and slid their forms to the bottom of the pile, knowing that when the clerk collected them and reversed the pile, theirs would emerge on top.

Geoff noticed Tony Bradley sitting in the corner of the room. He sat with his head bowed, seemingly wallowing in his own little aura of gloom, almost as though in a trance - locked in suspended animation, as Craig put it.

"Hello, Tony, how's things?" said Geoff, walking over to him.

Tony looked up, startled, then beamed at seeing someone he knew. "Oh, hello, Geoff. Still no work?"

"Not yet. Are you having any luck?" It was a pointless question, the answer was obvious.

Tony's face fell again. "No, no good at all. I can't see that things are going to improve much, either."

"Of course they will. There'll be a stack more work about after Christmas."

"Do you really think so?" Tony's voice momentarily held a glimmer of hope. "But the trouble with my job is the system is so different. I was a wages clerk back home, but the way they work the tax and everything is so different here, I would need to learn the job from scratch again. At my age, of course, nobody is prepared to teach me. It's easier for companies to employ a youngster, and train them."

The expression of gloom was back on his face. Geoff had noticed that the little cleft between his eyebrows seemed to get deeper as the weeks went by. He tried to visualise Tony at an interview asking, almost pleading, for a job, his hesitant voice and negative persona shouting far louder than the words he spoke, that here was a man sadly lacking in self-confidence, unable to act on his own initiative should his work deviate from the repetitious pattern he knew. An able employer would read him at a glance, and promptly dismiss any notion he may have had of offering him the position.

"You'll find something soon, Tony. They won't let you stay on the dole much longer, it's costing them too much money."

"The only job available at the moment is labouring on the railways. I'm not built for that type of work, but if things don't improve after Christmas, I may have to take it. A man has got to do something for a living. I hear the unions are planning to stop migrants from landing here, unless they have jobs waiting for them. Apparently, a few days ago they refused entry to fifty Spanish families and sent them on to Melbourne."

"I didn't see anything about it in the papers. Probably just another of George Ryan's rumours. But perhaps you should have gone on to Melbourne when you had the chance. There's a stack of work over there. I bought a Melbourne paper last week and it had thirteen pages full of jobs."

"I wish I had now. But Janice wanted to come here; she has an aunt living in Bassendean."

"Cheer up, Tony. Things will get better... if they don't get worse," Craig joked as he walked over to join them.

"They can't get much worse," moped Tony, his eyes dropping to the floor.

"Hutchins!" a voice called solemnly from behind the counter.

A man rose from his seat, tucked his paper under his arm and walked to the counter to collect his weekly benefits form.

Craig looked down at Tony with a mixture of amusement and pity. He certainly had his troubles. He doubtless considered it a near catastrophe to be without the security of his work. And now his bitch of a wife was becoming the talk of the hostel by running around with the chef. Life was getting all too much for little Mickey.

"Never mind, Tony. If things get too tough, you can always join the army." Craig indicated the recruiting posters that were pinned to the walls. "They're always looking for suckers. I do believe the Foreign Legion still have a few vacancies, too. But from what I hear, that's almost as bad as working for the Australian railways."

Tony looked up anxiously. "What's wrong with the railways?" he asked.

"Hard work, little money and appalling conditions. That's why the job is always available." Craig looked at him sternly. "Now, Tony, don't tell me you are thinking of going on the railways?"

"I don't want to, but if nothing else comes up, I may have to."

"You don't have to do anything of the kind," Craig scolded him. "The government brought you out here, and it is their responsibility to find you suitable employment. If they can't, then they will have to keep feeding you and paying you unemployment benefits till they can. You don't have to worry about a thing."

"Curran!" A voice boomed from behind the counter.

"That's me." Craig strode across to collect his form.

Tony stared after him with a puzzled expression. "That's funny," he said. "You were one of the last to come in."

"Luck of the draw," said Geoff.

"The same thing happened last week, too."

Geoff smiled at him and winked. He had noticed a few other men looking quizzically at each other, but nothing was said.

Geoff always felt a twinge of guilt while waiting for the clerk to process his form. He half-expected a deputation of government officials to appear and inquire why he was still not working, and what efforts he had made to find work. But of course, they never did. When he had first registered for employment, he had been offered a job as a lube operator. He had declined the offer, telling them politely that he was a mechanic, not a greaser. Since then, it had been a routine matter of returning the form each week and waiting for his cheque to arrive.

They left the employment office and made their way back to their car, an old Morris Minor they had bought between them.

"Ah, the start of yet another fabulous week's holiday," Craig proclaimed with a broad smile, while flinging his arms wide in an all-embracing gesture. "I wonder what the girls have lined up for the weekend."

"Only one way to find out," said Geoff. They climbed into the car and headed it towards Cottesloe Beach.

Classy, was how Geoff would have described Elaine. She was tall and slim, with long dark hair, and carried herself with all the poise of a fashion model. She was a nurse and worked at the Royal Perth Hospital. Craig had met her during his extended stay in Sydney, and while she was holidaying there. They'd had a whirlwind affair, which had meant far more to Elaine than it had to Craig. When he'd arrived in Perth and contacted her, she had, quite wrongly, assumed that he had travelled halfway round the world specifically to see her, and that this, therefore, must be the start of a big romance.

But a committed relationship was far from Craig's mind. The only thing he had ever been committed to was the pursuit of his own pleasures, and if it were not for an ulterior motive, he probably wouldn't have bothered to contact her at all. But Elaine had lodgings in the nurses' residential quarters at the hospital and this had persuaded him to call her and rekindle their relationship.

"The nurses' quarters are great hunting grounds for women," he confided to Geoff with his roguish grin. "The nurses' irregular shift patterns mean that the recreation rooms are rarely empty. Invariably, there are lovely, young off-duty nurses milling around - studying for exams or watching TV. Usually they're bored, so most of them will jump at the chance to go out on a date with a handsome young stranger." He gave a knowing wink. "And being nurses, they know the score. Well, they hardly have to be told the facts of life, do they?

Having a girlfriend living in the nurses' quarters means that once you are known to security and able to walk unannounced into the recreation rooms, it will be women on tap." He boasted smugly.

And so it had proved, for him and for Geoff. They were rarely short of female company.

Geoff felt a little sorry for Elaine. She was a good-hearted girl, if somewhat gullible – and she was obviously in love with Craig, believing him implicitly when he told her the other girls meant nothing to him, that they were just meaningless dates - someone to have a drink and a chat with whenever her work roster dictated she could not be with him.

Craig was a great character: witty and amusing, and always a laugh to be with. He and Geoff had had some great times together. But there was a side to him that Geoff didn't particularly care for; the side that used people, disregarding their feelings, and the hurt he caused them in his selfish pursuit of personal pleasure.

"Hi there! Who told you we were here?" Elaine sprang to her feet and tossed her long, dark hair back over her shoulders.

"How suspicious the female mind," Craig said airily, as though reciting from a poem. "She never asks how you are or says how pleased she is to see you – always she begins by checking up on you."

"I can't help being a woman. You wouldn't want me to change anything, would you?" She twirled alluringly in front of him. She was fully aware of her trim, well-proportioned figure – perhaps a little too aware of it.

Craig gave her a quick, rather dismissive, peck on the cheek and began preparing for his afternoon on the beach.

On seeing Craig and Geoff arrive, the rest of the girls came out of the water and started back up the beach. Jill came running. She had a bounding vitality and never walked if it were at all possible to run. With her athletic figure, glowing suntan – set off by a white bikini – and her short, platinum blonde hair, she reminded Geoff of the girl in the advert for a sparkling health drink. She threw herself down beside him, showering him with sand.

"G'day, Pomes. What's new?"

"Nothing much, except my back has started to peel - again," said Geoff. He tossed her a bottle of suntan lotion. "Get to work, masseur, and see you do the job properly this time. According to the label, I should have a deep, bronze tan by now."

"The label wasn't written with pink Pomes in mind. You'll end up with skin cancer if you're not careful."

"Are you two coming to the barbecue tomorrow?" asked Julie, a plain, rather plump girl.

"If you ask us nicely," agreed Craig. He sat on his towel and began applying suntan lotion to his legs. "How much beer have you got in?" he asked.

"None! Us nurses don't earn a fortune, you know. If you want to get drunk, you can bring your own beer."

"When are you lazy Pomes going to start work and stop wasting your time on the beach?" complained Jill. "My tax has doubled since you two arrived."

"Work? Nobody said anything about having to work when they took my ten pounds' passage money," said Craig. "As far as I'm aware, the government brought us here specifically to populate the country for them." He smiled smugly. "And I can assure you that we do our very best in that department. Some times, of course, the Aussie Sheilas are not quite as agreeable as they might be." He shrugged philosophically and placed his hand on his heart. "But I can say, in all sincerity, that I'm doing my utmost for the cause."

"You chauvinist pig," Jill snapped back, with a curl to her lip.

"That's me." Craig smiled agreeably and continued applying lotion to his legs. Jill became visibly irritated.

"Don't argue with him, Jill, he's in one of his funny moods again," said Elaine.

"Most people have better things to do with their lives than bumming around on the beach all day and drinking themselves stupid," Jill said cuttingly.

"What could possibly be better or more rewarding than this?" he said with a sweeping gesture. "Sea, sand, sunshine, and surrounded by beautiful women - we have it all. Work is a mere distraction from all the free and gratifying pleasures of life. Personally, I have no great wish to join the ranks of those ambitious, hard-working citizens with taxes to pay, and families and mortgages to support." He gave a deep, aggravating chuckle as he stretched himself in the sun. "The life of the dedicated beach bum suits me just fine."

"You are a total waste of space, a no-hoper," snarled Jill. "You think you're smart, but you are just a bludging Pome. You will never amount to anything in life. And you'll probably end up an alcoholic." With that, she threw herself down onto the sand. Geoff knew from experience that she was now going to sulk for the rest of the afternoon.

She was a moody girl, very prone to tantrums and fits of sulking if she couldn't have her own way, and, for that reason, Craig revelled in teasing her. Geoff had dated her three times, and when in a good mood, she was a vivacious companion and a lot of fun to be with. But he couldn't abide her mood swings. He had made it perfectly clear that he wasn't looking for a committed relationship, with her or with anyone else. Like any red-blooded young male, he enjoyed female company and was happy to play the field and take advantage of his opportunities as they arose. However, he didn't allow the dating game to become an obsessive quest to expand his tally of conquests, as often appeared to be the case with Craig.

Geoff luxuriated in the sun until its hot rays began to sting his back, then he ran down to the water to swim and cool off. He was a strong swimmer, and had soon mastered the art of bodysurfing. Today, the surf was high and he was able to ride the breakers for thirty to forty yards. It was a most exhilarating sensation.

As he swam, he reflected that Australia was certainly living up to his expectations. The holiday of a lifetime, Craig had called it, and it was most certainly that. They had enjoyed a four-week cruise around the world, followed by weeks of swimming and sunbathing on golden beaches. It was proving to be exactly the relaxing break away from work commitments and responsibilities he had been seeking following his stint in the army. Yet he was not an idle person by nature, and several times over the past few days, as he dozed on the beach listening to the relaxing sound of the surf pounding in, then the rush of the water as it raced back out to sea, he began to feel restless. As pleasant as all this was, he was beginning to feel the need to be active. He needed to get some sense of purpose and direction back into his life; for that he needed to get back into work.

Also, there was the question of finances. Most of their dole money was paid directly to the hostel in return for their food and keep, meaning they received a mere two pounds a week as spending money. Not surprisingly, funds were beginning to run low. Geoff had already decided to start looking for a job immediately after Christmas.

As they drove back to the hostel, he informed Craig of his decision.

"I know exactly what you mean. My bank account is almost at rock bottom, too," Craig agreed in a matter-of-fact tone. Insolvency was nothing new to him, nor was it something that bothered him. "I guess all good things come to an end - temporarily, anyway. Kertesz has been hinting strongly that our time at the hostel is limited, as well. Still, look on the bright side: once we have incomes, we'll be able to rent a flat, or a house, even - somewhere half-decent to take women back to. And just think what great parties we are going to have."

CHAPTER EIGHT

Tom Henshaw made his way slowly up the drive, his head bowed, his eyes transfixed on the ground one pace ahead of him. Nothing was real - it was as though he was sleepwalking. The footsteps that echoed from the drive were not really his, for he was not *walking*. He was *moving* up the drive, but his mind was too numb to transmit orders to walk. He was floating as though in a dream - a nightmare, more like. A nightmare he wanted to wake up and forget.

A Morris Minor passed him on its way down the drive. Tom failed to see it; hardly heard the driver's cheery greeting. The only voice he could hear was Edna's, but what was she saying? What would she say when he told her his devastating news?

He left the drive and trudged his way through the fine sand between the chalets. Stupefied, he climbed the steps and opened the door. Edna was sitting by the window, darning a pair of Kenny's socks. She looked up as he entered.

"What's up with you? You look like you've seen a ghost," she said, and continued with her darning.

He stood frozen to the spot in front of her, fumbling for words. "I've... I've been given a week's notice," he choked out.

Edna went on darning, as though she hadn't heard him, her expression remaining blank. It didn't even occur to Tom that had she displayed any emotion at all, it would probably have been one of delight. He would not have believed she could be so impervious to his distress that her immediate thought would be that without the security of his job and a regular wage, Tom would have no option but to see things her way. As far as Edna was concerned, migrating to Australia had been a massive mistake, and the sooner they rectified it and returned home, the better. She had long since abandoned all notions of attempting to make a new life here.

"I've been stood off!" Tom almost shouted in an attempt to jolt some sign of response from her.

"I heard you the first time." She sighed and placed the socks back into her workbasket. When she looked up, her expression was one of indifference to his plight. She had made her own views on Australia plain enough. "Well, what are you going to do now?" The question was challenging and devoid of compassion; almost a demand that he bow to her way of thinking.

"I don't know." He sank into the armchair and gazed vacantly at the ceiling. "I really don't know. Not much chance of finding another job before Christmas. The shop steward phoned around all the big firms for me earlier today. But there's nothing. One of the smaller foundries might need a moulder early in the New Year - but it's doubtful. I could always try my hand at something else, I suppose..."

"Why should you? You have a right to be employed at your trade. That's why you served an apprenticeship. In any case, with all the young men that are unemployed, what chance would a man of your age stand of finding work outside his trade?" She snorted and added disparagingly, "And what else could you do? Foundry work is all you've ever known."

"I don't know. I just don't know, Edna. We can't afford to pack up and go home – you know we can't."

"My brother will lend us the money. He said he would if things didn't work out."

"Yes, and it will take us the rest of our lives to get ourselves out of his debt. We can still make a go of it here. We have to at least try. The boys have both settled in all right. John is doing well at his job, Kenny likes his school - and he has never looked so well in his life. I'll find another job after Christmas, we can rent a place, and..."

His words trailed away to nothing under Edna's incredulous stare. She was right – who was he fooling? Already a plan of retreat was beginning to form in his mind. It was the easy option. Back home, they would be amongst friends who would help them to resettle. He could get his old job back, and everything would be the same as before, except they would have to pay Ben back a few pounds a week. And he could put in a few hours' overtime to cover that. It would all be for the best, he assured himself. Anyway, he hadn't really wanted to move to Australia in the first place. It had all been Edna's idea.

During the two weeks remaining before Christmas, Tom made little effort to obtain work. Mostly, he moped around the hostel, conferring and commiserating with others who were unemployed, finally convincing himself, as the others had all done, that there was no work to be had. He adopted the attitude that he was a tradesman and should, therefore, be employed at his trade. Eventually, he began deriding Perth for its lack of big industry.

"That's the trouble with this place," he remarked to Tony Bradley, as they stood listening to the Salvation Army band playing carols in the square outside the reception hall. "The industries are too small, too reliant on orders from Sydney and Melbourne. Look what happened to me: the firm lost one contract from the Victorian Railways and had to stand off a dozen men. And they're the biggest foundry in Western Australia! I shudder to think how unstable the rest are. A man wouldn't know from one day to the next whether he had a job or not. That sort of thing is no use to a man with a wife and family to support."

"I quite agree with you," said Tony. "I wish I had never left England. I would go back tomorrow - if I had the chance."

"We're hoping to be on our way in a couple of months," said Tom. His attention had swung to the group of teenagers gathered on the reception hall steps. They had been whistling and jeering the band for some time, and had even brought along a transistor radio in an attempt to distract them. But the sound of the band easily drowned out that of the radio. The teenagers then began flicking pieces of gravel at the drum.

"There are some horrible brats in this place," said Tom. "Most of them were decent kids when they arrived. Living in the hostel does something to them. They lose all sense of values, of what's right and wrong. It's like the housing estates back home. The kids lose respect for their neighbourhood and start running wild."

As he spoke, he was looking at Peter Taylor, who was sitting on the top step, a cigarette butt stuck defiantly in the corner of his mouth. Tom had never considered Peter to be a particularly nice kid, but since he had been mixing with the local yobs, he was developing into an out-and-out delinquent. It was well known that several of the local youths were on probation. Tom wondered whether Stan was aware of his son's involvement with them.

"This place seems to change everyone," agreed Tony. He was thinking of Janice, rather than the youths. He didn't see much of her lately, and when they did meet, she was moody and would snap at him. But she was still his wife, and he loved her. If only he could find a job, so they could move away from the depressing influence of the hostel. He felt sure, once they had their own place, she would cheer up and everything would be fine between them again.

A car pulled up at the curb, and John stepped out. He had been swimming with some of his workmates. Tom was glad he didn't mix too much with the hostel teenagers. But then John had never been the type to idle his time away with a bunch of layabouts. He was a sensible, mature-minded young man who knew what he wanted in life. Once, Tom had been proud of his son's positive outlook. He still was, but now it served mainly as a painful reminder of the tensions building within his family, for the life John had set his heart on was here in Australia.

"But why, Dad? What's wrong with Australia? Why do we have to leave? You can easily find yourself another job," he had argued, on learning of their decision.

"John!" Edna had corrected him sternly. "Don't ever question your father's judgement. We have decided to return home - and that is final."

Though John respected his parents and would never have openly defied their wishes, he was now too old and too independent to believe blindly that their every decision was automatically for the best, certainly not for him. Australia was the place he wanted to live; he had known that since the day he arrived. He loved the healthy outdoor way of life, and was thrilled by the thought of being able to swim and play tennis all year round. Australians were so active and alive, always going places, doing things: fishing, shooting, surfing, having barbeques. It was all so excitingly different from the drab existence of life in Sheffield. Already, he felt he was more Australian in his outlook than British - and no way did he ever want to go back.

Since learning of his parents' decision to return home, John had lived within his own little shell of depression, hardly speaking unless spoken to. But now, as he approached his father, his stride had a fresh spring to it, and his smile was a beam of new hope.

Tom's spirits plunged to new depths as he sensed more friction and a heightening of the tension within the family. He had come to regard all changes of mood sceptically, especially changes from the now comfortable and accepted negative to anything that resembled a positive outlook; it could only signal yet another headache for him to endure.

"Hello, Dad. Hello, Tony."

"Hello, Son. Been swimming?"

"Dad?" John looked earnestly at his father until he was sure of his undivided attention. "What would you say, Dad, if I..." He hesitated, as though suddenly unsure of the plausibility of his question. "Well, if I were to stay here in Australia? What I mean is, my friend, Eddie, who I'll be serving my apprenticeship with, well his parents have offered to board me. They have a lovely big home in Osborne Park. It's not as though I'd be living out here on my own. I know them - and I'd be treated as one of the family. What do you think, Dad?"

Tom sighed heavily, and the crease in his brow deepened. "I don't know... We'll see what your mother has to say about it."

"But what do *you* think, Dad?"

"We'll see."

John bit hard on his lip. It was always: "See what your mother says". Why couldn't his father make a decision for once, or at least offer an opinion? John loved his father, but sometimes he wanted to shout at him, even swear, in an attempt to shock him into action – any action, as long as it was wholly his and not merely a placid adherence to his wife's wishes.

The ray of hope drained from John's face, and they made their way back to the chalet in silence. His mother would never consent to his staying in Australia on his own. He should have realised that before. The idea had sounded plausible enough at the time; after all, he was seventeen, he had a job, and he was capable of looking after himself. He had at least expected his parents to give the idea some credence, and discuss it rationally before coming to their decision. Had they done so, he could have accepted their rejection without resentment. But his mother's subsequent outburst of affected shock and indignation served only to harden his defiance.

She had stood with her hands planted firmly on her hips and glared at him - as though the question had been a slap in the face. Then she had lectured him, long and bitterly, condemning him for his selfish and ungrateful attitude to even consider such a monstrous idea. After all they had done for him, all the sacrifices they had made to ensure that he had always had the best they could provide.

It was the same old story over and over again; John had heard it all many times before. Lately, it seemed his mother was always harping on about how much they had done for him and how little appreciation he showed. Certainly, they had always done their best, and he would never have belittled their efforts. But surely it was a parent's duty to provide for their children – he would be expected to do the same for his own children one day.

And all the time, his father had sat there saying nothing, as though afraid to interrupt.

John failed to see any justification for his mother's irrational outburst, or that the idea of living apart from his parents was such an outlandish one. He was no longer a child; during the war, boys not much older than him were being taken away from their families and sent to fight for their country. He felt he was at least old enough and mature enough for his views to be given a fair hearing. Somehow he had lost that closeness he had once had with his parents. They no longer knew what was best for him; at times, he doubted they even considered him in their plans. It was not that they didn't *care* for him, but simply that they still regarded him as a child; a child whose only option was to tag along meekly wherever they chose to lead him. They refused to recognise that he was almost an adult now and had a life of his own to live.

But an adult he was, and John was now more determined than ever to live life to his own design.

He would not go back to England.

He made his decision quickly and resolutely, even while his mother was still browbeating him. If necessary, he would leave his family and hitchhike across to Sydney. He had friends there, Danny and Simon, two teenage lads from London he had met onboard ship. He'd had a letter from Danny and knew they had rented a flat. He felt sure they would let him stay with them for a while, just until he found himself a job and digs. Australia was a big country; once he was away from Perth, he would not be traced.

Later, when he had time to think about it more rationally, he realised the enormity of the journey he was contemplating. Sydney was over three thousand miles away, and over a thousand miles of that was via a mere dirt track that crossed the notorious Nullarbor desert between the states of Western Australia and South Australia. He had read harrowing reports of motorists breaking down out there and dying of thirst and dehydration before they could be rescued. It would not be an easy journey to undertake alone. He was bound to encounter problems and dangers along the way.

Ideally, what he needed was a friend to go with; a travel companion. He thought of Peter. They were not the closest of friends, but they shared the chalet together, and they got on okay. Peter had often spoken of wanting to leave home and get away from his father's strict and overbearing presence. Perhaps Peter would be up for it?

As the Salvation Army band finished playing and began packing away their instruments, a grudging, disinterested ripple of applause rose from some of the teenagers sitting on the reception hall steps. Peter tossed a piece of gravel and it bounced off a brass trumpet with a metallic ping. Louise Tate giggled and leaned towards him, resting her hand heavily on his knee.

"Say something, Peter," she said sweetly. "I want to hear your accent. It really sends me."

Louise had arrived in Australia a week earlier and had created quite a stir amongst the teenage males at the hostel. She was a tall, exceptionally well-developed girl. Her dark-brown eyes, full lips and long, well-groomed hair, together with liberally applied makeup, gave her a mature, sophisticated look that was way beyond her fifteen years. Peter imagined he had fallen in love with her, and could scarcely believe it, but she seemed to have taken a shine to him, too.

But the competition for her attention was fierce. Eddie Carter was always hanging around, trying to impress her with his silly jokes and smart remarks. Then there were the local youths, roaring around in their cars, showing off and offering her rides to the beach. But, amazingly, she seemed to prefer Peter's company.

"Here come our resident beach bums," quipped Eddie, as a black Holden roared up the drive and skidded to a halt in front of the teenagers.

In the car was Wayne Stanton and his brother, Robbie, local youths who often drove into the hostel '...looking for a bit of stray skirt', as Wayne put it.

Peter got on all right with Robbie, but Wayne he couldn't stand. He talked too much and thought himself a big shot because he was on probation, and claimed he was paying maintenance to a girl in Victoria. He had a deep tan that made his long blond hair look almost white. Whenever he was around, he would dominate the conversation with his crude jokes and tales of conquests. In spite of his crudeness - or perhaps because of it - he had become popular with the girls at the hostel – which was yet another reason why Peter didn't like him.

"G'day, lover boy, how are you doing?" Wayne shouted to Peter through the car's open window. "Do you want to borrow a rubber?" he smirked, giving a suggestive thumbs-up gesture.

Some of the girls giggled. With Louise's hand resting on his thigh, Peter felt uncomfortable at their laughter, and at the insinuation. He felt himself flush and hoped he wasn't blushing; that would be just too embarrassing. He made no reply.

"Don't fret, Louise, my darling, he wouldn't know what to do with it." Wayne winked at Louise as he leaned out of the car and asked, "How do you fancy coming for a spin along the beach with a *real* man?

"Why don't you get lost?" said Peter, feeling the need to make some sort of macho response. Robbie had once confided that his brother was all talk. Peter wasn't too sure about that, but intoxicated by Louise's smile, he was prepared to push his luck. In any case, Wayne wasn't that much bigger than him, so if it came to a fight, he wouldn't be afraid of him.

"Careful, sonny, you're getting way out of your depth here," warned Wayne.

Louise got lightly to her feet. "Come on, Peter, let's go for a ride along the beach. It'll be fun."

"No boys invited on this trip. What do you think I am, some kind of poof?" smirked Wayne.

"Well, you do dye your hair," quipped Eddie, giving a coarse rattle of a laugh. A highly-strung lad, he began shuffling his feet and twitching with nervous energy as his eyes darted from face-to-face, seeking appreciation of his joke.

Peter was relieved that the attention had swung away from him, and that the laugh now appeared to be on Wayne.

"Smart arse," Wayne retorted, pointing two fingers at Eddie, as though holding a gun.

"I'll go with you, Wayne," June, a slim, dark-haired girl volunteered. "Where's your car? It's more comfortable than Robbie's."

"Shagged battery," Wayne stated simply. "I'd go and nick a new one, but I'm on probation. If I got caught, it would be six months inside, at least. Not worth the risk for a poxy battery." He looked cunningly around the group, his eyes lighting on Peter. "What I need is a mate with some guts and a clean record. Someone who owes me a favour or two for all those free rides he's had to the beach. How about it, lover boy? Are you feeling brave?"

"Why should I nick anything for you? If you want a new battery, go and nick it yourself."

Wayne flapped his arms and made a clucking sound. "Look who's chicken. I bet he's never nicked anything in his life."

"Of course I have," lied Peter.

"Yeah, right. We all know how shit-scared you are," mocked Wayne. "You're even scared of daddy catching you out here after ten o'clock - the time when all good little boys should be tucked up in bed."

The group laughed mockingly, and this time Peter was sure he was going red.

"Liverpool lads are not chicken; they are rebels. They are afraid of nothing," Louise spoke up confidently in his defence. She ran her hand along his thigh and Peter felt emboldened by her touch; he couldn't disappoint her.

"Let's see you prove it then, hard man," Wayne goaded.

"Go on, Peter. Show him, show them all," Louise urged, excitement shining in her pretty, brown eyes.

Peter felt trapped. He didn't want to steal anything, especially for Wayne, but he had to measure up to Louise's expectations. If he refused, he knew he would lose her respect, admiration and all those intimate little glances that made him feel so special. He couldn't let that happen.

"All right. I will," he blurted, regretting it even as he spoke. "I'll show you I'm not chicken. I'll nick one tonight, when it's dark."

The hostel boasted two main car parks: one at the top of the hill, behind the reception hall, the other at the foot of the drive. All afternoon, an agitated Peter wandered from one to the other, agonising as to which posed the lesser danger of being caught. And all the time he wondered how he had allowed himself to be tricked into this act of crass stupidity. He hadn't wanted to steal a battery, or anything else. He was terrified of being caught, and having to face the police – and what would his mother think of him?

Backing out was not an option. He had to go through with it, or he would be a laughing stock amongst his friends. More importantly, he would lose the affections of Louise.

For the third time, he went to study the car park behind the reception hall. There were more people about at the top of the drive, though nearly all of them stayed at the front of the building. The car park at the foot of the drive was much quieter, but it was very close to a row of chalets.

After much deliberation, he finally decided that the lower car park would be favourite, as there was a gap in the perimeter fence where he could slip through and run off along the road should anyone spot him. But the close proximity of those chalets meant he would need to be very quiet.

It was gone midnight when, armed with a torch, a piece of wire and a shifting spanner borrowed from Robbie, he crept out of his chalet and made his way down the drive. He cursed under his breath at how light it still was. But, hopefully, everyone would be asleep by now. All day, he had been nervous, dreading the impending night, but now, as he approached the row of cars, he was gripped by an intense excitement that swamped all his fears. He was a grown man now, acting independently, committing an act of defiance and rebellion. It was an exhilarating feeling. Even the threat of his father's belt, the inevitable result of being caught, was swept from his mind. The belt was nothing new – he could take it.

Peter hated his father. It seemed he was always getting on to him about something, and even the most trivial of misdemeanours received a bark and a scowl; strange how he wasn't the same with David and little Debbie. With Debbie especially, he was a completely different man, tender and loving, always ready to read her a story, or take her to the park to play on the swings. Stan had never read Peter a story, never even taken him to the rec to kick a ball around, as he occasionally did with David. David never seemed to get the scowls, either. It was only Peter that Stan had a down on - or so it seemed.

Since they had been in Australia, Peter hadn't seen much of his father. Stan had been too busy with work to bother with him. The chalet he shared with John and another youth was like having their own flat. He was enjoying living away from the rest of the family. It gave him a sense of freedom – a taste of what it would be like to be grown up – and, already, he was looking forward to the day when he would leave home and strike out on his own.

At the bottom of the drive, Peter eyed the row of parked cars, looking for a Holden similar to Wayne's. He wasn't sure if all car batteries were the same, and didn't want to look an idiot by stealing one that was not compatible. He spotted a Holden and moved cautiously to it. Crouching in front of the bonnet, he poked the piece of hooked wire through the grill, searching for the cable that would release the catch. Soon, he snagged the cable and gave a tug. The bonnet sprang open with a loud metallic clang that echoed around all the adjacent chalets. The noise seemed to be amplified by the silence of the night; surely someone must have heard?

He crouched back down behind the bonnet and held his breath, ready to sprint for the perimeter fence, should one of the chalet doors open. Robbie had warned him to hold the bonnet down firmly when releasing the catch so as to prevent just such a noise. Stupidly, he had forgotten the advice.

He waited and watched, but saw no movement from the chalets - no doors opened and no lights came on. Peter breathed a sigh of relief. It appeared he had gotten away with it. Quietly, he lifted the bonnet and propped it open. The battery looked old and corroded. He unfastened one of the terminals and disconnected the lead, but the second terminal wouldn't budge. He pushed hard on the spanner. It slipped off the nut and he banged his knuckles. He cursed and tried again, but now the corners of the nut had been rounded, and, try as he may, he couldn't shift it. He swore again and reluctantly abandoned the task.

Three cars along, stood a similar Holden. Peter moved quietly to it and quickly released the bonnet catch, remembering this time to hold the bonnet down with his other hand. It sprang open quietly. The battery in this one looked new, and the terminals were clean.

He had soon unfastened them and was lifting the battery from its cradle. He smiled with satisfaction. All the nerves and sense of foreboding that had been plaguing him all day were gone, replaced now by an exhilarating sense of achievement. As the adrenalin pumped through him, he felt truly alive for the first time in his life. He was on an almighty high, and knew he would be compelled to seek out more experiences like this in the future.

He carried the battery through the hole in the perimeter fence to the road, where Robbie was to collect it; then he walked casually back up the drive to his chalet.

All the next day, Peter walked with a confident swagger, conscious of the new respect being accorded to him by the usual gang outside the reception hall.

Even Wayne appeared impressed. "That's a brand new one," he enthused on seeing the battery.

"Of course it is. No point in nicking rubbish," Peter told them nonchalantly, as though he had been stealing batteries all his life.

But the real prize was that Louise seemed really impressed. She sat close to him on the steps, one arm draped around his neck, and smiled up at him, hero worship shining in her big brown eyes.

"See, I told you all he would do it," she boasted proudly. "A Liverpool lad wouldn't chicken out." She slid her hand inside his shirt and began caressing his chest. Her hand slid lower.

Peter felt his stomach muscles contract. He was unable to speak. He pulled her clumsily to him in an attempt to kiss her, but she pushed him away.

"Not here, silly. You were going to show me the photos of your trip, remember?"

"They're in my room. I'll go and get them, if you like."

Louise danced lightly to her feet. "I know they're in your room. I'm coming with you," she smiled.

Peter's roommates were out, and Louise followed him up the steps and into the chalet.

"You're so lucky. I wish I had my own chalet," she said moodily. "I've got to share with my parents; what a drag that is. Oh, this looks comfortable." She flopped onto the bed and stretched out with her hands behind her head, thrusting her firm, young breasts into her flimsy blouse; smiling up at him provocatively.

Peter began fumbling through a drawer for his photos.

"I don't want to see your stupid old photos," she giggled. "I did the same voyage myself, remember?"

Peter closed the drawer. Somehow, he had known that. "But I thought you wanted to see them," he offered lamely.

He sat awkwardly on the edge of the bed beside her. The intimacy of her smile sent quivers running up and down his spine. When he leaned over to kiss her, she locked her arms tightly round his neck, pulled him down on top of her and whispered softly in his ear, leaving him in no doubt as to why she had come to his room, and what was expected of him.

Panic seized him. He couldn't go through with it. He had often bragged to his friends about the number of girls he had been with, but the truth was, he had never had sex – had never even had a girlfriend before. He had read a book about sex, but still wasn't sure what to do. He feared there was something else he should know - something that everybody else knew and he, through his lack of experience, didn't. He would be clumsy and do something wrong. Louise would know he was green and would laugh at him. He wanted to run. His mind began fumbling for an excuse to leave - somebody might come in, or...

Louise had been digging her fingernails into the back of his neck. Now she was thrusting her tongue between his lips and kissing him like he had never been kissed before. Urges began stirring within him; suddenly he had no fears - only unstoppable desires.

Peter relaxed on the bed, still breathing heavily. Every nerve in his body was alive and throbbing with pleasure and excitement. He had done it. He had actually had sex. He didn't need to lie about it any more. He was truly a man now; mature and experienced.

The adrenalin was still pumping, and he was on that almighty high again. At that moment, Peter hadn't a care in the world. The possibility of Louise becoming pregnant never occurred to him. If it had, he would have dismissed it. People had to sleep together regularly before they could have babies, he knew that. And carnal knowledge was just another of those phrased the lads bandied about when wanting to sound big. He knew what it meant, of course. But Louise wasn't under age, she was sixteen - she had told him so.

CHAPTER NINE

The reception hall had been decorated for the Christmas dance: paper chains, tinsel and clusters of coloured balloons hung around the walls and ceiling in abundance, and a string of fairy lights adorned the Christmas tree that stood in the corner by the stage. A quartet, dressed in blue silk jackets and bow ties, were on the stage churning out dance tunes. But only a few couples were taking advantage of the music. Most of the migrants sat in tight cliques around private supplies of liquor, and the hall held the strained atmosphere of a wedding reception where none of the guests had been introduced.

A group of Spanish migrants had gathered by the door and were laughing and joking loudly. The men were drinking from a canvas bag with a nozzle top, holding the bag above their heads and letting the continuous jet of wine squirt into their mouths. The group hushed. A man stood rigidly, his head tilted back, the canvas bag held high at arm's length, his other hand resting firmly on the back of his hip for balance. He stood for a long moment, seemingly without breathing or swallowing, while the wine flowed down his throat. Eventually, he lowered the bag with a flourish and his friends laughed and applauded him. Many of the British migrants frowned on the Spaniards' behaviour, while others made to ignore them altogether.

The door opened and a man in his mid-twenties entered. He was medium height, with broad shoulders and a good physique. His light, even tan had a superficial appearance, as though it had been sprayed on. But he was strikingly handsome with chiselled features, dark wavy hair and deep-set, blue eyes. As if to distinguish himself from the crowd, he wore a blue blazer and a bright orange cravat. Silver-framed sunglasses protruded from the top pocket of his blazer. He squared his shoulders and stood gazing around the hall with a fixed expression that may have been an attempt at upper-class aloofness, but which on his young features came across as distain.

The girl by his side was slim and pretty. Her light brown hair hung loosely to her shoulders, while her soft blue eyes darted timidly about the hall. She clung tightly to the young man's arm, as a frightened child might cling to its parent's hand for fear of getting lost amongst the crowd.

"Wow. Who's he? He's really handsome," said Susan. "He looks like a film star."

"He looks a bit of a poof to me," said Joan.

"Oh, he's a terrible sweetie. I'm sure you'll simply adore him," mocked Craig. They were sitting at a table by the corner of the stage. The young man spotted them and began to make his way over. The girl followed, still clinging to his arm.

"Just what the party needs," said Craig, "A genuine English gentleman to regale us with tales of his outstanding success and achievements in the world of business and high finance."

"Hello there. Everyone enjoying themselves, I hope. Mind if we join the party?" He drew a bottle of whisky and a bottle of gin from his blazer pockets and placed them with the bottles of beer standing on the table. "I've brought a little something to make the party swing," he said.

"Thank you, Michael, that's most generous of you," said Geoff. "I'm afraid we only have beer and soft drinks to offer in return."

"Don't mention it, old chap. They are duty-frees," Michael explained, waving aside Geoff's gratitude, and praise of his generosity.

Michael Dean and his fiancée, Gloria, had arrived in Australia by plane four days earlier, and Michael had been allotted the small room adjoining Geoff and Craig's room. Michael always stressed that they had arrived by plane, in the belief that it somehow distinguished them from the hordes of other migrants who had merely been shipped here.

"Of course, flying migrants out is something comparatively new," he would say, puffing out his chest. "At the moment, they are only exploring the economics of the thing with a select group of migrants: businessmen and professional people, mainly. As I held an executive position with an international company at the time of applying, naturally, we were offered the flight."

Michael poured himself a whisky. "Well, here's to a prosperous future for all," he toasted grandly, raising his glass. "Actually, I was hoping to have a word with you, Geoff. I'm looking to buy a car. A little Volkswagen, I think. I'm not very good mechanically, and I was wondering if you would be kind enough to cast your professional eye over it for me. I'll pay you for your time and trouble, naturally."

"I would be happy to do that for you, Michael. No payment required. We Pomes have to stick together, you know."

"Well, thank you," he said politely, his tone suggesting he was not too comfortable with being referred to as a Pome. "Of course, once I take up a position here, I expect to be allocated a company car. Then Gloria can have the Volkswagen as a runabout."

Geoff didn't mind Michael, as long as it was in small doses. True, he was a bit priggish and pompous, but beneath it all, Geoff sensed he was a genuine sort. Michael went to great pains to present himself as an upper-class gentleman, a man of impeccable breeding and good manners. Whether this image was merely a façade or whether he was the genuine article, Geoff had yet to decide. But he believed Michael to be a man of high principals, one who would always endeavour to do the right thing by anyone with whom he had dealings.

Craig's assessment of Michael was harsher and much more to the point. "The man is a complete and utter prat," he had stated dismissively after their very first meeting.

Michael Dean's main topic of conversation was Michael Dean, and somehow he always managed to swing the conversation round to himself, and how whatever was happening in the world related to him.

"In the last position I held - with Howard Electronics - I was charged with organising a huge sales drive throughout the whole of southern England," he was telling Joan, who was plainly disinterested. "I don't anticipate any difficulty in obtaining a position with one of the state's leading companies. Naturally, I have already been approached by several of the smaller firms, but they are not offering nearly enough in remuneration. I expect to receive a salary in the region of two thousand a year, to begin with. I couldn't possibly consider anything less."

"A man of your calibre should get much more than that," Joan told him, with a straight face. "Even tradesmen can earn forty pounds a week out here."

Her dry humour was wasted on Michael. He was far too full of his own importance to imagine anyone would not take him seriously.

Gloria smiled shyly. Her father had warned her that Michael was all talk before they became engaged, but she had refused to listen. She had led a very sheltered life, always longing to travel and see the world, but lacking the courage to set out on her own. Then Michael had come along and she had been swept off her feet by his good looks, his confident persona and his promises of travel and adventure. He had sounded so convincing, and she had believed in him whole-heartedly. Their courtship had been a whirlwind affair. They had become engaged only two weeks after their first meeting, and had applied for emigration to Australia the very next day. It had all been so fast and exciting, she had hardly given herself time to think twice. But now she was beginning to realise her father could have been right; that perhaps Michael was not quite the high-flyer he purported to be.

"How are things with you, Geoff - or have you not been bothering about work yet?" asked Ted, edging discretely away from his wife's one-sided conversation.

"I'll be out there looking for a job first thing in the New Year. I've lazed about long enough," said Geoff.

Not having seen Ted for a few weeks, Geoff had been struck by the change in him, but couldn't decide immediately whether the change was for better or worse. Gone were the bloated features and ruddy complexion of the shopkeeper. His face had become lean and heavily bronzed, and when he smiled, certainly, he looked a picture of health and alertness. Yet, when he was standing quietly, gazing around the hall at nothing in particular, Geoff noticed a slightly haggard expression enter into his eyes. It was as though there was a nagging problem at the back of his mind that would creep up and take possession of him whenever his brain was inactive. It occurred to Geoff that perhaps Ted was finding life as a truck driver a little too strenuous and demanding. Perhaps he was beginning to miss the comfort and security of his shop.

Joan, too, looked fed up, but then the hostel affected most of the women that way. With no shopping or cooking to do, they soon became bored and listless. But Susan was her usual self, and talked gushingly about her job as a counter assistant at Woolworths.

"It's much better than working in a stuffy old office. I meet lots more people, and I'm learning all the Australian expressions. They never say 'good morning', or 'good afternoon'; it's always 'g'day', or 'how are you going?' And their response to just about everything is 'no worries'. I love that expression, it's so Australian. It sums up their whole free-and-easy attitude to life. It's like I'm having to learn a whole new language."

Ted smiled and the blankness left his eyes. "I've even picked up one or two of the more colourful expressions myself," he said. "The truckers are full of them."

"And I bet they're not the same ones I've been hearing," laughed Susan.

"In Woolworths? I should certainly hope not, dear."

"And how is the trucking business, Ted? I haven't seen much of you lately,"

"It's hard work," he admitted with tight lips. "Harold has more contracts than he can keep up with. He's had a truck off the road for a couple of weeks, which hasn't helped any."

"Think you'll be staying in Perth?"

Ted shrugged. "Hard to say at the moment. We haven't settled in properly yet. As soon as I can get a few days off, we'll go house hunting. Find somewhere to rent, and get out of this place."

"Get out of this place". To Geoff, the phrase and the tone in which it was uttered highlighted the change in Ted's outlook. The bright new life he had embarked on so enthusiastically had lost its lustre, and all the excitement of finding a new home and getting his family settled was no longer an adventure - it had become a chore. Now he merely wanted to "get out of this place", and with as little personal effort as possible.

After a lengthy interval, the musicians were back on the stage, and with the flow of liquor, more couples were inclined to dance.

Peter was sitting with his parents, who were talking to the Jacksons. He sat apart from the little group, sipping at a glass of lemonade and wishing it was beer. It was a crummy dance, and he was bored. He wouldn't have gone at all, except that he knew Louise would be there. But she had walked in with Eddie Carter and they had sat together all evening, laughing and holding hands. Peter watched venomously as they whirled around the floor. Why was she dancing so close to him, and smiling at him that way, when she was supposed to be his girl? As they whirled by in front of him, her skirt brushed against his knees and he caught a whiff of her perfume - the same sweet smell that had filled his nostrils as she moved rhythmically beneath him. He wanted her again, now. He felt an urge to rush over and punch Eddie on the nose – and he would, the very next time he saw him alone.

"Don't scowl so, Peter," said his mother. "Why don't you ask one of the girls to dance?"

"I don't want to dance. I'm going back to my room." He got up and went outside where he sat moping on the steps.

Gloria hadn't wanted to dance. She would have preferred to sit quietly sipping her gin-squash all evening, trying not to be noticed. She was always very shy and ill at ease amongst strangers. When Craig asked her to dance, she had wanted to refuse, but that would have drawn attention to her, and caused her even more embarrassment.

Geoff watched her step timidly onto the floor, like a frightened little canary about to be devoured by big, bad Sylvester. Perhaps Craig had felt sorry for her and was merely trying to draw her more into the spirit of things. But Geoff didn't believe that for one moment. Craig had taken an instant dislike to Michael and would be out to get one over on him by chatting up his fiancée. It wasn't Geoff's idea of a joke. But then, it was none of his business.

Michael stiffened visibly when Craig asked Gloria to dance. Clearly, Craig had ignored correct etiquette by not first asking Michael's permission. As though not wanting her to stray too far from his side, Michael turned instinctively to Susan.

"May I have the pleasure?" he smiled, extending his hand and bowing politely.

"It doesn't seem like Christmas, does it?" Joan said after a short silence. "There's no atmosphere, if you know what I mean. It's as though everyone is thinking of their friends and relations back home, and wishing they could be there celebrating with them."

Geoff knew what she meant. He looked around the hall at the groups of gloomy faces and wondered why most of them had bothered to attend the dance at all. He felt sure they would all have been far happier drinking in the privacy of their own chalets.

"The Spanish are the only people who are enjoying themselves," observed Joan.

"Old George is happy, too," said Geoff, nodding towards George Ryan. "He's always happy when he has some new arrivals to ear bash. The Tates look absolutely terrified. He must be telling them about the poisonous spiders that crawl into the chalets of a night. If he stopped complaining and concentrated on finding himself a job, he'd get on a whole lot better."

"He's too lazy... like someone else I could mention," said Joan. "When are you going to start looking for a job?"

"That depends on how long it takes the employment office to catch up with me," he joked. "Seriously, though, I'll be out looking directly after Christmas. Come on, let's dance." He stood his glass down on the table and led Joan onto the floor.

"I'm not the one who wanted an invite," she said pointedly, glancing towards Susan.

They entered the dance close to Craig and Gloria. Gloria was smiling and looking almost relaxed in his arms. Craig was looking intensely into her eyes; giving her his earnest, Mister Sincerity look, and Gloria's smile said she appeared to be buying into it.

"What's his game?" Joan asked icily.

Geoff shrugged. "You know our Craig, always turning on the charm. He can't help himself." He sensed that Joan was about to respond with a cutting remark when they were distracted by a rush of excitement by the door. There was a fight. People were crowding the entrance, trying to see out.

Outside, Peter and Eddie were swinging wildly at each other while Louise looked on, her face alive with excitement. Men grabbed hold of the boys and held them apart.

"What have you been up to?" screeched May Carter, pushing her way through the crowd. She was flushed and looked close to hysterics.

"Nothing, Mum." Eddie looked away, trying to hide the blood oozing from his lip.

Peter glanced anxiously towards the door, praying that his father wouldn't come out. It had been madness to start fighting in front of the hall. Neither of them had wanted to, not really, but Louise had egged them on, making it look as though they were both afraid to fight.

"I might have known you would be at the bottom of this, Peter Taylor. You are a born troublemaker. A good strapping is what you need."

"Cool down, May, there's no harm done," said Bernard Carter. He strolled up casually, as though he had merely been passing the disturbance and had no deeper interest in it than a wish for the noise to cease so he could get back to his drinking. He was a placid, even-tempered man; it would take more than an excited crowd or a shrieking woman to rattle Bernard.

"No harm done? Look at his mouth."

"It's nothing. Teach him to keep his guard up next time."

"What goes on here?" Stan was shouldering his way through the crowd. Peter froze. Now he would be for it.

"Your son has been picking on my Edward, that's what. Look what he's done to his mouth. Why don't you teach him to keep his hands to himself?"

"It takes two to make an argument, May," said Stan. He turned to the boys. "Well, what's it all about?"

There was an awkward silence. The boys stood with their heads bowed. "Nothing much," muttered Eddie.

"In that case, shake hands and let's hear no more about it."

"He needs a good strapping, that one," said May. "He's always causing trouble. Is that all you are going to say to him?"

Stan nodded. "That's all, May. And I'll be the judge of what he needs, thank you."

"An occasional scrap never did a lad any harm," declared Bernard. He inspected Ted's lip, and then ruffled his head. "You'll live. Get off home and bathe it."

Peter walked despondently back to his chalet. He was relieved, and a little mystified that his father had taken it all so calmly, had even stood up for him - that was a first. Peter was never sure how his father would react to anything. He had taken his belt off to him for far lesser things. Why couldn't he have a father like Bernard Carter? Bernard was solid and dependable - the sort of dad you could go to when you needed advice, a dad you could talk to and confide in.

His thoughts drifted back to Louise. She had been the cause of all the trouble. She had stirred up the argument; she had wanted them to fight over her. He and Eddie had been friends before she arrived. He wondered if Eddie had had sex with her. He expected so. She was a flirt and a troublemaker, he could see that now. He didn't really like her much anymore. But, inexplicably, he still wanted her, perhaps more than ever. The memory of her soft body moving rhythmically beneath him filled his mind, overshadowing all her faults.

When he got back to his chalet, John was there, studying a large road map that was spread across the foot of his bed.

"How are your plans going?" Peter asked casually, as he looked down at the vastness of the map. "Have you worked out your route yet?"

"More or less." John pointed to a cross on the map. "This is where I'll start hitchhiking, Midland Junction. I'll go that far by train. It would be hopeless trying to thumb a lift through the suburbs, and it would take far too long. I'll need to be away from Perth quickly."

"It's a hell of a long way," Peter said dubiously. "Over three thousand miles. How long do you reckon it will take you?"

John shrugged. "It all depends how lucky I am with lifts. I'll have to make it as fast as I can, though, or my money will run out. I don't want to be broke when I arrive in Sydney."

"*If* you get there," Peter said gloomily. He sat down on the edge of his bed. "I can't see why you want to stay in Australia, anyway. If I had the chance to go back to England and see all my old mates, I'd take it like a shot."

"I like it here. I don't want to go back to England."

"But Sydney is bound to be a lot different to Perth. I've heard it's like London: fast and overcrowded. Suppose you don't like it there? Or what if you can't get a job? What will you do then?"

"I don't know," John admitted ruefully. He had asked himself the same question many times. Peter was right - Perth was where he wanted to be. He had friends here now, and a good job. He didn't really want to go to Sydney any more than he wanted to go back to Sheffield. But he was determined to remain in Australia, if only to prove to his parents that he was grown up now, capable of looking after himself and making his own decisions in life.

Peter looked pensively at the map. "It takes a lot of guts to attempt a journey like that on your own," he said with genuine admiration.

"You can still change your mind and come with me," John said hopefully. "It would be much better with two of us; we could look out for each other."

Peter didn't answer immediately. He had already given John's offer serious thought, and he was tempted. "No, my old man would kill me," he said eventually.

"Not if you don't come back, he can't. That's the whole point of going," John said, looking up from the map.

"The police are bound to trace us sooner or later. It's all right for you - once your parents have gone back to England, you'll have nobody to answer to. But I would really be for it."

Secretly, Peter would have loved to accept John's offer, if only to get away from his father, but he wasn't sure he could survive on his own without the support of his family. He wasn't a mummy's boy, but he would miss her, and his brother and little sister. What if he couldn't find a job, or somewhere to live? For all his bravado and big talk in front of his friends, deep down he knew that he lacked John's mental maturity and self-reliance. He wasn't yet ready to leave home and strike out on his own.

The onlookers began drifting back into the hall. Mary Tate grabbed her daughter by the arm and pulled her roughly aside. "Did you have anything to do with that?" she demanded sharply.

Louise winced at the tenacity of her mother's grip. "No, of course I never. Why is everything always my fault?" she whined.

Her mother's eyes narrowed spitefully. She was a tall, gaunt woman with high cheekbones that made her eyes appear dark and frightening. "You little liar," she spat. "I've seen the way you've been making up to the pair of them."

"I have not."

"Don't lie to me. Get to bed before I give you a good slap."

Louise's mouth twisted sulkily. "Oh, what for? It's Christmas."

"Don't be too hard on the child, Mary," said Simon Tate. "It wasn't her fault."

"You know it was, as well as I do. You're always making excuses for her. And... she is not a child."

Louise could do no wrong where her father was concerned. She was their only child, and he idolised her.

Simon followed his wife back into the hall, where they had been sitting with George Ryan and his wife, and Shirley Bates. Tom and Edna had now joined the little group. Simon was not enjoying the company, but they had not been at the hostel long and, as yet, hadn't made many new friends.

Shirley had smartened herself up for the Christmas dance, and the return of her husband. She'd had her hair done, and applied her make-up with extra care. In her snug-fitting red dress and high-heeled shoes, she was looking more like the attractive young woman she really was.

Terry and Sandra Masters' husband, Trevor, had wandered over to the group of Spaniards, and, between roars of laughter, were being instructed on how to drink from the wine bag.

Trevor was keeping a suspicious eye on his wife, who was sitting opposite. Two weeks earlier, he had received an anonymous letter telling him that she was having an affair while he was away.

"Well, it certainly wasn't me!" Shirley had blazed indignantly when Terry had questioned her about the letter. "I'm not a troublemaker, or a gossip. And, anyway, I'm not in the least interested in anything she does."

"But has she?" Terry insisted.

Shirley turned away. "It's none of our business."

"I'll take that as a yes, then."

She spun back to face him. "Look, Terry, I know he's a mate of yours, but just leave it. Their marriage is no concern of ours. But, between you and me, yes, she has had a string of blokes in there." She wrapped her arms around his neck. "I haven't seen you for two months, Babe. Don't let their problems spoil our time together. Just stay out of it."

"Here's another one with a job waiting for him," George said with his deep, rumbling laugh, as Simon and Mary rejoined the group. "Tell him what happened to you, Tom."

"My job is secure enough," Simon replied tersely.

"This is Australia," said Shirley. "No such thing as security here. The whole country is in hock to the Yanks."

Simon toyed with the idea of asking her to explain the remark, if only to discover whether her facial expression could possibly become any blanker. It was obvious the girl hadn't a clue what she was talking about.

"Look at that monstrosity of an opera house they're trying to build in Sydney," Shirley whined on. "It's already years behind schedule and millions of pounds over budget. They haven't a clue how to do things here."

"That hideous structure never will get finished," George agreed authoritatively. He gave another deep laugh. "The men working on the opera house are the only ones in Australia with jobs guaranteed for life. Even the Aussie press are calling it the biggest white elephant in the country's history. It's a disaster. The whole world is laughing at it."

George's wife, Christine, looked a little embarrassed as he laughed loudly, yet again. She was a quiet woman, with pleasant, rounded features. Few people bothered to ask what her opinions of Australia were. They assumed them to be the same as her husband's.

Terry Bates swayed his way back across the room and slipped his arm around Shirley's waist. He was a cheerful character with sharp brown eyes and a rather comical goatee beard he had been cultivating while away in the bush - much to Shirley's annoyance. He had a lean, wiry build and a naturally dark complexion that, deepened by his time spent working in the sun, made it difficult to distinguish him from the Spaniards. A large stain discoloured the front of his shirt, evidence of an unsuccessful attempt to drink from the wine bag.

"You've ruined that shirt. That won't wash out," grumbled Shirley.

"Stop your whining, woman. If it won't wash, I'll throw it away and buy a new one. We're living in the land of plenty now. Ain't that right, George?" He patted George's ample paunch. "Oh ho, I'll say. Look at that, never had it so good. Ten stone he was when he arrived in Australia - now look at him. Living off the fat of the land, and not a day's work has he done to earn it."

"That's the trouble," said George. "They won't let you work here, so a man goes to fat."

Terry threw his head back and laughed heartily. "Come on now, Georgie boy, you know that sort of drivel won't wash with me. I'll soon find you a job if you want one. Come back to Bridgetown with me and Trevor after the holiday and spend a few months working on the pipeline. We'll soon have you back in shape."

"That isn't permanent work," George countered quickly. "What happens when the pipeline is finished? I'll be no better off than I am now. I want a permanent job, preferably in my own trade."

"You'll be no worse off, either, and at least you'll have a few quid in your pocket. Perhaps even enough to get you back to England, if you are still daft enough to want to go."

"That's no good to me. I'm not chasing all over the country after scraps. I need a regular, secure wage."

"You don't know what you do want," said Terry, his eyes alive with amusement as he taunted the fat man. "I'm sadly disappointed in you, George. When we came over on the ship together, I thought you really intended to get stuck in and make a go of it out here."

"So I did, but what's the use, with the employment situation the way it is? It's no good starting work one day and being stood off the next. Look what happened to Tom here. How can a man build a life for himself and his family under those circumstances?"

"What would you know about the employment situation?" Terry continued his teasing. "You haven't looked for a job since the day you arrived."

"Rubbish!" blurted George. "Anyway, I don't walk around with my eyes closed. I know the way things are," he floundered.

Terry chuckled in satisfaction and grabbed himself another beer.

Simon listened with interest, finding it reassuring to know that someone in the group wasn't wholly dissatisfied with life in Australia. He knew it couldn't possibly be as black as George had painted it. "But I understood from your wife that you were ready to pack up and go home, Terry?" he queried.

"Me? Not on your life," said Terry. "I might send the old woman packing if she doesn't brighten her ideas up. But I love it here in Australia. We know when we're well off, don't we, George?" He gave another hearty laugh and patted George's paunch again, repeating: "Never had it so good."

George laughed with them. He wasn't about to give Terry the satisfaction of thinking he was riled. "Never been had so good, that's what you really mean. How I ever allowed myself to be conned into coming to this hellhole of a country, I'll never know."

"I'll give you a word of advice, Simon," Terry said, placing a confiding hand on his shoulder. "If you want to give Australia a fair go, the first thing you need to do is ignore most of the people in this place - your ever-cheerful campmates." He waved his arm to include the entire hall, but there was little doubt in Simon's mind that the criticism was being aimed mainly at George. "The trouble with most of them is they won't make any effort to adapt to the Australian way of life. They sail halfway around the world for the express purpose of starting a new life, and when they get here that is the one thing they won't do. They expect the whole of Australia to change to suit them."

"The country would be a damn sight better off if it did," said George. "Some of their ideas are archaic, and positively ludicrous."

"I'll admit they are behind the times in some things," conceded Terry. "But it is still a comparatively young country, with a lot of learning and catching up to do. You must always remember one thing: we are the foreigners here, therefore, it's up to *us* to adapt to the Australian ways, not them to ours. Look at Andrew Lambert over there." He pointed to a tall, thin-faced man sitting on the opposite side of the room. "I'll tell you how interested he is in Australia and starting a new life here. He buys one paper a week, and that's the one with the British football results in. He will tell you there are two things he misses out here - his football and his pint of brown-and-mild in the local on Saturday night. And his wife is just as bad: apparently, all she misses is walking home from the local bug-hutch with a bag of fish and chips wrapped in newspaper. It's like a flaming comic opera with them. All their hopes and dreams of an exciting new life, abandoned for the want of a pint of warm beer and a fistful of soggy chips."

Terry danced a jig of delight, and roared with laughter at having made his point, and momentarily silencing even George. But Simon didn't let the element of truth escape him. Most of the complaints he had heard so far had been over just such trivial things.

The discussion was cut short as another disturbance erupted by the door. Trevor was gripping the front of a man's shirt and had his fist drawn back threateningly. "Is this the joker you've been having it off with?" he was raging at Sandra.

"I haven't been with anyone!" Sandra shouted back defiantly, trying to push her way between the two men.

The man pushed Trevor away. "You're crazy. All I did was ask her for a dance," he protested.

"I know your type, always on the prowl. We'll settle this outside."

Terry dashed over and pushed his way through the crowd, but by the time he got there, other men had stepped in to separate the antagonists.

"Ease up, mate, it was just malicious gossip, there's no truth in it, you know that," he said, pulling his friend away.

Trevor spun back and grabbed his wife roughly by the arm. "Back home, you. We've got to sort this out once and for all." He hustled her through the door, and the cluster of people started to disperse.

For most of the evening, the band had been scrounging drinks from the small groups around the stage, doing particularly well from Craig, who had replenished their glasses with liberal shots of Michael's whisky. Their playing became progressively worse as the evening wore on. At one stage, the pianist and accordionist were churning out a quickstep while the drummer, stripped of his jacket and tie, pounded away at a rock number of his own composition. By this time, nobody was dancing anyway, and many people had already drifted back to their chalets.

The band stopped playing and held a brief discussion in the centre of the stage. They resumed with a rendition of "Auld Lang Syne", played at double time to a still unenthusiastic audience, loaded their equipment into their station wagon and left.

Nobody seemed to miss them and gradually the hall emptied. Eventually, the caretaker came along to lock up. For the residents of Seaview Hostel, the Christmas celebrations were over.

CHAPTER TEN

On the first Monday of the New Year, Geoff set out to find a job. He didn't anticipate having too much difficulty - he had been keeping an eye on the employment columns for some time, and there seemed a liberal demand for mechanics.

There were three vacancies in the morning paper. He located the suburbs in his street directory and headed the Morris across the Swan River into South Perth to find Western Motors. They were Holden dealers. Geoff had heard them advertising on the radio often enough, and expected to find a much larger showroom than he did.

The receptionist smiled and directed him through the workshop to the service manager's office. Three men stood waiting at the door, and through the glass front, Geoff could see a fourth man inside being interviewed.

One of the waiting men nodded to him. He was in his early thirties, unshaven and looked to be still suffering the effects of his New Year's celebrations. "Strewth, things must be pretty bad around town, with five of us chasing the same job," he commented while pacing impatiently. "Been out of work long?"

"No, I've only recently arrived in the country. This is the first job I've applied for," said Geoff.

"A newie from the Old Country, are you?" The man gave a lazy smile. "Well, I'll give you the drum, mate, you don't want to waste your time working in the city. The pay is no good for a youngster like you. Take my advice and go bush for a couple of years, that's where the money is. A good diesel mechanic can write his own pay cheque on some of the mining and irrigation schemes up north. Just down from Mount Magnet myself. I earned a packet, but I was getting a bit bush-happy. Needed another spell of city life."

Geoff was about to ask where Mount Magnet was, when the first applicant emerged from the office and the man he had been talking to went in.

A few minutes later he reappeared, a satisfied grin creasing his whiskered face. "That's me out of the running, mate. Told him where to shove his job." He chuckled and walked out without further comment.

When it came to Geoff's turn to be interviewed, he handed the manager his trade certificates and references, answered a few questions about his previous employment and filled in the application form the manager pushed across the desk to him.

The manager, Mr George Watson, was a thin, hard-faced man. Mostly he seemed disinterested in Geoff, or his answers. His eyes were constantly roving the workshop, presumably intent on spotting any slackers.

Geoff noticed that Mr Watson's desk was exceptionally tidy and free of paperwork. Clearly, he was a man who knew how to delegate his work to others, leaving himself with little to do but bark out orders. He reminded Geoff of another garage owner he had once worked for who kept a similarly tidy desk. "I'm a teller, not a doer", was his boast. That and: "My main function here is to kick arses". Not a pleasant man, and Geoff got the uneasy feeling that working for George Watson would prove to be an equally disagreeable experience.

He flicked through Geoff's references, grunted, then tossed them back onto the desk, as though he considered them to be of little interest, or value.

At this point, Geoff found himself on the verge of becoming the second applicant that morning to tell the manager what to do with his job. He resisted the temptation, and listened while the manager explained that he would prefer an older man with a wider experience of Holdens. But he said that all the applications would be considered on Wednesday, and that Geoff should phone in on Thursday morning for a decision.

Geoff went back to his car and headed it towards High Wycombe for his next interview. He wouldn't bother to phone on Thursday.

At the High Wycombe garage, he discovered that the position had been filled over the weekend. He decided to head back towards the hostel, applying for work at the garages and service stations along the way. There proved to be quite a few of them and it seemed to Geoff that he must have climbed in and out of the car more than a dozen times before he eventually drove back across the Narrows Bridge to the north side of the river. There he turned right and drove on through the commercial heart of the city, then continued through the eastern suburbs, still applying for work at every garage he happened upon.

Several garage owners repeated George Watson's view, stating that they preferred their mechanics to have a comprehensive knowledge of Holdens. Geoff began to wonder whether this was merely another way of saying that if there were any jobs going, they would be offered to an Australian rather than a Pome.

During the afternoon, he stopped at a café for a snack and sat reviewing the situation. Things were not going well. Evidently, it wasn't going to be as easy to find work as he had thought. However, it was still only his first day of looking, and he hadn't really expected to walk straight into a job. He knew men at the hostel who had spent weeks searching for work. True, most of them were not tradesmen, but their failure must reflect the general shortage of employment.

The prospect of spending the next two or three weeks chasing around Perth attending interviews did not thrill him. He wasn't broke, but his bank balance was beginning to run low, and he wanted to have the comfort and reassurance of a regular wage packet as soon as possible.

Officially, Craig had started job-hunting today, too, but at the moment, he would be lazing on the beach, or swimming. Craig considered the possibilities of finding a job on the first day of looking to be near non-existent; therefore, he would spend today at the beach and start looking in earnest tomorrow. The strategy made a lot more sense to Geoff now than it had that morning.

He left the café and strolled along the parade of shops in search of a tobacconist's. On the opposite side of the road, he noticed there was a service station with a small garage attached. Having purchased his cigarettes, he crossed over to inquire whether or not they were in need of a mechanic.

"Wouldn't know," shrugged the pump attendant, a lanky youth wearing a baseball cap and large sunglasses. "Had a joker leave before Christmas, though, so Biggsie might be starting someone. Hang around, when I've got a mo, I'll go and have a word with him."

Having served the customers queuing at the pumps, the youth disappeared into the workshop. He returned a few moments later to escort Geoff through to the office. "Looks like you could be in luck," he said. "Biggsie wants to see you. Not a bad old bugger to work for, as long as you don't arse around too much," was his uninvited opinion of his boss.

The sign on the office door informed Geoff that "Biggsie" was the manager, and his more formal name was Mr Daryl Biggs. He was a well-built man with sandy hair, going grey, and a round face, that was mottled with freckles.

"Sit yourself down, young man," he smiled, beckoning to the chair beside his desk.

Geoff lifted a pile of files and folders from the chair and placed them back on the already cluttered desk. Biggsie was clearly no George Watson.

He sat down and read quickly through Geoff's references. "Just arrived, have you?" he observed without looking up.

"That's right." Geoff didn't expand on his answer, in case it prompted awkward questions as to why he hadn't been working already.

But the manager continued to probe. "I see you haven't worked here yet?" he said with a faint smile. "Have you been acclimatising yourself to the country, or having a good bludge on the beach?" he asked casually.

"Enjoying the beach for a while, I guess," Geoff answered, just as casually.

Biggsie smiled broadly. "Nothing much wrong with that. I went a bit beach-crazy myself when I first got here. That was over fifteen years ago now. I've never regretted making the move. Perth is a great place to live."

"I wouldn't have taken you as being English," observed Geoff.

"It pays to acquire the accent and blend in, Geoff, especially if you're in business. There's nothing an Aussie enjoys more than putting one over on a Pome. Most of the time there's no malice in it – it's a bit of a game we tend to play. It probably stems right back to the days of transportation, with the convicts striving to keep their spirits up by scoring points off their guards." He rubbed his hands together. "It all adds to the spice of life here. But I'm sure you are going to fit in well."

He studied Geoff's reddened face with a trace of amusement. "That brings back a few memories. Try as I may, I never did obtain that golden tan. I doubt you will, either. For us pale-faces, a deeper shade of red is as good as it gets."

Satisfied with the references, he leaned back in his chair. "Your timing is spot on, Geoff. I was just about to prepare an advert for the papers. It looks like you have saved me the trouble. I can offer you a job starting at twenty-three pounds a week. There's no regular overtime, I'm afraid, though we do a little now and then. If you would like to give us a try, you can start tomorrow."

"That would suit me fine, Mr Biggs," said Geoff.

Biggsie gave a sharp intake of breath. "Daryl, please. Nobody gets the "Mr" tag here in Australia, Geoff, only the Prime Minister, and that's accorded more as a term of abuse than anything."

They shook hands and Geoff left. The interview had been so brief and informal that several times on his return drive to the hostel, he felt that perhaps he should go back and confirm that he had heard Daryl correctly - that he really had offered him a job.

"This calls for a celebration," said Craig. He produced a bottle of rum from his wardrobe and began sloshing liberal amounts into their enamel mugs.

"Steady on with that stuff," cautioned Geoff. "I don't want to turn up with a hangover tomorrow."

"So, you've landed a job on your first day of hunting. That must be something of a record for the hostel. I'll have to go some to top that. Actually, the way things are looking, I can see myself having to join the railways, or even worse, hawking encyclopaedias around the streets." Craig gestured, as though these were positively the last things he was prepared to do for a living.

"I can't see you lowering yourself to labouring on the railways, but what's so bad about selling encyclopaedias?" queried Geoff.

"What's so bad about it? The job is easier to get than a dose of pox – and about as useful. I'm not too sure whether the social status of an encyclopaedia salesman is one step above or below that of a toilet cleaner. It's a standing joke in Sydney - there are more bods bumming sets of encyclopaedias around than know how to read them."

Geoff sipped at the rum, then returned the mug to the top of his bedside cabinet. "How do they all make a living at it?" he asked.

"Most of them don't; that's why it's such a crap job. But there are a certain number of businessmen who will buy an expensive set of books and have them displayed in a glass-fronted cabinet in the lounge, hoping to impress visitors. It seems the world has labelled the Australian businessman as uncouth and illiterate – which, of course, a good percentage of them are – and he has developed something of a complex about it. He will go to any expense to convince people that he is really a man of culture and sophistication. Even so, for every status-seeking businessman, there are at least a dozen encyclopaedia salesmen chasing his order. One gets a sale and eats; the rest go hungry."

Michael had come in and they could hear him moving about in the adjoining room.

"I wonder how many fifty-pound-a-week jobs the captain has rejected today," said Craig. He winked and went to the door.

"Ah, there you are, Michael. Come in and join the celebration. Geoff here has broken into the hostel's elite society of wage earners."

Michael came in to offer his congratulations. He had been attending an interview and was still wearing his blue blazer and tie. "What sort of money are they offering?" he asked in his aloof, disinterested voice.

"Australian currency, I should imagine," quipped Craig.

"Oh yes, of course," he laughed thinly. "I really meant how much of it?"

"It's nothing to rave about, only tradesman's wages. Twenty-eight plus overtime," lied Geoff. "It should average out between thirty and thirty-five a week."

"Which isn't too bad – for a tradesman, that is," added Craig. "How did you get on at Westlec, Michael?"

Michael cleared his throat, always alert to the opportunity of discussing himself. "Officially, of course, they are reserving their decision until Friday, though, between you and I, the position is mine, should I desire it. I really can't see myself accepting, though." His face took on an expression of profound disappointment. "I must say I am finding it rather difficult to understand the attitude of companies out here. They all demand outstanding references and qualifications from their sales executives, but they are reluctant to offer anything like top salaries. I'll give it another month or so. If nothing has eventuated by then, we may have to move on to Sydney."

There came a soft tapping at the outside door.

"That will be Gloria. Must go," said Michael. He congratulated Geoff again and hurried through the door.

Craig and Geoff looked at each other and grinned. "What an idiot." said Craig. "I'm sure he believes his own bull half the time."

"If he doesn't, nobody else will. But I think he is wise to you, he doesn't allow Gloria in any more."

"As though I am interested in his woman," Craig said, shrugging his indifference.

"Well, of course not – the very thought of it: gentleman Craig, he of the impeccable principals and moral values, moving in on another's betrothed? Absolutely unthinkable."

Craig poured himself another rum. "Betrothed, my eye. Gloria wants out and I can't say that I blame her. But I can assure you, I am not going to be the knight in shining armour she dreams will ride up and whisk her away from the clutches of Captain Blowhard - and a fate worse than death."

"I'm glad to hear that. I hope you mean it," Geoff said in a serious voice. "Causing the break-up of someone's marriage or relationship is not something that should be done for a laugh, or to get one over on them, simply because you don't like them. Anyway, Michael isn't so bad. He's all right once you get to know him. His aspirations are a little higher than most, that's all."

"As are his opinions of himself," countered Craig. "The man is a prat. Having a posh accent doesn't give him the right to look down his nose at people, no more than it entitles him to walk into a high-flying executive position. The Australians have obviously not been taken in; that's why he hasn't been offered a job yet. I'll lay odds he hasn't any qualifications at all for the positions he's applying for. He's lying through his teeth, trusting that his upper-class accent will swing something for him."

"Whatever he did for a living back home, it must have paid well. He shelled out five hundred pounds in cash for that car, and didn't quibble about it."

"Well, whatever his trade or profession is - or was - he is not executive material, that's for sure. And I predict he is going to fall flat on his face. The only question is, will that be before or after sweet little Gloria dumps him?

CHAPTER ELEVEN

Geoff was not the only one to take a special interest in the paper's employment section that Monday morning. It would have astounded many to learn that for the first time in months, George Ryan had been seriously scanning the columns.

George had lain awake for a long time on New Year's night, making a critical assessment of his situation, and the future did not look at all promising. The demand for his skill as a French polisher was virtually non-existent in Australia, he couldn't afford to return to England, and what money he did have was slowly ebbing away. Migrating to Australia had been a drastic mistake - there was little doubt about that. The question was, what could he do about it? For six long months, he had agitated and complained to the immigration authorities, the employment office, the hostel management and anyone else who would listen, but his complaining had achieved precisely nothing. Nobody was in the least interested in his plight. As far as the authorities were concerned, he could stay where he was and rot. And unless he faced up to the facts, that was exactly what he would do - rot, in this hellhole of a place. Somehow he had to get back home to England; for that, he needed money, and to get money, he needed a job.

So, grudgingly, George had bought the morning paper, and now sat in the doorway of his chalet, sifting through the employment columns. As he expected, there were no vacancies in his trade. He disregarded the building trade. He was no lover of hard work, and made the excuse that he was too big and sweated too much. Bus conductor: now there was something he could do. The job didn't particularly appeal to him, but it sounded easy enough, talking to people, and taking their money.

"I don't believe it. Don't tell me you are actually looking for a job, George?"

Of all the people to be passing his chalet just as he was underlining the advert, it had to be Terry Bates. George felt oddly guilty and embarrassed, as though he had been caught in an act of treachery against his sworn beliefs. Then he adroitly turned the situation to suit his argument.

"I've been chasing work every day since I arrived here," he lied, with a straight face. "But there's none to be had. That's what I've been telling you all along."

Terry grinned his disbelief, but at that moment, a fitting retort eluded him. "Why not do as I say and come back with me and Trevor? I can get you a start down there. The money is good, and we'll soon have some of that blubber off you."

"I don't think so, Terry. My blood pressure would never stand that kind of work. Besides, the wife would be scared stiff if I left her here alone. I'll find something sooner or later."

"Sure, you'll be right," Terry agreed optimistically. "I've a few bottles to kill off before I leave tomorrow. Come on over and give me a helping hand."

The front of Terry's chalet had become a much-frequented area over the Christmas and New Year period, and it wasn't long before half a dozen men had gathered to wish him farewell. Terry liked having plenty of company and a drink, and enjoyed nothing more than to instigate a good-natured argument.

George could usually be relied on to take up the challenge, no matter what the subject, but today he was uncharacteristically quiet. His thoughts were focused on the money he could save working in the bush. Eight or nine months at the wages Terry was earning would enable him to square his debt with the government and be well on his way to having his fare home. It would be hard, hot work, but if his attempts to find work around the city proved unsuccessful, perhaps he might consider it.

Trevor emerged from his chalet and slouched over to join the group of drinkers. His mood appeared dark and brooding.

"G'day, Trevor. All packed up, ready to go?" Terry greeted him cheerily.

"I don't know if I'll be going back at all yet," he moaned, accepting the beer that was held out to him. "It's Sandra. We've been arguing all night – again. I don't know what she wants any more. One minute, she wants to go home to England, and the next, she's talking about going over to Sydney. She always wants something different to what she's got – never satisfied. It was the same just after we got married. She could never settle anywhere, always wanting to be on the move; different towns, better houses. Then she got the emigration bug and wouldn't let go of it. I was never that keen on coming here in the first place. Now she wants to go back home. Well, I'm blowed if I do. Now I'm here, I like it - and I'm staying."

"Show her the papers from home," one man suggested. "They say Britain is having the worst winter on record. There's a picture of the Thames frozen over, and that's the first time that has happened this century. She must be crazy to want to go back to that."

"If that's England, they can keep it," said Terry. He took a long swig of beer and sighed deeply as he looked up at the cloudless blue sky. "This will do me."

"I really don't know what she wants any more," Trevor continued his lament. "In truth, I think it's me she is fed up with. I'm certainly getting fed up with her. I can't see our marriage lasting much longer. If I go back to Bridgetown now, I doubt she'll still be here when I get back. Either that, or I won't bother coming back at all. I'll get in the car and just keep on going."

"She'll come round," Terry consoled him, without conviction.

"It's this place that splits couples up," said George. "There are dozens of marriages that break up within a few months of couples arriving here. Come to Australia and make a new life for yourselves, that's what the adverts tell you." He chuckled smugly. "And it seems a lot of couples take the invitation a little too literally."

"Give it a rest, George, you're not helping," Terry snapped at him irritably. "Sandy is just homesick," he assured Trevor." My Shirley is the same, misses her family and friends. It's a woman thing." He turned back to George. "You of all people should understand that, George, being a bit of an old woman yourself."

Terry ignored George's words of protest, and seeing Tom step from his chalet, called him over, thrusting a glass of beer into his hand.

"Thanks but I'm waiting for the boys," explained Tom. "We're going to the beach for a couple of hours."

"Have a last drink with me," insisted Terry. "I'll be leaving tomorrow and I'll likely not see you again."

Tom accepted reluctantly. "Well, here's wishing you luck, Terry."

"And to you," said Terry. He drained his glass and reached behind the door of his chalet for another bottle. "So you've really set your mind on going back to England, have you, Tom?"

"Yes, we'll be on our way in a couple of months," confirmed Tom. He didn't want to discuss the matter, but Terry persisted.

"I suppose you know what the figures are? They say that over ninety per cent of those who go back reapply to come out again."

"So I have heard," admitted Tom. "But we'll not be amongst them. If a man can't get work at his trade, what is there for him to come back to? I'm too old to start in a new profession now."

"Rubbish! You are not old. I'd spent all my working life in an office till I came out here. You have to be prepared to adapt, try anything. If anyone had told me when I left England that I'd be working as a labourer on a construction site, I'd have told them they were crazy. But here I am - and loving it. My advice to anyone is to give Australia a real good go before making a decision to return. Look around you. The opportunities are here, for you and for the kids. And with all this free sunshine thrown in, it's far too good a dream to give up on."

"I prefer to be employed at my trade," insisted Tom. "There's no point in serving an apprenticeship if you are going to accept pick and shovel work." As he spoke, Tom was painfully aware that these were Edna's words, not his.

"What's the difference, as long as it pays the bills and gives you a good standard of living?" argued Terry.

Tom felt a tug at his sleeve. It was Kenny, wanting to know when they were going to the beach. Tom finished his beer and set the glass down on the steps, grateful for the excuse to get away.

"Well, all the best to you, Terry." They shook hands and Tom left the little group to their drinking, knowing that, apart from George, most of the men there thought him weak and foolish for wanting to return to

England.

As they made their way to John's chalet, Tom was agreeably aware that Kenny no longer wanted to hold onto his hand whenever they were walking together. Invariably, he would run on ahead, never appearing to be short of either breath or energy. It was wonderful to see him looking so well. If nothing else, coming to Australia had certainly done little Kenny the world of good.

But there were other advantages, too. Several times during the past few days, doubts as to whether or not they were really doing the right thing had crept unobtrusively into his mind. As soon as he was aware of the presence of such thoughts, he would dismiss them, telling himself that their decision had been made, and that it would all turn out for the best. But still the doubts persisted.

Over the next few weeks, Tom made no effort to find work, considering it pointless. Edna had decided she wanted to go home, so he accepted that that was what the family would do. He always left Edna to make the big decisions, it was easier that way.

A few days into the New Year, the hostel had buzzed with the unbelievable news that George Ryan had gone back to Bridgetown with Terry and Trevor, and had started work on the pipeline. Tom wondered vaguely whether he could have done the same. He wasn't young, but he was probably fitter than George, and Terry had said the work wasn't really that hard. But no, leaving the family alone at the hostel was out of the question. Edna would never hear of it. And... what would be the point? Even if he had a job, it wouldn't change Edna's mind about going home. So again, he thrust any thoughts of positive action from his mind.

Tom left all the arrangements for their return voyage to Edna. Nothing too unusual there - she was always the organiser and driving force in whatever the family did. But on this occasion, Tom displayed a particular apathy towards the proceedings. He spent his days either at the beach with the boys, or strolling around Kings Park, admiring the views over the city.

Tom wasn't a great beach fan, but the boys loved it, and it was good to be able to spend so much time with them. He felt immensely proud as he watched John cutting through the surf with strong, easy strokes. Even amongst the beach-loving Australians, his prowess as a swimmer stood out. As for little Kenny, the change in him was staggering: he looked so well that friends and family back home would barely recognise him. It was going to hurt the boys to leave Australia. Neither of them wanted to go.

The only downside of spending so much time with his sons was that they kept questioning him as to why they must return to England when life here in Australia was so good.

"But there are other jobs, Dad," John argued. "Lots of men at the hostel have taken jobs they have never done before. And even George

Ryan is working now."

"But he has had to leave his wife here and go two hundred miles into the bush to find work. We are a family, we need to be together," Tom explained unconvincingly.

"Why don't you look through the papers, or ask at the employment office? There must be lots of jobs you could do. Why can't we stay?"

"I want to stay here, too," Kenny would chip in, jumping up and down with excitement. "I love swimming. Soon I'll be surfing, like John. We can't do that in England, it's too cold. Why can't we stay here, Dad?"

Tom could never find a credible or convincing answer to their questions, not even in his own mind. He felt more comfortable after the holidays, when John was back at work and Kenny had resumed school.

Most days, he would leave Edna to her planning and head for Kings Park, one of his favourite places in Perth. The park encompassed a thousand acres of gardens and preserved natural bush land, right in the heart of the city. Tom loved to stroll along Anzac Way, the park's main thoroughfare, in the shade of the tall eucalyptus trees while admiring the lawns and gardens. Another of the park's features he particularly enjoyed visiting was the huge greenhouse where wild flower seeds gathered from the remotest parts of Australia were being propagated. Unique species of plants with stunningly vibrant colours were on display, and, amazingly, most of these plants were to be found exclusively in Australia.

But perhaps his most favoured spot of all was the park's high viewing area, situated at the far end of Anzac Way. There, he would sit on one of the bench seats and look down on the tall white buildings that comprised the city's commercial heart, and watch the tranquil Swan River, reflecting a brilliant blue sky, as it swept gracefully through the suburbs and parklands. A wide dual carriageway followed the curve of the bay, and then turned and crossed the river into the city's southern suburbs. There really couldn't be many cities in the world with a more picturesque view of itself than Perth.

As he sat there one day, quietly admiring this scene, he couldn't help but recall and compare the view he'd had from his allotment overlooking the suburbs of Sheffield. There was nothing picturesque about that scene. It was cold, grimy and depressing. Tom shivered at the recollection, and at the unpleasant thought of being back there.

But then, picturesque views never paid any bills. In Sheffield, at least he would have a job and a regular wage. Edna had already taken it upon herself to write to the personnel manager at the foundry, and he had replied with the news that the company would be more than happy to welcome him back. There was job security waiting for him at home in Sheffield.

Tom's thoughts drifted to the foundry where he had spent most of his working life. The huge cranes carrying heavy ladles of molten metal across the workspace, the showering sparks as the metal was poured into the moulds, the constant din and rumble of powerful machinery, the deafening clatter of iron against iron. It was a hazardous and unpleasant workplace where you needed to keep your wits about you. He had often likened it to a scene out of the dark ages.

The foundry had afforded him a reasonable standard of living, certainly, but Tom had never really enjoyed his work there, or the foundry atmosphere. He was a gentle, studious man, and had never been cut out for all the rush and tear of heavy industry, or the pressures associated with deadlines and production runs. But when you were brought up in a steel town, it was accepted, almost from birth, that you would work in the foundry or the steelworks, like your father and his father before him. Your whole upbringing and education steered you in that direction. There wasn't really much choice.

He turned his head and studied the huge floral clock set into the embankment behind him. He had always admired the clock. Two gardeners were tending it now, changing some of the brightly coloured flowers in its face. Now *that* was the sort of job he would have liked. With a job like that, it would be a joy to go to work each day. Had he been given the choice, he would probably have gone for a career in horticulture, perhaps even agriculture - anything to do with the land and growing things.

But the foundry, he hated.

Yes, he really did hate it, he realised with a start. And he was loathing the thought of having to go back there. The stark reality was that once he did return, they would be in so much debt that he would have no choice but to remain there for the rest of his working days. That prospect filled him with dread, and seemed to be hanging over him like a prison sentence.

He gave an ironic smile, reflecting that they had emigrated to start a new life. Was it really too late for that? As Terry said, he wasn't too old to try other things. At that moment, anything seemed preferable to returning to the foundry. Why not make a clean break and try for that new life they had set out to find? Why not, indeed?

On his way out of the park, acting on an impulse, Tom stopped at the curator's office and enquired about employment. He had met the curator several times in the greenhouse. He was a pleasant, interesting man, always ready to discuss the plants and their locations. Of course, there were no vacancies. Tom had not really expected there to be; the curator took his name and promised to get back to him should anything come up.

Tom left the park that day with a renewed spirit of purpose and determination. He had made a decision, and he had taken the first preliminary step towards his goal. He was going to do what he had set out to do - start a new life, here in Australia. It was what he wanted, and it was what his sons both wanted.

He decided not to tell Edna of his intentions – not yet. She had her heart set on going home, and would doubtless do her utmost to dissuade him. When he had secured a job, then he would tell her. His resolve wavered slightly even at the thought, for he knew it was bound to trigger an almighty disagreement – one that would severely test the very foundations of their marriage.

CHAPTER TWELVE

An ancient steam train screeched and jolted to a stop beside a quiet bush-town station, a hundred and fifty miles east of Perth. The sign on the platform informed Tony Bradley that he had arrived at Merredin.

Tony poked his head through the carriage window, and as the billowing steam cleared, he could see a few weatherboard houses dotted haphazardly amongst the mallee trees. To his right, behind the station, lay the main town, a mere dozen or so streets in all. Beyond the rooftops, a vast acreage of salt bush and mallee; a flat, characterless landscape, stretching to a distant horizon that was distorted by a quivering heat haze.

Tony reached into his pocket for his travel warrant, rechecked the name of the station, and then turned back into the carriage to gather his luggage.

The big man still lay huddled in the far corner, snoring loudly. He was dirty and untidy, and smelled strongly of alcohol. Tony thought perhaps he should wake him and tell him they had arrived, but he was reluctant to disturb him, for fear he might fly into a drunken rage. Cautiously, he shook the man's shoulder. There was no response. He shook a little harder. The drunk stirred and emitted a deep groaning sigh that seemed to fill the whole compartment with the stench of stale alcohol, but there was no further response. Tony gave up and carried his bags out onto the platform.

When, two days earlier, he had returned to the hostel to find Janice's farewell note awaiting him, it had come as the final, crushing blow to his hopes of reconciliation. Although they had not shared a bed for some time, she was still his wife, and he had refused to concede that she would really leave him. While he could see her dresses in the wardrobe and her shoes under the bed, he could somehow manage to convince himself that she would soon tire of Rudy and come back to him.

But now there was nothing. Frantically, he searched the room for something to pin his hopes on – some little thing that she would have to return for, but he found nothing; this time she had really gone. Suddenly, he felt empty and alone. He needed her, now more than ever. How could he face all the people he knew at the hostel knowing what they would be thinking; watching their pitying glances. He had to get away – far away – and he had done so by the only means he knew open to him. He had accepted a labouring job on the railways.

The moment he stepped from the train, a swarm of flies descended upon him, and he felt the fierce sun burning its way through his thin shirt. A swarthy, thick-set man was striding along the platform towards him. He had a leathery complexion and hard, alert eyes. He walked with the quick, purposeful steps of a soldier and swung his arms as though he was used to marching.

"You Rogers? He barked at Tony in a harsh, domineering voice that held a thick foreign accent.

"No, I'm Tony Bradley. I have to report to a Mr Vargha."

"I'm Vargha. Give me your starting docket," he ordered.

Tony gave him the slip of paper he had been issued with at the employment office. "I think that must be Mr Rogers in the carriage. He's sleeping rather heavily. I tried to wake him, but..."

Another man came strolling along the platform and peered into the carriage. A slow, easy smile spread across his wrinkled face. "Your mate's had a bit of a skinful, I reckon. We'll soon have him right." He extended a calloused hand to Tony. "I'm Frank Doyle," he smiled.

"Get that man out of there," Vargha ordered impatiently.

Frank climbed leisurely into the carriage, and a few moments later he came out with Jack Rogers leaning heavily on his shoulder. Frank called another man over and together they half- carried, half-dragged Jack to the row of wooden huts on the far side of the track.

Vargha watched Jack's suffering with sadistic pleasure. He had seen many men arrive on the job in this condition. It was typical of the no-hopers who sought employment on the railways. They were always either drunks or worthless drifters, and Vargha had no time for any of them. He looked again at the timid little man in front of him. This one was obviously of a different breed.

"You worked on the railways before?" he asked brusquely.

"No, I'm a wages clerk," said Tony.

"You don't look strong enough for this job. It's hard work - and I don't tolerate any slackers. Follow me."

Tony followed him across the track to the row of small, wooden huts with sloping roofs. Vargha kicked open one of the doors. "This one is yours," he said, and walked on.

The hut was little bigger than a garden shed, and totally devoid of furniture. A low, slatted platform had been built along the back wall to support a mattress, and beside it was a narrow shelf that extended to the front wall. The moment Tony stepped into the room, his nostrils were assailed by a multitude of vile smells. The walls were plastered with nude photos and obscene drawings, and the floor was littered with papers and empty bottles. A discarded pair of underpants had been thrown into a corner under the slatted platform. Tony stared at them in disgust and disbelief. They were caked with excreta and alive with flies. He felt he would be sick if he didn't get out into the fresh air.

Vargha came back carrying a palliasse and a kerosene lamp, which he thrust into Tony's hands. "These are yours. If you lose them, you must pay. There's straw in the end hut to fill the palliasse."

"A straw mattress?" Tony muttered in mild disbelief.

"Why should we provide better. The men get drunk and piss and spew everywhere."

When Tony brought his attention to the underpants, Vargha remained unmoved. "It's your hut, clean it up," he ordered tersely.

Tony walked into town to buy soap powder and disinfectant, then set to work scrubbing the floor and walls. It was pointless to unpack, for there were no drawers or cupboards in which to store his clothes.

By the time he had finished cleaning, and made his bed, it was 4:30 and the gang were returning from their day's work. Tony watched from the doorway as they trudged towards the huts. They were a rough, ragged-looking bunch, and he could hear many different foreign accents.

He moved back to his bed and sat down. Inevitably, he began to dwell on the hopelessness of his situation. He longed for the comfort and security of his office job back home, and the companionship of his wife. He hoped that Janice would soon tire of Rudy. Perhaps if he stuck it out here and earned some money, he could win her back. He dropped his head into his hands and started to sob. He knew it was never going to happen. He had to accept the facts: he had lost her and he would probably never see her again. With all his friends and relations thousands of miles away in England, he was all alone in the world now, and already he was feeling desperately lonely and insecure.

After a while, a hand bell sounded outside. Men emerged from their huts and began making their way to the mess-room, a long, flat-roofed building made from timber and asbestos sheeting. Tony hadn't eaten for hours, and he was hungry. He got listlessly to his feet and followed the line of men.

He was sitting at one of the long, wooden tables, supping at a bowl of soup, when he heard a string of abuse being voiced behind him. It appeared he was sitting in the man's seat. He apologised and slid himself further along the bench seat. The man sat down, still muttering to himself, as though he was thinking aloud. He was an old man with dry, wrinkled skin. His face was thin and pinched; seemingly devoid of cheekbones, and large eye-teeth protruded like yellow fangs from an otherwise toothless mouth.

"Always I sit here," he muttered between mouthfuls of soup. "Everybody know this my seat. But new men come, always sit first in my seat. Why? For two years I sit here. Nobody steal my seat."

Another man had seated himself opposite them. He was young and had long, dark hair and a bushy beard. "What are you muttering about now, Rat-face?" he said in a thick Scots accent.

The old man looked up sharply. "Scottie, you don't call me like that, I say. You show respect."

"Respect, for a drunken old wombat like you," goaded the young Scotsman. "Take no notice of him," he said to Tony. "He's senile; his brain's been pickled in cheap plonk."

The old man's eyes narrowed into slits of hatred. His hand shaking with rage, he gripped his spoon and pointed it threateningly. "Scottie, you don't make fun of me I tell you. I kill you. One day, for sure, I cut out your guts."

"No with that, you'll not, you old fool, that's your soup spoon," Scottie jeered. "You go to kiss Vargha's arse tonight, Rat-face?"

"Rat-face Ricky kisses Vargha's arse every night," called another man. There were jeers and mutterings of agreement.

"I kill you, Scottie. One day, for sure, I kill you, you Pome bastard," Rat-face ranted on.

Tony kept his head down, not wanting to be involved.

The door opened and Frank Doyle walked in.

Rat-face jumped to his feet. "Frank, you are leading hand, you must talk to the Scottie. He insults me – he threatens to kill me. I am an old man, I say nothing bad, always he pick on me."

"Go away, Ricky," was Frank's unsympathetic response. Frank was a patient, easy-going man, but he was tired of listening to the old man's constant ranting and complaining.

Amidst a chorus of jeers, Ricky flung his spoon to the floor and stormed from the mess-room. "I go see boss-man. I fix you all, bastards."

"You'll get used to that sort of thing on the railways," Scottie assured Tony with a light-hearted laugh. "With all the pissheads in this place, it goes on all the time. It's all part of the colourful tapestry of life here in the bush. What did you think of our illustrious leader, Mr Vargha?"

Tony shrugged. "I didn't see much of him, really."

"That's a definite plus. The less you see of that Hungarian Gipsy, the better. Reckons he was in the secret police during the war. One day out on the line, he was telling us how they used to string prisoners up by the thumbs and beat confessions out of them. A really nasty piece of work, is our ganger. He stands and watches over us all day, as though he is still a guard in a concentration camp."

The young Scotsman laughed at seeing Tony's concern. "Don't let it bother you too much. He has no real authority. If he starts coming on a bit strong, tell him to go to hell. There's not a lot he can do about it. The railways are too desperate to retain men to allow him to sack anyone."

The next day out on the line, Tony realised how right Scottie had been about Vargha; he watched them like a hawk. Occasionally, he would stride up and down the track inspecting the work, but mostly he stood in the shade with his arms folded in front of him, as though he was a warden guarding a gang of prisoners sentenced to hard labour. His sharp, squinting eyes darted everywhere, yet Tony was sure he had a special interest in him, and hardly dared to straighten his back for fear of being shouted at. He had been given the task of packing ballast under the sleepers with a beater pick. It was hard work, and by midday he was tired, and already his hands were beginning to blister.

When lunchtime came, he sought the shade of the mallee lining the edge of the track. After a while, Scottie came over to join him.

"How's it going, Tony?" he asked cheerfully.

"All right, I suppose. But it's hard. I'm not used to this kind of work."

"There's nothing hard about it. Just take your time. Most importantly, don't let Vargha push you. If he thinks you're afraid of him, he'll ride you right into the ground. That's the kind of sadistic animal he is."

Jack Rogers had looked ill all morning. Several times he had gone to the water bag, consumed large quantities of cold water, then returned to the track and worked laboriously while the perspiration poured from him. He was sitting next to Frank Doyle now. Frank had taken the meat from a sandwich and refilled it with salt.

"There you go, Jack, me old mucker, get this into you. If you don't replace some of that salt you've been sweating out, you'll end up with the cramps."

Jack bit sullenly into the sandwich and washed it down with gulps of black tea. Moments later, he was heading for the scrub, retching loudly.

"That's the way, Jack, get it out of your system," Frank sympathised.

Vargha stood watching Jack's discomfort with obvious pleasure. He gave a thin, humourless laugh. "You must get yourself well, so on payday you can drink yourself stupid again, and become even more ill."

Nobody else found the remark amusing, not even Rat-face Ricky, who usually considered it his sworn duty to agree with Vargha's every word.

"What's so bloody funny?" snarled Jack. He glared at Vargha as though he was about to grab a pick handle and batter him over the head with it.

The colour drained from Vargha's face in sudden alarm. Here was a man you obviously didn't poke fun at. "Next time you are drunk, you do not come out on the line," he stammered in an attempt to reassert his authority.

Frank took Jack by the arm. "Easy, Jack, old son, you'll only do your job in. Here, get some more of this salt down you."

Scottie grinned knowingly. "The brotherhood of drunks. They fuss over each other like broody hens."

"Is Frank an alcoholic, too?" Tony asked in mild surprise. Frank seemed such a sensible and dependable type.

"I'll say. Frank is a good drunk, though. He'll sing or curl up somewhere and sleep it off. But that Jack looks like he'd be a real mean bastard. Most of the gang hit the bottle pretty hard – that's why they're here. The railways are the last refuge for all the no-hopers who can't hold a job down anywhere else. They are a pathetic bunch, and some of them were very clever men before they took to the drink too. Look at old Rat-face over there: you wouldn't think that degenerate half-wit was once a chief engineer, would you?"

Tony looked in disbelief at the shaking, tramp-like figure. "You can't be serious," he said.

"I'm not pulling your leg. He was an officer in the Danish navy. He showed me his papers once, and a photo of himself in uniform. A smart, intelligent-looking man, he was, too. Now look at him: stuck in the world's worst job and having to kowtow to an upstart like Vargha to hang onto it. That's what the bottle does for you, Tony. It's enough to turn a man teetotal."

"So, if the job is that bad, how did you come to be working on the railways?" asked a puzzled Tony.

Scottie laughed. "Good question. I'm *not* a secret alcoholic, if that's what you're getting at. No, I'm part of what they call Australia's floating population - drifters who travel around the country, from town to town and job to job. I suppose you might call us modern-day swagmen. I've been working my way around the country. I'd just driven over from South Australia when the camper van broke down on me. I needed a job to build up a bit of cash before moving on to Perth. I'll be shooting through next payday."

"I won't be staying here very long, either," said Tony. "Only till I've saved my fare back to England."

As the days dragged by, Tony began to doubt his ability to stick the job even that long. His hands became badly blistered and his body ached in every conceivable joint and muscle. Vargha always seemed to single him out for the hardest jobs, and stood over him constantly.

Jack Rogers, too, had taken a dislike to him. Jack made no secret of the fact that he hated all Pomes. He would stand and laugh mockingly while Tony struggled to carry sleepers that were far too heavy for him.

In the evenings, Tony would sit in his room and gaze at the walls and ceiling. He would think of Janice, and how much he missed her, and their comfortable little flat in Ilford. It had all been so wonderful in those first few months of their marriage. He had been so happy then.

But Janice had been unable to adapt to her role as a housewife. She had no concept of housekeeping or budgeting. She was like a spoilt child, wanting everything that caught her eye, and Tony had never been strong enough to refuse her. He had squandered most of his savings buying expensive clothes and trinkets to please her.

Then, one day, she had said she wanted to go to Australia. To Janice it was simply a matter of paying their ten pounds and boarding the first available ship. Tony had tried to discourage the idea by explaining what it would mean to them financially if he gave up his job. But she had cried and sulked. She wanted to move to a new country like she wanted a new pair of shoes or a new dress, and eventually Tony had given in to her wishes, as he always did.

But for all her faults, he still loved her. Sometimes he would wake in the night and reach out for her, and finding her gone, he would ache with longing, then clutch his pillow to him and whisper her name.

The day after payday, the gang was down to half strength. Scottie and two other men had left, and several others were still suffering the effects of their pay-night drinking bout. Tony had been kept awake most of the night by a rowdy group in the next hut. Frank Doyle and Jack Rogers had both been there, but had managed to sober up enough to make it to work.

When they were out on the line, Vargha gave one of his thin, humourless laughs. "There is no Scottie to carry you today, Pome, now you must do your full share of the work." Then he had hounded Tony all morning, delighting in watching him jump whenever he shouted.

During the morning, Tony found himself packing sleepers alongside Jack Rogers. Jack had been wandering off at regular intervals and taking large swigs from the bottle of cola he had brought out with him. Every time he returned to the line, he would work a little more clumsily, and Tony could tell from his breath that the cola had been heavily spiked. As lunchtime drew near, Jack was beginning to stagger about and curse to himself as he swung the beater at the base of the sleeper. Suddenly, he turned on Tony.

"Who do you think you are looking at, you little Pome bastard? And what are you doing working next to me? I've told you before, I don't work with no Pomes, they stink, now piss off." He shouted, as he pushed Tony away.

Vargha came running up. "What goes on here? Why do you push this man?" he demanded.

"I don't work next to no stinking Pome," snarled Jack.

"I am the boss here. I say where the men must work, not you."

Jack leered at him contemptuously. "You can go and get stuffed too, you bloody Hungarian Gipsy."

Vargha backed away and picked up a ballast fork. "Now try abusing me," he challenged.

Jack cursed and spat defiantly at the ground, as though the menacing tines, poised a few feet from his face, were of no consequence to him. "I'm not stupid enough to fight on the job." He tapped the side of his nose cunningly. "Fighting on the job is the one thing that will get me instant dismissal. That's what you're after. But I'm not falling for it... Gipsy man!"

Jack stumbled over to the bushes and picked up his jacket and the bottle of cola. "I'll be waiting for you tonight when you leave the yard. Then we'll see how tough you are..." He threw his jacket over his shoulder and set off down the track for the two-mile walk back to camp.

During the afternoon, Vargha made a call on the field telephone, and when they arrived back at camp, Jennings, the local police officer, was waiting for them.

"What's the trouble this time, Mr Vargha?" he asked intolerantly. It wasn't the first time he'd been called out to escort the ganger home.

"The man in hut number six, he threatens to attack me when I leave the yard. I want him arrested."

"I can't arrest a man for making threats, as well you know. If he assaults you, then it becomes a police matter, not until."

"So... in this country you wait for violent criminals to attack innocent people before anything is done?"

"We are a civilised society here, Mr Vargha. Innocent till proven guilty is our belief - and our law. I will have a word with him, that's all I can do."

They went along to Jack's hut, where the three of them stood talking. Vargha gestured vigorously while Jack slouched casually against the doorframe, shaking his head and grinning in flat denial of everything. Vargha became increasingly agitated, and after a while, he called Tony over.

"Pome, you heard this man insult me and threaten me with violence. Tell the officer."

Tony hesitated, not wanting to get involved.

"Don't be afraid to speak up, this is a police officer, tell him," Vargha insisted.

"Well... er... yes, I suppose he did," stammered Tony.

"There you are, officer, this man is an independent witness."

Jennings was unimpressed. "I still can't arrest a man for making idle threats, Mr Vargha," he shrugged. "Disagreements between you and your men are of no concern to me." He turned sternly to Jack, whose interest had now wandered beyond the officer to where wagons were being shunted around the yard. "But I know all about you and your record, Rogers. And if you cause me any trouble while you're here, I'll have you inside that fast you'll wonder what's hit you. Do I make myself understood?"

"You've got me all wrong, officer. I'm going straight now, I don't look for trouble," Jack said, his voice thick with plausibility.

"See that you keep it that way," warned an unimpressed Jennings. He turned and strode away, his abruptness making it clear that he had no time for either man.

Vargha shot Jack a taunting sneer, and then hurried off after the constable.

Jack sat in the doorway of his hut with a glass and a flagon of wine and began drinking heavily. A hate-filled scowl crept across his face, and he began abusing all who walked by.

"I'm an Australian. I fought for my country," he muttered. "What right has that bloody Hungarian Gipsy to walk into my country and tell me what to do? I fought to keep the likes of that Nazi bastard out of Australia - and I'll do it again. I'll fix you, Gipsy, you see if I don't. And I'll fix that crawling, lying little Pome, too."

There was no dinner prepared for the gang that night. The cook had been drinking steadily all day and was found lying on the floor of his hut in a drunken stupor. A few of the men cursed him as they passed the door of his hut, but mostly they shrugged the incident off. It was only natural for a man to get drunk after payday.

Tony walked into town and had his dinner at the Gumtree Café, a shabby weatherboard building, badly in need of redecorating. Despite the café's appearance, Tony found the food to be very good and would eat there whenever the camp meals were inedible.

Tony sat at his usual corner table and, as always when alone, he began to worry about his future. He calculated it would take almost a year to save the money he needed to return to England. How could he possibly hope to stick the railways that long? Already he had taken more than he could stand, of the job - and of Vargha. But how could he leave? Where would he go, and what would he do? It seemed he had no choice. This was the only job he could get, so somehow he had to stick at it.

And there again, what was the point? Would life be any less unbearable for him back home, having to face all his friends and relations and explain to them how his wife had deserted him and run off with another man? No, deep down he knew he could never go back and face them. He sank his head into his hands in despair. There was nowhere for him to go, nowhere to hide, no refuge or respite from his torment. At times there seemed but one solution to all his problems – only one way out.

Frantically, he tried to hustle the thought from his mind. That was the coward's way out. He must never allow himself to get that low. There was always something worth living for. But still the thoughts persisted, and the more he tried to ignore them, the stronger they became, and the more positive he was that the future held nothing for him.

When he returned to camp, Jack was still slumped in the doorway of his hut. He looked very drunk now and his face was dark with hate and pent-up rage. Tony decided to creep along the back of the huts, rather than pass in front of him, but as he came to the front of his hut to unlock the door, Jack spotted him.

"Come here, you little Pome bastard, I've been waiting for you," he bellowed.

Tony was terrified. He pretended not to hear. Quickly he opened the door and slipped inside, bolting the door after him.

Jack struggled to his feet and swayed unsteadily along to Tony's hut. "Open up, Pome. I want a word with you," he shouted menacingly, and began pounding on the door with his fists. When there was no answer, he lifted his foot and swung a savage kick at the door. It burst open. Tony watched petrified as Jack's bulky frame towered in the doorway.

"Try to lock a man out in his own country, would you? Bloody Pomes are all the same, think they own the place." He slumped against the wall, and, for a moment, a vague, lifeless expression clouded his eyes, as though he had forgotten where he was and why he was there. Then he blinked in recollection. "Yeah, you're the lying little rat who dubbed me in to the law. A typical snidey Pome, throwing in with the enemy when the going gets tough."

Without warning, he bunched his fist and smashed it into Tony's mouth, knocking him to the floor. As he lay there momentarily dazed, Jack aimed a vicious kick into his ribs.

"All Pomes are the same – gutless. Get up and fight like a man, you little shit."

Tony pushed himself to his hands and knees, wincing at the sharp pain in his side. Then Jack's heavy boot smashed into his face and everything went blank.

"And where were the Pomes when the Japs were about to invade Australia? Wouldn't raise a finger to help us. Gutless, all of them." He kicked again and again at Tony's unconscious body.

"That's enough, Jack." Frank Doyle stood in the doorway, an unusually stern expression on his placid face.

"Come on in, Frank. You are just in time to help me teach this Pome traitor a lesson. He went to kick Tony again but Frank grabbed him by the shoulder and spun him round.

"I said that's enough, Jack."

Caught off balance, Jack staggered back against the wall. He stared at Frank, a puzzled expression in his eyes. "What's the matter, Sarge, you pulling rank on me?"

"That's right. Get back to your own hut and stay there."

Jack straightened up, towering above Frank. For a moment, it appeared as though he was about to defy the order and turn on Frank. But some animal cunning seemed to warn him that whilst he was very drunk, Frank was still sober.

"You're all right, Frank," he slurred. "I've got no argument with you. You're an old digger, a desert-rat, like me. Come and have a drink." He allowed Frank to guide him out and back to his own hut.

Blood was still oozing from Tony's nose and mouth when he regained consciousness. He spat out the fragments of his front teeth and struggled painfully to his feet. Vaguely, he was aware of Frank coming back in and thrusting a glass of something into his hand. He gulped it down, not noticing that it was neat whisky, only that it was strong and made him cough a little, which hurt his ribs. He made no attempt to stop the blood from dripping down the front of his shirt, or to bathe his cut mouth. It didn't matter – for what he was contemplating, nothing mattered. The beating had been the final straw that had tipped him over the edge. His misery was complete. His life was worthless. He could take no more.

When Frank had gone, Tony staggered painfully to the tool shed, took out a rope and made his way to the high, timber-framed coal stage.

"Janice, Janice, where are you?" he sobbed as he climbed.

For a long time, he sat shivering on the thick, wooden crossbeam, telling himself that this was the only thing left for him to do, the only thing he *could* do. He had plunged to the depths of human existence, was being forced to live amongst animals, and he was not strong enough, either physically or mentally, to prevail. The future held nothing for him, he had nowhere to go, no friends to turn to. Without Janice, his life was pointless.

He tied the end of the rope around the crossbeam and slipped the noose over his head. Mentally, he repeated all the valid reasons for ending it. Then he repeated them again, this time thoroughly convincing himself that there was no possible reason to go on.

He slid himself to the edge of the blackened beam and looked down. Glistening in the moonlight were the steel tracks where the trains would stop to have their tenders filled from the gigantic hopper that towered above him. Another few inches and he would overbalance and be hurtling down towards those silver tracks. A quick jerk on the rope, the snap of his neck, and it would all be over. There would be no more pain, no more torment. He willed himself forward. Just a few inches, and he would be gone – but there was a sickening tenseness gripping at his stomach, holding his whole body rigid. He began to cry. He couldn't go through with it. This wasn't the coward's way out. They lied. It needed courage to make that final move - courage that he simply didn't have.

"Janice! Janice!" he sobbed in despair. "I can't go on without you... I can't... I can't."

He didn't know how long it was that he sat there on the beam, and afterwards, he could never remember climbing down, or how he came to be in Frank's hut. His mind was numbed into nothingness. He found himself sitting on the edge of Frank's bed, clinging onto a glass of red wine. Frank was sitting beside him, telling him to drink. Tony obeyed mechanically. He felt the warming liquid sliding down his throat and begin to glow inside him. Presently, it reached the contorted ball of tension that was his stomach and he dived for the door, retching deeply until he thought he would suffocate. Eventually, he drew in a long, gasping breath and began to shiver violently.

Frank guided him back to the bed and placed another glass of wine into his hand. The mere smell of it turned Tony's stomach. He shook his head, but Frank insisted that he drink it, said it would do him good. Tony knew it wouldn't. Nothing could do him any good, least of all drink; that never helped anybody. But he was too weak to argue. He accepted the glass and began to sip at it while Frank talked. He recounted parts of his own life, how he himself had once hit rock bottom and tried to commit suicide. Vaguely, it registered that Frank must have seen him up on the coal stage, and knew what he had intended to do. But it didn't matter – nothing mattered.

As he listened, the wine began to settle his nerves, and he stopped shaking. Frank refilled his glass, and presently, refilled it again. Tony felt the warm glow growing inside him and he began to feel dizzy and a little light-headed. He found that he could think over everything that had happened and it didn't hurt any more. In fact, it barely registered. It was as though a barrier had risen between him and reality, and he was seeing life through a haze that filtered out all the unpleasant thoughts that would hurt him. He could see a man sitting on the coal stage, wanting to jump. But it wasn't him, just a character in a faded dream. For some unknown reason, he found himself laughing He knew then that he was drunk and all the people who said that drink never helped were wrong - it helped - it helped a lot.

In the morning, when he was sober, the barrier would have gone and the hurt would return. But it would be less, and he could bear it during the day, knowing that at night, he had found a sanctuary where no amount of worry or hurt could reach him. And he knew that this was the way it would be every night from now on. Everything would be fine - as long as he had a drink.

CHAPTER THIRTEEN

"Well, what do you think of it?" Susan asked, her eyes alive with excitement as she showed Geoff around the house. "Of course, we're nowhere near straight yet - we only moved in a week ago and there's a lot of redecorating to be done. I'll enjoy helping Dad with that. I love painting."

It was a large, older-style building, occupying a corner plot in the suburb of Inglewood, just north of the city. Ted and Joan had taken out a lease, with the option to buy at a later date. It had stood unoccupied for a while and was in need of considerable modernising and redecorating. But they were all happy to call it home, and were relieved to have moved away from the communal living and transient existence of the hostel. Joan in particular was looking forward to making a new home here for her family.

"It has great potential," Geoff agreed, going along with Susan's enthusiasm. "But, like you say, there's a lot of work to do. You are all going to be busy for a while."

"Don't even ask about the garden. Nobody has lived here for months, and it's very overgrown. Come into the kitchen, there's something I particularly want to show you."

They walked back through the living room, where a dozen or so guests were gathered for the housewarming party. Mostly, they were people Geoff had never met before, neighbours and a few of Ted's workmates, but the Henshaws and the Taylors had been invited.

"What do you think of that?" Susan asked jubilantly as they stepped into the kitchen. She was referring to an old, wood-burning stove built into a recess in the wall.

"What about it?" said Geoff, not sure whether he was supposed to admire it for its antiquity or laugh at it.

"Don't you think it's great? I've never seen one before. Of course, we're not going to use it - we have an electric cooker. I'm going to polish it up and buy some old-fashioned copper pots to stand on the shelf. Then it will look like a proper farmhouse kitchen. It will be fantastic."

"It may have been regarded as something of a novelty in England," said Edna, who was helping Joan with the refreshments. "I haven't seen one of those things in use since my grandmother died - but from what I hear, half of Perth is still cooking on them, they are that far behind the times." Her jowls dropped and her face became stern and disapproving.

"I think it will look fab, anyway," smiled Susan. "It will create a homely look. Do you need any help, Mum?"

"No thanks, dear, we're managing." Joan looked happy to be busy again and back in control of her own housekeeping.

"That's good. I hate pouring beer. I always make such a mess of it."

When Edna had gone back into the living room, Susan laughed. "Poor old Edna, nothing is ever right for her. Everything new is cheap and shoddy, and everything old is behind the times... I bet she complained about everything in England when she was there. By the way, did I tell you my job is permanent now, Geoff? Three girls left over the holidays, so the manager has asked me to stay on."

"You've only told me about four times so far," said Geoff. "I take it you're pleased about it."

"Why don't you try for a typing job again, love?" suggested Joan. "There might be more about now the holidays are over. Gloria has found one without much trouble, in a bank. She starts in a couple of weeks, I believe."

"But Gloria is a really good typist, and she does shorthand. I'm not up to her standard. Besides, I like working in Woolworths. It's more interesting than sitting in an office."

"So, how does it feel to be living in a real house again, Joan?" asked Geoff.

Joan looked to the ceiling with an expression of sheer bliss. "Wonderful," she sighed. "I never thought it could feel so good just to stand in a regular-shaped room and feel a solid floor beneath your feet. And to have your own kitchen and be able to cook your own food again, well... it's absolute heaven."

"I know what you mean. It's little wonder so many migrants become homesick, cooped up in the hostel. But now you have made that final leap of faith and moved out, I'm sure you are all going to be fine."

"It is something of a let-down when you leave a comfortable home and good business behind, then you find yourself living in a tin shed... in a refugee camp! It's a bit of a shock to the system." She laughed. "Now I'm beginning to sound like a member of your Shilp, aren't I? But we really did have a beautiful home in England, and a successful business. It took a lot of hard work and the best part of our lives to achieve it. It was a huge decision to leave it all behind. Sometimes, during the day, I used to sit in that tin shed at the hostel and stare at the bare walls, and I would thoroughly convince myself that we must have been completely off our heads to sell up and come out here to start all over again."

She glanced around her kitchen and new home, as though to confirm she was not dreaming. "But things seem to be turning out all right now. I think everyone goes through a period of doubt. Oh, you youngsters wouldn't appreciate that - to you, it's one big adventure. But when you get to our age and find yourself uprooted and having to start again from scratch, you begin to wonder whether it really is worth all the effort and heartache."

"But we did consider it all very carefully before we decided to come, though," said Susan.

"Yes, I know we did," said Joan. "Everyone considers it very carefully.

The trouble is, when you're at home talking about migrating, you automatically picture yourself already there and settled - living in a smart new home. You tend to overlook all the worry and upheaval that comes in between."

"Dad has had a lot of worry lately, trying to organise everything at once - the house and his business. Did you know he is buying his own truck, Geoff?"

"He mentioned that he might be, the last time I saw him. I haven't had a chance to talk to him yet tonight. I must go and have a word."

They made their way out into the garden, where more guests were gathered around a brick-built barbeque and a large plastic tank containing crushed ice and cans of beer.

"You can see what I meant about the state of the garden," said Susan. "We've managed to cut the lawn and clear a path to the barbeque so we can hold the party, but the rest of it is like a jungle, especially down the bottom. There is a pond down there somewhere. I expect some drunkard will stumble into it before the night is out."

"What are you looking at me for?"

"I wasn't. But if the cap fits... " She laughed, and Geoff noticed that as always, her laughter began in those clear, hazel eyes, then spread to light up her entire face. He was saddened by the thought that he wouldn't be seeing much of her now that the family had moved out of the hostel. He was going to miss her company, especially in the dining room where they invariably ate together. He really must get around to taking her out to dine more formally - on a date.

They found Ted talking to Craig. He was laughing at one of Craig's jokes, and Geoff noticed that the laugh was tension-free for the first time since they had left the ship. It wasn't too difficult now to picture him sitting confidently behind the wheel of a truck.

"I've been telling Craig about my new truck," he greeted them. "I take delivery of it next month."

"That's great news," said Geoff. "So you have finally conquered all your doubts and decided to take the plunge. What are you doing for contracts?"

"I'll be running her in with Harold's fleet. I've taken out a three-year sub-contract with him. I had to have that to get the finance pushed through."

"So, it's all systems go: a house, business - the whole works. It looks as though you are in Perth to stay," said Geoff.

"It looks that way," agreed Ted. "No turning back now. We all like it here. We had one or two wobbles at first, but things are gradually ironing themselves out."

"When are *you* going to start work, Craig?" Susan asked impishly. "I'm getting worried about you now that I'm a taxpayer. You're a major drain on the economy."

"Your concern for my welfare is most touching, even though prompted by self-interest," smiled Craig. "You probably won't believe this, but I've decided to renounce all worldly pleasures and dedicate myself to the cause of obtaining honest labour."

"Says he, guzzling another beer. You're right, I don't believe you. You've even let George Ryan beat you into employment. Did you know he went to Bridgetown to work on the pipeline? Terry Bates got him the job."

"It would be hard not to have heard - the whole hostel has been discussing nothing else since he left. I've been considering opening a book on how long he'll stick it."

"You never know, he might like it there."

"Like it! This is George we're talking about. He has almost as much love for manual labour as I do. The general feeling at the hostel is that he'll be back within a month. And he'll be brimming with outrageous tales of unbelievable hardships, Stone Age living conditions, and perhaps even cannibalism, with which to terrify the new arrivals. No, I'm afraid our George is far too obsessed with the idea of getting home to his warm beer and fish and chips to like anything about Australia."

"Like too many Pomes," said Harold, who had been flipping burgers on the barbeque. He wandered over to join them. He put an arm around Susan and gave her a hug. "Here she is, my favourite little niece," he said in a loud, beery voice.

"That's because I'm your only niece," said Susan.

Harold was sweating and looked slightly flushed with drink. Unlike his brother, he was broad and rugged. In his shorts and open-necked shirt, Geoff thought he looked the typical Australian bushman, in town for a weekend's drinking.

"You wouldn't think he was a Pome, would you?" said Susan. "He even talks like an Aussie."

"I'm ninety-nine per cent Australian now. As far as I'm concerned, they can pull the plug out on that fart-arse little island and sink it any time they like. I wouldn't miss it."

"He doesn't mean that. He's very patriotic, really."

Harold gave a deep, beery laugh. "Don't you kid yourself, I'm that much of an Aussie I'm even developing a dislike for whinging Pomes - only the whinging ones, mind. They give us all a bad name. If they don't like it here, send them home and let them freeze, that's what I say. But my little Susan is no whinger." He squeezed her to him.

"Little Miss Sunshine, always wearing a big smile, no matter what. That's what you've got to be able to do here in Australia, face life with a big smile, no matter how tough it gets. When I arrived out here, I didn't have a bean in my pocket. I carried my swag all over the country, earning a quid any way I could. Those were the days - young and fancy free. That's what I love most about Australia, the free-and-easy way of life. A man can live any way he wants out here. He can be a beach-bum and do absolutely nothing, or he can work his backside off to get on and become rich, the choice is his."

"England is a free country, too," said Susan.

"Bah humbug! Britain has had it. It's so overcrowded and overdeveloped that it's choking itself to a standstill. Its industries are being crippled by the constant war between greedy bosses and communist unions. I'm afraid the days when you could call it 'Great' Britain are well and truly over."

"I'll have none of your soap-boxing in my house, Harold Harvey," said Joan. She came out carrying a tray of rolls and sandwiches. "Here, chew on one of these and keep your opinions to yourself," she ordered.

Harold laughed loudly, and put an arm around her, too. "It's taken me fifteen years to persuade you and your family to come out here to our little paradise, Joanie. I'm going to make sure you don't start getting any stupid ideas about going back."

Stan Taylor and Tom Henshaw were standing next to the little group and could hear Harold clearly.

"He's right there, Tom," said Stan. "It may not be paradise, but it's certainly a much fairer place to live than Britain."

"I couldn't agree more," Tom replied, much to Stan's surprise. "The boys love it here, and I quite like it myself."

Stan looked at him quizzically. "So why are you still so hell-bent on taking them back to England?" he queried.

Tom shook his head slowly, suddenly feeling the need to share and discuss his newly-formed plans with someone. He glanced furtively about to check that Edna was not within earshot before continuing. "I'm not, not any more, Stan. To be honest, I'd like to stay and make a go of it here, or at least try. I owe it to the boys." He gave another furtive glance over his shoulder. "Between you and me, Stan, I've been looking for a job - any sort of a job. But there's not much going in the papers, and the staff at the employment office are not a lot of help. It's not easy."

"I can vouch for that," said Stan. "I spent weeks chasing all over this city trying to find work. In the end, I just got lucky. All I can advise you to do is keep on trying. You're bound to get there in the end." He placed an encouraging hand on Tom's shoulder. "What does Edna think about it?"

Tom felt a twinge of embarrassment as he admitted, "I haven't told her yet. She's still planning the voyage home. If I can get a regular job, I'm hoping to persuade her to change her mind and give it another go. To be honest with you, I'm desperate. The boys both love it here so much, and I don't want to let them down, or even worse, have them think their father is a quitter. I'll do whatever it takes - sweep the streets, or even clean toilets if necessary, as long as it pays a wage."

"That's the kind of attitude I like to hear," Harold cut in brashly. "Good British fighting spirit, that's what works out here. Okay, so work is a bit tight around town at the moment. Call it the country's growing pains, if you like. But keep plugging away and you'll get there, Tom."

He gave another beery laugh, then confided, "The trouble with a lot of Pomes is they don't expect to have to graft when they come out here; they expect to walk straight into cushy, managerial jobs. Their attitude seems to be that of the old colonialists, coming to a backward country to modernise its antiquated industry with their technology and expertise, and expecting the whole of Australia to be eternally grateful. Then someone thumps a shovel in their hands and says 'There you go, cobber, let's see how you handle a day's work', and suddenly it's shock-horror time, and let's all get the first boat home."

"Harold! Button it," Joan called a stern warning.

Harold chuckled and blew her a kiss. "Don't you just love that girl? Anyway, lads, your glasses are looking a mite low, let me get you both a refill."

Harold swayed over to the tank of crushed ice, pulled out a couple of cans of cold beer, and swayed back. "Here's to Australia," he said, looking around the gathering and holding up his glass, as if in a grand toast. "Talking about work, Tom," he said, still speaking loudly, as though to everyone within earshot. "There's an old reprobate over there who is looking for a good worker." He pointed to a tall, grey-haired man standing by the barbecue. "Hey, Clive, I was just telling our friend, Tom, here that you are looking for a good man to tidy up that rubbish tip you call a timber yard."

"Am I? That's news to me," said Clive.

"Bloody right you are. It's a disgrace. Whenever I make a delivery to you, it takes me longer to negotiate the rubbish in the yard than it does to drive the load up from Fremantle. And I haven't yet come away without a puncture. The state of your yard is costing me a fortune."

"Yeah, I must confess it has got a mite untidy of late. I've got two men off sick, and two more away on long-service leave," Clive lamented sheepishly.

"That's what I'm saying. You need help," said Harold. He nodded towards Tom. "Here's the man to sort it out for you. Come and meet Tom. He's a moulder by trade, worked in a foundry all his life. There are no easy jobs in those places, so I can guarantee he's a real grafter. He'll soon lick that yard into shape for you."

Clive strolled over. "I'm afraid I haven't anything permanent on offer, Tom," he said apologetically as they shook hands. "Once we're back to full strength, I'll be fine. But if you are prepared to accept a casual post for a while, I would certainly be more than grateful for the help."

Tom gripped his hand eagerly. He didn't care that it was only a few weeks. It was a job. It would prove to Edna that there was work about, and that he could do other things. It was a start.

"Well, I suppose the money will come in handy," Edna conceded grudgingly when they were back in their chalet, preparing for bed. "It will help us to get resettled. Goodness knows we'll have enough debts to pay off once we are home."

"Earning money to get us resettled is not why I took the job," Tom said evenly. "A few quid isn't going to make one iota of difference to the mountain of debt we will be facing back home." He took a deep breath; this was the moment he had not been looking forward to, knowing it would lead to the kind of confrontation he had always strove to avoid in his marriage. "I took the job because I want us to settle here – or at least make the effort to do so. I quite like Perth, and the boys absolutely love it, as well you know. We owe it to them to make an honest effort."

Edna dropped what she was doing and stared at him, her face a study of utter incredulity, an expression she always employed when the infallibility of her opinion was being called into question.

"What do you mean, make an honest effort? We're making plans to go home. We've already decided. Ben is sending the money."

"Cancel the plans," Tom said firmly, thankful he'd had a few stiff drinks that evening to fortify him.

"We will do no such thing. I'm not staying in this hell on earth a moment longer than I have to."

Tom was undeterred. "Then I'll cancel mine and the boys'. You can return home if you've a mind to," he found himself saying to his own amazement, and instant regret. He hadn't intended to go quite that far.

Now genuine incredulity filled Edna's eyes. "I think you've had too much to drink," she said, planting her hands firmly on her hips. "We'll continue this discussion in the morning – when you're sober."

"My mind is made up," he said resolutely. "We are going to make an honest attempt at making a new life for ourselves here, just as we planned when we left England. If we find we can't, then we'll consider going back. But not before."

Having taken the initiative, Tom found it surprisingly easy to be firm. Perhaps Edna was right, the beer had helped. Yet, as he drifted off to sleep, new worries began to plague his mind. A casual labouring job was one thing, but would he be able to find regular, full-time employment? Above all, would he ever be able to convince Edna that they would be better off staying in Australia? It certainly wasn't going to be an easy ride.

CHAPTER FOURTEEN

Craig stepped from the tall, white office block on Saint George's Terrace, knowing that his application form would already be a crumpled ball in the waste paper basket. He had no real qualifications for the job; in fact, Craig had no proper qualifications for any job. Most of his adult life had been spent flitting from town to town and job to job, working at a variety of things but never staying anywhere long enough to become qualified at anything.

His longest period of employment had been with the Merchant Navy, and he had only stuck with that long enough to become exempt from National Service.

He had been seeking employment for over three weeks, and although his attempts had so far been tentative and few, and the afternoons invariably saw him sprawled on the beach, he was becoming irked by his lack of success.

Due to the many and varied positions he had held, Craig had become very adept at playing the interview game. He knew all the right answers to give; where and when to insert the yes Sir, no Sir, three bags full Sir, in order to present the right attitude to make him appear the ideal, reliable, and conscientious applicant. He prided himself that he could usually talk his way into a job, even without the necessary qualifications. But not so in Perth. Here, they appeared to be more interested in a man's references than in the man himself.

He walked along Hay Street, where the buildings were still decorated with flags and banners welcoming visitors to the recently finished Commonwealth Games. Above an intersection hung a gigantic crown, jewelled with dozens of coloured lights. The crown's presence was a clear statement of Australia's patriotism, and loyalty to Britain and the monarchy.

While in Sydney, he had heard much in praise of Perth and its beauty, and, certainly, with its tall, white buildings, wide streets and well-laid-out shopping arcades, it was all very picturesque. Craig, however, preferred Sydney; that was a real city. Perth seemed too much the architects' model. He felt there was something too cultured and artificial about its neatness.

He stopped walking and stood on the edge of the pavement, gazing about him in an attempt to pinpoint the essence of his notion. Everything was quiet and orderly, and the atmosphere was that of a country town on a Sunday morning. He watched the traffic lights with their changing green and red "Walk", "Don't Walk" signs that no pedestrian dared to disobey for fear of courting a jaywalking fine. He recalled having once seen a drunk stagger from a bar and make his way along the sidewalk. The drunk hadn't gone far before a patrol car pulled up and two burly policemen bundled him into the car and whisked him away - almost as though he was a piece of unwanted litter that had been blowing along the street.

Perhaps that was it: everything was far too tidy and orderly. The city wasn't to live in, but to look at - a showpiece, maintaining an image of quiet respectability for the benefit of tourists. It was an image that the citizens were being regimented into becoming as much a part of as that huge, brightly lit crown and the bunting. It seemed they were somehow being denied the chance to be individuals, to act out of character with their city's pristine image, or to behave like untidy slobs if they chose to.

Satisfied that he had aptly categorised the mood of Perth, Craig decided he had better move on before the city's police performed their garbage-disposal duties and arrested him for loitering.

It was two o'clock. Would he try another firm today or not? No, to hell with it, the weather was much too good to waste away, sitting outside an office waiting for some prat of an official to interview him. He walked back to the car, and then drove to the hostel for his trunks and towel.

Gloria was sitting in Michael's room, reading a magazine, when Craig burst into the chalet. On seeing her, he stopped in mid-stride.

"Well, hello, Gloria. How are you? I must say it's a pleasant surprise to find you unescorted for a change," he joked. They were both aware of how diligently Michael chaperoned her whenever Craig and Geoff were about, and Craig could only guess what base opinions of their characters he would have thrust upon her in their absence.

She smiled up at him. "I'm very well, thank you," she said. "I hope you don't mind my being here. I've brought some clean shirts in for Michael. He's attending an interview in the city at the moment."

Craig looked from her to the pile of neatly ironed laundry and smiled. "Some guys have all the luck. Why can't I find a nice girl like you to take care of me? Guess I'm cursed to remain a lonely bachelor all my life."

"I'm sure you won't," she said, blushing slightly.

"Michael tells me you've landed a job in the city," Craig said, changing the subject before she had time to feel any embarrassment at the allusion to their marital status.

"Yes, shorthand typing. I start on Monday."

"Congratulations. It's consoling to know the country's commerce hasn't ground to a complete standstill." He was about to continue into his own room when he thought: to hell with Michael. "I can't allow you to sit here all alone on one of your last days of freedom. You should be out enjoying the sunshine. I'm on my way to the beach. Grab your things and I'll drive you down there."

Craig's voice held a note of finality, as though it had already been decided. He strode through into his own room before Gloria had time to utter a polite refusal. When he reappeared carrying a towel across his shoulder, and held out his hand to her, she felt she had no choice but to let herself be drawn to her feet and escorted from the room.

Later, she thought it somewhat strange that she had gone with him so readily. It was most out of character for her. She hardly knew him, and was usually so shy and retiring in the presence of strangers. Yet, somehow she didn't feel shy or ill at ease with Craig - he was far too smooth and confident in himself to create any awkwardness in others. She had been aware of this strong physical presence when he had danced with her at Christmas, and had known even then that she would be unable, and unwilling, to reject any advances he might make.

It was a still day, and the sea was calm, with barely a wave to ripple the surface.

"Flat as stale beer," commented Craig. "Sorry we can't inject a little life into the surf for you."

"I prefer it like this. I'm not a very good swimmer. The surf frightens me when it's too rough."

They waded into the water and swam side-by-side in silence. Craig didn't attempt to force the conversation, or flirt with her, as she had half expected him to. Instead, he seemed to blend himself with the tranquil mood of the water, floating on his back and watching the gulls gliding gracefully overhead.

"Isn't it strange how when the sea is calm, it makes everything appear so peaceful and serene," she remarked, eventually. "It's a really beautiful day. All the cold and snow of Britain seems so far away."

"It could almost be on the other side of the world, in fact," Craig reflected humorously.

"Yes, almost." She gazed timidly about her, as though suspicious of the very stillness. "Do you ever get worried about sharks?" she asked. "There's supposed to be lots of them around the Australian coast. I've been terrified of going swimming ever since reading about that man in Sydney who had his leg bitten off."

"That's Sydney. There's not much danger here in Perth," Craig reassured her. "They've only had two deaths here in the last fifty years."

Gloria found little comfort in the fact. "That isn't much consolation if you happen to be the next one," she worried.

Craig couldn't resist a chuckle, noticing that Gloria was constantly gazing about, as though expecting to find they were suddenly surrounded by man-eating sharks. "No, I suppose not. But don't worry, I'll take good care of you." He flashed her a rakish grin. "Though Michael would probably prefer to entrust you to the safety of the sharks. His opinion of me is biased, of course. None of it's true, I'm a very shy lad really."

"That I can't believe," said Gloria. There was no tenseness in her laughter now.

They talked and swam for a long while, and by the time they left the water and ran back up the beach to sunbathe, Gloria felt more at ease with Craig than she had ever felt in the presence of any man – even Michael, she realised with surprise.

"What do you do for a living, Craig?" she asked.

"As little as possible," he assured her airily.

"You appear to be very good at that. But seriously, what *do* you do?"

Craig scooped his towel from the sand and began to dry himself briskly. "Barman, truck driver, salesman, labourer, seaman – you name it, I've done it."

"It sounds a very exciting way of life. You must have travelled a lot. That's what I've always wanted to do, travel all round the world."

Gloria spread her towel onto the sand and stretched herself in the sun. A rush of excitement and anticipation swept through her as Craig lowered himself beside her. He was tall, dark, and not so much handsome - not in the classically good looking way that Michael was - but he exuded a strong masculine magnetism. And he was so infuriatingly sure of himself. She could imagine him reaching out and casually drawing her into his arms – wished, in fact, that he would. But instead he lay quietly on the sand beside her, as though nothing was further from his mind. Perhaps he really was shy, or perhaps it was simply that she wasn't his type, or that he didn't find her attractive.

"America is the country I would really like to see," she said, not wanting the conversation to lapse. "But I don't suppose I'll ever get there. It looks as though migrating to Australia will be my life's one and only big adventure. I think Michael wants to settle down here. He talks a lot about going all over the world and doing all manner of things. But he's not like you - he's not really a spontaneous person. Talking about it is as far as he'll ever get."

"It takes all kinds," said Craig. "But you're not married to him yet. If that's the way you feel, why don't you break it off and strike out on your own?"

"Sometimes I think I should, but it's not easy for a girl travelling alone. I'm not sure I could cope on my own, I've never had to. It's not that I don't love Michael," she added quickly. "He is a good man; kind and considerate - and very generous. I'm sure he would make a very good husband. I suppose, like most women, I feel a little insecure. I'm twenty-three and a little afraid of being left on the shelf, afraid that no one else will ask me to marry them."

Craig reached out and squeezed her hand. "That's absurd. You are very attractive, and you would make any man a wonderful wife."

She smiled shyly. "It's nice of you to say so."

Craig didn't press the point. That she smiled and left her hand in his said it all. If he wanted to take her from Michael, he could.

When they returned to the hostel, Geoff and Michael were both there. Geoff was wearing that peculiar, about-to-burst expression of his that meant he was trying to suppress his amusement.

"Ah, I see you've been out job hunting again," Geoff said, referring to the towel slung across Craig's shoulder, then using the observation as an excuse to release a laugh.

"Been to the beach, darling?" Michael asked Gloria.

"Yes, Craig drove me down there. You don't mind, do you?"

"No, of course not." His exaggerated gesture of indifference conveyed that Craig was being offered no thanks for the task.

"I'm afraid I have rather bad news for you, Craig," said Geoff. "As from Monday, you will be the only unemployed resident of chalet fifty-six."

Craig turned to Michael with an approving smile. "So, you've finally cracked it and found a position worthy of your mettle. Congratulations."

"Worthy indeed," said Geoff. "As a matter of fact, you were only telling me the other day how it's one of the highest paying positions in Australia."

Suddenly, it clicked and Craig understood the reason for Geoff's amusement. He stood with his finger poised. "Don't tell me. No, surely you couldn't have been lucky enough to break into the lucrative encyclopaedia market. Now that truly would be a position worthy of your mettle."

"Right first time," said Geoff. "How lucky can a man get?"

"Lucky! I'll say. Why, some of those guys I knew over in Sydney were knocking out close on a hundred pounds a week. No doubt you will be on a similar astronomic salary, Michael. You must tell us all about it."

Michael cleared his throat. "Well, actually, I have accepted the position of senior sales executive for the Parsons Encyclopaedia Company. They are an American company, about to introduce a new range of products to the Australian market. They are comparatively new to this country, so it seems I will be in right on the ground floor, so to speak. And yes, they assure me the sky is the limit as regards remuneration."

"Don't tell me a position of that calibre was actually advertised? You must have had inside contacts somewhere," said Craig.

"Actually, it *was* advertised – but very discretely, of course."

"Is it door-to-door selling?" Gloria asked curtly.

Michael flinched visibly. "Well... er, I may be involved with a little canvassing for the first week or two. Mainly to obtain first-hand knowledge of the product and the type of customer we will be targeting. But once the company becomes established, I will be managing the promotion and sales campaign throughout one of their four areas around Perth. Eventually, I will be running a team of a dozen or so representatives."

Gloria studied Craig and Geoff's faces and quickly became aware that their humour was at Michael's expense. Michael, however, seemed oblivious to the fact. He was too full of his own importance to realise he was being made fun of. He was revelling in being the centre of attention, posturing as though he was a celebrity surrounded by admiring fans. He couldn't see that they were ridiculing him, that they knew as well as she did that all his fabulous job amounted to was walking the streets hawking an expensive set of books nobody wanted to buy. She also knew that he was being forced to accept the job because it was the only one he had been offered. Suddenly she felt nothing but contempt for him. You great, stupid, pompous ass, she thought, and stormed from the room.

Sensing that something was wrong, Michael followed her out.

"Well, I'll be blowed," said Geoff. "I didn't think things were going that badly for him. He must be desperate to stoop to door knocking, especially after all the fantastic positions he's supposed to have turned down."

"I told you he was full of crap," Craig said triumphantly. "He won't make enough at that game to cover his boot leather. He would have been better off joining Tony on the railways. At least that pays a regular wage."

"And what have you been up to with Little Red Riding Hood? Plotting her seduction, I shouldn't wonder - or executing it, maybe?" Geoff raised his eyebrows, questioningly.

"On a public beach? Don't be ridiculous. We went for a quiet, innocent swim, nothing more. But, like you, Michael will never believe that. He's probably rushing her to the doctors as we speak, to check on her virginity."

"You think she is still a virgin, then?" queried Geoff.

"It wouldn't surprise me," Craig said, shrugging his indifference. "Michael has never touched her, and I doubt he ever will. He's too intent on playing the perfect gentleman, doing the right thing and struggling to maintain that stiff upper lip. 'Gentlemen do not indulge in sex before marriage, don't you know, old chap. It's not the done thing'." Craig mimicked with a poker face. "Anyway, he's due for the elbow any time now - with or without my assistance. Gloria wants out, and I can't say as I blame her. But I'm not going to be her excuse. Frankly, I can do without that kind of aggravation." He looked at his watch. "Time for me to eat," he decided. "I'm feeling rather peckish after such a hard day's job hunting. I'll see you over there."

He gathered his cutlery and mug from the top of the dressing table. Job hunting - that was something he really must start taking more seriously.

Craig had barely seated himself at a table when, of all people, Stan Taylor came and sat opposite him.

"How's your job hunting going?" Stan asked, without preamble.

"I'm still looking," said Craig, mildly surprised at Stan's sudden show of interest. Apart from nodding the time of day, they had hardly spoken since arriving in Australia. It wasn't that they openly disliked each other, or had had a disagreement, but instinct had somehow communicated that they were two vastly different people with nothing much in common to talk about.

Craig was well aware that Stan had a particularly low opinion of him, that he considered him a sponger and a layabout, incapable of doing an honest day's work. Craig, on the other hand, saw Stan as a relic from a different age, when a man's work was his life, and when dedication to duty and loyalty to one's employer were traits to be proud of, and valued way above trivial indulgences such as personal freedom or the enjoyment of life.

"So you haven't found anything yet?" Stan persisted.

"Not yet," admitted Craig. "But to tell you the truth, I haven't been looking too hard. I've been having a bit of a bludge; enjoying the sun and the beach while I can - and, of course, while I'm being provided with free meals and accommodation." He smiled debonairly, knowing that Stan was well aware of the facts, and that he thoroughly disapproved.

Stan did not return the smile. "My boss wants a man for three days' work, if you're interested," he said tersely.

"Three days? Well, that's better than nothing, I guess. What's the job?"

"We're digging the foundations on a new building site. It will be hard work, but that shouldn't bother a young man like you."

"Three days on the pick and shovel is just what I need to get back into shape," Craig said cheerfully. "Thanks for the thought, Stan. I'll be glad to take it on." He consciously voiced a far greater enthusiasm than he felt, sure that Stan had expected him to refuse pick and shovel work.

"And how's the family keeping? Craig asked. "All well, I trust?"

"They're well enough," said Stan, his brevity making it plain he had no interest in discussing personal matters. Having said what he came to say, he got to his feet. "I'll phone Joe and let him know you'll be in on Monday."

"Thanks again, Stan. I appreciate the thought."

Craig propped his elbows on the edge of the table and watched Stan's squat form stride away. Now why the hell should Stan Taylor do me any favours, he puzzled. He must know dozens of men at the hostel who would be glad of a few days' work. Craig was still pondering the point when Geoff slid his tray onto the table.

"You're looking very thoughtful. If I didn't know you better, I'd say you were stewing on a problem," said Geoff, lowering himself onto the chair opposite.

"The only problem I ever allow to bug me is where my next shag is coming from, but thanks to our lovely nurses and the permissive maidens of Septic Hill, that's not a problem right now. As a matter of fact, I think I have just been challenged."

Geoff laughed. "I did warn you Michael might be the duelling type. What's it to be, short arms at midnight behind the toilet block?"

"Nothing so sordid," said Craig. "I think our friend Stan doubts my ability to do a day's work. The duel is to be fought with picks and shovels in a three-foot trench."

On Monday morning, when they were preparing for the day's work, Craig appreciated how close to the truth he had been. Joe was leaving the pair of them to dig the foundation trenches on a new site, and Stan made it crystal clear from the outset that he expected Craig to do his share of the work.

"Shouldn't take you any more than three days," said Joe. "The boys will be finished at Manor Road tomorrow, and I want this site ready for them by Thursday."

"Finish it in two if the big fellow proves any good at all," said Stan.

"Looks big enough to knock it over on his own," admitted Joe, eyeing Craig, who equalled him in height and build.

"Can't always go by looks. We'll soon see how good he is." Stan laughed the remark off, but his intentions were quite clearly to work Craig into the ground.

Craig laughed, too. If that was the way the old fool wanted it, then so be it. This wasn't the first time he'd had to resort to pick and shovel work to earn a living, and he was capable of working as hard as any when he had to.

Craig had always taken pride in his fitness and, though he hadn't worked for over three months, he had been keeping himself in trim by swimming and jogging along the beach. His supple young muscles took to the task without complaint, and soon he was surging ahead; laughing to himself at the way Stan kept looking furtively across at him, trying to appear as though he wasn't having to hurry to keep up.

Eventually, Stan paused and stood watching Craig thrashing away with the pick. "It's a long day," he commented dryly, hinting that Craig would never last at the pace he was going.

Craig straightened up. "But then I'm a long man," he quipped. He knew how touchy Stan could be about his lack of height and sensed that the remark hadn't gone down too well - he hadn't intended it to. One up for me, he smiled. But Stan was right - it would be a long day. So, satisfied at having drawn first blood, he began to ease up.

Stan pushed on steadily all day, his pace never varying, his pick falling with the regularity of the tick of a clock. Craig amused himself with the thought that he was like a miniature trench-digging machine - a machine with the mental capacity to contemplate with pride its own ability to dig. He could imagine Stan winning a fortune on the pools and still turning up the next day to put in his eight hours with the pick. Work was the only way of life he knew, and he had long since resigned himself to loving it.

The afternoon was hot, and as Craig began to tire, he became increasingly aware of the stupidity of the thing. It reminded him of an old-time comedy film, with the characters acting out an argument in complete silence. If they adhered to the script, they should start lobbing clods of dirt at each other any time now, closely followed by battering each other about the head with their shovels; still without a word being spoken. He cursed for having allowed himself to be drawn into the farcical situation of having to prove anything to a numbskull like Stan Taylor.

Stan seemed too absorbed in the job to notice the heat, or to suffer any fatigue. He plodded on obliviously, as though he was capable of working all day and all tomorrow too, and would be quite blissfully happy doing so. Somewhat reluctantly, Craig began to admire the sheer stamina and resoluteness of the man.

Eventually, late in the afternoon, Craig straightened up and looked around the site. They were well over halfway. "I could be working myself out of a couple of days' pay here," he observed casually. "There won't be enough work for the two of us tomorrow, let alone wednesday."

"Don't let that bother you," said Stan. "Joe is a man of his word. He'll give you the three days, like he promised." He straightened up too, and leaned on his pick. "That's not a bad day's work, not bad at all," he admitted proudly.

Craig agreed, assuming an air of satisfaction, as though he, too, thought there was something fine and noble in forcing oneself to work like a horse.

Stan climbed out of the trench and went to the shed where a water bag was hanging in the shade. He unhooked it and drank. "Well, I don't mind admitting when I'm wrong," he said, wiping the back of his hand across his mouth, and offering the bag to Craig. "I had you down as being workshy. But I've got to hand it to you - you've put in a damn good day's work today, and no mistake."

"Well, thank you, Stan. That's most gracious of you – but you were probably right the first time. I'm not lazy, but I'm certainly workshy. There is a subtle difference." He tilted his head back and drank, leaving Stan waiting on an explanation.

When he lowered the water bag, he continued, thoughtfully. "It's not the physical aspect of work that bothers me as much as the mental repression of it. It's the thought of being committed to the daily grind, and having the spectre of a lifetime of mundane drudgery stretching before you. That's what makes me shy away. I enjoy my freedom too much to sign up to that."

"Have you no ambitions to better yourself in life?" Stan asked. "You can't live like a beach bum for ever."

"If by ambition you mean having a huge mortgage to maintain and H.P payments to keep up with, to pay for all the trappings we associate with success, then no, I don't have ambitions. There's got to be more to life than working your socks off for years, simply to pay off debts for a lifestyle you didn't want to commit to in the first place."

"There are times when we all feel a bit that way, as though we're treading water," admitted Stan. "Times when you wonder whether it is all worthwhile. But there are some things that are worth taking on responsibilities for, and working a lifetime to achieve. But, there again, you need to have your own family around you before you can fully appreciate that."

The conversation ended when a ute pulled up at the kerb and Joe stepped out.

"By the Jesus! What have you pair of mad Pomes been up to? You have bloody nigh finished." He stood with his arms folded and surveyed the job approvingly. "If you think you're going to screw a bonus out of me, you can forget it. A beer's all you're getting. Throw the tools into the shed and hop into the ute."

Craig needed no second invitation to down tools. He'd done quite enough digging for one day.

"I'd like to keep you on permanently, but we're at full strength at the moment," Joe told him, when they were in the pub downing their first round of beers.

"I'll find something soon enough," Craig assured him.

"I'll do a bit of scouting around for you as soon as some of the regulars get in. One of them should be able to put something your way."

At ten past four, the rest of the gang barged in. Lee ambled up to Stan and slapped him on the back. "How's it going, Stan? Been having another easy day of it, I see. How long have you bludgers been in here?"

"Since lunchtime, and we've still done twice as much work as you lot," Stan retorted with a barely perceptible grin.

"That'll be the day. You'll have to finish growing before you can keep up with me, Stanley. Did Stan ever tell you how he got out here for a fiver on the ten-pound scheme, Craig? He put his son's school uniform on and they let him through for half price."

Stan made to elbow him in the ribs. Lee saw it coming and jumped clear. "Dead ignorant, these Australians, but you get used to them," said Stan, his grin widening.

Craig was surprised to see dour, mirthless Stan take the ribbing in such good spirit. He had never imagined him to have much of a sense of humour. Apparently, even Stan had come to realise that a thick skin was necessary for survival here in Australia.

The bar soon became crowded as men poured in to quench their thirsts before making their way home. Joe, from his superior height, constantly watched the door. Presently, he nodded to Craig.

"Come over and meet Rodney. He's the foreman at Keer's Paper Products." He led the way to a group of men who had worked their way to the bar.

"How are you doing, Rod? I'd like you to meet Craig. He's a friend of mine and he's looking for a job. What do you know?"

"Then why don't you give him a bloody job?" Rod gave a beery laugh. "Good to meet you, Craig. Any friend of Joe's is a friend of mine. A job? Well, I don't know off hand. What do you do?"

Craig ran through a few of his previous positions.

"You sound versatile enough. Should be able to find you something. Not fussy what you do, are you?"

"I'll do most things for money," Craig assured him.

"I can see you're a man after my own heart, Craig. Bowl up next Monday, I'll fit you in somewhere. Any more little problems I can solve for you, Joe? How's that footie team of ours coming along?"

"Shaping up real well," said Joe. "We'll take the premiership out this year, no sweat."

"I'll drink to that," said Rod. He did. "Craig here looks like he might have the makings of a good footie player. What do you think?"

"He's got the build for it," agreed Joe.

"Ever been to a game of Aussie Rules, Craig?"

"Sure, many times. It's a fast, exciting game," said Craig, sounding enthusiastic. "But it's not for me, not as a player."

"Nonsense - a lad your size was born to play footie, same as Joe here. One of the best players in Western Australia is Joe. He takes a ten-foot mark with his feet still on the ground." He gave another beery laugh and slapped Joe on the back. "You're not going to tell us you're a soccer man, are you, Craig? You can't be a mate of Joe's and be interested in that sissy game."

Craig resigned himself to a boring discussion on the differing merits of footie and soccer, a common bar room topic whenever the British and Australians mingled. Craig hadn't much allegiance to either game, but being English, he knew it was expected of him to defend soccer. Dutifully, he put forward all the usual arguments in its favour, taking care to let his future foreman win most of the points of debate, and even hinting that he might be persuaded to try his skill at playing rules one day. By the time he and Rod parted company, they were firm friends, and Craig was confident of being placed in the best job available come Monday.

"I hear Rodney has offered you a permanent job," said Stan when they were driving back to the hostel in the Morris.

"That's right, he has - and I have you to thank for that, Stan. Your help is much appreciated. I owe you one."

"I'm glad to see you fixed up. It's not good for a young man to be out of work too long; it makes him idle. You'll have to keep out of Rod's way, though. He'll drive you mad talking about footie, especially a lad of your build and height. He won't rest till he has you playing for Subi."

"He seems a decent enough bloke, but I can't see myself playing footie for him," said Craig. The conversation then lapsed, the two still finding little in common to talk about.

"So, how are you and the family finding life in Australia?" Craig asked eventually. "Is it living up to your expectations, or are you planning to join the exodus back to England?"

"We'll not be going back," Stan assured him staunchly. "We're much better off out here. More money, better climate - it's a better way of life altogether. At least it will be once we get settled into our own place. Yes, I can honestly say it is living up to my expectations."

Craig smiled. "Well, at least we can agree on one thing... Australia is a great place to live."

"I can't understand people wanting to go back... though... to be honest, I think the wife might be tempted, given half a chance. She is still a bit homesick, that's the trouble. But she'll get over it. As soon as we find a place of our own and move out of the hostel, she'll be fine."

There was a thoughtful, somewhat concerned, note in Stan's voice, suggesting that perhaps he had more family problems than he was letting on. Craig might have pursued the point further had they not already been turning in through the hostel entrance and mounting the drive.

Maureen sat at the window and read her mother's letter for the umpteenth time that day. Her mother had written every few days since they had arrived in Australia, telling her how much she missed them all, especially little Debbie, who had always been her favourite. Maureen's eyes were red from crying. She had always been very close to her mother and sisters, and she missed them all. She hadn't wanted to leave England, but Stan had been set on it. He said Britain was finished and he wanted to get out and give the children a better start in life.

She stood up and went to the dressing table to powder her face. Stan would be home soon, and she didn't want him to see she had been crying - he had enough to worry about as it was. If only she had something to occupy her mind: cooking, shopping - anything. That was the trouble with the hostel, there was too much time to sit and think. It wasn't so bad for the men, they were out all day, either working or looking for work. They had something to think about to take their minds off home and the things they missed - but then men didn't get homesick, anyway.

She sighed and went to the door. It was a beautiful day; there had hardly been a bad day since they'd arrived. Debbie was playing in the sand with the Spanish children from the next chalet. They were all having great fun, shrieking with laughter as they tried to understand each other using sign language; it didn't take children long to readjust and make new friends.

Her eyes wandered to the number on the door of the chalet opposite: sixty-eight. It was there as a constant reminder of her mother's age. Strange, how when you were away from loved ones, you became more conscious of how old and vulnerable they were.

In all probability, she would never see her mother again. It was a hard and bitter fact to have to accept. Of course, they had discussed that possibility before leaving home. It had been easy then to talk about not seeing friends and family again and say you would be brave about it for the children's sake. But while at home, they had been empty words, their bitter truth didn't become a reality till later - how could it? While you were at home, seeing people every day, talking to them and involving them in your plans, it was impossible to realise what it would mean to you never to see them again.

Never! Such a harsh and final word. It meant they were gone from your life for good - almost as though they were already dead.

Maureen blinked back a fresh surge of tears.

Stan rounded the corner of the building. Debbie saw him and ran to meet him. He lifted her onto his shoulder and carried her up the steps, kissing Maureen lightly on the cheek as he went through the door.

"Good news, love. I get my bonus next week," he said. "Then we'll be able to start looking for a proper home."

"Really? That's wonderful." Maureen smiled bravely and followed him into the chalet.

CHAPTER FIFTEEN

"I'm four weeks overdue with my period." Louise's big brown eyes were wide and challenging.

Peter grunted and turned away. He was no longer interested in her. It was Saturday afternoon, and she had caught him alone as he was about to enter the youth club.

"I said I'm four weeks overdue," she repeated, grabbing his arm and pulling him back to face her.

"Peter gaped at her vacantly. "So what?"

"So... it means I'm pregnant, you dummy. Don't you know anything about women?"

"Of course I do. But why should I care if you're pregnant?"

"Because you're the father, stupid."

"No, I'm not!" Peter blurted in sudden panic. "You can't blame that on me. You've been with dozens of blokes since then. It could be anyone's."

"It's yours because I say it's yours. They always believe the girl. What are you going to do about it?"

"Nothing. Why should I? I'm not going to marry you, if that's what you mean," he sneered. "You're nothing but a little scrubber – everyone knows that."

Louise's eyes blazed in fury. "Don't you call me a scrubber," she seethed. She flew at him, her long, sharp nails clawing at his face. Peter reeled back in pain. He pushed her away and slapped her hard across the face, sending her spinning against the wall. She glared back at him, like a wild animal, her lips trembling with rage.

"All right, you bastard, I'll fix you," she snarled. "I'll make you wish you had never been born. I'll tell the police you raped me. I'm under age and you'll get five years' hard labour, at least – and a good flogging with the birch. You didn't know they still use the birch in this state, did you? But they do – you'll see." She turned and ran off down the steps.

Peter stood staring after her, his mind stunned and confused. She didn't mean it. She wouldn't go to the police. And she certainly couldn't prove the child was his - nobody would believe her. He raised his hand to his face and fingered the painful marks beside his eye. When he drew his hand away, there was blood on his fingers. She meant it right enough. And she was right - they always believed the girl.

Fear and panic gripped him. He would be sent to jail – and the thought of the birch sent waves of cold terror running through him. What could he do? Who could he turn to for help? Certainly not his parents; his father would kill him, and he couldn't possibly approach his mother with such a delicate problem.

In his moment of desperation, one name sprang immediately to mind:

Craig Curran. Yes, Craig was a man of the world, a man he admired and looked up to. Craig was sure to know what to do.

He raced to Craig's chalet and began pounding on the door. There was no answer. Peter sank to the steps in despair; there was no one else he felt he could confide in.

After a while, he stood up and began pacing up and down in an agitated state. The more he dwelled on his predicament, the blacker everything became. Already, he could hear the prison gates slamming behind him and see the barred windows looming in front of him. In desperation, he ran up the steps and thumped the door again.

Where the hell was Craig? What would he do in this situation? But, of course, someone like Craig was far too smart to ever land himself in this sort of mess. It was only naive, inexperienced fools like Peter who allowed themselves to get trapped.

He slouched despondently back down the steps, his head bowed, stewing in the depths of despair. What was he to do?

"A tank full of gas and a heavy right foot." The phrase echoed up from a recess of Peter's troubled mind. They were Craig's very words - Peter remembered them distinctly. It was on the voyage over. Craig had been talking to a group of lads in the bar, saying what a great country Australia was for amorous young men looking to sew their wild oats without fear of entrapment, and telling them that the country was so big that "...with a tank full of gas and a heavy right foot", there was no woman problem that couldn't be resolved, and be a thousand miles back down the road in no time at all.

Placed in this situation, that was what Craig would do, for sure, and what he would no doubt advise Peter to do.

Peter kicked in frustration at the sand as he paced up and down in front of the chalet. A fat lot of good that advice would be - he had no car, and he couldn't drive.

Then, his panic cleared abruptly as something clicked in his mind. Suddenly, the solution was right there staring him in the face. He turned and sprinted at full speed for his chalet.

John's case was under his bed. Peter dropped to his knees and dragged it out. The maps John had prepared for his hike to Sydney were all there, tucked neatly into a folder, together with a notebook he had filled with information gathered from youth hostels and motoring organisations. Peter had no qualms about taking them; John had no further use for them now that his father had decided to stay in Australia.

But as he opened the notebook, five five-pound notes fluttered to the floor; money John had been saving for his trip. To his credit, Peter's first instinct was to stuff the notes back into the case, but as he did so, his hand froze around them. It was going to be a long journey, and he would need money. The eight pounds or so he had of his own wouldn't get him very far. He hesitated. John was a friend; he couldn't steal from a friend. But suppose he hadn't opened the notebook? Then he wouldn't have known the money was there till after he'd left the hostel. Or he could look on it as a loan; he would return it when he started work in Sydney.

He knelt by the case, wrestling with his conscience for a long moment, more time than he could afford. As much as he needed the money, and no matter how much he tried to justify taking it, it was still stealing. So what? He was in big trouble, anyway - what difference was one more little charge going to make to the length of his sentence?

He crammed the money into his pocket and pushed the case back under the bed. Then he quickly threw a few clothes into his travel bag, and ran from the hostel as fast as his legs would take him.

The train rattled into Perth Central station and stood there for what seemed an age. It was already mid-afternoon, and Peter wanted to get as far away from the city as possible before he was missed. Louise would have told her parents by now, and perhaps they had already alerted the police. His nerves began to twitch with the inactivity. He watched the people milling about on the platform, and felt sure they were all looking at him. They all knew who he was and what he had done. Any minute now, the police would arrive to arrest him and take him away.

Eventually, the train moved slowly away from the platform, and he began to breathe more easily.

At Midland Junction, he stepped out of the train, and, walking from the station, found himself on a quiet side street. Surely this couldn't be the main road out of Perth? He must have made a mistake.

He reached into his bag for John's notebook. On the first page was a pencilled map of Midland Junction. He followed the instructions and soon came out onto the Great Eastern Highway. The traffic was quite thick, and most of it seemed to be heading out of Perth.

Peter began waving his thumb at the cars as he walked along, feeling a little foolish and self-conscious at first. Presently, an old Hillman Minx pulled up beside him.

"Where are you going, son?" asked the driver, an old man with a bald head and a pair of rimless spectacles that were perched so far down his nose that he was peering over them.

"Sydney," Peter replied without thinking.

"Sydney, eh? Well, I'm not going quite that far," the old man chuckled. "But I can take you as far as Northam."

Peter thanked him and climbed into the car.

"Travelling kind of light for a journey like that, aren't you, son?"

"Yes... well, actually, I'm going to Kalgoorlie first," stammered Peter. "I have a brother there. He has the rest of my luggage." The lie didn't sound a very convincing one, even to Peter. He would have to prepare a better story than that for future lifts. Fortunately, the old man didn't persist with his questioning, but became more intent on relating his own experiences of Sydney.

The Hillman bumped along at a steady thirty-five, while other cars sped by at fifty and sixty. Peter became edgy again. The police were bound to be looking for him by now. He would need to thumb a much faster car next time.

Eventually, they arrived at Northam and the old man stopped the car in the main street. Peter thanked him again and got out. There were a number of people about, and rather than draw attention to himself by hailing cars in town, he decided to walk.

It was a small town, and he was soon through it and back on the highway. The traffic was much thinner now, and he walked for a long time without being offered a lift. Again, he began to feel edgy, wanting to be on the move, feeling the need to be speeding away from Perth as quickly as he could.

When the big American car pulled up a few yards ahead of him, Peter ran to it and jumped in jubilantly. This should move along much faster than the Hillman, he thought. And he was right - but the manner in which it did so terrified him. The big car rocketed along, bouncing and swaying all over the road. Every time they met an oncoming vehicle, Peter was sure there would be a collision. The road was so narrow that, were it not for the road signs, he would have doubted that this was the main east-west highway. Back home, even the B-roads and farm tracks were wider.

Peter had no need to relate the cover story he had prepared, as the roar from the engine and the wind howling by made conversation virtually impossible. And the driver, a hefty man with heavily tattooed forearms, seemed disinclined to talk.

They were in open country now, and Peter settled back to watch the scenery slip by. The sun was sinking behind them, so that the trees cast long shadows and the fields took on a deeper, richer colour. All around him appeared so tranquil and serene, he could almost forget the trouble that festered behind him.

Soon it was dark, and the big car roared on, eating up the miles; chasing the two wide beams of light fanning out in front of them. The driver had said he was going to Southern Cross. Peter had no idea how far that was in miles, but he remembered seeing the name on the map and it appeared to be about halfway between Perth and Kalgoorlie, making it a comforting one hundred and fifty miles or so from Perth.

He dozed a little and, when he awoke, there was a new nip in the air, and his legs and feet were cold. He was glad he had thought to stuff his jacket into the bag - he would be needing it.

At Southern Cross, he stepped out of the car, thanked the driver, then made his way to the edge of town and stood by the side of the road. It was cold and there was no traffic - and he was hungry. After a while, he gave up and began walking back into town to seek food and lodgings for the night.

He stopped abruptly. No, this was a stupid idea. There would be police in town and he would be spotted. He turned and walked back again, and kept on going along the highway for about a mile.

The huge pipeline carrying water to the gold mining town of Kalgoorlie had been running alongside the highway for many miles. Peter turned off the road and walked through the scrub towards it. He would bed down beneath it for the night.

Peter remembered that on their voyage over they had attended a talk on Western Australia. This very pipeline had been mentioned, and had been described as one of the state's greatest feats of engineering. The longest water pipeline in the world, they had said. Over three hundred and fifty miles of it, with many pumping stations along the way.

He couldn't remember exactly how many pumping stations, but what he did remember was that when the pipeline was completed and commissioned, the water had been so late in arriving at Kalgoorlie that the engineer who designed it had been ridiculed and derided as a failure, and a complete and utter fool to ever imagine he could pump water that far into the desert. So fierce had been the criticism that the beleaguered engineer had been driven to suicide.

The very next day, to a great fanfare and cheers, the water had come gushing through at Kalgoorlie. All the people who had criticised and berated him, then began hailing the engineer as a genius and a national hero, and proclaimed his pipeline as one of the country's greatest feats of engineering.

A fat lot of good all their praise and adulation had done him - he was dead, Peter thought cynically. He had been hounded to it by his critics. In the end, what did it matter what anyone thought or said about you? It was only your own opinions that counted, only your own self-belief and self-reliance that would see you through.

He ate the remainder of the bun he had bought in Northam, and washed it down with lemonade. That was all he had had since breakfast, and he was starving hungry. He wrapped his jacket tightly around him and lowered his head onto the travel bag. He was cold and tired, but his mind was far too active for sleep. He stared up at the underside of the huge pipeline, wondering what tomorrow would bring. Would he manage to cross the border into the safety of South Australia? Or, would he be arrested and sent back to Perth to face trial - and jail? South Australia was still a long way away, and his mood was far from hopeful.

He was feeling alone and isolated. He had never lived away from his parents before, and already he was missing them, and his brother and little sister. Perhaps he would never see any of them again. And he hadn't even had a chance to say goodbye. Tears began to fill his eyes. He choked them back quickly, reminding himself that he must be strong. Only sissies cried.

He thought of Louise, but there was no sense of guilt, no nagging conscience. He could not accept that he had done wrong – at least, not in the criminal sense. It was nature. Louise had wanted it to happen as much as he had, perhaps even more. She had been the experienced one; she had instigated it. And, as the chances of the child actually being his were remote, he refused to allow any feelings of guilt.

But there was the money. The rest he might explain away and convince himself that he had merely been the victim of circumstances, but not the money. He had wilfully stolen that, and from a friend. Peter liked John. True, he was a bit of a square, but he was solid and dependable, the sort of friend he could have turned to for help; who would probably have lent him the money had he asked for it.

John wasn't like Wayne Stanton and the rest of the gang that hung out around the youth club. They would doubtless be treating the whole thing as a big joke, laughing at his misfortune. They were nothing but a bunch of idiots; stupid kids trying to impress each other with their smart talk, their petty pilfering and their sly drinking. He would never have landed in this mess had he kept away from them. He would steer well clear of their kind in the future. And he would return John's money the very first chance he got.

The next morning, Peter was up as dawn broke. He hadn't heard any traffic yet, but he couldn't afford to miss the possibility of an early lift. He had to put as many miles between himself and Perth as he could - and quickly.

Making his way back through the scrub to the road, he became aware of a scratching sound, and as he got nearer the road, he could see that shadowy figures were moving about there in the half light. Surely nobody would be about at this time of day? It was far too early for road gangs to be working. He crept quietly through the scrub and peered out.

"Kangaroos! Real kngaroos," he whispered.

He counted seven of them. They had come out of the bush and were drinking; licking the early morning dew from the tarmac surface. As one turned sideways, Peter spotted a tiny head protruding from the pouch. He watched, spellbound.

As the sun began to rise slowly behind them, it glistened from the road's damp surface, turning it into a ribbon of gold; silhouetting the kangaroos against it. This was magic. Pure magic. This was the mystical outback he had heard so much about; this was the *real* Australia. He wanted to linger and savour the experience, but knew he should be pressing on.

The scene was disturbed when a car came speeding out of the rising sun, its blazing headlights getting ever nearer. The kangaroos continued to drink, seemingly oblivious of the danger. Nearer and nearer sped the headlights.

In desperation, Peter broke his cover and ran towards them, shouting and waving his arms. The kangaroos turned and bounded gracefully away, disappearing into the safety of the bush. The car sped harmlessly by.

Seeing the kangaroos had brightened Peter's mood. He whistled as he strode purposefully along the highway. He had studied the map and, with luck, hoped to be safely over the border and into South Australia before nightfall. There was an early morning nip in the air, so he walked briskly to keep warm. There was little traffic on the road as yet, and he walked for almost an hour before putting his bag down and resting.

There was warmth in the sun now. He slipped off his jacket and stuffed it back into the bag. He observed that this was a particularly bad stretch of road for hitchhiking, as it appeared to run straight for miles, and what cars there were flashed by at too fast a speed to be bothered stopping for a hiker. He thought it best to keep walking till he came to a bend where they would have to slow down.

He walked and walked for what must have been miles. The town behind him had long since disappeared from view, and his hopes of making a good start to the day faded with it. It was ten o'clock before he received his first lift, and this on the back of a farm truck that was only going a few miles up the road. The farther he travelled from Perth, the harder it was becoming to obtain lifts. Finally, and reluctantly, he had to abandon all hope of reaching South Australia before nightfall.

He trudged along, tired and with his mind clouded in despondency. Just when he was reaching his lowest point, a huge semi-trailer rumbled and hissed to a halt a few yards ahead of him. Peter sprinted up to it, his heart leaping for joy at the sight of its South Australian number plates. Yes! He was going to make it over the border today after all.

"Are you going to South Australia?" He asked excitedly, as he climbed up into the cab beside the driver.

"That's right, son, but not by road."

Peter stared at him in bewilderment. How else was he going to get there – fly?

"Stick her on the train at Kalgoorlie," the driver informed him with a wide grin.

"You put this on the train?" Peter didn't know whether to believe him or not, it seemed a daft idea.

"That's right. Drive the whole rig onto the train and freight her across."

"But why? There's a road, isn't there?"

"Some people call it a road. Nothing but a dirt track, really. Over a thousand miles of it, right across the Nullarbor desert."

"But isn't it expensive, taking it all that way by train? Wouldn't it be cheaper to drive?"

The driver shook his head emphatically. "Not in the long run. That dirt track knocks all hell out of a truck. No garages out there, either, one or two petrol stations, that's all. Cost a mate of mine five hundred quid once for a tow through to Port Augusta. Yes, sir, she's wild old territory, is the Nullarbor. I hope you know what you are up to trying to hitchhike across it, young fellow. People have died out there. It gets so hot a man could dry up and blow away, and nobody would ever know." He laughed brashly, though Peter failed to see what was funny about people drying up and blowing away.

"...and lifts are not easy to come by, either," the driver continued. "Couple of lads I picked up once reckoned they spent four days sitting by the road at Norseman before they got a lift across."

"Four days!" gasped Peter. "I didn't think it could be that bad."

"It's that bad, all right, and worse, especially this time of the year. There wouldn't be any more than four or five cars a day going across by road. And they'll all be holiday-makers, too well loaded to take passengers." The driver shook his head sombrely. "You think long and hard, young man. My advice is to catch the train. It will cost you about twelve pounds from Kalgoorlie to Port Augusta. It's expensive, but at least you'll get there alive."

Twelve pounds. He couldn't afford it. He would need that money when he arrived in Sydney. "I'll try hitching a lift first," he said stubbornly.

"Just thought I'd warn you," said the driver. He gave another unnecessary laugh. "Just be sure to take plenty of water with you. We don't want you drying up and blowing away, do we now?"

The wheat-belt lay far behind them now and they were entering the gold mining areas, driving through dense bush-land, mile after mile of dull, uninteresting country. So this was the Australian outback? Peter was impressed by its vastness, yet he couldn't tear his thoughts away from the far vaster Nullarbor that lay ahead of him. A thousand miles... a thousand miles... he kept repeating to himself.

The words were meaningless sounds echoing within his head. It was beyond his powers of comprehension to visualise anything so big - and so empty. A thousand miles - a mere dirt track longer than the entire length of Britain, stretching through a vast wilderness where it got so hot that "a man could dry up and blow away". The thought terrified him. But the thought of prison and the birch terrified him more. Somehow, he had to cross that desert.

Eventually, they rolled into the gold mining town of Coolgardie, twenty-three miles from Kalgoorlie, and the driver brought the truck to a halt.

"This is as far as you go on this road," he told Peter. "There's a road that runs south from here down to Norseman. That's the last town before crossing the Nullarbor."

As they shook hands, he gave Peter a concerned stare. "If you are venturing into the desert, remember what I said and be sure to take plenty of water with you. The Nullarbor is a dangerous place. People really do die out there," he said earnestly. And this time, he wasn't laughing.

Peter thanked him and climbed down from the cab. The big truck rumbled away, and he was left standing by the side of the road amidst a cloud of swirling dust.

Norseman: the last town before crossing the Nullarbor, the last outpost of civilisation. The name took on an ominous, almost sinister, note. Would he, too, have to wait there for four days – perhaps even longer? He prayed not. He felt sure that even one day's hold-up would mean certain arrest. The police were sure to be looking for him by now. True, he was over three hundred miles from Perth – four hundred by the time he reached Norseman. But he would not feel safe until he was over the border and into South Australia.

An idea occurred to him: if he went to Kalgoorlie, he may be able to jump the train, that way he could save the fare, and save time, too. It might be worth a try. Anything sounded better than facing the horrors of the Nullarbor. He would think about it.

It was late in the day, and he hadn't eaten for hours. He picked up his bag and walked into town in search of a café.

Coolgardie was exactly how he had imagined an old mining town to be. The dusty main street was flanked by shabby buildings - some of timber, some of brick. Many were falling into disrepair with their doors and windows boarded up. Two large, solidly-built hotels stood on opposite corners in the middle of the town. Large, ornate verandas protruded to shade the wooden sidewalks - the type Peter had only seen in Westerns. The street was empty, and with his footsteps echoing eerily from the boards as he walked along, he could almost imagine he was playing out a scene from a cowboy film.

He stopped and let his eyes roam the dusty street. This was an exciting town; it had character and atmosphere, something that big cities never had. He could picture it as it might have been years before, with horse-drawn carts and buggies churning up the dust as they rolled through town. Hardy prospectors would have gathered on this very boardwalk to exchange yarns of big finds. Gold fever would be in the air, and everyone would be hoping and praying for that one big strike that would make them outrageously rich. How he would love to stop here for a while and soak up the atmosphere; explore the old diggings - perhaps even do a little prospecting himself. That would really be something to tell all his mates back in Liverpool. But, of course, that was impossible. He must keep moving, and fast.

There was only one café in town. Peter pushed open the door, and a bell above his head clanged loudly. It was cool and dark inside, and it took his eyes a few moments to adjust to the gloom.

"What'll it be?" a husky voice asked from beside him.

Startled, He turned and saw a tall, gaunt woman standing at the large curtainless window. Her face was drawn and weather-beaten, and her dark eyes seemed to pierce his, unnervingly. She looked every bit the tough, hardy type of character he would have expected to find in a place like Coolgardie. She would be part of the very fabric of the town.

"I'd like something to eat, please," he said.

"Didn't think you came in to buy a shirt," she drawled. There was no trace of humour or sarcasm in the remark, merely a dry, matter-of-fact reply. "Going far?" she asked.

"No... only to Kalgoorlie."

"So was the truck you climbed out of." Again, her voice was flat and unemotional. He had made another silly mistake, and the woman was well aware of it. It was almost as though she didn't have to ask questions - she already knew all there was to know about him, and where he was going. She made him feel uneasy, and so very guilty.

Peter ordered his meal and the woman went through into the kitchen to prepare it. He was gripped by an impulse to run before she came back. There was something odd about that old woman. He could still feel her dark eyes piercing his, like hot coals burning their way deep into his mind, reading his every secret thought. Somehow, he was sure she knew who he was and what he had done. He took a deep breath and steadied himself. That was absurd. How could she possibly know anything? He was tired and hungry, his nerves were playing tricks on him, that was all. He forced himself to sit still and try to look at ease.

Eventually, the woman returned and placed a tray on the table in front of him. She stood there studying him with an intensity that made him fidget guiltily.

"Run away from home, haven't you?" she stated in the same flat, matter-of-fact voice.

Peter's jaw dropped open. "No, I... I'm going to see my brother in Kalgoorlie," he stammered.

She nodded knowingly, then left him to his meal and returned to her position at the window. "Seen them all come through here in my time," she said quietly, almost to herself. "Hardened criminals, escaped convicts, runaway kids, even one or two murderers. They get this far into the bush and think they're safe, think nobody's going to catch them. But they're all proved wrong. They all get caught. I've never seen a one of them manage to jump the state border."

"Why's that?" Peter asked, unable to control his need to know.

She turned back from the window. "Stands to reason, don't it? There's only one road, and only one railway. Anyone leaving Western Australia has to go through Kalgoorlie or Norseman. And the law is red hot in both places. They all get caught."

She was right, of course, he could see that now. The hundreds of miles he had put behind him didn't mean a thing. When narrowed down to one road and one railway, the vast wilderness that was the outback was really very small after all.

The old woman was still studying him intently. "Why did you run away?" she demanded.

Peter attempted to relate John's story about his parents going back to England, and his wanting to stay in Australia. But he soon found himself faltering under that piercing gaze, and eventually he broke down and told her everything, never doubting for a moment her supreme right to know.

It was all right, though, she wasn't going to hand him over to the police. There was a sympathetic note in her gruff voice that said she wanted to help him, wanted to prevent him from falling into the police trap at Norseman.

"How can I get through to Sydney, then?" he asked.

"You can't. I just told you that."

"But I can't go back to Perth. They'll throw me in jail."

"You will have to go back and straighten it all out eventually, you know that. What you need right now is somewhere to rest up and think on it for a while, get it sorted in your head." She returned her attention back to the window and peered out onto the street.

"But where?" Peter urged.

There was a long pause before she continued thoughtfully. "There's a quarry fifteen miles north of here. I'll get you a job and you can live in the camp out there. Nobody will find you." She turned back to him and raised a monitoring finger. "I'm not hiding you away, mind, just giving you some breathing space to get your head sorted out, that's all. You'll come round to doing the right thing soon enough."

Peter wasn't at all sure what she meant by 'the right thing', but he nodded his consent to the plan; he appeared to have no choice.

"All right," she said. "The first thing you need to do is write a letter."

"A letter?" he repeated in alarm, his panic suddenly returning. Was the woman trying to trick him into signing some kind of confession? "Who to?" he asked uneasily.

"To your mother, of course. You youngsters are all the same. Strike out across the country whenever you feel like it, never a thought for your mothers and how they are worrying themselves sick about you."

She brought pen and paper and placed them in front of him. "Don't tell her where you are, or what you're doing. Just say you're all right and you are staying with friends."

"But they will know where the letter came from."

"No they won't. I'll give it to one of the truckers to post in Adelaide. That way they'll think you've made it to South Australia."

Peter smiled; starting to relax for the first time in two days. This shrewd old woman had all the answers. If she said he would be safe at the quarry, then he was sure he would be.

CHAPTER SIXTEEN

Louise's screams rose high above her mother's shrill voice. Simon Tate heard them as he rounded the corner of his chalet. He ran up the steps, ignoring the group of muttering women who had gathered opposite.

Louise was cowering in a corner, screaming hysterically. Her mother stood over her, her face contorted with rage as she swung the leather strap again and again.

"You dirty, disgusting child," she screeched.

Simon snatched the strap from her hand. "For goodness sake, Mary, you'll kill the child!" He picked his daughter up gently and she clung to him, sobbing loudly. Mary was breathing heavily, her face still red with rage. They stood that way for a long moment, the tension between them growing more intense with every second.

"Will somebody tell me what this is all about?" Simon demanded, looking from one to the other in bewilderment.

"Your darling daughter is pregnant, that's what," seethed Mary.

Simom's mouth dropped open in shocked disbelief. No, not his Louise, not his lovely little girl, surely this couldn't be. It could happen to anyone else's daughter, but not his Louise.

"Don't be ridiculous! She... can't be..." he stammered.

"It wasn't my fault," sobbed Louise. She wriggled free from his grasp and threw herself onto the bed, burying her face deep into the pillow.

Simon stood frozen to the spot, his arms extended in front of him, as though he was still holding her. "There must be some mistake... she's only fifteen... just a child," he muttered.

"There's no mistake. She's a little tramp, that's what. I told you and told you to be firmer with her, but no: 'She's only young once', you said. 'Let her have fun, let her stay out all hours of the night, let her run around with every Tom, Dick and Harry. Can't do any harm', you said. 'They're only kids', you said. Now look what's happened. After all I've done for her. God knows I've tried my utmost to see she grew up clean and decent – and this is the thanks I get."

She clasped her hands to her face and collapsed into a chair, emitting a long, remorseful groan. "Oh, my God! What have I done to deserve this?"

Now mother and daughter were both bawling. Simon was at a loss to know what to do - whether he should attempt to comfort them, or give way to his own feelings and fly into an almighty rage.

"Oh, God. Please forgive me. Please forgive me," Mary kept repeating, her hands still clasped firmly to her face.

His wife's religious fervour had long since been a source of antagonism to Simon. He seized on it now as an outlet for his rage. "You and your narrow-minded religion," he bellowed. "Constantly harping on about morality, and lecturing the child on the evils of the flesh, scaring her half to death till she sees her every natural urge as something dirty and disgusting. You can't suppress nature. Your precious church twists and tortures a child's mind till they see every natural instinct as something sinful and perverted. You... " Simon gave up; Mary's only response was to wail even louder, drowning his words.

"Louise, you sit up now and tell me what happened. Who did this?" he demanded.

"Peter Taylor," Louise sobbed into her pillow. "I couldn't stop him. He made me."

"He forced you? Are you telling me he raped you?"

"Yes," she sobbed.

"This is a matter for the police. I'm going to phone them," Simon asserted. As the statement met with no objections, he turned and strode from the room.

The group of women were still gathered opposite their door. Mrs Hollins's owl-like face was prominent amongst them, her mouth slightly open; her eyes wide and eager, delighting in the spectacle.

"Is anything the matter?" she asked in her insipid voice.

Simon shot her the most contemptuous glare he could muster, and hurried by. The gossip would be all over the hostel before the hour was out.

The telephone box at the foot of the drive was occupied. Simon paced up and down impatiently, cursing everything he could think to curse. What a monstrous thing to happen. Their move to Australia had been going so smoothly. He had landed a good, secure job, they all loved Perth and its climate, and they were looking forward to making a new life for themselves here. And now this. But justice would be done - he would see to that.

By the time the phone box became vacant, he had simmered down a little and began to think more rationally. Having the police - and perhaps the newspapers - probing into their lives, asking insensitive and embarrassing questions, wouldn't help Louise; neither would being dragged through the courts as the victim in a rape case. The most important thing now was to think what was best for Louise, and, of course, for her child. The Taylor boy must do the right thing, and provide for them. Simon was determined to make sure that he did. But realistically, the lad wouldn't be able to fulfil his commitments from a prison cell.

Simon held the buzzing receiver in his hand for a long time, agonising over whether to dial or not. Perhaps he should have a quiet word with Stan Taylor before doing anything rash. He didn't relish a confrontation with Stan. He was a tough-looking character, and from what he knew of him he could be quite abrasive. But Simon was in no mood to be intimidated. This was about his Louise, and, one way or another, he was going to see that she got justice. Stan had a daughter - surely he would see reason and ensure that his son did right by Louise. Perhaps they could work this out between themselves and avoid any further trauma or animosity by involving the law.

Reluctantly, he replaced the receiver and made his way back up the drive.

Stan was sitting on the steps of his chalet, reading the paper. He looked up as Simon approached. "Good day, Simon. How are things with you?" he asked.

"'Things'" are not good," Simon said pointedly, then hesitated, not quite knowing how to begin. "I want a word with you about young Peter."

Stan closed his paper and sighed. "What has he been up to now?"

From the corner of his eye, Simon noticed the same group of women were now edging their way to the end of Stan's chalet. Their snooping reawakened his anger and frustration.

"Go home and mind your own business," he shouted at them. "You're nothing but a bunch of nosy, gossiping old bags."

Stan stood up in alarm. "Steady on there, Simon," he said, coming down the steps and placing a restraining hand on his shoulder. "Best come inside and tell me what this is all about. You look as though you could use a stiff drink."

Stan ushered him into the chalet. Once inside, he drew a bottle of whisky and two glasses from the cabinet and poured out large measures. "Now, what seems to be the problem? What has that idiot of a boy been up to now?"

"Are we alone?" Simon asked, glancing towards the other room.

Stan nodded. "Maureen is over at the laundry. You can speak your mind."

"Well... I'll come straight to the point, Stan. My Louise is pregnant and your Peter is the father. Not only that, but she tells me he forced her." He paused awkwardly and made to sip the whisky. The smell turned his stomach. "We are talking rape here, Stan," he said as tactfully as he could. "And as Louise is only fifteen, Peter could be facing some very serious charges, and a long prison sentence." He put the whisky to his lips again, but didn't drink, waiting for the gravity of his words to register.

Stan stood studying his own tumbler of whisky, but said nothing. His jaw began to tighten, and Simon could sense his anger rising.

"I've no wish to see the boy go to jail," Simon offered by way of conciliation. "But he will have to shoulder his responsibilities and provide for the child. If we can all agree to that between ourselves, I see no reason why we can't keep the matter out of court."

Stan downed his whisky, and ground his teeth, more angered than shocked by the accusations. This was going to devastate Maureen. Damn that fool of a boy. He would like to strap the very hide off him for this. Yet, even in his anger, he was aware that there were two sides to every story. He had seen the way Louise dressed, and how she flaunted herself in front of the teenage boys. He didn't believe for a moment that she was a totally innocent victim in this.

"Louise is sure it was Peter?" he asked tentatively.

"Of course she is sure. How could she possibly be mistaken?" Simon fired back.

Stan stood his glass back on the dressing table. Simon had missed the whole point of the question. He was still too aghast that his daughter should misbehave at all to have considered the possibility of her having done so on more than one occasion - or with more than one boy. Stan let the point drop. They could thrash that out later, along with the dubious question of rape.

"Damn it all, I can't believe this is happening!" exclaimed Simon. "It's all so... so. Well, you have a daughter of your own, Stan. Imagine how you would feel if anything like this happened to her. Debbie is only a child yet, I know, but to a father, they are always children. One minute they are the size of young Debbie, running about and climbing onto your knee, and somehow you never get to think of them as being any older. They are always Daddy's little girl. Then, out of the blue, something like this happens, and it's... well, it's a shock." He hung his head, feeling the inadequacy of the word, but his mind was still too stunned to delve for a more fitting one. "It knocks your whole world for six, I can tell you."

His words had touched a nerve. Stan idolised little Debbie; she was his treasure. Of course, nothing like this would ever happen to Debbie, but the possibility was there, and looking into the drawn lines of Simon's face he could almost feel the pain that could one day be his. "If Peter is to blame, he'll do the right thing. I'll see to that," he said firmly. "But first we need to hear his side of the story."

Stan led the way to Peter's chalet, but when they got there, it was empty.

"Probably at the beach," he said. Then he noticed that the drawers had been turned out and Peter's travel bag was missing. "Did Louise say anything to him about this?" he asked Simon.

"I don't know. I don't think so." He looked up sharply. "Why do you ask? Do you think he has taken off?"

"It's a possibility," Stan said trying to play it down.

"He can't do that! He will have to be brought back," insisted Simon. "He can't be allowed to simply run out on his responsibilities."

"He can't have gone far," Stan said calmly. "He hasn't much money. And where would he go? He doesn't know anyone here. He'll be back in a day or two, when he starts feeling hungry."

Simon was not convinced, nor was he going to be placated. "In a couple of days, he could be over the other side of Australia. I want the police alerted," he panicked. "I won't press any charges right now, but he'll have to be found. Tell the police he's a runaway - anything. But he has to be brought back to face up to what he's done."

Stan had no choice but to agree. If they were to iron this out, Peter had to be found and brought back.

Rumours, both true and false, were soon buzzing around the hostel. John heard the news from Eddie Carter as they entered the dining room together.

"Wouldn't like to be in Peter's shoes when the police catch up with him," Eddie said with a sly, unsympathetic grin. "Carnal knowledge is a very serious offence in Australia. I hear they still use the birch in some cases."

John picked up a tray and made his way to the servery. "But why Peter? He wasn't the only one to go with Louise," he reasoned. "The kid could be anybody's – yours, even, you went with her, too."

"It's his because Louise says it's his. A kid can only have one father, and Louise has pointed the finger at Peter. That lets the rest of us off the hook." He fanned his face with his hand and grinned in relief.

John was annoyed that Eddie seemed to be treating the whole thing as a huge joke, especially when he was supposed to be Peter's friend. "Louise is more to blame than anyone," he adjudged. "We all know what she is."

"Yeah, she's a right little goer." Eddie agreed with another sly grin, rolling his shoulders and shuffling his feet cockily. "Still, I hear she got hers, too. They say her mother beat all hell out of her with a broom handle." He laughed and shuffled his feet again, in nervous excitement, like a string puppet, John thought. "But that's nothing to what Peter will get when the police catch up with him. Boy, am I glad my name isn't Peter Taylor. Where do you reckon he is heading?"

"How the hell would I know?" John snapped impatiently. He knew exactly where Peter would be heading. He would be on his way to Sydney. They had talked about the trip so much, and studied the route together. Peter would have taken the maps and be on his way to Sydney, for sure, and good luck to him. John resolved to say nothing. Then he remembered his savings and hurried back to his chalet.

He knelt by his case and cursed, more at himself than at Peter. He should have put the money in the bank. He doubted Peter had taken it intentionally; he'd probably been in too great a hurry to even check the contents of the folder. Twenty-five pounds was a lot of money to lose, yet if he told anyone about it, he would have to tell them about the maps, too. The police would know where Peter was going, and he would likely be caught. John didn't want to do anything that would ruin Peter's chances of getting away, but it had taken him a long time to save that money, and he wanted it back.

Maureen had recovered from her initial shock, and sat at the dining table looking composed, if still a little pale, as Stan explained the position to her.

"The police will bring him home safely," he assured her. "At the moment, he is only registered as a runaway, so there's nothing they can arrest him for. It won't become a police matter unless - and until the Tates file an official complaint."

"I still don't like the idea of the police chasing him. He's only a boy. He'll come home soon enough."

"I know," said Stan. "But the Tates are naturally concerned, too. They want to feel that something is being done."

Maureen looked nervously about her. Everyone in the crowded dining room seemed to be talking about them, whispering and nodding in their direction; some with stern, disapproving faces, others with sly, sneering grins.

"I can't stand this place," she said. "There's something depraved about the people here. They positively delight in other people's misfortunes."

"You're imagining things, Maureen."

"Am I? Look at them all." She withdrew her hand from under his as the tears began to fill her eyes. "Where do you think he's gone, Stan?"

"I've no idea. There's nowhere he can go, really. The police think he will try to cross the border into South Australia, but I doubt that."

"How can he? He has no money."

"I know, and that's why it's better to have the police find him and bring him home before the little fool starves somewhere."

"I suppose you're right," sobbed Maureen. "But I still don't like it."

"There's nothing to worry about," Stan comforted her. "They'll soon have him back safe and sound."

"Safe? And then what's going to happen to him?"

"That all depends on what he has to say for himself, and what line the Tates decide to take."

"We all know what line Mary is taking. It's not her daughter's welfare she's overly concerned about; it's the stigma of her being an unmarried mother. That and her own shame at having an illegitimate grandchild. It isn't right for Peter to be forced into such a marriage - he is not much more than a child himself. And Louise isn't so innocent, either. People have told me things about her."

"That's as may be, Maureen, but she is under age, and Peter has committed a serious offence. For the moment, we just have to be thankful that the Tates are not pressing charges. Things will work out right eventually, give them time, and try not to worry."

Telling Maureen not to worry was as futile as telling her not to breathe. "I can't stand any more of this place, Stan - I want to go home," she suddenly blurted out. "I miss Mum and the family. I need them around me."

"You'll feel differently when we get this behind us and we move into our own place, away from the hostel."

"No, I won't. I've had enough. I don't like it here. None of this would have happened if we had been at home, where we could have kept an eye on him. I want to go home. As soon as Peter is back with us, I want us to pack up and go."

Stan pursed his lips, but said nothing. He had sensed this coming for some time. He had hoped Maureen would get over her homesickness eventually and get to like Perth as much as he did. But a crisis like this was always going to shatter her fragile confidence and send her running for home and the comfort of her family. It was all Peter's fault. Damn that idiot of a son.

By the time Peter's letter arrived, a week later, Maureen was beside herself with worry; imagining all manner of morbid fates that may have befallen him.

She plucked the letter from the rack and, recognising the scrawling handwriting, tore at the seal with fumbling fingers. Her heart stood still as she read quickly, expecting the worst. Then she breathed a huge sigh of relief. He was safe. Thank God. She grabbed the rest of their mail and hurried back to the chalet.

"It's a letter from Peter," she exclaimed, smiling for the first time in days as she waved the sheet of paper in front of Stan. "He's safe, thank God!"

Stan looked up. "Where is he?" he asked tersely.

"He doesn't say - just that he is safe and is staying with friends. It's postmarked from Adelaide."

Stan took the letter and read it himself, relieved that the boy had shown good sense enough to write and reassure his mother. Stan wouldn't have credited him with being that thoughtful, but credit where it was due.

"I doubt he's made it to Adelaide," Stan said, turning the envelope in his hands. "And he certainly doesn't have any friends there."

The letter's calming effect on Maureen was visible. "As long as he is all right and someone is looking after him, I don't mind where he is," she beamed. "In a way, I hope they don't find him. He is probably safer where he is."

Stan was inclined to agree. The boy would do well to keep his head down for a while. Perhaps, given time, the whole thing would blow over. That was wishful thinking, of course - nothing was going to go away. This was a respite, at best. Peter's chances of remaining hidden for more than a few weeks were remote. He wouldn't be smart enough or lucky enough to evade the police for long.

Maureen's peace of mind was short-lived. The next letter she opened was from her sister. She caught her breath and the colour drained from her face, leaving it a deathly white. "Stan!" she gasped, her hands clutching the thin paper rigidly. "It's Mother. They think she's had a stroke."

Stan's attempts to pacify her were to no avail.

"She needs me, Stan. I've got to be there. We'll have to go home," she insisted.

"All right, all right," Stan said, not meaning to sound impatient or insensitive. "If that's the way you feel, we'll pack up and go. I should have realised you would never be able to live away from your family."

He paced the room for a long time, reluctantly forming a plan for the family's return to England, while silently cursing the old woman. He had never been in favour with his mother-in-law, nor she with him. She was far too possessive, and fussed over her daughters like some broody old hen. Stan didn't believe for a moment that she was seriously ill at all. It was not beyond her to feign sickness in order to win sympathy and have her daughter come rushing back to her side - and how she was succeeding. Damn her.

"You had better leave first and take Debbie with you," he said eventually. "We have money enough for that saved already. I'll follow on with the boys later."

"What about Peter?" panicked Maureen. "We can't leave him here. I don't want the family broken up."

"We may not have a choice. Peter will probably be back in a week or two at the most. We can't decide anything concrete until then."

"What about the girl? And the charges... what if the Tates press charges, Stan?" She was near to hysterics again.

"Oh, Maureen! I don't know. I don't have all the answers. It's a mess, whatever way you look at it. But we'll get through it somehow. Just you stop worrying, or you'll make yourself ill."

The days slipped by and still Peter did not return, nor did they hear from him again. Maureen was silent on the subject. Her main concern now was her mother, and getting home to be with her.

Reluctantly, Stan began planning for their return to England, cursing every step he was being forced to make. In a few short weeks, all his hopes and plans for the family's bright new future in Australia had been shattered.

CHAPTER SEVENTEEN

Michael Dean sipped moodily at his after-lunch coffee and reflected that his move to Australia was not working out at all to plan. For a month now, he had been traipsing the streets with his briefcase crammed full of pamphlets and advertising bumf, and not one sale had he made.

Although he had little sales experience, he refused to blame himself for the failure. The books were far too expensive, that was the problem. It was a waste of time hawking such costly tomes of wisdom around working-class areas when the working man had no desire to read anything more enlightening than the racing pages of his morning paper.

At first glance, the proposition had appeared promising. He had only to sell one set of books a week to earn a reasonable wage, and two or more sales would put him on big money, but there was simply no demand for the books, and, as his employment was strictly on a commission-only basis, no sales meant no money.

To everyone he met, Michael Dean was a sales executive, and had always been a sales executive. Not even Gloria knew that until a month before they met, he had been working as a chef. Michael was in fact a very good and highly-qualified chef who had worked in some of the finest hotels and restaurants in London. He had developed his passion for the culinary arts at an early age, and he loved his work - well, the creative aspect of it, at least. But servitude was not his forte, and customer relations were not something he had ever considered to be an important part of his profession.

Michael saw himself as an artist, a master of his craft whose creations were to be admired and appreciated, certainly not devoured mindlessly by ignorant, overpaid gluttons from the city. Many such customers would look down on him with contempt, as though he were little more than a servant.

By far the worst offenders were the sales executives: whole teams of brash, classless yobs with their big commissions and bonuses - and even bigger mouths. For them, complaining appeared to be something of a sport - a competition to see who could shout the loudest and draw the most attention to themselves; always at the staff's expense. All too often, management would require him to appease such high-paying and valued customers by suffering the indignity of making a grovelling apology in front of a crowded restaurant, when, in truth, it was the customers who were at fault.

How Michael hated those obnoxious sales teams. Yet he couldn't help but notice the amount of ready cash they always had to splash around, and the expensive company cars they drove. Disgruntled with his lot, Michael had decided that a new career in sales was for him.

He never doubted for a moment his ability to make good as a sales executive. He was smart, educated, and imagined he could speak eloquently and convincingly on most subjects. What else could possibly be required of a salesman?

In England, however, the profession appeared to be something of a closed shop. The big companies, it seemed, had a criteria of their own by which they selected staff - a criteria that, for some reason, excluded Michael. The only positions open to him were in what the profession termed "direct sales" - better known as door-to-door selling. Those jobs were always offered on a commission-only basis with no retainer, and definitely no company car.

He had heard that Australia was the land of opportunity, a land where everyone competed on equal terms, with no closed shops. It was a young country, where the lodges and old boys' networks that he suspected were blocking his progress in England would not have established themselves.

Certainly, the Australian papers he had bought while in England appeared to support this view, for they all carried many pages of adverts calling for dynamic young salesmen, and offering mammoth salaries and excellent prospects of promotion for the right applicants. Michael never doubted for a moment that with his cultured accent and polished manners, he could soon talk his way into a top position here.

But once in Australia he soon discovered that, as in England, the majority of the adverts offering high salaries 'with no experience needed' were placed by direct sales companies. *Genuine* sales positions still required applicants to have experience and references.

It was all a hoax, and Michael had had enough. That afternoon, tired and disillusioned, he returned to the office and handed in his resignation. He then he drove dejectedly back to the hostel, having no idea what he would now do for a living.

Since Craig and Geoff had moved out of the hostel two weeks earlier, Michael had had the chalet to himself. He'd been happy to see them go; they were coarse types, and he loathed the idea of people associating him with them.

He sat down, intending to write a letter home, but finding himself out of aerogrammes, he got up and went to Gloria's chalet to borrow one. Gloria had not yet returned from work, but Michael knew where she hid her chalet key, and let himself in. He was rummaging through her writing case when he came across an address scribbled on the back of an old luggage label: "Craig Curran, 10 Warwick Street, Mount Lawley."

He stood staring at the label, dumbfounded. What on earth was Gloria doing with Curran's address? The answer was all too obvious - she must be seeing him, or planning to see him. His fiancé was cheating on him, running around with another man – and a no-good, low-life like Curran at that. That's where she would have been the other night, when she had supposedly gone to the pictures with a friend from work. She had been with Curran all the time. How they must be laughing at him!

He stormed back to his own chalet and paced the floor impatiently, waiting for Gloria to return. He would have this out with her right away. Nobody was going to make a fool out of Michael Dean. It had happened before, yes, but it wasn't going to happen again.

Gloria lingered in town doing some after-work shopping that day, and by the time she returned to the hostel, Michael had thoroughly convinced himself of her infidelity.

"You're late - where have you been? Round to see Curran again, I shouldn't wonder," he challenged the moment she stepped into the room.

Gloria stared at him, bewildered. "I've been shopping. You wanted a birthday card to send to your sister, remember?" She placed the card on the bedside cabinet.

Michael was unconvinced. "That didn't take you all this time. I know you've been seeing him. I'm not stupid. You were with him on Tuesday night, too, weren't you?"

"No! Whatever gave you that idea? I haven't seen Craig since the day he left here. Why would I?"

"Then what was his address doing in your writing case?" He held the damning label up in front of her eyes.

"What right have you to go searching through my belongings?" she replied indignantly. This belligerent attitude was a side of Michael she had not seen before, and one that she didn't much like.

"Don't evade the question. You've been seeing him. I know you have."

"I have not!"

"Then why did he give you his address?"

She took the label from his hand. "If you must know, he gave it me so I'd have a friend to turn to for help, should I ever come to my senses and walk out on you."

"How touchingly chivalrous of him," he mocked. "I've met his type before. There's only one place that snake would help a girl, and that's into his bed."

"Just what are you suggesting? What do you think I am?" Gloria asked, angrily.

"You know very well what I'm suggesting."

"In that case, there's nothing more to say, is there?" She slid her engagement ring from her finger and tossed it onto the bed. "If that's what you think of me, there's your ring, take it. We're finished." She turned and hurried from the room.

Michael stood staring after her, open-mouthed. He hadn't intended it to go this far, had never imagined that Gloria would be spirited enough to break off their engagement. She couldn't be serious. She needed him.

He hurried to the door and called after her, but she ran on, without looking back.

Once in her room, Gloria threw herself onto the bed and sobbed her heart out. Afterwards, she never understood quite why she cried, except that it seemed the natural reaction to a broken engagement. She had been aware for some time that Michael was not right for her. He had his good points, of course. He was very caring and considerate, and she was still very fond of him – but he was not the one.

Initially, she had been blinded by his good looks and polished manners, been taken in too easily by his tales of executive positions in big business, and she had wanted desperately to believe in his plans to travel the world. But Michael had proved to be a dreamer. He was certainly not the solid, dependable tower of strength that she needed in her life. She should be glad he had finally given her the excuse to break off their engagement; she should be happy about it. Yet still she cried.

Presently, there came a tap at the door. "Gloria, let me in. We have to talk."

"Go away," she said into her pillow. "I don't want to see you."

"Stop being so childish and open this door."

She sat up rigidly but made no reply. So now she was being childish. That was rich coming from him. It was just the sort of priggish remark he would make.

"Gloria, I want to talk to you. Please open the door," he said, his voice softening.

"Go away. We're finished."

"Gloria, I'm sorry. I... " He stopped abruptly, suddenly realising how absurd he must look, standing there pleading with the door. The surrounding chalets all had eyes and ears, their occupants must all be sneering at him. Michael Dean was being made to grovel – again.

He straightened himself, haughtily. "Very well," he said with finality. "When you have come to your senses and want to talk, I shall be in my room."

Gloria stood up now, furious. The pompous ass expected her to go running after him, pleading forgiveness. He was so full of himself, he didn't believe she could be serious in her rejection of him. She was serious, right enough; they were through, and she wasn't about to give him the opportunity to smooth-talk her out of it.

Hurriedly, she began packing her cases, not giving a thought to where she would go. Her sole objective was to leave the hostel and get far away from Michael.

Her cases packed, she phoned a taxi and went to wait in front of the reception hall. She felt very conspicuous standing there alone with her cases beside her. She only hoped that Michael would not come by and see her. A public scene would be so embarrassing.

Eventually, the cab arrived. The driver loaded her luggage into the boot and inquired where she would like to go.

"I don't really know," she said uncertainly. In her hurry to get away, she hadn't thought that far ahead. It was too late in the day for flat-hunting. "Do you know any boarding houses?" she asked.

"Sure, dozens of them. What area do you want?" asked the driver. He was a burly, middle-aged man with a friendly, reassuring smile.

Again, she didn't know. "Somewhere close to the city, if you can, that's where I work."

"Not too many around that cater for female boarders," he pondered. "But we'll find you something, girlie. Hop in."

As they moved off down the drive, the driver gestured to the rows of corrugated iron chalets. "The living here too rough for you, is it? Can't say as I blame you - I wouldn't fancy living in one of those tin huts myself."

"It isn't a very pleasant place," Gloria agreed quietly.

They drove around the city for a long time, but everywhere they stopped was either full or had no provision for female boarders. Gloria watched with some concern as the taxi's meter ticked higher and higher. After noticing her reluctance to knock on strangers' doors, the driver obligingly got out and made all the inquiries for her. Eventually, he brought the cab to a halt in front of a large, old house in East Perth, and after conferring with the landlady, he beckoned to Gloria.

The landlady was short and fat with frizzy ginger hair that hung untidily to her shoulders. She regarded Gloria without comment. Her blank, wide-eyed expression unchanging, she turned and led the way up a narrow staircase to a small, dimly-lit room.

"It's a share room, I've no singles," she said, indicating the two single beds. "The other woman is out most nights – working." She jutted her chin disapprovingly. "None of my business what she does, of course. Pays her board, that's all I care. Six pounds a week, paid in advance." She folded her arms and slouched against the door frame in a take-it-or-leave-it attitude.

Gloria peered past her apprehensively. The room's few pieces of furniture were old and shabby, the floor was bare, and large, dark patches stained the walls and ceiling. It was a horrible room. But the taxi fare was soaring higher all the time, and might even double again before she found anything better. This would have to do, just for a day or two, until she found herself a flat. Reluctantly, she accepted.

She unpacked only the things she would need, and then sat down to write a letter home. Her father would be pleased to hear of her break with Michael, but he would be worried now that she was on her own and would want to know her plans. She sat thoughtfully chewing at the end of her pen. She didn't rightly have any plans, not yet, except to find herself a flat as soon as possible. She daren't tell them she was living in a boarding house - her mother would have a fit. Eventually, she screwed up the letter, resolving to write when she was more settled.

From downstairs, there came the uproarious sound of several high-spirited male boarders stomping along the passageway, followed by a loud crash as something - or someone - fell heavily. Then the landlady's shrill voice rose in abuse of all. Gloria found it all very depressing, and a little unnerving. She settled down to read, but the light was too dim and strained her eyes, so she climbed into bed for an early night. She would start flat-hunting first thing tomorrow.

She slept till the early hours of the morning, then she awoke with a start - someone was moving about in her room. She sat up, terrified.

"Relax, sweetheart, it's only me," a gruff voice reassured her.

Gloria blinked and stared across the room to where a woman sat on the edge of the bed, peeling off her stockings. At first, Gloria imagined the woman to be about her own age, perhaps a little older. She had a young figure, slim and well-proportioned, but her face was that of a much older woman. There were lines around her eyes and across her forehead that even her thickly-applied make-up failed to hide. The woman lit a cigarette, and the flickering flame illuminated a pair of deep blue eyes, set above high, rounded cheekbones. She had doubtless been a very beautiful woman not too many years ago – might still have been considered attractive were it not for the leering ugliness of her wide, thin-lipped mouth.

A bottle of cheap wine stood on the dressing table beside the woman's bed, and Gloria could see she was more than a little drunk.

"Don't mind if I smoke, do you, sweetheart?" It wasn't really a question. "Ruby's the name. What's yours?"

"I'm Gloria."

"Gloria," she pondered thoughtfully. "Pretty name for a pretty girl." She reached for the bottle of wine and sloshed some of its red liquid into a dirty cup. "Have a drink with me, Gloria."

"No, thank you. I don't drink."

"She doesn't drink," Ruby repeated drowsily into the cup. She looked up, her expression a mixture of amusement and distain. "I suppose you're a bloody virgin, too?" she sneered.

Gloria made to ignore the remark, but Ruby's eyes were riveted to hers, demanding an answer.

"No..., I'm not a virgin," she said quietly.

Ruby gave a deep-throated chuckle that sent shivers of fear running down Gloria's spine. In the room's dim orange glow, her dark eyes were like sinister hollows, sweeping the thin blanket that covered Gloria's body. Perhaps it was only the light playing tricks on her, but there seemed a savage lust in those eyes, as though they were willing the blanket aside and leaving her naked on the bed. She drew the blanket tightly to her in sudden alarm. The woman's a lesbian, she thought. She's going to molest me.

Ruby chuckled louder, as though reading Gloria's fears. She drank the wine at a gulp, coughed, and refilled the cup.

"What does a pretty little girl like Gloria do for a living?" She asked with a sarcastic edge to her voice.

"I'm a typist," confessed Gloria.

"I thought it would be something bloody stupid," Ruby cackled, then gave a rasping cough. "You want to know what I do...? I'm a prostitute. That shock you, sweetheart? I'm one of those horrible low creatures of the night who sell themselves to men." She drank more wine, then stared mournfully at the floor.

"But I'm past it now. Men don't want a shrivelled up old bag like me, they want sweet young chicks, like you. Yeah, that's right, they're all looking for sweet little virgins. You know what, Gloria? Men would cough up big for a night in the cot with you. Think what a great life you could have. No more slaving away at that stupid typewriter. Every day could be a holiday. And you would have pots of money to buy all those beautiful clothes you've always dreamed of; just for being young and pretty."

Ruby drew deeply on her cigarette, and then bowed her head pensively as she exhaled a thick cloud of smoke. "I was beautiful once – really beautiful. They all wanted me then." She gave a harsh, cynical laugh. "I was even a virgin once. Hard to believe, I know. You want to know how I became a prostitute, Gloria? Well... I was engaged to be married, see, only we didn't have the money to get started right, with a home and furniture and all that. So *he* comes up with the idea of me going on the street for a while. 'Only till we have the deposit for a house of our own', he says. I didn't like the idea at all. I'd been brought up very strict, you see. He was the only man I'd ever been with – and that wasn't till after we were engaged, either. But he made it all sound so simple and sensible."

She sniffed, and then turned to stub out her cigarette. "I'd have done anything for that man," she reflected with a deep sigh and a slow shake of her head. "I felt I'd be letting him down by refusing. Well, if it didn't make any difference to him how many men I'd been with, what the hell, I thought. So I started on the game for him." She smiled ironically. "Like I told you, they all wanted me back then. I made big money. And like the stupid, half-baked cow I was, I handed it all over to him. 'Only a little longer', he kept saying, 'then we'll get married, move into a lovely home and raise a family'. God, I wanted that so badly, I believed his every word. Then, one day, I discovered he was selling the same story to two other girls. The lousy bastard."

She sloshed yet more wine into her cup, and banged the empty bottle down onto the cabinet. "He laughed right in my face. 'You don't think I'd marry a whore, do you?', he says, all indignant like. What a fool I was." She started to sob, then checked herself and spat contemptuously at the bare floor. "They're all the same, sweetheart - cheating, lying bastards, every last one of them. Don't ever put your trust in a man, Gloria – not ever."

She finished the wine at a gulp and fell silent, staring drunkenly into the empty cup. After a while, she went out to the toilet and Gloria could hear her vomiting down the pan. When she returned, she flopped onto the bed and fell immediately into a deep sleep.

Gloria sat up for the remainder of the night, terrified to sleep, lest Ruby should wake and come over to her. The thought of being touched by such a degraded creature made her squirm. She had never met a more revolting woman in her life, yet she couldn't help but feel a twinge of pity for her; the way she might for a sick animal.

Gloria rose early the next morning and crept out quietly before Ruby woke. She had to find a flat and move in right away. To spend another night in that room was unthinkable.

There were a few flats advertised in the morning paper but most of them were in districts she had never heard of. She wanted somewhere close to the city, to be near her work. Craig and Geoff had found their place through an agent, she recalled. Perhaps if she went to see them they might still have the agent's address, and that would save her chasing all over the city after advertisements.

She hired a taxi, telling herself that this was her only reason for wanting to see Craig. True, she liked him - liked him a lot. But she wasn't really thinking that there could be any possibility of a relationship between them. He had offered his help and support should she ever need it, and right now she needed it. She was alone and feeling insecure and vulnerable in a foreign land. She needed the strength and support of a close friend - someone like Craig.

Craig was everything that Michael was not: self-assured, masterful. Nothing in life seemed to faze him. She needed a man like Craig beside her. She would feel safe and protected with him.

No, she really mustn't think that way. Her only motive in contacting Craig must be to acquire the agent's address.

Geoff stretched, slipped on his dressing gown and wandered through into the lounge. Craig had left to drive Gwen, his latest conquest, back to the nurses' quarters for the early shift, and Geoff had the dubious pleasure of having the aftermath of the previous night's party all to himself.

He was still deciding whether to start preparing breakfast or crawl back into bed when there was a knock at the door. On answering it, he was surprised to find Gloria standing there, looking pale and apprehensive. For a brief moment he stood looking at her, trying to fathom out how on earth she had obtained their address, and what she could possibly want.

"Well, hello. This is a pleasant surprise," he said eventually. "Michael not with you?"

"No. We've had an argument. We have split up. I... I'm looking for a flat," she began hesitantly, realising now how thin her excuse for coming to see Craig really was. "I was wondering...."

"I'm sorry, I'm forgetting my manners," said Geoff, suddenly snapping awake. "Come in and make yourself at home."

As Gloria followed him through into the lounge, Geoff grinned apologetically. "As you can see, we had ourselves a swinging time here last night. The place isn't always this untidy - believe it or not, it's usually much worse," he joked.

Gloria gave a faint smile as she glanced shyly around the room.

"So you have broken up with Michael? I'm not sure whether I should be sorry or pleased for you. But what can we do to help?"

"Craig gave me your address. He said if I ever needed any help, I should contact him," she said awkwardly. "I'm looking for a flat, and I wondered whether you still had the address of the agent you went to?"

"Sure, we have it kicking around here somewhere," said Geoff. She could tell he was not fooled as to the real purpose of her visit.

"You look hungry. You can't have had breakfast yet."

She shook her head. "I left my digs in rather a hurry."

"No worries, you can eat here." Geoff turned towards the kitchen, then stopped and studied her thoughtfully. "This is not a good idea," he began tentatively, but firmly. "Looking up Craig, I mean. It's none of my business, of course, but... how can I put this? I don't know what he has said to you, or what he may have led you to believe. Craig says a lot of things he doesn't really mean, especially to women. Oh, sure we'll help you find a flat, that's no problem. But..." He sighed thoughtfully as he cleared a chair and beckoned her to sit down.

"Perhaps I'm getting it all wrong here," he began slowly, "...and, if so, I apologise. But if you are hoping Craig will become some kind of support system, or boyfriend, even, someone you can rely on to look out for you, then forget it."

She flushed visibly. "I don't see him as a boyfriend," she said, too quickly. Her spirits sank. Geoff was right. She was being foolish. Craig would not want to be lumbered with her. He had many girlfriends, she knew that.

Geoff sat on the arm of the chair opposite her. "Craig is Craig," he explained simply. "He is what you might loosely describe as a man of the world. To me, he's a great mate, we get on well and we have a lot of laughs together. But..." He paused, with finger raised. "Let me put it this way: if I had a sister and he so much as looked at her, I would shoot him. Craig is a predator, pure and simple. Where women are concerned, he is only interested in one thing - and that certainly isn't a committed relationship, or helping maidens in distress. All I'm saying is don't pin any hopes or any future plans on Craig; they will be dashed." He spoke firmly but gently, not wanting to exacerbate her already distressed state.

"No... I wasn't thinking of that... I just need somewhere to stay - a flat," she insisted feebly. In her head, she could hear Ruby's drunken voice telling her: 'All men are the same. Lying bastards every one of them. Don't ever put your trust in a man, Sweetheart - not ever.' Craig wasn't a pimp, of course, but she was aware of what Geoff saying. He was a user. He was never going to provide the support and security she needed. She was being a fool.

"You are right; this wasn't a very good idea," she said, getting to her feet. "I should go."

"Nonsense," Geoff said, standing up too. "Not before you've had breakfast, and certainly not before I've helped you find that flat," he said, steering her through into the kitchen.

"Looks like you had a great time here last night," she said quietly, eyeing the littered floor and worktops with scarcely concealed distain.

"You could say that," said Geoff mildly embarrassed. She was right, of course; the place was a mess, this was no way to live. The constant round of rowdy parties, heavy drinking and crashing hangovers was all becoming a bit boring. He had begun to ask himself what was the point of it all. For Craig, of course, partying and making sexual conquests was a way of life – an obsession, even, but Geoff had always known that for him it was only ever going to be an interlude in his life.

After the rigours of the army, he had felt the need to have a fling and let off some steam. Well, he'd had his fling and now he sensed it was almost time to start getting his life back on track. Now that he had a steady job, he was feeling the need to get more stability and a clear sense of direction back into his private and social life, too. And perhaps even begin a steady relationship.

As he prepared breakfast for them both, he began thinking of Susan. He hadn't seen her since the day of the housewarming party, and he had missed her. He enjoyed her company, and that was far more than he could say for many of the girls he had dated recently. Why was he bothering with meaningless one-night stands? He had known all along that he and Susan would get together eventually. What was he waiting for? More to the point, why was he making her wait? He wasn't being fair.

"I've just had a great idea!" he said suddenly, while slipping fried eggs onto the plates beside the bacon, beans and toast. "What you really need right now is a spell of home life with people you know. I haven't seen the Harveys lately, but I know they have a spare room at their place. You get on well with Susan, and I know that Joan would be more than happy to board you. It will be far better for you than being on your own in a pokey little flat. What do you think?"

Gloria seemed to like the idea, but was unsure. "I don't really know them that well," she protested. "I couldn't possibly just knock on their door and ask them to take me in. It would be a bit of a liberty."

"Don't worry, I'll do the asking," he smiled broadly. "I'm almost one of the family."

After breakfast, he phoned the Harveys' to broach the subject of Gloria lodging with them. He had hoped that Susan would answer the phone, but apparently she was out. As he expected, Joan said she would be delighted to help Gloria and have her come to stay with them. So, later that day, he drove Gloria back to the boarding house to collect her luggage, and then headed the Morris to the Harveys' place in Inglewood.

It would be great to see Susan again. He knew she would be delighted to see him, especially when he asked her out on their first date. She would probably give him a ribbing for being slow and not asking her before. Perhaps he would take her to a restaurant; he had discovered one or two good ones. Or maybe he would take her for a drive. They could even go to a drive-in movie. That would be something new for Susan - she wouldn't have been to a drive-in before.

Susan was still out when they arrived. Joan showed Gloria to her room and left her to unpack. Geoff wandered through into the lounge. It was freshly decorated, and new furniture had been installed. Joan had added homely touches with personal belongings brought from England, and photos of family members left behind. Geoff was pleased to see that the Harveys appeared to be settling into their new home well.

Joan returned and went through into the kitchen to put the kettle on.

"It's all coming together very nicely," said Geoff, following her. "It's looking a lot more like home now."

"It's a big place, and there's still a lot of decorating to do. But we are all enjoying planning what we're going to do, and in what order. Yes, I'm happy to say we are all settling in well."

"Wow! The stove is looking great," said Geoff, referring to the now gleaming wood-burning stove. "I can see Susan has been putting in a lot of elbow-grease on that."

"She has made that thing her pet project. Personally, I'd still prefer to rip it out."

"So where has she skived off to today?" he asked smiling.

"She's out with her boyfriend," Joan said pointedly.

"Her boyfriend?" he gaped.

"Oh, my! Clock the face! Pick the chin up off the floor, please," said Joan. Then she spun to face him, bristling with indignation. "How dare you be surprised? Why wouldn't she have a boyfriend? She's a beautiful girl, and she works in the public eye. Every day young men are stopping by her counter and asking her out on dates. Did you think she was going to sit at home twiddling her thumbs, waiting for you to wake up to yourself? It's high time you stopped all this boozing and whoring around. It's not your style, Geoff. If I thought for one moment it was, I'd have made sure she kicked you into touch months ago."

"Ouch! That hurt. But I deserved it." He had a sinking feeling. What an arrogant fool he had been, expecting Susan to put her life on hold while he was out having his fling, partying and playing the field.

"So... is it serious?" he asked awkwardly.

"Who knows? He's a nice boy with good prospects. He's an accountant - pots of money, new car. Typical Aussie, tall, bronzed."

"Rub it in, why don't you?"

Joan poured boiling water into the pot and arranged the cups. "I'll tell you one thing," she said wagging her finger sternly. "If you want to take her out now, you will have to wait in line. She's not the kind of girl to two-time anyone or play the field. So, while she's with Paul, I don't want you bothering her. Do I make myself clear?"

He nodded sheepishly. "Absolutely. I've been a complete idiot, haven't I?"

Joan nodded emphatically. "Too right, you have."

CHAPTER EIGHTEEN

Tony woke with a thumping headache and a vile taste in his mouth, as he had done most mornings since that traumatic night when he had climbed onto the coal stage in an attempt to end it all.

He remembered little about the previous night's bout of drinking. He had drunk himself into oblivion, and collapsed onto the barroom floor. He was vaguely aware that some of his workmates had helped him back to his hut and dumped him onto the bed to sleep it off.

Groaning, he rolled from the bed, grabbed a towel, and swayed unsteadily to the shower block to splash cold water over his head. Next, he moved robotically along to the mess where he downed a cup of black coffee, grabbed a piece of dry toast and chewed on it as he made his way out to the track where the Casey Jones was waiting to ferry the gang out onto the line for the day's work.

Neither the cold water nor the black coffee had served to revive him much – he had not intended that they should, for being sober meant that his mind would start to function, and he would then begin to dwell on all the things he would rather forget: the helplessness of his situation, Janice - and the excruciating pain of losing her. He needed the mind and emotion-dulling benefits of the previous night's drink, in order to blot it all out.

Vargha sat upright and arrogant on the Casey's high driver's seat. "So, Pome, yet another night you spend drunk and rolling around on the barroom floor," he mocked as Tony climbed aboard. He pushed the clutch lever forward to engage the Casey's ancient belt drive system. "You must work extra hard today, Pome, or you lose your job, for sure." He gave a thin, cynical laugh as the Casey moved away.

Tony ignored him. As the drink and a fuddled mind helped nullify the pain of his personal life, so it helped him to ignore Vargha and his sarcastic jibes. And, anyway, Frank had assured him that he would not lose his job. He had confided that Head Office had received so many complaints about Vargha and his harsh, abusive treatment of the workforce, that now it was Vargha himself who was on a final warning, and would not dare risk another enquiry by trying to sack anyone.

While Vargha and losing his job were things that Tony no longer felt the need to fear, there were others that still tormented him. He closed his eyes tightly as the Casey gathered speed and trundled its way passed the coal stage. But in his mind, it was still there, as vivid as ever: a huge blackened ogre towering above him, a sinister vision from his nightmare, the painful memory of which no amount of drink was able to erase.

And there was also the constant, menacing presence of Jack Rogers, glowering at him whenever they were working in close proximity, as though waiting for the merest excuse to give him another beating.

As time went by, he found the work on the line becoming easier and more within his physical capability, and together with his newfound disregard for Vargha, he was managing to get through the days without suffering too much distress. It was the evenings, when he returned to his hut, now sober, that were the hardest to bear. The first thing he would see on entering his hut was the large framed photo of Janice. She was looking at him with a soft, loving smile on her lips, the way she had on their wedding day. Life had been so wonderful then; they'd had so much to look forward to.

He knew that gazing at the photo would break him up, it always did, but his eyes were drawn to it like a magnet; he couldn't bear to take it down. He still loved her, and he hoped upon hope that one day she would come back to him.

But, of course, she would not. The pain would grip him, the tears would start to flow, and he would stem them the only way he knew how – by reaching for the bottle. And so another bout of drinking would begin. Such had become the routine of Tony's life.

After a few weeks, he imagined the hurt and pain was becoming less. Some evenings he could look at the photo objectively, almost as though it was just a picture of a pretty girl, any pretty girl, one he didn't know and had never met. Perhaps he was getting over her, or perhaps he had drunk so much and his whole system was becoming so saturated with alcohol that his senses were becoming permanently dulled. If that was the only cure, then so be it. Drink up.

On the fourth payday, Jack Rogers quit his job and headed to Perth on a bender. He never returned, and Tony was grateful to be relieved of at least one of his tormentors.

The gang was in a constant state of flux, with men coming and going all the time. Most were heavy boozers. Tony was never short of drinking companions, and, when necessary, friends to help carry him back to camp.

The week after Jack left, six new men arrived to swell the gang's complement to twenty, the largest it had ever been. This triggered the union's ruling that should any gang number over eighteen men, then the ganger would be permitted to assign one man to remain in camp to clean the facilities and assist the cook by chopping wood for the stove.

That morning, as Tony was about to board the Casey for the ride out to work, Vargha eyed him with a contemptuous sneer. "No, Pome, not you. You are no use to me out on the line. You stay here and chop sleepers for the cook. Clean up the showers and the toilets." He turned and laughed to the rest of the gang members. "That is all the little Pome is fit for, cleaning toilets."

But the ganger's insults were nothing to Tony, not anymore. He watched the Casey move away and thought fondly of the bottle of wine in his room.

"Come on then, Tony, my son," called Ernie, the cook, as the Casey trundled into the distance. "Our first job is washing up after the rabble. Then we'll fix ourselves a breakfast feast. You look as though you could do with a bit of building up."

Ernie was an East London lad who had arrived at the camp two weeks earlier, when the previous cook had left. Like Scottie, who had befriended Tony when he had first arrived, Ernie was one of an army of young Brits who were working their way around the country. This was his first job in Western Australia after travelling extensively in Victoria and South Australia in his Volkswagen caravanette.

"I'm what they call a Sundowner," he had told Tony proudly when they had first met. "That's someone who's constantly on the move. Home is wherever they stop to put their head down for the night. *The Sundowners* was a great film with Robert Mitchum and Deborah Kerr. Did you see it? That's what made me want to come to Australia - well, one of the things, anyway. I thought what a great way to live: free as the wind, shackled by nothing and nobody. And when I found out that the Australian Government was offering to waft me away to this paradise for a measly ten quid, well... how could I refuse?" He laughed loudly and brashly, his rotund figure quivering with merriment.

Tony had taken an instant liking to the new cook, and was more than happy to be left in camp in his company.

"This beats slogging your guts out on the line," Ernie asserted cheerily, as Tony clattered the enamel plates around in the sink, and he busied himself preparing them a hearty breakfast. "They tell me that hard work never hurt anyone - well, it kills horses. Me, I steer well clear of it," he said with a crafty wink. "An easy job in the kitchen suits me fine. Well, look at me, I'm not exactly built for hard work in a hundred degrees of heat." He laughed heartily, drawing attention to his bulk.

The cooking done, he slid two loaded plates onto the table. "There you go, my son, get that down you," he invited. "The best of everything for the kitchen staff, which is yet another reason why I like being the cook. I do enjoy my tucker." He sat down and began attacking his breakfast, gesturing for Tony to do the same.

The contents of the plates made Tony want to heave: fried eggs, bacon, sausages, chops, beans and fried bread.

"I really couldn't eat all that," he protested. "I'm not very hungry."

"Nonsense. Get it down you," Ernie insisted with a full mouth.

Tony sat down and began picking gingerly at the food.

Ernie laughed, noticing Tony's changing colour. "Throw it up if you have to," he insisted. "There's plenty more, and it will stay down eventually."

But Tony wasn't sick, and ate what for him was a hearty breakfast. He spent the morning cleaning, and chopping sleepers to feed the wood stove, and the boiler in the shower block. In the afternoon, Ernie called him into the kitchen to help prepare the vegetables for the evening meal.

"This beats working out on the line, don't you think?" Ernie asked as he slid a tray of chops from the fridge.

"It's certainly a lot easier," agreed Tony.

"That's what we are all after, an easy life. No stress, no obligations, and definitely no hard work. Tomato soup and lamb chops tonight." He indicated to a bowl of potatoes on the worktop. "You can start peeling the spuds while I prepare the chops and vegetables. The soup comes out of a tin - what could be easier than that?" He opened the stove door and rammed two more chunks of sleeper into the fire. He washed his hands, and then turned back to Tony.

"So, you have a drink problem, Tony?" He asserted without preamble. "There's a lot of it about out here in Australia, especially around these work camps. A lot of it is down to the weather, I guess. Blokes need a drink after a hard day's work in the sun. They have to replace all the fluids they sweat out somehow. But then drinking becomes a habit, especially in a place like this, where there's nothing much else to do. Before you know it, the habit becomes an addiction. Either that, or it's woman problems that kick it all off. Have you had woman problems, Tony?"

"My wife left me," Tony admitted reluctantly. He had no real wish to discuss it.

"That explains a lot. Women can be a curse. Don't get me wrong - I like women well enough. But usually they don't go a bundle on me. Well, I ask you, look at me: I'm twenty-four and already going bald. Plus, I'm short, fat, and ugly. Not too surprising that I don't have woman problems, is it?"

Tony laughed, knowing it was intended as a joke. Ernie's personality was as big as the man himself, and no doubt women would feel comfortable and reassured in his company, just as Tony did.

"I've had a few knockbacks, who hasn't, but like I always say, you can't take life too seriously. Laugh it off and move on, that's my motto. Would you have her back? Your wife, I mean?"

"Yes, of course I would, she's still my wife. I love her." He paused and then added positively, "She will come back to me, I know she will." He surprised himself by the statement, mainly because he had actually started to believe it.

Ernie filled a huge pot with water, and slid it onto the stove. "That's not good news," he commented sombrely. "It's not until you *don't* want them back and don't give a damn that you are over them and on the mend." He sprinkled salt into the water while shaking his head. "There's not one of them that's worth ruining your health over, believe me."

After dinner, Tony did the washing up and cleaned the kitchen. The chores done, he and Ernie sat down with mugs of coffee. They talked mainly about places they both knew back in England, and their experiences of life in Australia. It was quite late before Tony eventually retired to his hut and realised he had not had a drink that day, and, more surprisingly, that he hadn't missed it.

"Keep your mind occupied, that's the secret," Ernie had said. "Don't allow yourself time to stew on things."

Perhaps he was right; though Tony wasn't at all sure he wanted to be without a drink, not permanently. He knew that, deep down, he was still hurting, and still needed the comfort of the bottle and the mind-numbing oblivion it provided.

All week, his evenings were spent washing up and cleaning the kitchen, followed by those long chats with Ernie over coffee. Consequently, he no longer had to sit in his room staring at Janice's photo and feeling the pain of missing her, and then having to resort to drink to abate that pain. Thus, he managed to get through the week without once needing to get drunk.

On Saturday, he finally succumbed when a group of his regular drinking partners insisted on dragging him along to the pub. Once there, he enjoyed the company and the pub atmosphere well enough, but oddly he no longer felt the urge to drink himself into oblivion - there seemed no need. He drunk only enough to dull his senses a little, and become merry in the company of his fellow drinkers.

He did not dare to imagine that the drink no longer had a hold over him, or that he had beaten the craving within. It was merely that with the change in his job and routine, he no longer had time to dwell on his problems.

"What are you going to do when you leave here, Tony?" Ernie asked one evening when they were cleaning up after dinner.

Tony shrugged. "I haven't really thought about leaving. This was the only job I could get. There is nothing for me in Perth. I was saving up to get back to England, but I'm not even sure about that anymore. I don't think I could face my family, or friends... not without Janice." He thought for a moment. "I suppose I'd like to travel around a bit, like you. Work in different places and see something of the country. That's what Janice and I intended to do when we came out here. Perhaps we still will - when we get back together."

"Why not strike out on your own?" suggested Ernie. "Become a sundowner. It's a great life."

Tony hesitated. "Well, jobs are not easy to find, especially when you don't have a trade to fall back on."

"Rubbish. I don't have a trade to fall back on, either, and I get by all right," Ernie smiled.

"But you're a cook!"

Ernie laughed heartily. "Fooled you too, have I? Anyone can be a cook, Tony. It's the same as cooking for yourself, only in larger quantities. All you need is half a dozen tried-and-tested recipes and the confidence to have a go. And it's the easiest job on earth to get. There are hundreds of work camps like this one in the bush: railways, roads, water works, mines. Wherever there are men working, they need cooks to feed them. And they are all cushy little numbers," he assured Tony. "If you can handle working out on the line, you can certainly do this job. You should give it a try."

Tony was not convinced. "I've never done it before. I don't have any references," he protested.

Ernie grinned and gave conspiratorial wink. "I'll write some references for you," he offered, then laughed again at Tony's blank stare. "Well, who the hell do you think wrote mine?" he boomed. "This is Australia. They don't go a bundle on red tape or certificates here. If you say you can do something, they'll give you a go at it. As long as you don't poison anyone, you're in."

So, under Ernie's supervision, Tony started to learn the basics of being a cook. It proved to be just the interest and distraction he needed to keep his mind occupied and away from Janice - and his craving for drink.

It was always quite late by the time he had finished in the kitchen, and he invariably made it to bed sober. He would often look long and lovingly at Janice's photo, only now, in his new positive frame of mind, he could convince himself that all was well, and that she would soon write saying she was ready to come back to him. Soon they would be together again.

He did suffer one sharp setback; on the day he had cause to walk past the coal stage. He smiled defiantly as he strode by, telling himself that his problems were all in the past, and that there was nothing to fear from this black, towering structure. It had no power; it was only dead, blackened pieces of wood.

But when he looked up at the cross beam where he had been sitting that night, he saw to his horror that the noose he had placed around his neck was still up there, dangling from the beam. An icy shiver ran up and down his spine, and his legs turned to jelly. In panic, he fled to the safety of his hut, and, with shaking hands, poured out a large tumbler of whisky.

As the tumbler reached his lips, the smell of whisky fumes filled his nostrils, and nauseating memories of how ill he had often made himself came flooding back. He really didn't want to go through all that again.

He steadied himself, then, with hands still trembling, he poured the amber liquid back into the bottle and triumphantly screwed the cap back into place.

He knew then that he was going to be all right. He no longer needed to drink himself into oblivion in order to cope with life. He had been through hell, but he had finally beaten his demons. He was stronger now than he had ever been. All he wanted now was that letter from Janice saying she was coming back to him, and everything in life would be just perfect.

Tony went immediately to the kitchen to share the news of his victory with his friend, Ernie.

"I've beaten it," he proclaimed proudly on entering. "I needed a drink so badly, and I resisted. I poured it back into the bottle and screwed down the top. It doesn't have a hold over me any more."

"That's marvellous," said Ernie, giving him a hug. "But then you were never a true alcoholic, anyway. You just had a temporary need for drink to block out the trauma in your life; there is a big difference." He held Tony at arms length and studied him searchingly. "And what about your other weakness? Have you conquered that, too?" he asked.

"If you mean Janice, I still want her, of course. She's my wife. But it's all right, she will come back to me soon, I know she will."

"Sure she will." Ernie smiled his agreement, but his mood was no longer congratulatory - his eyes were filled with concern for his friend's wellbeing.

The next payday brought the usual batch of leavers, and the gang's complement fell back below the magic figure of eighteen. To his disappointment, Tony was forced back out on the line.

On the ride out, he felt proud that he no longer had to close his eyes as the Casey trundled passed the coal stage. He looked up at the blackened timber structure and gave a self-satisfied smile. "You don't frighten me, not any more," he told it.

"So, Pome, you have cleaned up your act - for a while, anyway." Vargha mocked when they were out on the line. "But not for long, I wager. Once a pisshead, always a pisshead. Soon, you will be back on the bottle, and back crawling around in the gutter where you belong." He gave his thin, cynical laugh, revealing the two gold teeth, Tony had always thought looked cheap, and very Gipsyish.

"You go and boil your head, Gipsy man," was Tony's instant response. If he could beat the bottle and defy the dreaded coal stage, then he certainly wasn't going to kowtow to the likes of Vargha. A measure of his newfound strength and self-assurance was that he didn't even consider he was being brave or defiant by standing up to the ganger - it was just Tony being Tony.

Vargha looked as though he was about to explode with rage. "You don't talk to me that way, Pome. I am the ganger here. You show me respect, or I sack you for sure."

Tony found the ganger's petulant display of anger amusing rather than frightening. He began to laugh. "For calling you a Gipsy? I don't think so. You call me a Pome, so I call you a Gipsy - an insult for an insult. If you have a problem with that, we will take it to Head Office and see what they have to say – and who it is they decide to sack."

Tony turned away and continued with his task of packing ballast under the sleepers, whistling nonchalantly as he did so, confident that Vargha would not be taking the matter any further.

He was much more comfortable with the work on the line now, and always worked well within his ability. Vargha's attempts to provoke and bully him into working harder no longer had any effect. Eventually, the ganger left him alone and looked around for other, newer, weaker members of the gang to focus his attentions on.

Tony had enjoyed his time in the kitchen with Ernie, and was keen to get back there. He watched the trains eagerly, hoping that the next one would bring in a batch of new arrivals to swell the gang's numbers.

He still spent his evenings in the kitchen, helping Ernie with the washing up. The work done, they would sit and chat over coffee. Mainly, they talked about travel and the places Ernie had been to in South Australia. Tony had decided that that was where he wanted to go – where he *would* go, when he and Janice were back together.

"Whyalla is the best place for you to head to," Ernie assured him. "There are thousands of jobs going there. It is the second fastest-growing town in Australia. BHP has a huge steelworks and shipyards there, and they're always looking for men. They run two massive hostels to house their workforce. It's probably the best workers' accommodation anywhere in Australia, a thousand times better than these railway camps. But, more importantly from your point of view, the hostels have a lot of catering to do, and they are always in need of cooks and kitchen staff. A few months spent working in the kitchens there, and, with my references, you will be more than qualified to take on a cushy little cook's job anywhere."

But Tony was reluctant to make any definite plans, How could he, without Janice? His future was still with her. When she was back with him, then he would make plans.

Ernie was sceptical, telling him flatly that Janice would not be back and that he should accept the facts, forget her and move on.

Tony was aggrieved that Ernie refused to believe that Janice would ever come back to him, or even acknowledge that Tony's desire for such a reunion was a positive thing. It seemed so petty and mean of him to attempt to stifle Tony's hopes that way. It was so unlike Ernie to be negative about anything. Tony surmised that Ernie must be jealous, because he didn't have a wife, and, therefore, had no happy family life to look forward to.

Somewhat petulantly, Tony spent fewer evenings in the kitchen helping Ernie, and more time in his hut reading. But he soon became bored with books, and the kerosene lamp in his room wasn't really bright enough for reading, it strained his eyes. He took to going for a stroll around town and invariably ended up in the pub with his old drinking mates. He was aware that the pub visits were becoming more regular. But it was just for the company, he told himself. And he stayed resolutely away from spirits.

Then, one Saturday, when he walked into the Post Office to collect his mail, Tony's faith was rewarded. His heart leapt for joy as he recognised Janice's handwriting on one of the envelopes. It had been forwarded to him from Seaview Hostel. This was the letter he had been waiting for. He had been right all along, she wanted him back.

With fumbling hands, he tore the envelope open, and read quickly. Yes! She wanted reconciliation. There had been a brief niggling fear that she may have written asking for a formal separation, or even a divorce. But no, she really did want them to get back together. He had always known she would. This called for a celebration.

He hurried back to camp, and made first for the kitchen to share his good news with Ernie.

"I've heard from Janice," he announced jubilantly as he burst in, waving the letter under Ernie's nose. "I told you she would write. She still loves me and she wants us to get back together. Isn't that the greatest news ever?"

"I'm very happy for you," Ernie smiled unconvincingly. He continued preparing the vegetables for the evening meal, shaking his head slowly and solemnly, his eyes expressing disappointment rather than pleasure at the news.

"What's the matter with you? Why can't you be pleased for me?" Tony demanded irritably. "You're just jealous because you don't have a loving wife. Well, to hell with you. I think it is good news, and I'm going to celebrate. I'm not getting drunk, but I am going to drink to the future, our future - mine and Janice's."

He went back to his hut where he unscrewed the bottle of whisky and poured a large measure into his tumbler. "She wants me back. She wants me back," he rejoiced.

He unfolded the letter, and then sat on the edge of his bed to read and savour Janice's every word. It appeared that everything had gone wrong for her since she had left him. Rudy had been unable to find work and he had gambled away their savings. He had started drinking heavily and become violent towards her. Then he had walked out, leaving her with nothing. She'd had to take a cleaning job in a pub. It didn't pay very much, and now she owed a lot of money on the grotty room she rented. She concluded: "Please, please come and get me, and let's start over again."

Tony read through the letter several times, his mood turning from joy to annoyance, and finally to outright anger. Nowhere could he find a single word of concern for his welfare. No hint that she had missed him, or that she still loved him, and certainly no hint of contrition for the hell she had put him through. "Me, me, me..." Tony muttered. It was still the same selfish, self-centred Janice.

He placed the letter down beside the tumbler of whisky. What was he to do? The smell of the whisky was wafting towards him, rekindling memories of all the pain and suffering he had been through - that she, Janice, had put him through. Nothing had changed. With Janice, nothing would ever change.

On the shelf behind the whisky bottle were several books he had been reading, and amongst them was a copy of *Gone With The Wind*. He likened Janice to Scarlett O'Hara - self-centred, always wanting, always taking; giving nothing in return.

He was beginning to feel nauseous from the smell of the whisky. He was not going to put himself through that again - not for Janice, not for anything. Like Rhett Butler, he had finally had enough.

In a moment of inspiration, he took his writing pad and wrote in big, bold letters: So sorry to hear of your distress. But frankly, my dear, I no longer give a damn.

He contemplated the note for a long moment, and then chuckled in satisfaction. Yes, that just about said it all.

He folded the note carefully and slipped it into a long, white envelope. But before sealing it, he decided to take it along to show Ernie.

"I've written back to Janice," he said handing his friend the folded page. "You probably think that contacting her at all is a mistake, but I have to."

Ernie took the note without comment and flipped it open. His face lit up. "Oh, yes!" he shouted, punching the air in celebration. "That's what I call a result. And executed with a real touch of class. Well done, my son. I'm proud of you," he said enfolding Tony in a huge bear hug.

"So... what now, Tony?" Ernie asked later, over their evening coffee. "Now that you are finally free, of her, and of the drink, you are in full control of your life again. Where do you go, and what do you do first?"

Tony shrugged. "Move on, I guess. Go to South Australia, like we've been discussing. I've got a few quid saved, so perhaps I'll buy on old banger and go."

Ernie held up a monitoring finger, moving it back and forth in front of Tony's eyes like a metronome. "No, no," he disagreed emphatically. "The old-banger mentality belongs to the old Tony. The new Tony must learn to think positively; look after number one and put his own needs first every time. As a sundowner, your car is your most treasured possession. It is your transport and it is your home. And now that you no longer have an expensive wife or a drink habit to support, what else have you to spend your money on but yourself? What you really need is a Volkswagen caravanette, like mine."

"I can't afford anything like that, they're far too expensive," protested Tony.

"Of course you can. This is the new Tony, remember. Nothing but the best for number one. If you want something then have it, that's my motto." He reached over for the coffee pot that was percolating on the stove, and replenished their mugs. "To a sundowner, his transport is his best friend. I know mine is. If you hit hard times or find yourself in a place you don't much like, it will whisk you away to somewhere better. If you're broke and without a job, then it will give you shelter and a bed to sleep in. A Volkswagen caravanette is the sundowner's perfect companion. Benton Motors in town have one for sale. I had a look at it the other day and it's in great condition. A hundred pounds deposit and you can be driving off into the sunset."

Tony hesitated for a moment. The old Tony would have worried about getting into debt. What if he couldn't get a job to keep up with the payments? What if it broke down and he couldn't pay for the repairs? But he was a different man now. To hell with it, why not?

A week later, he was driving the gleaming Volkswagen from the showroom and, a few days afterwards, he was saying farewell to Ernie, and the town of Merredin, and hitting the road bound for South Australia.

The Volkswagen purred along under a cloudless blue sky, eating up mile after mile of tarmac. Tony sang along with the music blaring out from the radio. He had an overwhelming sense of freedom and independence, yet, at the same time, he felt safe and secure within his own little space.

After half an hour or so, he pulled over onto the hard shoulder. Having stretched his legs, he put the kettle on and set about the task of polishing his windscreen till it was crystal clear. This was a ritual Ernie said he always performed whenever he was on the move.

Tony sat in the driving seat with a mug of coffee and gazed at the empty road stretching before him. The blank canvas of a brand new life was how Ernie had described it. Tony smiled - he liked that analogy. A blank canvas on life, a fresh, new start. Peering through his windscreen at the sun-drenched road ahead, that's exactly what it was. All the fears and insecurities that had plagued him were in the past; they lay scattered along the road far behind him. He was moving on, and looking forward to colouring in that blank canvas. Whatever the future out there held for him, Tony now felt strong enough to not only cope with it and to survive, but also to enjoy it.

Initially, he hadn't wanted to move to Australia. He would have been quite content to remain in his dreary little office job. But he was more adventurous now, and he was far happier than he had ever been. His future along that road ahead was looking good.

CHAPTER NINETEEN

Peter sat proudly behind the wheel of an ancient tipper truck and drove it – expertly, he imagined – up the rough, winding track leading from the quarry. The truck was battered and doorless, and its tired old engine groaned painfully at the task of hauling its load up the rise, but for the thrill it gave Peter to drive, he could have been sitting at the wheel of a sleek new E-type Jaguar.

This was a vastly changed Peter Taylor from the boy who had set out from Seaview Hostel barely six weeks earlier. His body was heavily bronzed, and streaked now with dust-choked sweat. His hands were hard and calloused where blisters had come and gone, and, to his immense pride, his hair grew thick about his ears, and hung in an unruly mass across his forehead - a symbol of his newly-acquired independence.

The quarry camp was no place for a boy, especially a green Pome boy, and at first the rough bushmen had tormented him with their crude jokes, and terrified him with supposedly poisonous snakes and lizards. But Peter had learned fast, and there wasn't much the older men could fool him with now.

Halfway up the rise, he brought the truck to a halt and waited. Presently, from down in the quarry, there came the sound of an explosion, then another. He looked back and saw puffs of white dust and stone being shot high into the air. A satisfied smile spread across his grimy features.

Beside him sat a thick-set man whose broad shoulders were mottled by a mass of dark freckles; his fair skin having been tanned red by the fierce sun. His mates called him "Blue", supposedly on account of his sandy-coloured hair. Peter was still at a loss to understand the nickname. When the men had explained that in Australia all redheads were called Blue, he'd thought it was another of their leg-pulls. But after six weeks at the quarry, it was still the only name he knew the foreman by. Peter was never too sure how to take Blue. Mostly, he was jovial and easygoing, even if his jokes were the crudest Peter had ever heard. But at other times, he was sullen and moody, and at such times, the men knew better than to anger him.

Blue sat in silence now, sucking at a loosely-rolled cigarette as he counted off the charges. "That's her," he drawled as the last explosion sounded. "All good'uns. We'll make a powder-monkey of you yet."

Peter grinned proudly. It was the first time Blue had allowed him to set the charges. "Shall we go back and see what they've brought down?" he asked eagerly.

Blue gave a slow smile. "You're getting too keen, young'un. Plenty of time for that on Monday. Me, I've got a weekend's drinking to catch up on. Take her back to camp."

Peter crashed the truck back into gear and drove it on up the rise. Their camp consisted of a dozen or so wooden huts, grouped together in a small clearing that had been bulldozed through the scrub.

"Have you still got all your fingers, young Peter?" a man called in a broad Irish accent, as Peter brought the truck to a halt amidst a cloud of dust. The call had come from Paddy, a tall, bearded man who was leaning over a water trough, rinsing the dust and sweat from his body and wringing out his shirt.

"What do you take me for, a stupid half-wit of an Irishman?" Peter retorted.

"Watch yourself, boy, or I'll wop you good."

"Any time you think you're man enough," Peter taunted him.

The Irishman bounded over to the truck, grinning from ear to ear. "Getting mighty cheeky for a young'un. Time I gave you another licking."

He dragged Peter from the cab and rolled him in the dust. Peter made a dive for his legs, but Paddy danced nimbly clear.

"Miles too slow, sonny," he laughed.

Peter sprang to his feet and they began to spar. Paddy ducked and weaved with all the skill of a trained fighter. "You're improving, young'un, but keep the guard up," he said, and clipped Peter on the ear. Peter retaliated with a hard right that bounced unnoticed from the Irishman's brawny shoulder. Paddy laughed and clipped him on the ear again. Then, tiring of sparring, he rushed Peter, grabbing him round the middle and heaving him effortlessly over his shoulder. He carried him to the water trough and dropped him unceremoniously into it.

Men gathered round laughing as Peter sat there luxuriating in the cool water.

"We can't have a joker arsing around with geli before he's had his end away, can we, Blue?" said Keith, a lanky, heavy-boned youth who, in spite of his size, was only a year older that Peter. "He might get the shakes and blow himself to pieces. What do you say we take him into Kal with us tonight and get him his first shag?"

"Sure, we'll toss him head first into Ma Ketchal's brothel, she'll look after him," said Paddy.

Apart from his weekend prospecting trips with Blue, Peter hadn't ventured outside the camp since the day he'd arrived there, and he was becoming bored and restless. He would have loved to go into Kalgoorlie and drink with his workmates, but he feared the police would still be on the lookout for him.

Every weekend, he had managed to find a credible excuse for staying in camp; this week, however, Paddy and Keith were giving him no choice in the matter. They carried him from the trough and thrust him under the shower.

"Get cleaned up, young'un, you're going into town to get drunk and have your first shag," they insisted.

"It's a big day for you. Sure, you'll come back a man."

"I had my first shag years ago," Peter protested weakly.

"Hark at the patter, will you. Sure he still thinks it's for peeing out of."

"He'll soon realise what it's for when Ma Ketchal's lovelies get hold of him."

"Don't bullshit me. There are no brothels anywhere in Australia," Peter asserted confidently, sure they were pulling his leg again. "I ain't going to Kalgoorlie."

His protests went unheeded and, later that evening, he was being bundled into the back of Blue's car between Paddy and old Billy, the Aborigine. Billy was already more than half drunk. He slumped in the corner seat, his head lolling from side to side as the car lurched along. He had neither washed nor changed for his weekend in town. As far as Peter knew, the clothes he now wore were the only ones he possessed – and the smell of him was overpowering.

Yet, in spite of his lack of hygiene, Peter rather liked the old Aborigine. He was quiet and didn't mix much with the rest of the gang. Blue said all Aborigines were that way.

Peter remembered when he had first started at the quarry and the men had tormented him. They had him hopping around, terrified of everything that crawled, from bull-ants to goannas, lest they should possess a deadly bite or sting. Billy had taken him aside and assured him quietly, "When I say jump, you jump. If I say nothing, there is no danger." True to his word, Billy had never tried to trick him, or make fun of him.

But Peter soon discovered that any closer friendship with the old Aborigine was not possible. He refused to be drawn into conversation. Not because he was moody and unsociable, as the other men described him - he was always ready with a wide, friendly grin - but his answers were laconic to the extreme and never invited further discussion.

One hot evening, when Peter had been sitting outside his hut catching the benefit of a cool breeze that had sprung up, he had thought the old Aborigine was at last going to favour him with a closer friendship. Billy had stepped from his hut holding a charred and bent piece of wood, at one end of which was a vicious-looking notch that jutted at an angle, like the crest of a parrot.

"Here, boy, you want this?" he said gruffly.

Peter turned it cautiously in his hands. He knew it was a boomerang, but he had never seen one like this before. He had always thought of them as novelty toys you saw in department stores, or in souvenir shops as polished ornaments, but this ugly piece of wood was quite obviously a weapon.

"Not like you see in shops, eh?" smiled Billy.

"No, I'll say. Does it work?"

"Course he works, I make him." Billy replied indignantly. He took it from Peter's hand. "Watch the fork in that mallee."

He brought the boomerang back behind his ear and threw it with a short, sharp action similar to that of a darts player, and seemingly with little more effort. The boomerang flew across the clearing with amazing speed and stripped the branch from the mallee.

"Wow!" exclaimed Peter. "Boy, does that thing go! Can you make it come back to you?"

Billy whistled, then gave another wide grin. "No, he don't come back."

It took Peter a moment to realise that Billy had actually made a joke. He had never heard him joke about anything before. Blue said that Aborigines had no sense of humour. But then Blue always spoke of Aborigines that way: as a race, rather than as individuals – at times, almost as though they were another species.

Peter ran to retrieve the boomerang. "Will you teach me how to throw it, Billy?" he asked eagerly.

"Why you want to throw him?" Billy shrugged lazily. His attitude was once again one of aloof indifference, conveying to Peter that their longest-ever conversation was at an end.

Peter sensed it wasn't so much that Billy didn't want to teach him to throw the boomerang for fear of giving away some tribal secret, but rather that he couldn't be bothered to explain it all, or simply didn't want to have that close and prolonged a contact with anyone.

It was almost dark when they drove into Kalgoorlie. Buildings of all shapes and sizes lined the main street, their rooftops rising into the dusk like a row of uneven teeth. Peter's immediate impression was that the town had not been designed or planned at all, but had merely grown into existence following some master plan of its own. It was as though in the early days businessmen had staked their claims along the main thoroughfare and erected whatever shape and size building best suited their needs. Some were brick-fronted with large windows; others were of timber with jutting verandahs, and none, it seemed, had any design feature in common with the establishments flanking it.

From every angle, however, Peter was reminded that this was a gold town, with the fascias on the buildings proclaiming: 'Lucky Strike Cafe', 'Sluicebox Hotel', 'The Golden Nugget' and 'Pay Dirt'. The whole town throbbed with all the colour and excitement of its goldrush days.

The thing that struck Peter most was the width of the streets. He had always imagined the streets of mining towns to be narrow and dusty, with the buildings crowding in on each other from either side. In Kalgoorlie, this was not so; the main street was wider than any he had seen in Perth, and the streets that intersected it were equally spacious.

Blue parked the car in front of the Sluicebox. Peter stepped out and stood gazing at the town. It was like Coolgardie, only much bigger. Billy got out and started ambling along the street on his own.

"Where are you off to, Billy?" Peter called after him.

Billy kept walking, as though he hadn't heard.

"He's got mates in town," said Blue.

"Isn't he going to have a drink with us?"

"He's an Abo," said Blue. His tone was flat, implying nothing more than the simple statement of fact.

Peter was too engrossed in the town to pursue the point. "Why are the streets so wide, Blue?" he asked.

"They were made that way in the early days, when they used to drive the big bullock teams and stage coaches into town. That was the only form of transport back then, and the streets had to be wide enough for them to turn around in."

"You see that up there, young'un," Paddy pointed to the far end of town where a row of towering constructions stood silhouetted on the horizon. "Those mines are part of Kalgoorlie's famous golden mile. It's the richest strip of land in Australia – possibly the world. Millions of pounds in gold are hauled out of those mines every year."

"You've often heard of the streets of cities being paved with gold," said Keith. "Well, Kalgoorlie is the only place in the world where it's true. There's real gold dust built into the roads here."

"Don't bullshit me," Peter scoffed. "Nobody would be daft enough to build roads out of gold."

"It's true, we wouldn't lie to you. Ask Blue."

"True enough," Blue said nodding. "Kalgoorlie's roads were made out of low-grade ore from the mines. The price of gold back then wasn't what it is today. Any ore yielding less than an ounce a ton wasn't worth processing, so rather than throw it away, they built the roads with it."

"And every time they resurface a road nowadays, they send the old surface along to the state battery for crushing. The gold they extract from it more than pays for the new surface."

"Is that true?" Peter asked in half-belief. It sounded feasible, but he Peter had heard so many of Paddy's tales.

"Sure it's true. Why, when it rains here in Kalgoorlie, you can see the specs of gold glistening up at you from the streets. And there will be a row of prospectors sitting along the pavements, panning the rain water as it flows along the gutters."

Peter's face creased into a grin of awareness. "You lying toad," he said, punching Paddy's arm.

Blue gave a loud, bellowing laugh and slapped him on the shoulder. "You'll do, young'un," he said. "Come on, let's see how you handle a beer."

"We'll do a crawl of Hannan Street first, then we'll take you along to Ma Ketchal's and throw you to the mercy of her little lovelies. It's going to be a big night for you, young Peter: your first bender and your first shag – all in the same night."

There were thirteen hotels in Hannan Street, and all were packed with tough, brawny-looking miners, intent on having their pay-night bender. Peter's head was spinning long before they had drunk their way along the north side of the street, and by the time they crossed over and started down the south side, his legs felt oddly rubbery and were reluctant to carry him on a straight course.

Paddy and Keith were both in high spirits. It seemed the big, jovial Irishman knew everyone in town. But Blue began to sink into one of his sullen moods, and Paddy and Keith gave up talking to him.

In one hotel, Blue's ill humour almost started a fight. He shouldered his way impatiently to the bar, pushing aside a group of miners. One of them cursed loudly as beer slopped down the front of his shirt. Blue turned on him menacingly and, for a moment, it seemed the two would come to blows, but the miner thought better of it and backed down.

Keith said that Blue always got that way with the beer, and that there was bound to be a brawl before the night was out. Peter took Keith's advice and left Blue to the depths of his own thoughts.

At a number of hotels, Peter had noticed groups of Aborigines gathered around the entrance. They were invariably dirty, tramp-like figures. Some sat drunkenly on the pavement, leaning their backs against the wall, while others waited expectantly by the door. Keith explained that they were waiting for their mates inside to slip them out beer or plonk.

"Why don't they go in and get their own?" Peter asked.

"They're Abos," Keith explained, in much the same tone that Blue had used earlier.

"You mean they're not allowed inside the pub?"

"Not unless they have their white man's rights."

"What's that?"

Keith gave a disinterested shrug. "It's a sort of licence allowing them to have a drink."

Peter noticed that the Aborigines allowed inside the hotel had to produce a card before the barman would serve them. It was like a small passport with the holder's photo stuck to it. After one or two drinks, the holder would go outside and hand the card to one of his mates who would then go in and take his place at the bar. Peter couldn't understand the set-up at all, but by this time, his main concern was remaining upright.

At the beginning of the pub-crawl, he had been in high spirits, the same as Paddy and Keith. But now he was feeling nauseous and dizzy. There was a numbness creeping through his limbs, and an uncontrollable slur in his speech. He knew he was already drunk, and by his befuddled count, there were still four or five pubs to go. But he was determined to prove himself as good as his companions and complete the crawl.

He stumbled his way to the Coach House in the wake of a loud and jubilant Paddy and Keith. A group of Aborigines loitered at the entrance. They were as dirty and shabby as any he'd seen, and if anything, a little drunker. He was about to follow Keith through the door when he felt a tug at his sleeve. He turned and saw Billy standing beside him.

"Hey, boy. You buy me a bottle of wine," he was saying, his speech very slurred.

"Sure, Billy. I'll buy you a bottle," said Peter, thinking Billy must be broke and wanted him to pay for it. But Billy fumbled in his pocket and came out with a crumpled pound note.

"Here, you buy me a bottle of plonk," he mumbled.

"You know better than that, Billy," Blue intervened roughly. "What are you trying to do, get the boy arrested?" He thrust the money back at him, and Billy shuffled away into the shadows like a scolded dog.

Blue hustled Peter inside and told him sternly: "Don't ever buy booze for an Abo. It's a serious crime out here. If you're caught, you'll be breaking rocks for the rest of your days."

"Why, Blue? Why can't they drink? There's no colour-bar in Australia, is there?" Peter asked as they entered the bar.

"Not exactly, but Abos aren't allowed to drink. They can't take it. They're too weak in the head."

"Who's weak in the bloody head?" challenged a tall, dark-skinned man, standing beside him.

Blue glared at him, disgust written plainly on his face. "Thought I could smell a f'ing cast in here somewhere," he said.

Without warning, the man took a wild swing at Blue's head. Blue reached up, almost casually, and blocked the blow, then drove a hard right into the man's stomach and he crumpled to the floor with a groan.

His mates immediately crowded in on Blue, forcing him back against the wall. Peter rushed in to help him. He pulled one man away and swung a punch at his middle, hoping to see him crumple the way Blue's adversary had. But his swing was weak and uncoordinated, and he was never sure whether the punch landed or not. He felt himself flying backwards and hitting the floor with a thump. The side of his face was numb where the miner had struck him. He tried to regain his feet, but couldn't. Every time he rose to his knees, he would lose his balance and fall back to the floor. He was hopelessly drunk.

Through the blur, he saw Paddy and Keith come bounding over from the bar to Blue's assistance. Paddy waded into the thick of the fight, a wide grin on his face as he jabbed and hooked at every head within reach of his long arms. Everywhere Peter looked, men were fighting; it seemed the whole pub had taken sides in the matter.

Someone was lifting him to his feet. It was Keith. "Come on, Peter, let's get the hell out of here before the police arrive," he was urging, "or we'll both go down for under-age drinking."

Keith dragged him outside and together they staggered away down the street. Peter had to lean heavily on Keith's shoulder to get along. When they stopped, Keith told him to put his fingers down his throat and vomit into the gutter. Peter did so, and afterwards he felt much better, but his head was still spinning.

It was not long before the paddy-wagons arrived. Peter noticed they were nothing more than standard Holden utilities with metal cages built onto their trays. Keith and Peter watched as the police bundled men into them. Blue and Paddy appeared from a side entrance and came swaggering along the street with their arms about each others' shoulders. Paddy was singing and laughing loudly. Blue's mouth was bleeding, but his sullen mood had vanished and he, too, was laughing loudly.

"Nothing that pair enjoy more than a good brawl," explained Keith.

"You've the makings of a beaut shiner there, young'un" said Paddy. "But don't fret none, I gave him a good thumping for you." He winked to the others. "Sure, I think he's looking fit enough to go a couple of rounds with one of Ma Ketchal's lovelies right now. What do you say?"

They had been bandying the joke about all evening and Peter had ceased to take it seriously. Brothels only existed in foreign countries, he knew that. The strict laws in Australia would never permit them.

"Okay, let's go and see your brothels," he said cockily, calling their bluff.

"That's the spirit," said Paddy. He clamped a big hand over Peter's shoulder and guided him down the street.

They walked along for a few blocks till they came to a row of small weatherboard houses, fronted by large verandas that had been enclosed with chicken wire. Behind the wire, women paraded in flimsy nightdresses and bikinis, revealing more of the female body than Peter had ever seen before. At some of the houses, men stood in front of the wire partitioning, bargaining with the women. The snatches of conversation that floated back to him left Peter in no doubt as to what the girls were selling.

"Aren't they beautiful?" grinned Paddy. "Take your pick, young'un. You can have any of them for a fiver."

"He still doesn't believe it," laughed Keith. "Look at his face. They're real, right enough. Only town in Australia with legalised brothels, that's Kalgoorlie. They are all a bit old up this end of the street, though. Wait till we get to Ma Ketchal's, there are some real dolls there."

They walked to the end of the block, where a house a little larger than the rest stood on its own behind a low white fence. A sour-faced woman sat at the door. Her hair was dyed bright red and piled on top of her head in tight curls; absurdly big earrings dangled onto her shoulders. Compared with the other women seated along the veranda, she was grossly overdressed.

"How are you today, my darling?" Paddy called a cheerful welcome.

"Don't you, 'my darling' me," she growled, but with a trace of humour. "I don't know as you reprobates are welcome after what happened last week."

"You wouldn't turn us away, Ma. Sure we are your best customers," the Irishman said, trying to charm her.

"My best customers are them that pay most, not them that indulge most," she countered. "I want no trouble from you lot tonight."

"We never cause any trouble, Ma. Sure, we are peace-loving lads. Come over here, Julie, my darling. I have a boyfriend for you."

A tall, dark-haired girl smiled and moved towards them. She wore a tight-fitting brassiere that swelled the top of her breasts, causing them to bounce lightly as she walked. Peter couldn't tear his eyes away from them, but his senses were still too numbed by beer for him to become aroused by the sight.

"This is Peter. I want you to look after him for me," Paddy told her with a knowing wink.

"Hello, sweetheart." Julie smiled; tell-tale lines appearing about her mouth and eyes. She was older than Peter had at first thought.

"What's the special rate tonight, Julie, my darling?" Paddy asked confidently.

"No specials on Friday nights, you know that," cut in Ma. "Five quid standard charge. Pay it or go."

"Ah, but sure he's only a lad. You can take him in for half price."

"They're all men when they come in here," said Ma.

Peter was still unable to take his eyes off Julie's bulging breasts. He was becoming hypnotised by the milky-white mounds, rising and falling gently in rhythm with her breathing. Something began to stir within him. This was a new kind of excitement, much deeper than the thrill he'd experienced while watching bikini-clad girls on the beach. This was a mature woman standing before him. She was available, and he was about to have sex with her.

"He's no boy. He knows what it's all about," Julie said softly. She opened the wire-covered door. "Come on in, sweetheart."

Peter obeyed mechanically. He paid Ma his five pounds and followed Julie along the corridor to a small, well-furnished room. She closed the door behind them and crossed the room to a low coffee table. On the table was a chamber pot, full of what looked like disinfectant water. Wads of cotton wool stood beside the pot.

"Come over here a moment, sweetheart," she smiled.

Peter went over to her and she unfastened his fly and began to bathe his privates. He became aroused at her touch. Julie smiled up at him. It was an intimate smile that made him blush at the desires stirring within him. He felt he had no right to be there, that he was just a green, immature boy. Julie was a mature woman, very beautiful and very experienced. It was as though their relationship was to be an impersonal doctor-to-patient one, and the physical act of sex between them was to be no more emotional than a part of the treatment.

There were heaters burning in the room, making it hot and stuffy. The heat and all the beer he had consumed were making him feel very drowsy. When they rolled onto the bed together, he began to sweat profusely. The physical exertion sapped at his energy and he could feel his ardour starting to cool before he'd reached his climax.

The next thing he knew, Julie was sprinkling cold water over his face, and slapping him.

"Wake up, sweetheart, you can't sleep here, I've got a living to earn," she said, pulling him to a sitting position.

Peter's head felt as though it was splitting in two, and he wanted to be sick again. He stood up shakily and, forgetting his trousers were still loose about his ankles, took a step towards the door. He tripped and fell headlong over the coffee table. There was a deafening crash as the table overturned and the chamber pot shattered. Peter found himself slumped against the wall, sitting in a pool of disinfectant water. Julie flew into a rage and shouted at him. From outside there came the sound of more raised voices.

"That big Maori bouncer is in there. He's rolling young Peter for his pay packet." It was Blue's voice. Ma Ketchal screeched something back at him. There was another crash as the wire door burst open, followed by the sound of heavy feet running along the corridor.

Blue and Paddy charged into the room, closely followed by Ma Ketchal wielding a millet broom at the Irishman's head and screeching hysterically for them both to get out and never come back.

The bouncer was next into the room; a huge Maori who, it seemed, had to turn sideways to get his shoulders through the narrow doorway.

"He's the one!" said Blue, and swung into him before the Maori knew what was going on.

The Maori brushed the blows aside, catching Blue in an armlock. They grappled together for a moment, then slipped on the wet linoleum and crashed to the floor in a heap. Then Keith came tearing in, minus his trousers, and dived into the tangle of bodies to assist Blue. Meanwhile, Paddy was still darting around the room, jumping over furniture and ducking away from Ma Ketchal's swinging broom.

Peter found it all very amusing, like a scene from a slapstick comedy. He propped himself against the wall and began to laugh uncontrollably.

The next thing he knew, the room was full of policemen - and they were all being arrested and taken out to the paddy wagon.

Blue and Paddy sang and joked all the way to the police station. They said it was the best night out they had had for a long time, and credited Peter with causing all the excitement.

Peter was unable to share their exuberance, and certainly wasn't feeling like the hero of the hour. He had sobered up a lot now, and he was scared. The police were bound to know who he was. He would be arrested and sent back to Perth to face trial. Only now there would be even more charges against him. What would his mother think when she learned about the brothel and the drunken brawl? All this coming on top of a possible rape charge. How could he ever look her in the face again?

Vaguely, he considered lying about his name, or making a run for it when they opened the wagon. But he knew he could never get away. He was far too drunk to outrun sober policemen, and running would only make things worse for him. This time, he had really blown it. He'd been caught. There was no escape.

The paddy wagon came to a halt. The door opened and they were escorted into the police station by a tall, stern-faced constable. Paddy and Blue were still laughing, but Peter was feeling sick with fear and apprehension.

Once inside the station, the stern-faced constable's mood changed dramatically. He laughed loudly and called through to an adjoining room. "Look who I've brought you, Blue!"

A sandy-haired sergeant came out holding a steaming cup of coffee. Peter didn't need to be told that he was Blue's brother; the two were identical, in all but dress.

The sergeant gave a growl of annoyance in anticipation of having his peace disturbed. "Oh, for Christ's sake, get them out of here, Bruce. They spend more time in this bloody place than I do."

Bruce slapped his hat against his thigh, still laughing loudly. "Funniest turnout you ever saw in your life," he said, and went on to describe the scene at Ma Ketchal's in graphic detail.

Paddy swaggered through into the staff room. "Ah, I see you have the billy on the boil. Good lads. Come and have a cup of coffee, young'un, it will sober you up. Very hospitable people, are the Kalgoorlie police."

It took Peter a few moments to realise what was happening. They were amongst friends, and were not going to be charged, after all. An enormous feeling of relief swept over him, as though he was awakening from a nightmare to find the terrifying monster vanishing before his eyes.

Elated at his last-minute reprieve, he followed Paddy and Keith through into the staff room.

"Who's the boy?" the sergeant demanded of his brother.

"Works out at the quarry with us."

"What's his name?"

"Peter Taylor. Why?"

"Thought so. We've been on the lookout for him for weeks."

"What for? What did he do?" Blue demanded open-mouthed.

"Just a runaway," shrugged the sergeant. "Seems he got some girl into trouble and did a runner. He'll have to go back."

"Ah, that's no crime," Blue said dismissively. "Give the kid a break."

"He'll have to go back," the sergeant repeated firmly.

"Don't be a bloody rat-bag," Blue flared, raising his voice. "He's a good kid. You never saw him, right?"

"How long is he going to stay a good kid, knocking around with you and the boys?" said the sergeant, raising his own voice. "I could slap a dozen charges on him right now. Use your head, man. He's got to go back to his family."

The twins were now shouting angrily into each others' faces, standing toe to toe and bulbous nose to bulbous nose.

"I'll go back," Peter intervened quickly, sure that the brothers were within a whisker of coming to blows. The sergeant was right. He had to go back and face it sooner or later. He couldn't live at the quarry for the rest of his life.

"Now you're talking sense," the sergeant said approvingly. "I could keep you in for the night and make it official. Look a lot better if you went back under your own steam, though. What's it to be?"

"I'll go back," confirmed Peter. "I'll catch the sleeper next week."

CHAPTER TWENTY

Paul Stevens, manager of Morton Employment Agency, sat behind his polished oak desk and flicked through Michael's references with raised eyebrows.

"These are most impressive testimonials, Michael," he said with an approving tilt of the head. "I've been to London and I know some of these hotels. They are top-notch establishments."

"The restaurants are somewhat more exclusive," Michael assured him, without intending to sound pompous or boastful.

"Oh, I can believe that. I am well aware of The Grove in Mayfair." He looked up and smiled faintly. "I was only a student while in London, and no way could I have afforded to eat there, but I was certainly aware of it."

He leaned back in his chair and patted down the lapels of his dark blue jacket. "With references like these, Michael, you could walk into any of the top hotels here in Perth and they would welcome you with open arms. But, of course, you are already aware of this." He placed the references back on the desk and opened his palms quizzically. "This being so, why are you here seeking my help?"

"I don't wish to work in Perth. I desire a position in the country," explained Michael. He had decided the only sensible course of action was to return to his profession as a chef. But he wasn't prepared to risk humiliation by working in Perth and encountering people he knew, and to whom he had boasted of his previous executive positions and high expectations.

For several days after Gloria's hasty departure, Michael had been moody and depressed. It wasn't so much the emotional pain of losing her that hurt him, but her rejection had come as a severe blow to his ego. He had never imagined for a moment that timid little Gloria could summon the spirit needed to walk out on him. He refused to humble himself still further by running after her. If that was the way she wanted it, then let her go, and see how long she could survive without him. He would wait for her to come crawling back, pleading forgiveness, as he was sure she would. But after a week of waiting and sulking, Michael had conceded that Gloria would not be coming back to him, and had begun to make plans for his own future.

He realised it was pointless to keep applying for sales positions when the openings were simply not there. Now that he was on his own, it was a relief to know that he could return to his profession without the need for embarrassing confessions, or having to invent lengthy and awkward explanations for his inability to land a top executive position.

So, reluctantly, Michael had dug out his references and headed for an employment agency, where he now sat facing an impressed but slightly bemused Paul Stevens.

"Country employment?" Paul pursed his lips and pondered the request. "You haven't been in Australia very long, have you, Michael?"

"Not long," Michael conceded grudgingly.

"Well, perhaps I should explain the position to you. Country towns here are not as you would think of them in England - picturesque villages nestling between rolling hills and green fields - and all that. Australia doesn't really have countryside, as such. We just have miles and miles of bush, followed by desert. Moving out of Perth isn't going to be like moving from London down to Surrey." He paused to let his point register. "To put it graphically, bush towns are as rough as guts, and, in general, so are the people who live in them. I don't want to belittle my countrymen, but I doubt whether any of your bush town customers would appreciate the fine cuisine you are accustomed to preparing. Most of them will never have heard of the word cuisine. Your clientele would be made up of miners, station hands and navvies from road and railway gangs." He shook his head and urged, "I would strongly advise you to reconsider. If you give me a day or two, I'm sure I can find you something far more suitable in the city."

"No, thank you. I prefer to work in the country," Michael insisted stubbornly.

Paul raised his hands in resignation. "The bush it is, then." He stood up and moved to a filing cabinet where drew out a blue folder. "Actually, as it happens, I do have something that could possibly interest you. It came in yesterday. The mining town of Norseman, about four hundred miles away, if you don't mind travelling that far?" He looked at Michael, expecting to see him shake his head.

"I have a car. Distance is not a problem," said Michael. The farther the better, as far as he was concerned.

"The establishment is called Rosie's Restaurant. Though, if I know bush towns, it's probably little more than a café. They are only paying the basic rate, but accommodation is provided. I wasn't too hopeful of filling the position, to be honest, but..."

"I'll take the job," said Michael, much to Paul's surprise.

Michael's principles dictated that there was something he should do before leaving Perth. He needed to contact Gloria and make sure she was all right. He had no thoughts or intentions of a reconciliation - that was plainly out of the question. But he wanted to do the right thing. He had been responsible for bringing her out to Australia, so he couldn't simply abandon her. Before leaving, he must satisfy himself that she was safe and coping all right, and, if necessary, pay for her fare home. That would be the decent, gentlemanly thing to do, even though he could ill-afford the money.

Michael's innate sense of decency and generosity had always been his weakness where women were concerned, and there had been a string of girlfriends who had taken advantage of his benevolence. He reflected morosely that he had never had much luck with women. He attracted girlfriends readily enough; indeed, with his good looks, women usually came on to him. But as for keeping them and forming a meaningful relationship, that was a different matter.

Initially, women were proud to be seen on the arm of such a handsome young man; flattered to be treated with respect and deference by someone with such impeccable manners. But they would soon tire of his pedantic behaviour, and eventually become irritated by those impeccable manners – and, after taking advantage of his generosity, they would invariably dump him and move on. Sometimes, Michael felt that he was trying too hard to please, by being over polite. What was the point, when it was rogues like Curran that the women invariably seemed to gravitate to? Michael had had his fill of relationships and playing the perfect gentleman. Women were only an encumbrance, and an expensive one at that. From now on, he would concentrate on his own needs.

However, the question now was what to do about Gloria . The problem was he had no idea where she had gone. Curran had given her his address, so perhaps she had gone to him for help in finding somewhere to stay. There was nobody else she knew in Perth. The very thought of having to go humbly to the likes of Curran, admitting that his fiancée had dumped him, and asking for his help in finding her was abhorrent, and completely out of the question. That really would be one humiliation too far.

When he inquired at the hostel's office whether Gloria had perhaps given a forwarding address for her mail, he was informed politely, but firmly, that she had, but she had also left strict instructions that her whereabouts were not to be disclosed to anyone.

He left the office fuming. He had been concerned only for her welfare, and he had been made to feel like an undesirable - worse, like some kind of sex pest. Well, to hell with Gloria, and to always trying to do the right thing. From now on, she could fend for herself. If she needed anything, let her come to him, or even go to Curran. And if she wanted her fare home, then let her father pay - he had pots of money. Michael had been played for a mug once too often. It was high time he stopped concerning himself with the welfare of others and looked to his own future.

Two days later, Michael checked out of the hostel to leave Gloria, Perth, and this chapter of his life far behind him. It had been a mistake to abandon his calling for the fickle notion of easy riches in sales, and he was looking forward to making a fresh start, back working in the profession he knew and loved.

After a long and tiring journey, he arrived in Norseman and drove the Volkswagen slowly down the main street. Norseman was like so many of the small bush towns he had driven through on his four-hundred-mile journey. The drab, dusty streets were flanked by old, run-down dwellings and businesses, some constructed from bricks and others from weatherboard, and most with rusting corrugated iron roofs. A large Victorian-looking hotel stood on one corner of the town's main intersection, and standing opposite it was a similar-sized building that looked as though it, too, must originally have been a hotel. This was now Rosie's Restaurant.

Michael's first impression was not one of instant approval or enthusiasm. The wooden frames of the wide, frosted-glass windows were flaking and badly in need of a lick of paint, as was the heavy wooden door that looked as though the customary mode of entry was to give it a hefty kick. A notice taped to the inside of its cracked window informed him that the establishment was closed till further notice.

Michael stepped out of the car and stretched his legs. He took a handkerchief from his pocket and wiped the sweat and grime from around his neck. Paul Stevens had been brutally honest about it: Australian bush towns had nothing whatsoever in common with English villages. And neither did the weather. The temperature here on the edge of the desert seemed far hotter than in Perth, and the flies were definitely more abundant. He flapped the handkerchief at them as they buzzed about his ears. Coming to Norseman was looking like a big mistake. Perhaps he should drive on to Adelaide - it would be more civilised there. The problem was that Adelaide was another twelve hundred miles away, and he was hot and weary.

When he tried the door, it swung open. Still with misgivings, he stepped inside.

The interior was cool, and much more pleasantly decorated than he would have imagined from the outside, with pastel-coloured walls and freshly painted woodwork. Clean net curtains hung in the windows. The light oak tables and chairs were dust-free and smelt strongly of furniture polish. He estimated that there was seating for fifty or more customers - larger than he would have envisaged, or than Paul Stevens had predicted. Unlike the building's exterior, the dining room gave the impression that someone took considerable pride in its appearance.

"G'day, you must be Michael Dean, the new cook. Been expecting you." The man spoke with a lazy drawl, aptly complemented by the way he slouched across the room. He wore a faded blue singlet and baggy, knee-length shorts. "I'm Chuck Mills. Glad to meet you, Mike. Me proper name's Charles, but everyone calls me Chuck." As they shook hands, he smiled inanely, like the simple-minded country yokel Michael had already assessed him to be.

"I'm not the Mr Mills that owns the place, of course," he rambled on. "I'm his son. What do you think of Norseman, Mike? You been here before?"

"No, actually I haven't. It seems a nice enough town, though."

"Nice?" Chuck gave a weak, incredulous laugh. "It's a rat-bag of a town. Every bum in Australia passes through Norseman some time or other. We get shearing gangs, road gangs, miners, prospectors, station hands - all the rowdy, drunken dregs imaginable. That's Norseman for you. Soon as I've got a bit of cash behind me, I'll be heading over East where it's more civilised. I'd best tell Dad you're here. He's a bit crook at the moment. He's had a heart attack, that's why we need a new cook. Dad's name is Charles, too, only they call him Curley, on account of his bald head." He gave another feeble laugh, then turned and went back through into the establishment's private quarters.

When he returned, he was followed by his father, a big man whose clothes hung on him as though he had recently lost a lot of weight.

Michael introduced himself, and noticed the man stiffen at the sound of his accent.

"You'll need to drop the la-de-da stuff here," he said bluntly. "This is a bush town - we cater for working men. Some of our customers have a rough sense of humour. They'll rubbish all hell out of you sounding like that."

"I already told him it's a rat-bag town," Chuck added, this time without the inane grin.

"That wasn't what I said," his father cut back at him, making no attempt to hide the animosity between them.

Curley sat down, breathing heavily from exertion. "I expect you'll want to freshen up after your journey, Michael. My daughter, Rosie, has prepared a room for you. Chuck here will show you around. I'm a bit bushed at the moment. I can't do much these days, I've got no puff."

Michael found his room to be adequate. It was clean, with a comfortable double bed and plenty of storage space. He unpacked only the few things he would need, still uncertain how long he would be staying, or even if he would be staying at all.

He showered and took a much-needed nap before making his way back down to inspect the kitchen. As as he expected, much of the equipment was old, but it was serviceable. It would do, he decided; after all, he did not expect to be called upon to prepare anything too exotic. Paul Stevens had predicted it would be nothing more challenging than meat pies or steak and chips. Michael shrugged. If that was what the customers wanted, he would prepare it - that was his job.

He wandered about the kitchen, familiarising himself with its layout. He was back where he belonged, preparing to do the job he had always loved, and his mood began to lighten at the prospect. It had been foolish to think he could be happy doing anything else, no matter how large the salary. This was his true environment, the place where he excelled, and it felt good to be back.

"You must be Michael. I'm Rosie. Sorry I wasn't here to welcome you." Rosie bounded into the kitchen with the energy and vitality of a carefree young girl. But as they shook hands, Michael noticed that her features were drawn and her eyes were beset with worry.

Rosie took a quick step back and studied him closely with a wide, approving smile. "Oh, my!" she exclaimed. "The agency told me what an accomplished chef you are, Michael. They didn't warn me you were such a handsome dish, as well."

Michael accepted the compliment without comment. Good manners dictated that he should say something complimentary in return, but he was still weary and in no mood for small talk. In any case, he would have found it difficult to find anything in Rosie's appearance to compliment her on. The long, rather unkempt, blonde hair hanging about her shoulders held more than a hint of ginger, a colour Michael hated. And with her red-and-white check shirt and blue jeans, she only needed a length of straw dangling from the side of her mouth to look the typical country bumpkin. If Rosie was coming on to him, she would be sorely disappointed. He had no intention of starting yet another disastrous relationship, no matter how brief, and certainly not with this hick-town hillbilly. He would stay in Norseman just long enough to replenish his bank account, then he would move on to Adelaide and get himself a prestigious position in one of that city's finest hotels.

"Sorry. Now I've embarrassed you," Rosie said a little awkwardly at Michael's lack of response. "I'm an Aussie girl. I can be a bit full on at times - and a bit trappy too, so I'm told. I don't mean anything by it. You'll get used to me."

"Don't he talk pretty," smirked Chuck, who had followed her in.

"That's because he's a gentleman, which is something you will never be," Rosie retorted cuttingly. Plainly, Chuck didn't get on any better with his sister than he did with his father.

"If he is a gentleman, and as good as the agency says, then he won't be sticking around this dump for long. Only bums and no-hopers stay here."

Rosie ignored him. "Sorry about our resident wombat," she said. "Is everything all right for you, Michael?" she asked indicating the kitchen.

"Everything is fine," he assured her, "...though I shall require a day to clean thoroughly before we open."

"What's wrong with it? I mopped it out myself," Chuck challenged, belligerently.

"I never work anywhere unless I have cleaned every surface and every utensil personally. Hygiene is paramount in any kitchen."

"Get her," Chuck exclaimed, exhibiting a limp wrist, then effecting a pronounced mince on his way out.

"Sorry about him," Rosie said, apologising for her brother for the second time. "Like I say, he is a bit of a wombat. Unfortunately, I'm stuck with him. If there is anything you need, please see me, not Dad. He is so ill, I don't want him bothered." The worry in her eyes deepened.

"I understand that he had a heart attack," Michael said for the want of something to say.

She nodded, then hesitated, as though feeling the need to confide in someone, but not comfortable at unburdening herself to a complete stranger.

"Dad has had this place for over thirty years," she began with a sigh. "It means a lot to him, and to me. I want to keep it open if I can."

"If you can? I take it that business hasn't been too good, then?" Michael opened the oven door and peered inside, a subconscious expression of disinterest in her family history, or problems.

Rosie shook her head. "Not anymore. In the old days, when the mines were going strong and the town was booming, the restaurant was full every night. But these days, we're lucky to get a dozen or so."

"That bad?" he said looking round at her in mild alarm. "It's a fair-sized town, and the restaurant has a good seating capacity. I would have expected more custom than that." His main concern was whether or not there was enough trade to pay his wages.

"The trade is there, but they don't come in any more." She perched herself on a barstool to explain. "You see, it was Mum's restaurant, really. She was the Rosie it was named after, not me. Mum was a great cook, not a qualified chef, by any means, but she served up good, wholesome meals, the kind working men need. When she died two years ago, the place went down hill fast. Dad soldiered on as best he could, but he's no cook, and, well, the trade simply fell away."

"And you, Rosie - you never took to cooking? I can see you have a great affection for the place."

"Hell, no. Mum tried to teach me," she smiled without humour, "but I'm such a clumsy cow, always burning myself - as well as the food. I'm not saying I'm stupid, mind," she added quickly. "Figures are my thing. Actually, I'm a qualified accountant," she boasted proudly. "Though, to be honest, I've become somewhat disillusioned with that profession, too. It can be so dull and boring."

Rosie slipped from the stool and began pacing the kitchen, a little self-consciously as she explained. "You're right, I am very fond of the restaurant. I was born here and it's been a big part of my life. But not the cooking side. I'm what you might call a people person. I always loved working in the dining room, serving the customers. I loved meeting new people, and sharing a joke with the regulars. It never felt like a proper job to me, more like an evening of socialising with friends.

"But like all youngsters brought up in small towns, I couldn't wait to see the bright city lights. So when I got my qualifications, I left home and headed for Sydney, and a job in banking. It was all right, I guess, but I was never really happy there. It lacked the friendly atmosphere and intimacy you find in small towns. I came back here two years ago, when Mum died. And I've been here ever since, running the restaurant and trying to balance the books." She sighed and pushed the long, ginger-blonde hair back across her head. "It hasn't been easy. We were ticking over all right, covering our costs - just. Then Dad had his heart attack and we had to close. I want to get the place re-opened for his sake."

She paused and faced him with a smile. "I'm boring you, aren't I? Sorry. I've no right to burden you with all of this."

Michael felt a twinge of guilt for letting his indifference show. It was bad manners, something he couldn't abide. "And how about your brother, has he no feelings for the restaurant?" he asked, attempting to make amends by a show of interest.

"None whatsoever," Rosie said with distain. "It's a harsh thing to say about your own brother, but he's only interested in one thing – the money. He's sticking around to collect his inheritance. Can you believe that? He's waiting for his father to die so he can sell up and go to Sydney and blow the money. How low can a human being stoop?" Her eyes momentarily flashed with anger, and then began to well with tears.

Michael wished he had never raised the subject. It wasn't as though he had any real interest in this feuding family, or their business.

Rosie turned away. "I'd love to keep the restaurant open permanently, but I really can't see how. To be honest with you, it's been running at a loss for some time. Now the bank is threatening to withdraw our credit. I daren't tell Dad - it would devastate him to see it close permanently. He and Mum put so much of their lives into it. I really have to keep it open while he is still with us."

She stopped suddenly. "I'm letting my mouth run away with me again, I always do," she flustered. "I shouldn't be telling you any of this. You've only just arrived, and I'm rambling on about closing the place. What must you think?"

What indeed did he think? The outlook was far from good. Was there a job here or wasn't there? And for how long? Perhaps he should simply cut and run, get back in the car and drive on. Perhaps he would.

Later that evening, he took a stroll around town, still pondering his future. The town's appearance did nothing to encourage him to stay; in fact, he viewed it as little more than a shantytown. He found the pub to be particularly uninviting, dirty and rowdy. 'Spit and sawdust' was a phrase that sprang to mind. The bar was filled with manual workers who had seemingly not bothered to wash or change before embarking on their evening's drinking. He imagined such would be the calibre of the restaurant's clientele.

Michael purchased a glass of red wine and took it to a corner seat. He noticed the barman had given him an odd look when he had ordered. Perhaps it was his English accent, or perhaps it was that he had ordered wine when the rest of the patrons were swilling beer. Nobody spoke to him, and the atmosphere was distinctly standoffish.

Later, Chuck walked in with a couple of his mates. They stood at the bar, laughing conspiratorially. Chuck started doing his limp-wrist gestures while nodding in Michael's direction, and Michael knew that much of their laughter was at his expense.

In his current frame of mind, Michael was tempted to go over and punch him on the nose, and see how that sat with his limp-wrist theories. But brawling in pubs would be most unseemly behaviour, not at all in keeping with the high standards he set himself.

He left the pub thoroughly convinced that Norseman was no place for him, and that he really should drive on. However, he'd had a long, tiring drive to get here and first he needed a good night's rest. He would decide tomorrow.

The next morning, he rose early and wandered into the kitchen, still undecided about his future. He couldn't go back to Perth, and Adelaide was so far away; he couldn't face another long journey so soon. More importantly, he needed to replenish his bank account. Reluctantly, he started cleaning the work surfaces. Now he was here, he may as well stay and see how things went, for a week or so.

During the morning, Rosie came to see him and discuss the menu. He found her stubborn and unenthusiastic about his suggestions.

"We can't afford to lay on exotic dishes, they won't sell here. And we can't afford to prepare too much food, either. I don't know how many customers we're going to get in," she said with a concerned frown. "We were barely breaking into double figures before Dad had his heart attack, and we've been closed for three weeks since then. Even our few remaining regulars may have found somewhere else to eat. Dad just used to put on meat pies with vegetables, steak and chips, fry-ups and that sort of thing. What do you think?"

"That's more in keeping with a transport café than a restaurant." Michael didn't bother to disguise his disapproval, or his irritation. "You don't need a chef to fry chips and warm up pies. I'm sure even you could manage that. But if you are expecting me to serve warmed-up factory-made meat pies, you can forget it. I'm a chef. I cook real food."

"Pies are cheap and easy, and there's a demand," Rosie offered weakly.

"They're disgusting," Michael told her bluntly. "The pastry is like wet cardboard and the fillings are all fat and gristle; barely fit for human consumption. I've seen them being made, and I refuse to have them on my menu. If you can't afford to provide me with quality ingredients to prepare, then I think we had best forget the whole thing."

He turned to face her accusingly. "And if you can't afford to buy ingredients, then how do you propose to pay me?"

"I'll get the money. I'll pay you up front, if that's what you want. Now that you are here, let's at least give it a go," she pleaded. He could see the concern in her eyes, and again they were beginning to well up.

"Oh, very well, we'll open and see what happens," Michael said in exasperation. His annoyance was more at his own inability to say no than at Rosie. Here he was being taken for a mug again by yet another young woman with a sob story. When would he ever learn?

"I'll bake a batch of proper steak and kidney pies. Even you will be able to tell the difference. I've won awards for my pastries and pies," he added gratuitously, not intending to be boastful. "I think we should have at least one good roast on the menu. I favour beef. Mixed grills, omelettes, etcetera can be done to order. How does that sound? Not a convincing menu, but the best we can muster under the circumstances. I take it the finances will stretch thus far?"

She nodded apologetically. "Thank you, Michael. I'm very grateful. I'm sure that once we open, things will be fine. The customers will come back."

She smiled at him and Michael became even more annoyed with himself. What was he doing wasting his time here? He just knew it was going to be a total disaster. He should drive on to Adelaide and take up a position more suited to his talents.

They opened at six o'clock the next evening and waited for customers. They waited and waited, but none came. Rosie became increasingly agitated, pacing up and down in her high heels, constantly going to the window and peering out.

She had worked hard preparing the dining room, and had it looking very smart, with clean white tablecloths, red serviettes and brightly polished cutlery. Michael noticed that she had smartened herself up, too. In her white blouse and slim-fitting navy blue skirt, she looked very efficient, and much more the proprietor than merely the waitress. Surprisingly, he found that she looked almost attractive, too... in a robust, sportswoman sort of way. He watched as she moved lithely between the tables, and could imagine her being good at physical sports like tennis or netball. She was far from the refined, elegant type of girl that Michael was attracted to, but with her outgoing personality, and curves in all the right places, no doubt she would have her admirers amongst the roughnecks of the town.

Finally, at eight o'clock, four station hands wandered in. Rosie greeted them exuberantly, like long-lost friends.

"Hello, Barry. How have you been?" she gushed, throwing her arms round one of the men and giving him a hug. "I knew you lads wouldn't let me down."

She seated the group at a table by the window, so that the restaurant would look busy to passers-by. The men all ordered the steak and kidney pies. Half an hour later, two more men came in and ordered roast beef.

"Is that the big rush over?" Michael commented dryly, when by nine, nobody else had come through the door.

"Things will pick up," Rosie replied optimistically. "Those pies looked awfully good. Once people get to know we've re-opened, they will come in."

At one point Chuck wandered in and sat with the station hands, making them laugh with rude remarks about the new chef. An angry

Rosie strode over, gripped his ear, dragged him to the door and pitched him out into the street. The station hands roared their approval. It was the highlight of the evening.

Michael was sitting on his barstool, wondering distractedly how long the restaurant was going to remain open, half planning his next move and thinking about the long journey to Adelaide, when he heard raised voices coming from the dining room.

"We want to see the cook," one of the station hands was demanding.

"Don't you start playing me up, Barry Smith," Rosie blazed back at him. "I'm in no mood to bandy words with you. I've got enough to worry about, what with Dad being ill, and that half-wit of a brother of mine. I can do without your antics."

"I want to see the cook," Barry repeated firmly, slapping the counter with his open hand to make his point.

Here we go again, thought Michael. I should have known these roughnecks wouldn't appreciate quality food. I should have served up the factory rubbish they are accustomed to – and added a dose of laxative for good measure.

"What seems to be the problem, gentlemen?" he asked politely, as he went through to stand at the counter, beside Rosie.

"No problem, sport," Barry beamed, then winked teasingly at Rosie. "Me and the lads have taken a vote and we reckon those are the best steak and kidney pies we have ever tasted." He extended a calloused hand. "Put it there, son."

"Well, thank you," said Michael.

Rosie skipped round the counter and kissed Barry lightly on the cheek. "Bless you, Barry. You're a diamond."

"Should have had the beef," called out one of the other diners. "It was cooked to perfection, and these roast spuds were to die for. Do I get a kiss too, Rosie?"

"Just be sure to tell all your mates how good the tucker is, and bring them back with you tomorrow. We need their custom," she pleaded.

The next night, they sold fifteen dinners, and by the end of the week, the restaurant was half full... they almost ran out of food.

Rosie was ecstatic as she finished balancing her accounts, and exclaimed, "We have actually made a profit on the week. I don't believe it. I really think we can make a go of this. Last night was great. I don't think we've had that many customers in since Mum was around. It's all thanks to you, Michael. You've been an absolute lifesaver."

Michael accepted her praise with indifference. He was well aware of how proficient he was. But he was quietly pleased that things were going well. He was happy, too, to be back doing the work that he loved. Why, oh why, had he ever allowed himself to be enticed away from this, his true vocation?

As the restaurant's popularity grew, Michael became a recognised figure around town. Whenever he went into the pub, men would welcome him into their circle and offer him drinks.

He had always believed that the only place for him was in the big cities. That was where the plush hotels and exclusive restaurants were to be found, so that was where his talents would best be appreciated. But, slowly, he began to warm to this small town with its intimate atmosphere. Here he wasn't just another chef; he was Michael, "the" chef, a title that afforded him almost celebrity status. And his ego loved it.

The only negative clouding his thoughts was the knowledge that his stay here in Norseman was destined to be short - that and the fraught atmosphere between Rosie and Chuck. Chuck was constantly antagonising his sister by reminding her that the restaurant's boost in popularity would be short-lived, and that no matter how well they did, he was still going to close it and sell up.

"This place is my inheritance, and I intend to cash in on it," Chuck said loftily one day as he strode between the tables. "I don't care how well it's doing; soon as Dad pops his clogs, I'm selling up and heading for Sydney."

"When Dad 'pops his clogs'?" Rosie repeated incredulously, her eyes flashing a mixture of anger and hurt. "You insensitive monster. That is your own father you are talking about. You are like a vulture, perched waiting for him to die so you can swoop down and pick over his bones. You disgust me."

"I love you too, sis. But don't worry, soon as I've got the money in my pocket, you won't see my arse for dust." He turned to Michael, mockingly. "And I don't know why you're so pleased with yourself, posh boy, there's no future for you here, either. No matter how good you are or how many customers you pull in, the restaurant is going to be sold, and you'll be out on your ear. I've been talking to George Price. He is interested in buying the place, and he don't need no posh Pome chef, so you'll be history."

"The restaurant isn't yours to sell," Rosie snapped angrily, tears beginning to well in her eyes.

"It will be," he assured her. "As the eldest, I'll have a fifty-one per cent say in the running of it. That's the terms of Dad's will. If I say we sell up, then we sell up. There's nothing you can do about it."

"This place is Dad's life. How can you talk that way with him so ill? Have you no feelings?"

Michael felt his anger rising at the sight of Rosie's distress. It offended his sense of decency to hear a woman being spoken to so cruelly, especially by her own brother. But she was of strong character and wouldn't have wanted him to intervene. It was a family matter.

Chuck sneered. "You may love the old bugger; I don't. He's never done anything for me."

"You absolute pig," she flared, anger finally winning the conflict in her eyes. She moved menacingly towards him and Chuck turned to make a quick exit, laughing as he went.

"Don't upset yourself, Rosie, he isn't worth it," Michael consoled her quietly.

"I know he isn't, but it still gets to me. How can anyone be so insensitive?" she seethed. "The annoying part is that he's right. No matter how well we do, it isn't going to last, not for either of us. I don't suppose you're too worried. With your talent, you can go and earn big money in the city - any city. You're far too good for a small town like this. I'm still puzzled as to why you came out here in the bush in the first place. I'm even more puzzled why you stay, knowing how things are."

She put her hands to her head. "Sorry, I shouldn't pry into your private life. I don't mean to. I'm just fishing for a word of reassurance that you are not going to shoot through and leave me in the lurch. The whole thing would fall apart again without you, Michael. Please tell me you will be staying, at least for a little while?"

Michael assured her that he had no plans to leave. He noticed the tremble in her voice as she whispered "for a little while". Plainly, she did not expect her father to be around much longer, so perhaps Michael's stay here would be even shorter than he anticipated.

Rosie remained upset and irritable all afternoon, but as soon as the restaurant opened, her mood changed, and she was once more the happy, jovial host. During quiet moments, he would often stand by the door and watch admiringly at the way she worked the dining room. Darting from customer to customer, sharing a greeting and a smile. He had to admit, she really was very good at her job.

As the business increased, she hired two young girls - one to help her wait on tables, the other to do the washing up. Michael was conscious of the fact that she went to great lengths to impress on both girls that their positions were only temporary. Again, Michael was reminded that his stay here in Norseman was to be a short one. The knowledge saddened him, for he was starting to like the place, and the friendly, appreciative customers. He would miss Rosie's company, too. After an uncertain start, they were working and getting on well together. She had a certain earthy charm and directness about her that he liked. And even that ginger-blonde hair was becoming acceptable.

One evening, when the restaurant was especially full, Rosie brought Curley down and sat him behind the counter to savour the atmosphere. The old man positively glowed with pride as he watched his restaurant swell with customers.

"This is just like the old days," he reminisced fondly. "I don't think even your mother used to pack them in like this. I'm so proud of you, Rosie, my girl. And this Michael of yours, he must be something special."

"He is, very special. But he's not *my* Michael," Rosie assured him. "Not in that way."

Curley chuckled. "Nonsense, I've seen the way you look at him, Rosie. You can't fool your old dad."

"It's not like that - don't get any ideas," she insisted, and then whirled away between the tables.

Curley did not stay long in the restaurant. All the hustle of business and the backchat with old friends and well-wishers soon tired him out. He retreated through to the relative quiet of the kitchen, where he sat on the barstool and fought for breath.

"You've done wonders here, Michael," he wheezed eventually. "I had my doubts about you at first, but you've come up trumps and no mistake. My Rosie thinks the world of you."

"I'm sure our success is mostly down to Rosie," Michael said with uncharacteristic modesty. "She's the attraction. She exudes a warmth and vitality that creates the restaurant's friendly ambiance. That's the secret of our success. The meals are secondary."

"She is a great girl," agreed Curley. "But it's teamwork that does it. You two make a great team, just like me and her mother, God rest her soul." He wheezed some more, then popped a little white pill into his mouth.

"Norseman is due to expand," he predicted after a short silence, while he caught his breath. "When they eventually put a sealed road across the Nullarbor to South Australia, all the interstate traffic will pass through Norseman. This is going to be a real boomtown. And Rosie's Restaurant will become an absolute goldmine - you mark my words. As a team, the pair of you could make a fortune here."

Michael made no comment. Obviously Curley was unaware of his son's plans to sell up and blow the proceeds. Rosie was right - the knowledge would devastate him.

Curley slid off his stool and turned to go. "She's a wonderful girl, my Rosie," he wheezed again. "You take good care of her, Michael."

That evening was to mark the height of the restaurant's success. Two days later, Curley had another heart attack and passed away. Rosie was weepy, but took his passing calmly.

"It's not as though it's a shock," she said bravely. "I'm so glad I brought him down here on Wednesday night, so he could see his restaurant thriving for one last time. He looked so proud. At least I was able to make his last few days happy ones. Thank you, Michael - for staying and, well... for everything. He was a good man. And, in spite of what Chuck might say, he was a good father, too."

As the tears started to flow, Michael put an arm round her shoulders, but couldn't find any words that might comfort her. Eventually, she pulled away and dabbed her eyes.

"What will you do now?" he asked.

She shook her head. "This is it, I'm afraid. I'm not opening the restaurant anymore. I couldn't face it, and there's not really much point. I was only keeping it going for Dad. Now he's gone, Chuck will be hell-bent on selling up, so let him. It's been great working with you, Michael. I'm sorry, but this is it, I'm afraid. Where will you go now?"

He shrugged and went to the stove where he began tidying away utensils. "Move on to Adelaide, probably. They tell me it's a lovely city, and there are many top-class restaurants and hotels there."

"I suppose I'll have to go back to city life, too, and boring old accounts. But I can't think about any of that yet."

"You would be wasted in an office," he told her. "You should go into restaurant management. You're a natural. You could have a very successful career."

"I don't think it's for me," she said shaking her head. "Serving in your own place as your own boss, and amongst customers you know, is one thing, but working for someone else as little more than a skivvy, and having to put up with a load of snobby customers, is quite another." She gave a thin smile. "I'm too outspoken. I'd tell them where to go."

Michael nodded his understanding. He knew a thing or two about complaining customers.

So, this was it. Yet another chapter in his life had closed, and on the all-too-familiar note of: "Thanks a lot, Michael, and goodbye". Again, it seemed that having served his purpose he was being cast aside. Of course, he and Rosie had not had an affair, and as there had never been any commitment between them, he had no right to expect anything else. But now that they were about to part, he realised he had become very fond of Rosie. He would miss her.

But right now, there were far more important matters on Michael's mind than Rosie. His stay in Norseman may have been short, but it had proved to be a life-changing one. He had seen the future and he now knew where he was heading in life. He'd had a taste of working in his own kitchen, as his own boss, and he liked it. He had developed a burning ambition to own his own restaurant; one with that intimate, small-town atmosphere where the diners were not just customers, but, as Rosie put it, more like a circle of friends; friends who would appreciate his talents, and compliment him on his success.

So, although he would be leaving Norseman with a little sadness, he would also be leaving with a new sense of purpose in life, and with a burning ambition to succeed as a restaurateur.

Michael went to his room and began to pack a few things in preparation for his departure. Later, he went along to the pub to say his farewells to Norman, the landlord, and a few of the regulars he knew would be there.

Chuck was there, sitting on a stool at the bar with two of his cronies. Irritatingly, he seemed in high spirits. He smirked as Michael walked in, then leaned towards his friends and made some remark which they all found amusing. Michael assumed it was yet another of Chuck's limp-wrist remarks, made at his expense.

Michael strode over to them. "What kind of a man is it that celebrates his own father's death?" he demanded in disgust. He spoke loudly so that everyone heard. The bar fell silent.

Chuck's mouth gaped open for a moment, then he fired back, "Well what kind of a man is it that pokes another man up the bum?" He laughed brashly, expecting everyone to laugh with him, but the bar remained silent.

Michael took a step forward and swung a hard right that caught Chuck full in the face, knocking him clean off his stool.

"Good on you, Michael. He's had that coming for some time," called one of the regulars. Others muttered approvingly.

Ever the perfect gentleman, Michael turned to the landlord. "I do apologise for that, Norman. I'm not a violent man by nature, but that was something I needed to do."

"Not a problem, Michael," said Norman. He placed a glass of red wine on the bar. "This one's on the house. We'll all miss you. And - just for the record - none of us believe it anyway."

Michael didn't stay long at the pub, as he knew he had a long journey ahead of him. He estimated it would take two or three days of hard driving to cross the desert and get to Adelaide. It made him appreciate just how vast a country Australia was compared to Britain. He did most of his packing ready for an early start the next morning, then retired, hoping for a good night's sleep.

But his mind remained active, thinking of his future, his restaurant and his newfound ambition. He had heard that Adelaide was a very beautiful city, with many fine hotels and restaurants. People had told him it was the most English of all the Australian cities; therefore, it followed that it would also be the most cultured. The people there would appreciate good living and fine cuisine. Adelaide would be the ideal city for him, and his new venture.

He had barely drifted off to sleep when he was disturbed by a tap at the door. He rolled over and switched on the bedside lamp. It was still only 11:30.

There was another tap at the door. On opening it, he was surprised to find Rosie standing there in a loose-fitting dressing gown.

"Can I come in, Michael?" she asked quietly. "I don't want to be alone - not tonight. Just hold me."

He did, and after a while they rolled into bed and he continued to hold her. He felt the firmness of her body pressing against his. He wanted her, and realised he had wanted her almost since the day they had met. He was reluctant to make the first move now, sensing that any advance would be a disaster if all she was looking for was comfort and reassurance in her grief. She slept in his arms, and it was not till they woke, in the early hours of the morning, that they made love.

"Are you going to handle the funeral all right?" he asked at breakfast. "What I mean is, do you need me there for support?"

"The funeral will be fine, I can handle that." She leaned over and placed her hand on his. "But I *do* need you, Michael. I know I come across as brash and over-confident at times – trappy, even. But it's all a front. I'm not good on my own. Wherever you are going, I want to be with you."

"You and me – as a couple?" Michael said in mild surprise. "I think that's a splendid idea," he stammered.

"A splendid idea," she mimicked. "Said with all the enthusiasm of the very stiff-upper-lipped English gentleman," she teased. "Thankfully, you are a lot more passionate in bed."

She leaned back in her chair. "There I go again. I'm being too pushy, aren't I? I'm assuming that you want us to be together as a couple, and I shouldn't. You have your own plans, and they probably don't include me. Look, if you do want us to be together, you go to Adelaide and find us somewhere to live - a flat or something. I'll follow on when I've tied up all the loose ends here. If you decide you don't want to be tied down to this coarse, unrefined, bush-town girl, you can simply keep going - shoot through, as we Aussies say."

He looked up with a start. "Run out on you? I wouldn't do that, Rosie. What kind of a cad do you take me for? No, I want us to be together, I really do," he reassured her. "But if you are sure you are going to be all right here on your own, then I'll drive to Adelaide and find us somewhere to live - a little love nest," he smiled.

Michael drove out of Norseman with a sense of unease, knowing this was not how it should be. He and Rosie should be leaving together. He had told her so, but she had insisted, and said that being apart for a few days would give him time to think about it, and be sure that being with her was what he really wanted.

When he had arrived in Norseman, he had hated the town. But the people had been warm and welcoming, and had accepted him into their community. He had loved the intimate atmosphere of the restaurant, too, and knew that this was where his future lay. With a restaurant of his own, and with Rosie by his side, life would be perfect.

When he had told her of his ambitions, she had been full of enthusiasm for the idea, and said that owning her own restaurant had always been her ambition, too.

"We can make it happen, Michael. We will. We can both earn good money in the city. I'll have some cash coming from the sale of the restaurant. We'll work and save hard for a couple of years till we have enough to open our own place."

To Michael, the future looked bright and exciting. He not only had a burning ambition to pursue, but he had also found a wonderful girl to share that ambition with; a soul mate who understood his passion. Yet, even with the outskirts of town shrinking in his rearview mirror, he began to have doubts. He had been let down so often. Why had Rosie insisted on them parting – was she having second thoughts?

As the miles slipped away, his discomfort turned to apprehension and then to real concern. Would Rosie really follow him to Adelaide, or would it be a case of 'out of sight, out of mind'? Was he heading for yet another big disappointment in his love life? As the distance from Norseman grew, so did his belief that it was all going to go wrong. He was going to be dumped, yet again.

He looked remorsefully into his mirror, but the outskirts of town had long since disappeared from view. Should he turn around and drive back? No, what would be the point, just to suffer the humiliation of being rejected face-to-face?

Still gazing forlornly into his mirror, in the distance, he could see a car, a mere speck that appeared to be travelling very fast. It grew quickly in the mirror; its lights flashing.

Damn lunatic, he thought and moved over onto the hard shoulder to let it pass. It flew by with a blast of its horn, and screeched to a stop ahead of him. Suddenly, he recognised it - it was Rosie's Holden. She jumped out, waving frantically for him to stop.

"It's ours! It's ours!" she shouted excitedly, running towards him and throwing her arms around his neck. "Mr Preston, the solicitor, came to see me. Dad changed his will. He's left it all to me. By law, Mr Preston shouldn't have said anything, of course, not till the reading. But he's a friend, and, well, we tend not to bother too much about petty points of law in bush towns. Dad has left the restaurant to me! Chuck doesn't get a thing. We have our own restaurant, Michael, isn't that wonderful? It's all ours, and, between us, we are going to make it the best restaurant in Western Australia."

CHAPTER TWENTY-ONE

Tom was thankful for his job at the timber yard. It kept him busy and, more importantly, kept him away from the hostel and Edna's foul moods and cutting remarks.

Clive had been generous in allowing him time off for job hunting, and, in gratitude, Tom had worked hard. He soon had the yard looking tidy, with all the lengths of timber stacked neatly in their appropriate racks, and the pathways between the racks all swept and clear of rubbish.

After two of Clive's regular workforce returned, Tom often found himself at a loose end, with nothing much to do. He kept himself busy by sweeping out the office and emptying the waste paper baskets.

"Still no luck on the job front?" asked Clive, looking up over the top of his spectacles from a mountain of paperwork.

"Nothing yet," said Tom. "But something is bound to come up soon - it has to. The boys are mad keen for us to settle here, and I truly believe there is a better future for them in Australia."

"There has got to be something around for a willing worker like you. I'd love to keep you on here - you're doing a great job, but as you can see, there isn't much for you to do now. To be honest, there's not even enough to keep you busy for the rest of this week."

Tom nodded. "I understand. I'll finish today if you like, Clive. You've been more than generous, and I don't want you paying me for sitting around."

"No, no! I didn't mean it that way, Tom. You're all right till Jack gets back." He sucked on the end of his pen and thought for a moment. "I'll tell you what, though. Would you mind doing me a big favour? I've got a huge garden at home, and I haven't had time to cut the lawn for weeks. It sounds a bit of a liberty, but if I drive you over there, would you mind running the mower over it for me?"

"No trouble at all," said Tom. "I quite enjoy a spot of gardening."

As Clive had said, his garden was huge, but the grassed area was not overly big. Tom strode up and down behind the mower, enjoying the sunshine and allowing himself to dream that one day he might own a property like this himself. Depressingly, the thought brought him back to the present, his dubious future, his quest for permanent employment - and his rift with Edna.

Having finished the lawn, and with time on his hands, he took a hoe from the tool shed and started to weed the flowerbeds. In the garden next door, an elderly gentleman had dragged a mower from his garage and was pulling hard on the starting cord, trying to get it going. He was a tall, upright man, wearing a khaki shirt and shorts. Tom had to smile at the sight of his iconic headgear - a wide brimmed hat with attached corks dangling in front of his eyes. Tom had only seen such hats in cartoons and, until now, had not believed that Australians actually wore them.

After a few pulls on the cord, the mower had not started, and the old man was blowing hard with the exertion as he leaned against the garage.

"Are you all right there?" Tom called over to him. "Would you like me to give you a hand with that?"

"That's very neighbourly of you, young man."

Tom chuckled. "It's a long time since I've been called that. Every time I apply for a job, they tell me I'm too old."

"Well, to me, you're only a youngster. I'm eighty-six, you know," the man said proudly. "This is too much for me now. I can't even get the thing started."

"You look in great shape," Tom assured him. "Don't worry, I can do the grass for you. I've got an hour to spare before Clive picks me up, and I'm sure he won't mind me helping his neighbour out."

"Just call me Pop, everyone does," said the old man. "My grandson used to cut the grass for me, but he's gone off to Kalgoorlie to work in the mines. He used to cut a lot of people's lawns around here. He had quite a nice little business going. Silly young fool - if he had stuck at it, he could have made far more money than they're paying him in the mines. But youngsters never listen.

"Then the ute broke down and he said it was going to cost too much to fix, so he gave it all up and went to Kalgoorlie. Youngsters are like that - no patience, everything on the spur of the moment. Now I'm stuck with a ute that doesn't run, and nobody to cut the grass." He sat down on a patio chair and smiled philosophically. "Perhaps it's as well, I'm too old to drive it anyway."

"He actually made a liveable wage from cutting grass, then?" queried Tom, a little surprised.

"He certainly did. More money than I ever made when I was at work. Mind you, that's a long time ago now." He chuckled. "The war was still on the last time I received a wage packet."

Tom's interest had been piqued at the intriguing possibility of someone making a living from cutting grass; he thought deeply on the matter as he strode up and down behind Pop's mower. He was in desperate need of a job, and this sounded like something he could do. The only stumbling block was the capital to buy equipment: a mower, and a ute to transport it around in. That would mean investing most of their savings on the venture. It would be a gamble. And that, of course, ruled the whole thing out immediately. He could only imagine what Edna would have to say about gambling away their savings.

When he had finished the grass, he sat at the patio table, sipping the cold drink Pop had prepared, and questioned the old man further about his grandson's venture.

"If you are really interested, the ute is there," said Pop. "If you can get it going, it's yours. It's only scrap; no use to me." His face creased into a wily smile. "You can pay me for it by cutting my grass once a week," he suggested. "And by popping over for a chat now and then. I don't get much company these days."

"It's a tempting offer," said Tom. But, in his heart, he knew the idea was a complete non-starter. Even with getting the ute for nothing, it still needed to be repaired, and then taxed and insured. No, it was a silly idea - it would never work.

Pop stood up and disappeared into the house. He re-emerged a few moments later holding a folder from which he drew out an exercise book and handed it to Tom. "This is a list of Ryan's customers. He's even put down how much he used to charge them. Of course, it's over a month now since he shot through, so many of his customers will have made new arrangements by now. But the real bad news is the ute." He handed Tom a written estimate from a local garage. "The water pump needs replacing, and the head gasket has blown. That means the whole engine has to be stripped down. They're estimating over a hundred pounds to fix it. To be honest with you, that's more than it's worth."

Tom pursed his lips as he studied the repair bill. "It's a lot of money," he agreed. "Too much."

For a brief moment, he had allowed himself to dream of an idyllic lifestyle - being his own boss, strolling up and down behind a mower in brilliant sunshine, doing a little weeding and pruning. It would have been absolute heaven compared to returning to the foundry. But obviously, it could never be. It would mean spending most of their savings, and there was no guarantee that the customers would still be there. It was all far too risky.

Anyway, Edna would never sanction spending money on what she would consider to be an insane idea. She would have a fit at the very thought. What money they did have, she had already earmarked for getting the family home to England, when he had 'come to his senses' as she put it.

Knowing what Edna's reaction would be, he didn't even bother to mention the idea to her. They were barely on speaking terms at the moment, and this was definitely not something they could have discussed rationally.

As something to talk about, that evening after dinner, he did mention it to John. He immediately wished that he had not. He should have realised that any idea, however insane, that had the remotest chance of keeping them all in Australia would be met with unbridled enthusiasm by his eldest son - enthusiasm that Tom would then have to cruelly crush.

"That's a really fantastic idea, Dad. Remember all the pocket money I used to make back home by going round trimming privets?"

"Pocket money is one thing, son, earning a regular, full-time wage is another," Tom replied soberly. "And there's the money it would cost to set up - over a hundred pounds just to get the ute repaired. No, forget I ever mentioned it."

"But you would be earning. Perhaps the garage would let you pay the bill off weekly. They do that a lot out here. And I'm earning a wage, I could help."

"No, John. It's never a good idea to get yourself into debt," Tom said, trying hard to make the statement sound positive and businesslike, and hoping John would not think he was taking a defeatist attitude.

"It must be worth looking into the possibilities, though" John persisted eagerly. "What if we called on all the customers in the book, and find out how many still want their lawns cutting? We would know for sure then whether or not it was a viable proposition."

Tom had no intention of getting himself into debt, with or without Edna's blessing, so he really didn't see much point in pursuing the matter. But he had no wish to completely kill off John's enthusiasm, either - or have him think his father was a quitter. So, somewhat reluctantly, he agreed, and on Saturday morning they set out for the suburb of Inglewood where Pop lived.

"There are loads of customers here, Dad. And look how much he was charging them. There's easily a week's wages here," John said enthusiastically, on opening the exercise book.

"But most of them have probably found someone else to cut their grass by now, it's been weeks," cautioned Tom.

John was not to be deterred. "We can find more customers. Everyone has got lawns," he insisted.

They split the book and set off in different directions. The roads were long, and the customers were well spread out. Tom was surprised to find that some fifty per cent of the customers were still interested in the service.

John was having similar results, and by knocking at houses with unkempt lawns, had even managed to find three new customers.

At John's next call, the front lawn was again long and unkempt. An old Morris sat in the drive. It looked vaguely familiar, but he didn't take too much notice of it, being more interested in the height of the lawn.

The door swung open and John was momentarily stuck for words at seeing Geoff Patterson standing there.

"Well... hello, John. This is an unexpected surprise. What can we do for you?"

"Geoff! I haven't come to see you... well, what I mean is, I didn't know you lived here."

"I don't," smiled Geoff. "The Harveys do. We're all out in the back garden, come on through."

Geoff had become a regular visitor to the Harveys' place, ostensibly to check up on how Gloria was coping, but the real purpose of his visits was of course to see Susan.

Ted was reclining on a sun lounger, wearing only a pair of shorts, exposing his now well-tanned body and limbs to the sun, and looking every bit a born and bred Australian; an image far removed from the pale shopkeeper who had left England only a few months earlier.

"That sounds like a solid business idea to me," Ted said, when John had explained his mission. "Most businesses go through periods of rise and fall in demand, but grass is always growing." He spread his arms in an expression of abundance. "Especially here in sunny Western Australia. It's summer all year round here. I'd say you're onto a real winner there. Tell Tom I'll be his first new customer. He is more than welcome to have a go at this lot."

"That repair bill sounds a bit steep, though," said Geoff. "Tell your dad I can get him the parts at trade prices. That would shrink it a bit."

"Can you really?" John asked eagerly. "That would be great."

Susan leaned forward. "If you ask nicely, he might even find time to fit them for you," she suggested.

"That's an even better idea," agreed Geoff. "Tell you what, I'll drive you back there now and take a look at it. See what it really needs."

Susan sprang to her feet. "I'll come with you, it will be nice to see Tom again."

Tom had already returned and was sitting at the patio table chatting to Pop when they pulled into the drive.

"Geoff is going to have a look at the ute for us, Dad," John called to him excitedly as he sprang from the car. "He can get all the parts at trade prices. And he might even find time to fit them for us."

Tom handed Geoff the garage report. "I fear it could be beyond redemption," he said apologetically. "But it's good of you to take a look. The water pump and the head gasket have gone. The head gasket is the main concern, as it's quite a big strip-down job I understand. The garage are saying that could lead to other issues - a decoke; valve seats to be reground. And if water has made its way into the engine oil, well... " Tom's voice trailed away in despondency. "It's good of you to offer, Geoff, but I fear it's something of a lost cause."

"Well, now I'm here, I may as well take a look at her."

Whilst Geoff opened the bonnet, Tom wandered back to the patio where Pop, delighted at having so much company, was setting out cold drinks for them all.

Geoff soon had the engine running. It emitted an uneven clatter, accompanied by a high-pitched screech.

Susan brought him a glass of squash and leaned into the engine compartment with him. "Can you perform miracles?" she shouted above the din. "That sounds as though it needs one."

"Engines I can fix," he said with a wry smile. "Other things I'm apparently not so good at."

When he had finished and switched the engine off, Tom came over looking glum. "That sounded terrible," he said shaking his head. "What's the verdict? Is it terminal?"

"It's not that bad, actually," smiled Geoff. "The screeching noise was the water pump. That's shot, right enough. Other than that all it needs is a good service and tune-up - plugs and points etcetra. It's a bit of a rust bucket, as you can see, but it will do the job you want it for."

"What about the head gasket?"

Geoff wiped the grease from his hands. "The good news is, there's nothing wrong with it. No water getting into the oil, and there's good compression on all cylinders. The engine sounds a lot worse than it is. A new pump and a service and we'll have it running like a top."

Tom raised his eyebrows. "So how much would it cost to fix, then?"

"A reconditioned pump isn't expensive, not through the trade. With the other bits and pieces, twenty quid should cover it."

"Twenty pounds!" exclaimed John, unable to contain his elation. "Is that all it needs? I've got twenty pounds. I'll pay for it, Dad."

"And what about the labour costs?" Tom asked cautiously.

"Call it a favour, to get you up and running," said Geoff. "I can get the parts and do it next weekend, if you decide to go ahead."

"I can't let you do it for nothing," Tom said shaking his head stubbornly.

"Well, if you insist, buy me a beer sometime. But don't tell Joan. I'm supposed to be on the wagon."

Susan prodded him in the ribs. "Don't make Mum out to be an ogre - and you are not on the wagon."

"We can do it then, can't we, Dad? It means you'll have a job, and we can stay here in Australia, can't we?" John pressed, hardly able to contain his excitement.

"I think it may well be a possibility," Tom agreed cautiously. Then his expression dropped. "But I'll still have to buy a mower. They're expensive. And then, of course, I'll have to square it with your mother. As you know, she still wants us all to return home to England."

"That was very nice of you, offering to do the job for free," said Susan, when Tom and John had rejoined Pop on the patio to discuss the ute.

"I'm a very nice guy, hadn't you noticed?" smiled Geoff, as he ducked back under the bonnet.

"Don't be so smug. And, if you recall, I came to that conclusion a long time ago. It was you who chose not to notice," she said pointedly.

"So... I'm a little slow on the uptake, but I'm still a nice guy."

"I think so." She leaned on his shoulder as he bent over the engine. "And now that you are finally taking notice?" she asked.

"And now what?"

"When are you finally going to get around to asking me out, of course?"

He straightened from the engine compartment. "I thought that you and Paul were... "

"Oh, I finished with him a couple of weeks ago," she smiled teasingly.

"And you've been stringing me along ever since?"

"Why shouldn't I? You made me wait long enough." She reached up and kissed him, then pulled away. "I'm assuming you have finished with all that partying, and sewing of wild oats?"

"Hell, yes. Your mother would skin me alive if she thought I hadn't."

"Just so there is no misunderstanding, it's not Mother you have to worry about," she cautioned with an impish smile.

Tom made his way back to the hostel, happy at how things had gone and hopeful for the future, but still a little anxious. Since the day of the Harveys' party, he and Edna had been at loggerheads. At every opportunity, she would deride his sudden change of heart as stupid and inconsiderate, and fire all his own previous criticisms of Australia and its lagging industry back at him with caustic sarcasm.

It had been a far from easy time for Tom. And now he had to confront Edna with the news that he intended to spend a good part of their savings on a lawn mower and a broken-down ute.

A few weeks earlier, he would doubtless have dreaded the encounter, and having to confess to deciding anything so rash without even consulting her. He had always been a placid, easygoing man, and had striven to avoid domestic friction when at all possible - usually by letting Edna have her own way. But he was nobody's doormat, and having finally made a stand, he was discovering that he, too, could be stubborn.

Remaining resolute was made much easier by the fact that, for the first time in their twenty-year marriage, he was genuinely angry with Edna. She was a strong-minded woman who could always be relied upon in times of hardship or crisis. Exactly the kind of wife a man would need by his side while building a new life for himself and his family in a foreign land - that was why he loved her. But just when he needed her support and strength of character the most, she had not only withdrawn it, but had turned it against him.

Her reaction to his plans was all too predictable.

"Now I have heard it all!" she blazed, her hands planted firmly on her hips; a dark scowl on her face. "You can't find a proper job, so now you want to run around cutting other people's grass; begging them for work, like some overgrown Boy Scout on bob-a-job week. This time you really have taken leave of your senses." She was pacing the room and becoming ever more agitated that her judgement and wishes were being disregarded.

"It will pay a full-time wage. That's all that matters," Tom reasoned, lowering himself into the armchair, whilst trying to remain calm.

"There is no regular wage packet. The money is not reliable. You won't know from one week to the next if you are going to earn anything at all. How can you build a future without job security, and a guaranteed wage?"

"Grass will always be growing. There's nothing more reliable or secure than that."

"Don't be flippant with me. You are a tradesman, not an odd-job man. Where is your pride?" she blazed.

"It has nothing to do with pride. I just want to make a living and support my family," Tom said evenly. "And I want to make that living here. It's what I want, and it's what the boys want. We are going to stay in Australia and make an honest attempt at settling here, just like we planned when we left England."

Edna bristled with indignation. "Don't you tell me what I'm going to do. I hate it here and I'm going home. You stay if you've a mind to. I'll borrow the money from Ben and take the boys home with me. They'll be far better off in England."

"You will do no such thing," Tom said springing to his feet. He was aware that he was losing his composure now, and raising his voice. The exchange was becoming far too heated, but he couldn't check the momentum. "The boys do not want to go, and you will not force them," he asserted. "John is an adult now, capable of making his own decisions. He's signed apprenticeship papers. He has his future mapped out. He wants to stay here."

"He won't want to stay here if it means splitting up the family," countered Edna. "But if he insists, he can. I'll go home, and take Kenny with me."

"No way!" Tom asserted even more forcibly. "Not while I'm still drawing breath will you take that child back to England. Have you taken a good look at him lately? Well, have you? Or have you been so wrapped up in your own petty little likes and dislikes that you've been blind to all else around you? That boy is a picture of health compared to what he was when we left England. There is absolutely no way I will allow you to take him back. Over my dead body. The boys are staying here with me."

Edna was stunned by the ferocity of his words. Tom took advantage of her shocked silence to storm out, knowing that things had become far too heated. Never in all their years of marriage had they ever had a bust-up like this.

He left the hostel and walked aimlessly around the streets of the local neighbourhood, trying to clear his head and analyse what was happening to them. Could it really be that after such a long, happy and contented marriage they had really reached an impasse, facing separation, and probable divorce?

They had met, courted and married during the darkest days of the war, when times were hard and futures were uncertain. Edna had been a tower of strength during those troubled times, not only to Tom but to the whole family, and many elderly neighbours, too. She had managed the finances frugally and conjured up filling meals, seemingly from nothing, when ration books and larders were empty. And when Tom's own mother had fallen ill, it was Edna who, without hesitation or complaint, had nursed her to the end. She was a wonderful wife and mother, and he loved her dearly.

He had gone too far, said things he now regretted. He should go back and apologise, he knew he should. If it were just about the two of them, he would doubtless have rushed to do so, as he always did - not because he was weak, but because he loved her and could not bear to see her unhappy or upset. But it was no longer just about the two of them; it was about the boys and their futures. And Tom was not about to let his sons down. Edna was clearly in the wrong; this time she must be the one to compromise.

But he knew she would not. After all those years, and all the struggles and hardships they had been through together, this was the end. Their marriage was over.

When, after much aimless wandering and much soul-searching, he eventually returned to the hostel and trudged wearily up the drive, he made for John's chalet. He must try to explain the situation, and prepare his sons for the family's impending break-up. John was a mature lad; he would understand and take it in his stride. But what of little Kenny? The break-up would devastate him. Perhaps he would choose to stay with his mother and return home to England. Tom prayed that he would not.

John was not in his room, and rather than return to his own chalet, and his row with Edna, Tom picked up a magazine and sat down to flick through its pages. He had no interest in the magazine and his attention soon began to drift around the room. A letter fluttered from the pages of the magazine. Tom retrieved it from the floor and tucked it back between the pages. But not before his eye had caught the sender's name and address: Peter Taylor, c/o- Post Office, Coolgardie. Deep in the darkness of his own thoughts, it took Tom a long moment to appreciate the significance of that address, and the fact that John knew where Peter was in hiding.

Eventually, he turned back to the letter and started to read. Apparently, Peter had returned some money he had borrowed and wanted John to write back telling him how things stood regarding him and Louise.

Tom replaced the letter, and continued flicking distractedly through the magazine, not sure what, if anything, he should do about the information. It was really none of his business. But perhaps he should tell Stan and let him decide whether or not he wanted his son found and brought back. The Taylors had their own problems right now, and they had a right to know.

"Damn it!" Tom slapped the magazine down angrily. This was one more problem he did not want to have to wrestle with. One more tricky decision he had to make. His head was beginning to spin with problems. Why did John have to get involved? He stood up angrily, and went out in search of his son.

He met him as he made his way between the chalets, on his way to the reception hall.

"Hi, Dad. Have you spoken with Mum about the ute?" John asked tentatively.

"Never mind that. How long have you had Peter Taylor's address?" Tom demanded without preamble.

John stopped in his tracks. "How did you...?"

"His letter fell out of the magazine. I couldn't help but see it."

"I only received the one, about three weeks ago. Peter wanted to know how things stood here. I told him to stay where he was for now, and I would let him know when it was safe to come back. I wasn't sure whether to tell you or not. Peter wrote to me in confidence. He trusted me. It wouldn't be right to betray a trust, would it?"

Tom sighed and rubbed his forehead. "Normally, no, but there's more to it than that. His parents are worried about him. They want to know where he is."

"I guess so, but he wrote to them. They know he is all right."

"That's not the point. They want to know where he is and what he is doing. Besides, as you know, the Taylors are planning to return to England shortly, and they will want everything straightened out before they leave."

"You think we should tell them, then?"

"I think they have a right to know. I'll have a word with Stan and let him decide what to do. We won't mention it to anyone else."

They made their way back to John's chalet, unaware that their conversation had been held outside Mrs Hollins's chalet, and that their intentions of keeping the information a secret had, therefore, already been thwarted.

Mrs Hollins had stood behind her door with baited breath, her ears straining in anticipation of learning Peter's whereabouts. To her dismay, she learned only that John knew where he was; even this, however, she considered to be a prized gem of information and hurried out immediately to capitalise on it.

A group of women stood huddled outside the laundry block; Mrs Hollins noticed with glee that Mary Tate was amongst them. She joined the group unobtrusively, not wanting it to appear as though she was running around for the specific purpose of spreading gossip. She had soon skilfully steered the conversation round to Louise and the hunt for the missing Taylor boy.

"Of course, there are some that have known where he is hiding all along," she said casually, almost as though this was common knowledge, something they should all know by now.

"It's the first I've heard of it," said Mary. "Even the police can't trace him."

It was the first the other women had heard of it too. They fell silent; hanging on Mrs Hollins's every word. She teased them along expertly, revelling in being the centre of their curiosity, and the power of possessing knowledge that they did not.

"I hear the police are even searching interstate for him," one woman offered in an attempt to coax more snippets of information from her.

"They probably are, if they are looking at all," she agreed offhandedly, wishing more than ever that she was able to dangle Peter's exact whereabouts before them.

Two of Mrs Hollins's cronies emerged from the laundry block; she beckoned them with an almost imperceptible nod of the head and they sidled over to join the huddle.

"If anyone is withholding information about Peter Taylor, the police should be told who they are," said Mary, suddenly tiring of probing game that Mrs Hollins was forcing them all to play. "And as it is my daughter who has been wronged, I'd be obliged for their names."

"Well, I don't know as I should say, really," said Mrs Hollins, determined to hold her audience in suspense to the very last. "But I suppose you of all people have a right to know, Mary. Mind you, I can't say how I came by the information," she added quickly; after all, she didn't want to appear an eavesdropper. "Well, the Taylors themselves know, naturally," she continued tantalisingly, thinking she was safe in the assumption that they knew by now anyway. "And I've reason to believe that the Henshaws know where he is, too."

"The Henshaws! Really, how on earth did they become involved?" the women quizzed her, eager to learn every last detail.

"Are you absolutely certain about this?" Mary asked curtly.

"I never say anything I am not perfectly sure of, Mary," she replied with just the right amount of indignation. "He's been corresponding with John Henshaw. I know that for a fact."

"Are you going to inform the police, Mary?" one woman probed thirstily.

"I would if I were you," said another. "It's high time that little louse was brought to justice. It's not as though he hasn't been given every chance to do the right thing and face up to his responsibilities."

"And what he's done to Louise can't ever be put right."

"Nor punished enough," Mary added vindictively. "I most certainly will be informing the police."

"You mean you're going to be pressing charges against him?" Mrs Hollins urged, her sharp little eyes alive with the prospect of a juicy scandal.

"We have been giving it very serious consideration."

The women were about to disperse to spread their newly-acquired knowledge when Edna walked by and began collecting her washing from the line. The women stopped and waited expectantly, placing Mary in the uncomfortable position of having to confront her or lose face.

"I'd like a quiet word with you, if you don't mind, Edna," she said in an even tone.

The edge to her voice made Edna bristle. She hadn't any more time for Mary Tate than she had for Mrs Hollins. And, after her row with Tom, she was in no mood for pleasantries.

"Well, go right ahead," she said, her voice as cutting as Mary's.

"I understand that you know the whereabouts of Peter Taylor. Is this true?"

Edna looked at her in blank amazement. "*I* know where he is? How on earth would I know that? I'm afraid you have been listening to idle gossip, Mary."

The women murmured amongst themselves, then glanced towards Mrs Hollins. Edna looked at her, too. "I might have known you'd have your nose stuck in this somewhere," she said accusingly.

"And what exactly do you mean by that?" Mrs Hollins said insolently, confident she was holding all the trump cards.

"Exactly what I say. You are always meddling in things that don't concern you; spreading malicious lies and gossip."

"Am I to take it that you deny knowing his whereabouts?" cut in Mary.

"I most certainly do deny it," replied Edna.

"Both your husband and your son know where he is," Mrs Hollins asserted airily. "I'll swear to that on the Hholy Bible if necessary. Your son has been receiving letters from him. What have you got to say to that?"

Edna folded her arms defiantly. "I have nothing at all to say to you, Mrs Hollins, except that you should mind your own business. If my son has heard from Peter Taylor, which I doubt, I see no reason for him to disclose that fact. There are such things as loyalty to friends, and knowing when to keep your mouth shut - something you really should try."

"It doesn't say very much for your son's choice of friends," Mary said sarcastically. "He'll end up in trouble with the law, the same as the Taylor boy, if he isn't very careful. Aiding and abetting a crime, and withholding information from the police are serious offences."

"I'm sorry, but am I missing something here, ladies? I wasn't aware that Peter Taylor was in trouble with the law, or that he had committed any crime," countered Edna.

"He raped my daughter, and well you know it," spat Mary.

"Rape, my eye!" Edna exclaimed with a jut of her chin. "Peter Taylor did nothing against your daughter's will, Mary, you know that better than any of us. That's the real reason you haven't pressed charges against him, in case the truth of the matter were to come out."

"And what exactly do you mean by 'the truth'?" Mary challenged weakly, aware of the delicacy of her position, but already having gone too far to retrace her steps.

"Hasn't your friend, Mrs Hollins, told you? Well, I am surprised! It seems she has made it her business to tell everyone else in the hostel. How she saw your daughter being escorted into Rodney Hill's chalet one night, followed by half a dozen local lads - all paying Wayne Stanton money at the door. Isn't that so, Mrs Hollins? No doubt that is also something you are prepared to swear to on the Holy Bible."

"I said no such thing... I..." Mrs Hollins began a floundering denial, but saw that other women were already nodding in agreement.

A stunned silence fell over the gathering. Mary went a ghostly white. "That is a filthy lie," she gasped, turning to Mrs Hollins. "Is this true?" she demanded.

Mrs Hollins was dumbstruck. A denial was out of the question, for most of the women present had heard the sordid details of that night from her lips. "There are some things it's kinder not to tell people," she stammered awkwardly.

"No, Mrs Hollins, what you really mean is some things are only said behind people's backs, not to their faces," accused Edna. She turned her gaze on Mary. "If I were you, Mary, I would disregard your daughter's accusations against Peter Taylor, together with any thoughts of prosecution. No court would ever uphold charges brought by a girl who accepts money."

Satisfied at having put both women firmly in their places, Edna took her leave of the group. She left her washing where it was and stormed directly to John's chalet, furious at having to learn things concerning her own family from the likes of Mrs Hollins.

"What's this I hear about you getting letters from Peter?" she demanded the moment she strode into the room.

"I only got the one. A few weeks ago. Did Dad tell you about it?" asked a stunned John.

"No, he did not!" Edna almost shouted. "It's all over the hostel. I had to suffer the embarrassment of hearing it from the hostel gossip. Doesn't my family tell me anything any more?"

"How is it all over the hostel? I haven't told anyone, only Dad."

"I don't know how, but it is. Where is your father?"

"He went to see Mr Taylor, I think."

"Is this the letter?" She scooped the letter from the top of the cabinet and started to read. "How come you lent him money to run away with?" she challenged angrily. "Apart from getting yourself involved, you may never have seen him or the money again. Twenty-five pounds! Have you gone completely mad? He's not that good a friend. Whatever possessed you?"

"I didn't exactly give it to him," John explained hesitantly. "He... he took it...."

"You mean he *stole* it from you?"

"No. Of course not. Peter wouldn't. He... he took it unintentionally. I was keeping it in a folder with some road maps I had of the route to Sydney. Peter took the maps without knowing the money was there. But it's all right; he's sent it back. I knew he would."

Edna stiffened, shifting her stare from the letter to her son "What were you doing with road maps to Sydney?" she demanded.

The unexpected turn in questioning caught John off guard. There was no reason why he should feel guilty about having road maps; there was nothing illegal about owning them. But his mother's stern scrutiny made him shift uncomfortably, as though he had been caught with a pocketful of dirty photographs.

"They were only road maps," he stammered lamely. "I wanted to go there, one day - for a holiday."

"When? And with whom?"

John shrugged. "I don't know. I just thought I'd like to go there."

"You're lying to me. What were you really doing with those maps?"

She was glaring at him now. John knew she would not relent until she had forced the whole truth out of him. "I was planning to go over there... rather than go back to England," he confessed with downcast eyes.

"You mean you were planning to run away from home?"

"I was only thinking of it. I wouldn't have gone though with it, not really. It was just a crazy idea, that's all." He sat staring at the floor, waiting for his mother to explode into an almighty rage, knowing he would then have to suffer the inevitable lecture on family love and unity, followed by a detailed account of the sacrifices his parents had made for him.

But the lecture never came. Edna folded the letter carefully and returned it to the top of the cabinet. Then she turned and walked slowly from the room, as though sleepwalking, her expression one of incomprehension - and hurt.

Tom heard Edna's tread on the steps leading up to their chalet door, and braced himself for the continuation of their bitter argument, or perhaps this time it would be a period of hostile silence. He resolved to remain calm and resolute, no matter what. He was not going to back down. If it meant separation, even divorce, he would not yield. He would not let his sons down.

"Did you know that John was planning to run away from home?" Edna asked quietly.

Tom looked up, surprised by her tone. There was no longer anger in her eyes - only sadness, and perhaps even a trace of contrition.

"With what I've learnt today, I guessed as much," he admitted.

Edna stood forlornly in the centre of the room, slowly shaking her head. "My first-born, my beautiful baby boy. He wanted to run away, from me, his mother." She dabbed a handkerchief to her eyes. "I've been so selfish, and so stupid, I failed to see what was happening within my own family."

"He wasn't running away from *you*, love," Tom reasoned softly. He had braced himself for another bitter argument, a battle of wills, in which he had resolved to be strong and unyielding. But at the sight of her tears, all his resolve crumbled; he couldn't bear to see his Edna hurting.

He went over and held her. "Don't upset yourself, love. He loves you, we *all* do - we just see our futures differently."

"It's mostly this place I hate, and the small-minded people in it," she said. "The sooner we get away from here and start living together as a family again, the better. As soon as you're earning, we'll start looking for a place to rent.

Tom was overjoyed at what he was hearing. "You really mean that, Edna? You're prepared to give it another try?"

"We are a family; if that's what you and the boys all want, then that's what we will do. I just hope you are right about this grass-cutting business."

He gave her a hug. He just knew everything was going to work out fine. Now that he had his rock, his Edna, back by his side, and *on* his side. How could they not?

CHAPTER TWENTY-TWO

Football season was under way in Perth, and Stan's workmates had insisted on introducing him to the game. As far as Stan could make out, for most of the supporters, the start of footie season had merely triggered a shift of drinking venues from the hotel bars to the grassy slopes around the oval. They turned up in their thousands, all carrying cool-boxes crammed with canned beer, and drank and shouted throughout the game. Stan soon came to enjoy his Saturday afternoons at the match, even though he was at a loss to fully understand the rules.

This week, Subiaco were at home to Swans, the champions. Joe was playing, and, as always, his muscular figure dominated the game. He seemed to be everywhere before the ball had arrived, leaping and plucking it out of the air from seemingly impossible heights. The catch, Stan now understood, was called a mark, and won the player making it an unimpeded kick of the ball. Halfway through the game, Joe went up for a high mark amongst a group of opponents. As usual, his big hands were first on the ball, but when he came down he crumpled into a heap on the grass.

"Feitz stuck the elbow in! Send him off, umpire!" raged Lee and Rodney.

A mixture of boos and cheers sounded round the oval as Joe staggered to his feet.

"Joe will have him for that," Fred asserted confidently. Joe always referred to Fred as his "little" brother, for he stood a mere six foot one. Fred usually played, too, but due to a pulled thigh muscle, he had been ruled unfit for this match.

During the fourth quarter, it became noticeable that Joe was sticking close to Feitz. "Joe's going to have that Feitz, for sure," Fred repeated. "Look at the way he's tagging him."

Soon a high ball came across and they went up together. Joe delayed his takeoff a fraction and this time he didn't succeed in making the mark. His elbow connected with Feitz's chin on the way up, and Feitz collapsed unconscious to the turf. Joe stood with his arms open in a gesture of bewildered innocence as the umpire came running up.

Fred threw his can high into the air in exuberance. "Yahoo! You little beauty!" he shouted.

One of the Swans's players, thinking that the umpire's attention was elsewhere, rushed at Joe with his fists flying. Joe ducked away, still protesting his innocence as the umpire changed the focus of his attention to intervene. A heated argument involving players of both sides ensued, resulting in Joe's attacker being put on report.

A group of enraged Swans supporters began throwing beer cans onto the pitch.

"What about that mongrel, Lampton, umpire?" roared one of them.

"Send the rat-bag off!" shouted another.

Fred, Lee and a couple of their mates made their way down to the group. A brief scuffle broke out, and then the stewards charged in to break it up.

It was an average game, packed with incidents, both on and off the pitch. Stan often wondered whether most of the spectators knew, or even cared, what the final scores were.

Most interest seemed to revolve around who had chopped whom, and whether the tribunal was likely to suspend anyone.

After the match, which Subiaco had won, they returned to the pub to celebrate. When Joe limped in wearing a triumphant grin, he was given a rousing cheer.

"You played a blinder, Joe," said Rod, slapping him on the back and thrusting a beer into his hand.

"By the Jesus, I feel like it too," said Joe. "Me ankle's that swollen it took me ten minutes to get me boot off. And take a look at that little lot." He lifted his shirt to reveal heavily bruised ribs.

"But you got him, Joe. Strewth, you caught him a real beauty – and got away with it, too."

"But, by Jesus, I haven't had a set of ribs like that since the day I ran into our Stan here."

"It's a pity we can't stretch you a bit, Stan. I reckon you would make a great footie player," said Rod. "What do you think of the game now? It makes soccer look like a sissy's game, don't it?"

"I don't know about that," said Stan. "But I wouldn't miss a game. It's a great atmosphere, as good as anything soccer has to offer."

"That's the way to look at it. You've got to get into the spirit of the thing," said Rod. "I'll tell you something, Stan. It doesn't matter a damn what game the jokers on the pitch are playing, as far as the spectators are concerned. The real object of the game is to get away from the old woman for a few hours, and have a good drink with your mates, that's what it's all about. It makes no difference whether the men in the middle are playing footie, soccer or even rugby. As long as a man can see plenty of action, have a shout and a swear, and let off a bit of steam, he'll go home happy."

"That's sounds about right," agreed Stan. "I don't fully understand the rules, but I always enjoy the game."

"The trouble with most migrants, especially the Pomes, is they won't see it that way. They'll live here for years and whinge on about how they miss watching a good game of soccer, and wouldn't dream of going to a footie match. They just don't want to adapt to our way of life. But I can see we are going to convert you into a real ardent footie supporter, Stan."

"You had better be quick about it," said Joe. "Stan's going to be back in England before the season is over."

Rod gave a hearty laugh. "That's bullshit. Stan wouldn't go back to England – he's almost an Aussie now."

"It's not by choice, I can assure you. I... have to go," Stan confessed with downcast eyes. "The wife is homesick, and the mother-in-law has been taken ill."

Rod looked aghast. "Mother-in-laws, eh? What would you do with them? They can be a real curse to a man. You'll be coming back, though?"

"Of course he's coming back. He wouldn't want to live in Pomeland after sampling life here in Australia," said Lee. "Don't get conned into going to Sydney or Melbourne though, Stan. They're foreigners over there. Melbourne's not so bad, but those Sydney jokers are Martians – they don't even play footie! They're all rugby freaks."

"There will always be a job waiting for you here, as long as I'm in business," Joe assured him.

"I can always find you a fill-in job at the factory," offered Rod. "Drop us a line when you're ready to come back. We'll have a whip-round at the club and see if we can help you with the fare."

There were murmurs of agreement around the bar.

"That's very generous of you all," Stan said, a little embarrassed at the offer.

"Don't mention it. You're one of us now, Stan. And, say what you like about the Aussies – and you Pomes usually do – but we look after our mates. If you need any help, you only have to shout."

Stan thanked them again for their generosity, regretting even more that he had to leave. Rod was right, of course - under normal circumstances, he would be the last one to think of returning to England. But the choice was not his.

He left the pub and made his way back to the hostel feeling more dejected than ever. He was halfway up the steps of his chalet when he heard Peter's voice – he was laughing. Stan felt his anger surge. After all the trouble the boy had caused them, he had the impudence to wander back - and laugh about it.

"Look what Peter has brought home, Dad. A real Aboriginal hunting boomerang," called David, the moment Stan stepped into the room.

Peter was sitting in the armchair, with Debbie perched on his knee. She was hugging a fluffy koala that he had brought her. Stan had to look hard to be sure that the young man sitting before him was really his son. He had been away barely two months, yet he seemed to have matured by three or four years. He had been well tanned before he left , but then it had merely been a pampered glow obtained from idling on the beach. Now, his features were much darker. The days of hard toil under the fierce sun had sweated the soft puppy fat around his eyes and cheeks into firm flesh, and filled out his arms and chest. His recent black eye added a touch of ruggedness to his appearance. Stan could find fault with only one aspect of the change: the long hair dangling across his forehead and curling about his ears.

"So... you've finally decided to come home, have you?" was all Stan could think to say.

Peter lifted Debbie from his knee and looked up at his father. "Yes, Dad, I've come home."

Stan saw something defiant, almost challenging, in the way he stood Debbie aside. As though by the gesture, he was saying: 'Here I am, offering no excuses, asking no quarter, let nothing stand between us.' It was an open, honest gesture, so unlike the Peter of old. And it was enough to convince Stan that the boy had matured in more than mere appearance during the short time he had been away in the bush – the boy had become a man.

Yet, in spite of his outward calm, Peter felt anything but confident or self-assured as he faced his father. On the train, he had taken a defiant attitude. His father was only a man; could only give him a beating. Maybe he would collect a few bruises, but what the hell? He'd learnt to rough it since he'd been away, he could take it. He had even considered following Paddy's advice and making a stand-up fight of it - he had nothing to lose, he was in for a good hiding anyway.

But now, as he faced his father, he wasn't so sure of himself. There was something about this man that unnerved him; made him regress to feeling the helpless, dependent child, incapable of making his own decisions, or even of having his own opinions. It was a fear and unease that went far deeper than the mere threat of physical punishment, and he was unable to reason with it.

Stan sent David and Debbie out to play. Peter sat waiting silently while his father turned the boomerang over and over in his hands, as though putting it through the most careful scrutiny. He moved to the dressing table and picked up the pill-bottle of gold dust Peter had panned. Still, he didn't speak. Peter imagined the silence was calculated to unnerve him. If so, it was succeeding. He called on every ounce of self-control he possessed to keep from fidgeting in his chair, determined not to give his father the satisfaction of seeing him squirm.

A faint smile crossed Stan's face, as though reading his son's thoughts. "Seems you've been having yourself quite a time," he said to Peter's surprise and relief.

Many times, Stan had considered what he would say and do when Peter eventually came home. Had he returned within the first couple of weeks, he would undoubtedly have strapped the very hide off him. But gradually his anger had subsided and he had begun to take a more tolerant view. Peter was no longer a boy, he was a young man - and when a girl was offering her favours freely, any normal, red-blooded young man was going to make the most of his opportunities. That didn't make what he had done morally right - far from it, but it was nature, and nature's march was not to be checked by the strap. Once a young man had reached the age of sexual awareness and desire, the only sensible thing to do was to tell him the facts of life and give him as much common-sense advice and guidance as to the legal and moral rights and wrongs of it all as possible.

But that could wait for another day.

"I hope you realise how lucky you've been," Stan said, his eyes still on the gold. "But for the skin of your teeth, you could be facing some very serious charges right now. You've emerged from the incident a whole lot better than you rightly deserve. I can only hope that you have emerged a little wiser, too. The Tates left the hostel in rather a hurry. Nobody seems to know where they have gone. Personally, I don't much care. We have enough problems of our own right now. I expect your mother has already told you about that?"

Peter nodded. "You mean about us having to go home on account of Gran being ill?"

Stan placed the bottle of gold back on the dressing table. "Your mother will be flying back with Debbie early next month. We'll follow by ship as soon as we have the fare. Going back is the last thing I want to do, but there are some things in life a man has no choice in. How do you feel about it?"

"I'd rather stay here," Peter said, without hesitation. His views on Perth had not changed - he had never been too taken with the place. Blue had described it as a "snob's" town - an overgrown bush town masquerading as a big, important city, and for want of a more fitting description, Peter was inclined to agree. But life in the bush, that was something much different. For him, that was the real Australia - a man's country. Peter had known it instinctively the first time he had walked along the dusty main street of Coolgardie, and he had known even then that it was the place for him.

Stan paced about the room thoughtfully. "Perhaps you're thinking you could make a go of it here on your own?" he suggested.

Peter thought carefully. "I have a job to go back to in Coolgardie, and I can look after myself," he said tentatively.

"I'm sure you can," Stan said proudly. "And, for my part, you could stay. But, well, your mother is a very possessive woman. It will take her a little time to get used to the idea that you're growing up. She will want you living with the family for a while yet, especially if the old lady takes a turn for the worse. She will need us all near her then. But we'll be back one day. I think your mother will want to come back, too, once she has had another look at England, and compared it with here. We'll have to pay our own passages next time, of course, so it isn't going to be easy. But we'll manage it somehow."

"I've got some money saved up, I can help," offered Peter. "Living in the camp out at the quarry, there was nothing to spend my money on," he explained. "And the gold is worth about fifty quid, so Blue said. We'll be back, Dad, no worries," he assured his father confidently.

Peter stood up. "I must go and see John. I've got so much to tell him.

I can't wait to see his face when I show him the boomerang - and the gold. I know he is mad keen to visit the outback. Boy, he is going to be so jealous. He still thinks boomerangs are ornaments. Wait till he sees this beauty."

"I rather had that impression of them myself," confessed Stan. "But then the only boomerangs us city types get to see are the Made In Japan variety displayed in souvenir shops."

"Yeah, this one isn't very pretty, but it's one hell of a souvenir. Rather an appropriate one for us, too. We'll hang it over the mantelpiece when we get home. It will serve as a constant reminder that we will be coming back."

CHAPTER TWENTY-THREE

"How much longer now, George?" called Terry Bates as he swung his rifle over his shoulder and strode on up the gently-sloping hill.

"About another four months I'd reckon," George called back. "Then I'll be heading home to good old England - and civilisation."

His three companions laughed heartily. The good-natured ribbing of George had become a part of their weekend hunting and fishing trips.

"Last week you told us it was only going to be three months," said Greg, a tall, muscular Queenslander. "Be honest about it, George - you don't really want to go. You're becoming addicted to our healthy, outdoor way of life. Where in England can you shoot or fish for your own tucker?"

"Plenty of good hunting in England," responded George.

"Sure, but no one's allowed to touch it, unless you were lucky enough to be born into the land-owning gentry," said Gordon, the fourth member of the party. Gordon had emigrated from England with his parents thirteen years ago, and his accent was now as strong as any Australian's. "The nobility own all the most beautiful countryside; the richest fishing rivers pass through their estates. The working man doesn't get a look in."

"The only fishing you'll do back in England is like you see in the Andy Capp cartoons, with Andy dangling his line in the local cut, pulling out bicycle wheels and old bedsteads," confirmed Terry.

They reached the top of the rise and looked down into a valley where Greg's Land Rover sat by a dirt track, some sixty feet below them. Sheep grazed peacefully on the lower hillside opposite, then the fields gave way to a row of tall eucalyptus trees that continued to the top of the rise, and then on to distant hills beyond. All was bathed in brilliant sunshine, not as fierce now as in the height of summer, and with the gentle breeze blowing along the valley, today could be likened to one of the better days of a British summer.

Puffing slightly, George topped the rise. He was chuckling at having succeeded in winding up his companions. Terry handed him the water bag. He drank from it and wiped the back of his hand across his mouth. George had lost little weight since he had been working. Nature had never intended him to be thin, and as much as he sweated in the heat, his dimensions remained much the same, though he grudgingly admitted to feeling a lot fitter now than he had while idling in the hostel.

"Just look at all that gorgeous countryside. We could be anywhere in England right now - Warwickshire, Herefordshire... don't you think so, George?" Gordon said with a sweep of his hand.

"It's nothing like Warwickshire," George responded obstinately. "The fields and trees are a proper green in England, fresh and vibrant looking, not this dull, grey-brown colour. Everything here looks half dead."

"Warwickshire is a bit greener, perhaps. That's because it's pissing with rain all the time," said Gordon.

"That's when it's not freezing your balls off - and snowing," added Terry. "The whole country was under six feet of snow for three months this year - the worst winter in history, they say. See what you've been missing, George? Only a complete lunatic would want to give up all this beautiful sunshine and open countryside to go back to that."

George gazed around with a philosophical air. "There is something really magical, almost mystical, about snow-covered hills," he said wistfully. Then he turned away from them to hide his involuntary chuckle. Even he didn't believe that, and they all knew it, but he felt it was his duty to keep the banter alive.

His companions laughed heartily. "Sure, George, we believe you. Snow looks great on a Christmas card," said Terry. "And personally, that's the only place I ever want to see it."

"At least the cold kills off all these perishing flies," said George, aware that his companions had long since ceased to take his negative comments at all seriously. But then by now, they were not intended to - it was all a wind-up, and they knew it.

While living in the hostel, George had never considered moving out of Perth; had never thought there was anything outside of the capital, apart from a few bush towns, followed by miles and miles of desert. Well, that was what they taught you about Australia in geography lessons at school. Ninety per cent of the country was desert, they said. And naturally, that was what he had believed.

George had always loved to get out into the countryside, and, in spite of his size, he was a keen walker and landscape photographer. Holidays at home in England had invariably been spent in either the Lake District or the Yorkshire Dales. He had been quietly impressed by the scenery around Bridgetown and conceded, reluctantly at first, that much of it could indeed be compared to parts of England.

He always enjoyed heading out of town on the weekend hunting and fishing trips with his friends. But, for George, the real revelation had come one weekend when Greg had driven them all to visit the Kerri and Jarrah forests. George had gaped open-mouthed at the splendour. As he looked up at the massive redwood trees towering some two hundred and fifty feet above him, and in the case of the kerri's almost fifty feet in circumference, he felt like a small child who, with eyes wide with wonder, was entering Disneyland for the first time. Surely this must be one of the most magnificent sights in the natural world.

Since that day, George had taken to buying the *Post*, a weekly magazine that was running a series of full-page landscape pictures from beauty spots all around Australia - the Flinders Range in South Australia, the Kimberlys in the north of Western Australia, the Blue

Mountains in New South Wales, the tropical rain forests of Queensland, and so many other areas of outstanding interest - scenery as stunning as anywhere in the world. It was a mystery to George why the Australians didn't boast to the whole world about the beauty their country possessed, instead of allowing it to be known almost exclusively for its massive "Red Centre", and letting the world think that Australia was nothing but one huge desert.

Weeks ago, George had admitted to himself, if not to his companions and workmates, that he had been completely bowled over by the countryside, and the pace of life he had found down here in the south. He wondered what Christine would think of it. He was sure she would love it. She had never really commented much on Australia, only on the hostel, and, well, nobody liked living there.

Unbeknown to Terry and the rest of his workmates, George had been taking a tentative look at houses for rent in Bridgetown. He would love to bring Christine down here to see the place for herself. Maybe, just maybe, they could settle here and make a new life for themselves.

George gave a secretive smile, knowing he would get one hell of a ribbing from his mates after all the negative comments he had made about Australia. But he would laugh it off. They all understood by now that most of his criticisms were only intended as a light-hearted windup.

"One of the things I love most about Australia is that the whole countryside is accessible to all," said Terry, as they started off down the hill again. "As long as you follow the golden rule: if you find a farm gate open, leave it open; if you find it shut, then shut it after you. Abide by that and no farmer anywhere in Australia will object to you crossing his land."

"Can you imagine setting foot on a gentleman farmer's land in England, let alone shooting on it? Heaven help any of us poor peasants who dared to trespass on the nobilities' land," said Gordon.

"Well, that, at least, is true," admitted George. "Trespass laws are very strict in England, and sentences are severe. Get caught and they clamp you in irons and deport you to Australia – unless the judge is in a good mood, of course, then he might pass the more lenient sentence of hanging."

Greg laughed and continued down the path towards his Land Rover. "True enough. My great-great-grandfather got out here that way. It didn't even cost him ten quid. I'm so thankful the old bugger was a thief, or I'd probably have been born a whinging Pome... like George here."

The banter was still going strong as they drove back into the camp. Trevor Masters came running towards them, holding a newspaper and waving his arms in hyper excitement.

"Hey! Terry! George! Take a look at this. We've only gone and won the lottery!" he shouted.

"We've done what?" exclaimed Terry.

"That lottery ticket we bought together. It's come up. We've won three thousand quid!"

George and Terry jumped from the Land Rover and grabbed the paper. Men gathered round as they checked the winning numbers with those of their ticket. "That's us right enough," confirmed Terry. "A thousand quid each." He threw the paper into the air and hugged his companions.

Greg and Gordon offered their congratulations and shook them by the hand. "I hope you will all be sticking around long enough to shout the gang a drink," said Greg.

"I've already taken care of that," Trevor assured him. "There's a couple of kegs laid on in the mess. Come and wish us luck before it's all gone."

The mess was crowded with workmen, all standing around the kegs, drinking beer, some from glasses and others from enamel mugs.

"Well, here's to a pleasant trip, George," Greg said raising a glass. "I take it you'll be leaving us and going back to England now?"

"I'm as good as on my way," said George, keeping up the pretence. He would have to tell them of his plans sooner or later, but for now it was much more fun to string them along.

"How about you, Terry? Don't tell me you and Trevor will be leaving, too?"

"No way," was Terry's instant response. "I'm certainly not heading back to England. Trevor and I will be taking a few days off to drive to Perth and give our wives the good news. We may even bring them back here with us, and see how they like the place. Maybe they'll want to settle here."

Later that evening, with the beer still flowing, a more thoughtful Terry confided to George, "I really don't know how my Shirley is going to react to the news, or what she'll want to do with the money. Judging by the last conversation we had on the subject, she was dead set on going back to England, much the same as you. I was hoping to persuade her to give it a try down here. Me and Trevor have been looking at houses to rent in Bridgetown. With a thousand quid, I could almost buy one. But will my Shirley want to live here? That's the question."

"I'm sure she will, once she's had a good look at the place," said George. "She'll soon change her mind." He hesitated, and then smiled. It was time to come clean. "Living down here has certainly changed my mind," he confessed softly. "To be honest with you, I've been looking at places to rent, too. I'm sure Christine will love the countryside around here."

Terry looked at him in amusement, and Greg, who had been standing beside, them laughed loudly. "Now I've heard it all. Listen up, guys: George says he likes it here. Does this mean you've changed your mind about going back to England?"

George laughed brashly to ward off any embarrassment. "I changed my mind on that one ages ago. I just can't resist winding you Aussies up. I must admit, it's a great way of life you have down here, I love the place - and even your beer's not too bad."

A raucous cheer rose from the little group within earshot.

"You've all got to hear this," Greg shouted to get everyone's attention. "George has something to tell you all. Get him up on the table, lads."

Four of them hoisted George up onto a table in full view of everyone. "Come on, George, tell them all what you just told me," Greg demanded.

"Fair cop," grinned George. "I'm not going back to England. I must confess I've become quite fond of this part of the country."

"'Quite fond?' That's nowhere near good enough," Greg insisted above the din of cheers and laughter. "We want a full confession."

George laughed in sheepish surrender. "Okay, I admit it." He raised his glass and announced loudly. "Here's to Australia. It's a real beautiful country - and I love it."

It was mid-afternoon when Trevor drove his car into the hostel car park behind the reception hall. They arrived just as Tom Henshaw was making his way across the tarmac towards his ute.

"Good day, Tom. I thought you would be long gone by now," Terry greeted him as he emerged from the back of the car and stretched the cramp from his limbs.

"We've had a change of heart," beamed Tom.

"Have you managed to find another job, then?"

"Not exactly. I'm working for myself. Of all things, I've started a lawn-cutting round."

"Lawn cutting?" puzzled Terry. "That sounds interesting. I thought you were dead set on sticking to your trade - like someone else I could mention."

"To hell with the trade," said George, easing himself out of the car. "The quality of life and the money to provide it is the reason we work, not misguided loyalty to any trade or profession. New country, new life - eh, Tom?"

"My sentiments exactly," agreed Tom. "As a matter of fact, I could have started back with Drew's a couple of weeks ago, but I turned them down. Cutting grass and being out in the sunshine is far more agreeable. I can't believe how much money I'm earning at it - far more than Drew's were offering. Young John has been like a human dynamo, running around knocking on doors, picking up more customers than I can rightly handle."

"That's marvellous news. I'm happy that things are finally working out for you," said Terry.

"I'm glad I've seen you before we leave," said Tom. "We'll be moving out of the hostel next week. We've rented a house in Mount Lawley. What brings you back here? I didn't think Shirley was expecting you home for a few weeks yet."

"We've had a spot of luck on the lottery," Terry informed him with a broad grin. "And perhaps even more unbelievable, George here has had a change of heart, too. We're all hoping to persuade our wives to come back to Bridgetown with us. So, if things go to plan, we could all be moving out of the hostel together."

"Daddy, Daddy!" Young Tracey came running up. Terry caught her under the armpits and swung her round, then cuddled her to him. "I've been playing on the swings, Daddy. Mummy didn't tell me you were coming home."

"Hello, my little treasure. Daddy has missed you. But soon we're all going to be living together again."

"Hello, Babe," Shirley came up and pecked him on the cheek. "What are you all doing back here? We weren't expecting you till ..." Suddenly she stiffened with a sharp intake of breath. "Oh, hell!" she exclaimed. "Must dash. I've left the iron on." Without another word, she turned on her heel and sprinted away in the direction of the chalets, leaving a bemused Terry to look after Tracey.

Shirley ran straight to Trevor's chalet and began thumping on the door. "You there, Sandie? Terry and Trevor are back on the camp..." They are here now!" she called urgently.

The door half opened. "So what do you want me to do about it?" Sandra asked sullenly.

"Well, pardon me," Shirley bristled indignantly. "I was trying to do you a favour. I thought you might have someone in there with you."

"Well, I haven't. And what business is it of yours if I had?"

"Oh, to hell with you, Madam. I was trying to warn you more for Trevor's sake than yours. You're nothing but a slapper. That man is far too good for you." She walked back down the steps and made her way to her own chalet to wait for her husband.

George charged jubilantly up the steps of his chalet and burst through the door. "Surprise! Surprise! I'm home, Christine," he called.

Christine stood with her hand over her heart in a gesture of shock. "For goodness sake, George. You frightened the life out of me, barging in like that. What are you doing here?"

"We've won the lottery. A thousand pounds," he rejoiced, enfolding her in a great bear hug. "Isn't that the greatest news ever?"

"A thousand pounds," she repeated, stupefied. "Well, that's wonderful, George." She released herself from his grasp and wandered back to the dressing table to continue with her tidying and dusting, as though his words had yet to register. "That's wonderful," she repeated with an uncertain smile. Then, after a moment of thoughtful silence, she asked probingly, "What do you intend doing with it, George? I really don't want to go back to England, if that's what you're planning. You know how I hate the cold. I couldn't take a winter like they've had this year." She turned back to face him. "I want to stay here, in Australia," she said assertively.

George gave a great, rumbling laugh. "That's marvellous, Chris. Just what I hoped you'd say." He went over and gave her another big hug. "I want to stay, too. The funny thing is, I thought I might have a job convincing you."

"*You* have a job convincing *me*? That is a laugh. I've always liked it here. What's changed your tune?"

George delved into his pocket and withdrew a packet of photographs. "If you like it here in Perth, you're going to absolutely love it down south. Take a look at these. With our winnings, I want to buy a car. I'll go back and find us somewhere to live in Bridgetown, then I'll come back and get you. We will start a new life down there... if you're sure that's what you really want?"

"Of course I'm sure. That was the whole point of emigrating in the first place, George. I'm so glad you have finally come to your senses."

Shirley was standing at the door waiting when Terry carried Tracey up the steps to their chalet. She kissed him passionately. "Good to see you, Babe. Sorry about that."

"So what was it all about?" he asked as they went inside. "You weren't ironing, were you?"

"Of course not. I ran off to tell Sandra that Trevor was back. I feel rotten for doing it; it's as though I'm helping her to cheat on him. Though, as it happens, she was on her own."

"But has she been seeing someone?"

Shirley nodded. "But leave it, Terry. It's for them to sort out. Anyway, why the surprise visit? You're not checking up on me, too, I hope."

"As if." He stood Tracey down and cupped his wife's face in his hands, preparing to watch her expression. "We've won the lottery," he told her jubilantly. "We've won a thousand pounds!"

Shirley screamed. "A thousand quid? No! That's fantastic!" She threw her arms round his neck, and they danced excitedly around the room. "A thousand pounds? Really? That's fantastic. That's more than enough to get us home."

The beam of joy faded from Terry's face, to be replaced by an expression of pain and disappointment. "Oh, Shirl. That's not really what you want, is it? I thought you would have gotten over all that homesickness rubbish by now."

"You know I hate it here, Babe," she sulked. "Perth is so lifeless. There's nothing here. Even the Aussies say it's nothing but a big bush town. It's pretty enough, but it's so dull - nothing ever happens here. As for going out in the bush where you are... " She screwed her face up. "I'd die there, I really would. No, let's go home, Babe. Please?"

Terry groaned, and lowered himself onto the edge of the bed. He was beginning to wish he had never won the money. Instead of uniting them, it had served only to bring to a head the issues that divided them, and that they had been trying to avoid for months.

"I'm a city girl. I need to be where there is life and action," Shirley explained in her whining voice. "I want big shops, and nightclubs. I want to be jostling along Romford Market, elbowing my way through the crowds, haggling for bargains. And, yes, I'm homesick. I miss my family and all the mates I grew up with. I can't settle here, Terry. Really, I can't. I hate it."

Terry lowered his head into his hands. "Oh, no. This is breaking me up. What are we going to do, Shirl?"

She shook her head slowly but resolutely. "I don't know, Babe. I don't know."

"I'm from the city, too, Shirl, a Londoner born and bred, like you. But I've found a better way of life. I've fallen for the wide-open spaces, fishing and shooting. I couldn't go back to London and face living in that concrete jungle - it would feel like a prison. I belong out here."

He sat for a long time, saying nothing. So many things were running through his mind, but a compromise or solution of any kind eluded him.

Eventually, he lifted his head and said firmly, "Think back, Shirley, and think very hard about this. We didn't have the life we wanted in England – that's why we came out here, searching for something better. If we go back, we still wouldn't have the life we want, and by the time we get there and get resettled, we will have blown most of our winnings and savings, and we'll be struggling again."

He got slowly, almost painfully, to his feet. "Well, I know what I want. Australia has proved to be all that I hoped it would be, and more. I'm happy to stay and start the new life we both said we wanted. Now it's up to you to decide what you want." He slid the new savings book from his pocket. "My winnings are in this account - one thousand pounds. It's all yours, Shirl. If going back to England is what you really want, and decide to do, it will pay the fare for you and Tracey and be enough to get you resettled."

"What, without you? You mean separate?" she asked incredulously.

"If you decide you really want to go home, then that's the way it has to be. The choice is yours, Shirley: England or me, you can't have both." He placed the savings book on the dressing table, and moved slowly to the door. "I really hope you are going to stay here with me. It's a big decision - for all of us. Think very carefully."

The first thing Trevor noticed as he entered his chalet was the half-packed suitcase on the bed, and Sandra stooped over it. "What gives?" he asked, mystified.

Sandra straightened and turned to face him. "I would have thought that was obvious," she said. "I'm leaving."

"Leaving? Where to?" he gaped.

"What I mean is I'm leaving you, Trevor. You know we haven't been getting on lately, not since we got here. No, even before that, if we are honest. We came out here looking for a fresh start, hoping that the shared struggle to build a new life might bring us closer together. But it hasn't happened. I've had enough of pretending - I'm finishing it."

"Is there someone else?" he demanded suspiciously.

She turned away from him. "I won't lie to you, there is. But it's hardly relevant. You and I have simply grown apart, Trevor, and that happened long before I met Ian."

"So you were just going to walk out on me without saying a word?" Trevor challenged angrily.

"No, I wouldn't do that to you. I've written you a letter. I was going to post it tomorrow, as I left. But now you're here, I can tell you to your face. I don't want an unpleasant scene, Trevor, and it's no use trying to talk me round - it wouldn't work. We have nothing in common anymore. It's time to call it a day."

Trevor sat down beside the half-packed case. "I can see your mind is made up. I won't try to talk you out of it," he said with resignation in his voice. "What we had died some time ago. Logically, it's best we both make a fresh start."

"I'm glad you see it that way. I really don't want us to part on bad terms," she said her voice softening. "You're a good man, Trevor, and we've had some good times together, but we're just not right for each other. Luckily, there are no kids to complicate matters. And we have nothing much to divide up - no money or property. You can keep the car. That's about the only thing of value we own. It will just be a clean break. We can both walk away and start new lives."

Trevor fingered the new savings book that nestled in his shirt pocket. "No, there's nothing to divide up," he agreed. What she didn't know wouldn't hurt her.

"If you want a divorce, you can name me as the guilty party, I won't contest it. It's all here in the letter." She handed him a white envelope.

Trevor stood up slowly and moved towards her, still stunned by the suddenness of it all. Sandra had never been faithful, not even in the early days of their marriage. He had hoped she would change as they grew older, and, hopefully, closer. But it was not to be. She was a tramp, he had always known that. And this Ian, whoever he was, would soon know it, too. Trevor was past caring, but still he felt hurt and cheated – and very angry. He was tempted to give her a good hard parting slap – many men would have - but what was the point? Keeping the money would be his consolation. He kissed her lightly on the cheek. "I wish you luck," he said simply.

"You, too, Trevor," she replied, as he walked through the door.

CHAPTER TWENTY-FOUR

The red lights were flashing and the boom gate was dropping slowly across the road. Craig cursed as he brought the Morris to a halt. Every morning, he was held up at the level crossing while The Kalgoorlie crawled out of Perth on its way to the goldfields. His head was throbbing and his tongue felt like a lump of dry boot leather. The party, and the company, had been a bore, and Craig had resorted to a bout of heavy drinking for want of something better to do. Geoff could usually be relied upon to liven up a dull party, but since he had been dating Susan, and apparently taken a vow of abstinence, he had become duller than the British weather forecast.

Later in the evening, Craig had carried Elaine into his room, and they had remained there for the rest of the night. It had been a good night he recalled with a contented smile, but the mere fact that he was beginning to double up on his old dates was a sure sign of monotony.

The Kalgoorlie was rumbling by in front of him, its wheels tapping out a rhythm on the track. People were crowding at the windows, gawking out at the congestion they were leaving behind. Some were laughing and waving, as though flaunting their freedom. They were escaping from that Monday-morning feeling and the rush and tear of the city - they were heading for open country and the romance and adventure of the goldfields.

Craig pictured the gold mining town that awaited them on the edge of the desert. It would be a rough town; the buildings would be old and shabby. Perhaps modern houses, even blocks of flats, had sprung up to contrast the town's original buildings. Maybe it now had drive-in cinemas and fast-food restaurants. But it would still be a town with real character - a town worth seeing.

Craig recognised the signs only too well. He was becoming bored and restless for a change of scenery - of life. He had planned to remain in Perth for another month yet, but the train wheels seemed to be tapping out a message, telling him it was 'time to be moving, time to be moving, time to be moving...' The rhythm became faster and faster as it faded into the distance.

The boom had risen and the drivers behind him were tooting their horns, anxious to rejoin the race to work. Acting on an impulse, Craig swung the Morris round in the middle of the road, thus halting traffic in the opposite lane. More horns blasted. The road was narrow and he had to reverse and make a three-point turn. Now traffic in both lanes was disrupted and horns were blasting at him from all directions. The drivers' frustration was just the tonic Craig needed to lift him from his gloom. He laughed heartily and jutted his fingers at the irate motorists as he drove away.

By the time he made it back to the house, Geoff had left for work.

Craig sang loudly as he darted about gathering his belongings and throwing them into his cases. He would leave today - no point in hanging about. Impulses acted upon immediately, with enthusiasm and spontaneity, were always the most enjoyable. He wouldn't even hang around to collect the wages that were owing to him.

He and Geoff had often spoken of hitting the road together, and working their way round Australia, but Geoff had been very quiet on the subject of travel lately. Since he had been dating Susan, he had somehow lost his spirit of adventure, and Craig doubted that he would be going anywhere. Nevertheless, he decided to drive to the garage and put the proposition to him anyway.

Geoff was leaning under the bonnet of a Ford Falcon. He looked up as Craig strode into the garage. "What gives? You prang the car or something?"

"Or something. I've had a sudden attack of wanderlust. I feel the itch to be moving on. How about you?"

"I'm not nearly as impulsive as you," considered Geoff. "I need a little time to think about these things. I wouldn't leave without giving Daryl a couple of weeks' notice. It would hardly be fair."

"Well, I'm shooting through today. You do your thinking, and if you decide to hit the road, you can catch up with me later. Now, what about the car?" He slid his wallet from his pocket. "I'll buy your half, if you're agreeable, or I'll spin you for the privilege of doing so."

"You take it," agreed Geoff. "It will be easier for me to pick up another here in Perth. Where are you heading first?"

Craig shrugged and gave his rakish grin. "I'm not even sure what direction I'm going in yet. Winter is coming on - such as it is - so perhaps I'll head north and follow the sun. I'll drop you a line and let you know where I make camp." He counted out the notes from his wallet and handed them to Geoff. "Well, all the best, Geoff. Maybe I'll see you in a couple of weeks."

"Yeah, maybe," mused Geoff. They shook hands and he watched as Craig drove away. He was still wearing that wide, carefree smile that said he was leaving all ties, commitments and responsibilities far behind him. Craig was on the move, and he was in his element.

Geoff stood at the workshop door and gazed after him, already feeling the loss. Craig was one hell of a character, and they had had some great times together. He knew, just as Craig had known, that their parting was to be permanent. He would miss him. Yet, strangely enough, he felt relieved that the parting had come. Now he could settle back into his own, quieter, lifestyle. The hectic round of parties and drinking had been fine for a while. But it had all become rather stale in its sameness. Craig had felt that, too - that was why he had left. Only Craig wasn't seeking a rest from it, just a change of venue. Craig wasn't the type to ever think of settling down.

In a way, Susan was right: although he and Geoff got on well, in reality, they had very little in common. Geoff was far too serious-minded to live at Craig's pace for long. Now he was on his own, he would move out of the house and find digs somewhere. Start thinking seriously about his future. And from now on, there would only be one girl for him.

One month later, Geoff and Susan were at the port of Fremantle to wave Gloria off. Luigi's heartbreak ship stood waiting at the dock, and the quayside was a hive of activity. New migrants were disembarking, some looking excited, others a little apprehensive. Homeward-bound migrants were trudging aboard, most looking dejected and disillusioned, their faces seemingly a foot longer than those of the new arrivals.

"There are quite a few people going home," commented Susan. "I wonder why they were unable to settle? I think it's a better country to live in, don't you? Though I suppose it doesn't suit everyone. I expect they all have good reasons for going back."

"I doubt whether one in ten could give you a valid reason," Geoff said dismissively. "Most of them are just homesick."

"Don't scoff. That's a perfectly good reason for going back. I wouldn't want to live here if Mum and Dad were still in England. Most people don't realise how much their families mean to them, until they're parted; then, naturally, they become homesick. I don't see as it's anything to be ashamed of."

"They would receive a lot more sympathy from me if they admitted it, instead of waving their Shilp diplomas under your nose and constantly running Australia down," said Geoff. "Ninety per cent of them are far better off out here than they ever were in Britain."

He took her hand as they walked along the quay. It was winter now, but still the sun shone down.

"Financially, perhaps they are better off here. But you're like Uncle Harold - you're too much of a materialist," she said. "You think everything can be measured by the size of your wage packet and the make of car you can afford to drive. There are some things that can't be compensated for merely by putting an extra fiver in a man's wage packet."

A party of new arrivals were being escorted along the quay to a waiting coach. A sign stuck to the inside of its windscreen informed them that their destination was Seaview Hostel. The children in the group were skipping along merrily in the sunshine, and all appeared happy to be exchanging the cold of Britain for the warmth of Australia.

"It's certainly a more affluent lifestyle," agreed Geoff. "But you are wrong; for me, it's not about the money. The thing that makes the biggest difference to life out here is the weather - this glorious, almost year-round sunshine. In Australia, you start work early and finish early. By the time you clock off, there are usually still four or five hours of sunshine left. So, it's a quick shower, and off out: down the beach to swim or surf, to play tennis or golf, have a barbeque - it's such an active, energetic lifestyle. Little wonder that Australia produces some of the finest sportsmen and women in the world. It's not that they are a race of super humans; it's all down to the climate."

Gloria had appeared on deck and was waving frantically to attract their attention.

"Look, there she is," said Susan, and began waving back. "But there are far more people who make a go of it here than go back," she observed.

"Oh, far more," he agreed, then added, "and not all those returning are disillusioned with Australia. Circumstances haven't left some with much choice." He had been watching a family group making their way towards the gangplank to board. At the head of them was the forlorn figure of Stan Taylor, trudging along with heavy suitcases.

"Poor old Stan. I feel for him. He had really taken to the Australian way of life. He had a well-paid job, and a close circle of friends. Returning to England was the last thing he wanted to do," said Geoff.

"Peter, too. What an eventful time he's had here. But they'll be back."

"You can bet your boots on it. Stan will move heaven and earth to get back here. Others, we're not too sure about." Geoff had spotted Terry Bates standing at the foot of the gangplank. He was holding young Tracey tightly in his arms, giving her a long, lingering hug, seemingly reluctant to release her back to her mother.

"One last roll of the dice," Geoff commented softly.

Susan eyed him quizzically. "What?"

"That's what Terry told me the last time I spoke to him. The statistics are that ninety per cent of those who return to Britain apply to come out again within a year. Terry's a gambling man, and he's taking the gamble of his life. He's paying for his wife and daughter to go home, praying that the odds run true to form, and that they'll soon be returning to him."

"Will they? I do hope so."

Geoff gestured his uncertainty. "Perhaps. We all like to see a happy ending. But there again, perhaps not. There are no guarantees in life, even if the odds are nine to one in your favour."

A group of Scots migrants were disembarking, looking resplendent in their tartan kilts and dark jackets. Some were marching proudly down the gangplank to the wail of bagpipes played by friends and family gathered on the quayside to greet them.

"Don't they look splendid," said Susan. "It makes you proud to be British."

"They are smart, indeed," agreed Geoff. "But at the risk of sounding cynical, I wonder whether theirs is the right attitude. Displaying fervent patriotism for a country you no longer wish to live in and flaunting it in the face of your new countrymen is hardly conducive to a harmonious or successful resettlement."

"There is nothing wrong with being patriotic. I know you still are."

"Yes, of course. I'm British and I always will be. But I love Australia, too. And I'm ready to admit that Australia is by far the better country to live in. But a lot of Pomes, even the ones who settle here successfully, are reluctant to do that."

"Perhaps it's a case of absence making the heart grow fonder."

"I don't think so. Too many Britons seem to be far more patriotic here than they ever were at home. I'm not saying you have to disown your own country, simply because you're no longer living there, but to a certain extent, you do have to break your ties and affiliations. If you don't, it can be like trying to drive a car forward while you still have it stuck in reverse gear."

When the new arrivals had disembarked, and the returnees had all boarded, the gangplanks were slid away, and the ship's horn blasted. They stood in silence and watched as the tugs pulled the heartbreak ship, laden with its cargo of disappointments and broken dreams, away from the quay. Gloria looked happy to be on her way, and waved cheerfully. They waved back and kept on waving until the people lining the ship's rails merged into a single blur of colour, then they turned and walked slowly away.

"We won't get ourselves stuck in reverse gear, will we?" Susan asked, taking his arm.

"No fear of that," he assured her.

"But we will always be British. I wouldn't like us to be like Uncle Harold and become anti-British. The Old Country still has a lot of good points."

"Of course we will always be British; we were born there, we can't alter that."

Walking ahead of them was the sad figure of Terry Bates, his shoulders hunched as he surreptitiously wiped a tear from his eye.

"I do hope Shirley comes back soon," said Susan. "But how about us? Will we have our happy ending?" she asked in a concerned voice.

"Naturally. But then we have it all planned out, don't we? After we're married, we will go up north, where I will work on one of the big new mining projects for a few years. I'll earn a fortune, and with the cash, we'll return to Perth and buy a brand new house in the suburbs, close to the beach. I'll open a garage, which will prosper. We will have three, perhaps four, children and live happily ever after – what could possibly go wrong?" He smiled.

She eyed him suspiciously. "Now you're going to say something really cynical, I just know it."

"Me? Perish the thought. But I am aware that however carefully you plan things, life has a habit of coming along and disrupting those plans. I guess that's what makes life so exciting." He started to chuckle.

"What now?" she demanded.

"I was just thinking of an observation that Daryl imparted to me. His experience is that if you study all the Aussies that have a grudge against the Pomes, you'll find that ninety per cent of them have British parents. His theory is that Pome-bashing is in reality nothing more than a rebellious child syndrome. As for my mirth? Well, I was just imagining what your reaction is going to be when all those little Aussies we're planning on bringing into the world, grow up and start referring to us disrespectfully - if not derogatively - as that pair of whinging Pomes."

Printed in Great Britain
by Amazon

84708103R00132